SECRETS FROM THE GRAVE

A British Murder Mystery

THE DEADLY WOLDS MURDER MYSTERIES
BOOK 5

JACK CARTWRIGHT

CP

CHESTNUT PRESS

ALSO BY JACK CARTWRIGHT

Deadly Little Secret

Waiting For Death

The DCI Cook Murder Mysteries

A Winter of Blood

A Secret to Die For

SECRETS FROM THE GRAVE

A Deadly Wolds Murder Mystery

JACK CARTWRIGHT

PROLOGUE

It had been a very British summer day. Long with showers and sunshine in equal measure, never quite staying dry long enough that the muddy footpaths that snaked their way through Snipe Dales Country Park dried. Oscar breathed in the Lincolnshire countryside, the petrichor waft of grass and wildflowers, trees and hedges, and streams and pools flowed through a version of the park he hadn't seen for nearly a year. His favourite place was bathed in the soft orange glow of the dying sun, casting long shadows from trees that swayed in the gentle breeze, like the ghosts of soldiers amidst the lush vegetation.

It had been the kind of afternoon that stretched on and on, later and later, as though apologising for the long, dark winter ahead. The sunlight seemed to linger only for them, sinking beneath the horizon as slowly as a peach into jelly. It was a gift. One that they shouldn't waste.

"Come on, Wesley," he yelled down the slope.

But Wesley didn't move. He was bent over on the narrow wooden bridge that spanned the stream, clutching a stitch in his side. At his feet, the roll of carpet they had found lay still and curved like a body.

Oscar looked past him to Louis, who grinned and rolled his eyes, then glanced up at the sunset.

"Come on, it's not far now," he said. "Let's just get it to the den so we can make a fire."

"It's alright for you," Wesley said, clearly in pain. "You're not carrying it."

"I carried the sofa," Oscar told him. "I'm not a bloody donkey."

"We've got marshmallows," Louis added, as a mother might attempt to convince a small child.

Despite his concerns that they may have to abandon the carpet, Oscar's heart was full. It had been the first proper day of summer. The Country Park was like their own private playground, and although the three boys could — and often did — enjoy the place in all weathers, they could now lose entire days in it. Snipe Dales offered all the comforts of their parents' homes and all the adventure of the world beyond childhood. There were trees to climb, streams to wade in, and springy grass to lie upon while staring up at the clouds.

What more could they need?

But everything ended eventually. Oscar knew that well enough by now. He watched the perfect day fade away, second by second, behind the trees, lowering behind one leaf and then disappearing behind the next, and those soldiers that swayed to and fro with the breeze, faded like a memory.

"Seriously, Wesley," he yelled down the slope, "can you hurry the—"

"It's heavy!" Wesley screamed back before Oscar could finish.

The retaliation had been on the tip of his tongue, just waiting for a trigger. Wesley was like that. He held it in and in and in — until he snapped. When they were younger, Oscar and Louis would test his patience by continuously poking him in the shoulder or pretending not to understand a joke, turning Wesley's crank over and over until he lashed out like a jack-in-the-box. In the last year or so, however, Wesley had grown more outward than upward, unlike Oscar, who'd grown tall and lean, and Louis, who'd somehow managed both, becoming an awkward bear of a teenager.

"Right, come on," Louis said when Wesley seemed to have recovered. "One, two..."

They shouldered the carpet like pallbearers, and with gritted teeth, they walked on shaky legs with dogged determination.

"I dragged it all the way from the car park," Oscar said as they reached the top.

"Yeah, downhill," spat Wesley between heavy breaths.

"It is bloody heavy," Louis said as they entered the trees and made their way up to the camp they had spent the day making.

He turned to Oscar as a removal man might.

"Where do you want it?"

They had already built the foundations. Leafy branches strung together formed the walls, an old tent cover draped across them formed a makeshift roof, and all of it had been built around the object that had inspired their project, the old, stained, red sofa they had found abandoned in the car park. The carpet was the final finish to smooth over the loose sticks and ant nests. Of course, in a perfect world, they might not have chosen a gaudy, red, diamond-patterned carpet with gold fringe along the edges, but you have to work with what you've got when you're a teenager.

With a final heave, they dumped the carpet, which landed with a heavy thump that scattered the nearby leaves.

"Oi! What are you lot doing?" The voice came at them like gunfire through the trees, and they all froze. "Get out of there."

Oscar peered through the trees, finding an old man on the footpath at the bottom of the hill, who held up a hand against the glare of the sunset to see them better. A long, loose raincoat hung off him, and a small, golden, curly-haired puppy bounced around his feet, curiously sniffing the mud and deciding if it was to his or her liking.

Oscar stepped forward. "What's it got to do with you?"

"You know this is a protected area, don't you?"

"I said, what's it to you?"

"It's a nature reserve," the man continued, stepping off the footpath and into the trees, encroaching on their territory. "You can't dump all that here."

"We didn't bring it here, sir," Louis said, stepping up beside Oscar. "Someone dumped it in the car park. We're just..." He looked back at the den. "Recycling it."

"Well, you shouldn't play around in rubbish. Could have anything in it, you know? Glass, knives. You should call the authorities if—"

But before he could finish, a large, thick stick landed at the old man's feet, causing his golden-haired puppy to whimper and scurry to safety behind its master's ankles. The man instinctively held his hands to his face, and then scowled at the boy who had thrown it.

"What the hell are you doing?"

But Wesley bent down to grab another.

"Playing fetch with your dog," he yelled, readying himself to lob another fat branch. "Hey, doggy. Fetch this!"

But before he could let go, Oscar turned and grabbed his arm hard, allowing the old man to pick up his puppy. He backed off, shaking his head and muttering to himself, as he slinked off along the footpath back towards the car park, throwing jaded stares over his shoulder.

Oscar glared at his friend. "What's wrong with you?"

"What?" Wesley shrugged out of his grip. "Got rid of the old bastard, didn't it?"

Louis laughed in that way his mother often did when she was trying to gauge his dad's mood from a comment.

"You're a bloody psychopath sometimes, you know that?" Oscar said.

Wesley seemed to take it as a compliment and threw himself down on the red, stained sofa with an insufferable grin.

"Budge up," Louis said, sitting beside him and saving space for Oscar, who shook his head but joined them nonetheless.

The three boys shared the two-person sofa and watched the orange passage of time through the trees. Oscar wriggled uncomfortably. The three boys sat so close together that he could feel vibrations through Louis's jeans pocket. Eventually, after a series of violent buzzes, Louis pulled out his phone and then groaned at the screen.

"Ah, biscuits," he said. "It's my mum."

Oscar's heart drained. "Can't you tell her you'll just be an hour? I thought we could stay a bit. Make a fire." He paused, then offered an idea that now sounded pathetic. "I bought marshmallows, remember?"

"I don't know, she's freaking out," Louis said, holding up a screen of notifications.

Oscar's phone hadn't buzzed once all day.

"Ah, come on," he said. "I mean, we could stay all night if we wanted."

"No thanks," Wesley scoffed, stretching. "I've got a roast dinner waiting at home."

But Louis held Oscar's gaze, reading his mind. "You've got to go home eventually, mate," he said quietly.

Oscar didn't reply. He just picked up the largest stick within reach and chucked it at the nearest tree, causing a chunk of bark to break off and fall to the ground.

"Come on," Louis said, jumping up and offering a hand. "We can come back tomorrow, yeah?"

"Fine," Oscar said eventually, allowing his oldest friend to pull him to his feet. He stretched and kicked out at the carpet. "Let's unroll this first, eh? A bit of air might get rid of the smell."

"If it rains, it'll get soaked."

"Better wet than stinky," Oscar told him, delaying the end of the day as much as he could.

"Fair enough." Louis smiled. "You going to help?" he asked Wesley, who reluctantly dragged himself to his feet.

After trying to kick the carpet open, to little avail, the three boys knelt on the ground to push it instead.

"One, two, three," Louis said as though directing a rugby play, and they began rolling the carpet open, one sluggish turn at a time, like a flat BMX tyre.

"Jesus," Wesley choked halfway through. "It stinks. It smells like a hospital or something."

"You'd stink too, if you'd been left out in the rain," Oscar said breathlessly.

"Come to think of it, you do stink," Louis added, earning him a playful dead arm.

"It'll be alright tomorrow. The roof will keep it dry," Oscar said, hoping to coax them on.

They continued their battle with the carpet until Wesley suddenly stopped. Without his bulk, Oscar and Louis stood little chance.

He squinted into the trees, then sat back on his ankles.

"What is it now?" asked Oscar breathlessly.

"Did you see that?" Wesley said.

"See what?"

Oscar looked around the clearing, noticing nothing but the elongated shadows fading to merge with the ground.

"It's just a shadow, Wesley. Come on."

"Wait—"

Even Oscar noticed it that time: the flash of a dark shape through the trees and an accompanying murmur.

"It's just a dog walker or something," Louis said, though his voice had quietened. "Come on."

He returned to the task of unfurling the carpet, but Wesley and Louis were transfixed.

"Come on, you two," he said. "Let's just get it done and then get out of here if you're scared."

Oscar fell onto his backside, pressed his feet against the roll, and gave everything he had. With every roll, the going became easier, and they shuffled along behind it for the next push, until at last, he felt the resistance give, and he fell onto his back to catch his breath.

"Jesus bloody Christ," he muttered, expecting the others to voice similar complaints.

But Wesley and Louis were silent.

"Some help you were," Oscar told them, groaning and stretching, prolonging the end of the day even more. He could have laid there all night. It wasn't the most comfortable he had ever been, but it was a far better prospect than going home.

"Oscar," Louis hissed.

"I'm staying here," he told them.

"Oscar!" Louis hissed again, with more urgency in his voice, and lazily he raised his head to peer at him. Both boys were staring at the carpet at their feet. "What?" he asked, shoving himself up onto one elbow to see what the fuss was about.

And then he saw it.

And the blood in his veins ran cold.

And the prospect of a perfect summer died with the last remnants of the day's sun.

CHAPTER ONE

The more George admired the Willow Tea Rooms' cute, bustling interior, the more details he noticed — a short, painted grandfather clock by the door, the British flag bunting along the ceiling, a ceramic bulldog on the wooden piano, an old accordion on a three-legged stool by the window. Through the window, people went about their day. Locals and tourists alike strolled the narrow streets, dipping in and out of vintage shops and clothing stores, weaving between each other like an ill-practised seventeenth-century dance, while ducking beneath stunning hanging baskets that caring hands had tended the length of the high street.

He gazed along the wall at the posters and flyers promoting small-town events. To his left, a cluttered pinboard showcased the best the Wolds had to offer in hobbies and workshops, from life drawing to woodworking to rambler weekends. One, in particular, caught his eye — *Pottery with Pauline* — if only for the crude, cartoonish sketch of a man sitting behind a middle-aged woman at a pottery wheel, which made George chuckle.

He sat back, enjoying the Sunday peace. It all reminded him of a deep comfort he couldn't identify. There was something soothing in the tinkling of spoons on porcelain and the hustle and bustle of the staff. Then, at the sight of an older lady walking towards him, drying her hands on an apron, he suddenly remembered spending long weekends at his grandmother's house when he was a young, carefree boy.

"Now then, my lovely," the woman said, flipping open a notebook much as a police officer might. "What can I get you, love?"

"I'm just waiting for a friend," George said, glancing at the door. "Do you mind if I wait for her to arrive?"

"No bother. We're closing up soon. It's been a lovely day, hasn't it?" she said, nodding at the golden-hour light outside and clearing his table of the previous customer's coffee cup. "When you wake up to glorious sunshine, that's when you know winter's really over."

"Or the first time you eat strawberries and cream," George replied

"Or the first time you smell a barbecue," she replied with a smile.

Weekends were important, George thought, if only to enjoy harmless conversations such as these. In another life, he might have enjoyed a job like hers, where he could chat about the weather with a stranger. Small talk was a privilege, he'd noticed. One that those in the force rarely got to enjoy.

"To be honest, I was surprised to find you open. I was quite glad of the sit down."

"Ah, we're not always open this late. A few days of the year. It's Alford's nineteen forties weekend. Biggest event of the year."

"Oh, I've heard of that," he told her. "Shame, I would have enjoyed that."

"If you'd have been on the High Street yesterday, you'd have thought you were in a strange episode of Dad's Army," she said with a laugh. "All the old military vehicles on display, the old clothes. Ah, it was a sight. They had a Hurricane in the square. A real success, this year."

"Well," he said quietly. "Maybe next year I'll make it. I should put it in my calendar."

"They made quite a fuss on social media. Surprised you didn't see it, if I'm honest."

"I erm... I'm not really on social media. It's a bit beyond me."

"It's not as bad as everyone makes out," the lady replied. "Let's face it. It's not going away anytime soon. Might as well embrace it."

"Yes," he said. "Yes, you're probably right."

"You can take one if you like, by the way," she said, nodding at the pinboard. "We've got plenty more flyers."

"Oh," George said. "No, that's okay. I was just looking, really."

"My friend Pauline does the pottery classes. Over by Tealby, if you know it?"

George smiled. "I know it well," he replied, though he didn't mention that he'd solved a murder investigation there only weeks earlier. As she continued to watch him, George turned back to the pinboard and removed the pottery flyer from its thumbtack, if anything, to be polite. "I'll think about it," he added.

"Very good. Just let me know when you're ready, dear, and I'll take your order."

"Thank you," he said as she toddled off and he folded the flyer into his coat pocket. "She won't be long."

But a minute later, when the charming little bell above the door announced a customer, he turned, not to find the woman he was waiting for, but a garish, sea-themed lampshade being forced awkwardly through the doorway. Turning down multiple offers of help, Ivy squeezed it inside the tearooms and heaved it over to George's table.

"What," he said, eyeing the monstrosity at her side, "is that?"

If there was any sort of coherent design to the lamp, George couldn't find it. Heavy beach shells and plastic pearls adorned the entire shade and half the stand. However, by the bottom, a more sci-fi-like style with a heavy, metallic, geometric base had completely replaced the ocean theme. The occasional flare of discoloured fringe only added to its chaos.

Ivy caught her breath and looked it up and down fondly. "It's a lamp."

"Looks more like a medical diagnosis," he replied, eyeing the growth-like shells. "Is that what took you so long?"

"I *loved* that shop," she said, beaming. She looked happier than she had in a long time, and George guessed it was because of more than just the lamp. Her skin looked healthier, her eyes brighter, like she shone from within. "Such unique vintage pieces. I found this out back."

"In the rubbish?" George asked innocently, and Ivy gave him a stern look. "And I know you loved it, Ivy, but twenty minutes in there was enough for me."

"Well, it's time to start buying. I've got a new house to decorate," she said. "That is when I finally move into it."

"Why don't you get started then?" George said. "Put that lamp in it now, eh?"

"I don't even have the keys. Not until everything goes through." Ivy stroked the ugly, purple fringe that dangled from the shade. "Anyway, you're the one who wanted me to stay with you."

"Yeah, for six months."

"Well, if you want me, I come with the lamp." She crossed her arms. "It's a non-negotiable."

George laughed at her stern expression. "Fine," he said. "I just didn't know you came with baggage."

It was Ivy's turn to laugh, and much harder than George had. "Oh, that you *did* know, guv."

"Do you want a coffee?" he asked, eyeing the pleasant lady at the counter who he didn't want to keep waiting. Ivy still hadn't taken a seat. He thought she might need a comedown from her buyer's high.

"Yeah, I'll take a—"

"Decaf oat latte," George said, standing. "Coming up."

"But let's take it to go, guv?" Ivy called after him, and George turned to look at her. He'd been rather looking forward to savouring the rare, old-worldly charm of the tearoom. "And make it caffeinated."

"What's the rush?" he asked, to which she grimaced and held up her phone.

"I've had a call," she said. "And it wasn't an insurance salesman."

CHAPTER TWO

By the time Ivy and George arrived at the crime scene, the sun was beginning to set. They pulled into the dirt track turning for Snipe Dales, and George depended on his memory to fill in the details. Large, open fields lay on either side of the road, protected by miles of hedgerows that cast long, fading shadows over the arable land. They passed through a bright yellow gate that, according to the little sign, was locked after five p.m.. Although today, in such circumstances, whoever ran the Country Park had thankfully left it open.

"Have you been here before, guv?" Ivy asked.

"Of course," he replied, slowing down for the bumps. "You don't live around here for as long as I did and not visit Snipe Dales for a picnic or two. There are some nice walks in these parts."

Ivy shrugged.

"I've never been here. Heard about it, but never been."

"Well, you haven't been here a year yet."

"I guess. In Mablethorpe, Jamie and I would often walk by the sea."

"Well, you're missing out," he said. "The Country Park is beautiful, especially at this time of year." He pulled into the car park and took one of the spaces not occupied by a police vehicle. In fact, the only car in the car park that wasn't liveried was a bright cerulean Ford Fiesta lit not by the sun, which had set, but by the glowing watercolour it had left in its wake. Tall trees shrouded the car park like sentries, guarding what lay within. "You'll see for yourself. It's a real pocket of nature."

"I'm not sure a crime scene will be the best introduction," she said. "Perhaps a walk in the daylight might shine a more positive light on it?"

In the silence of the car park, George unclipped his seatbelt and listened as it coiled into its holder. "You've got a point," he said and opened the car door.

But Ivy grabbed his arm before he could climb out.

"What's that?" she asked, staring forward.

George flicked the headlights on, casting a harsh beam over the grass bank beyond the parking space. There, amongst the trees, strewn in a haphazard heap, lay a mound of rubbish. Splintered side tables, broken chairs, and split bin bags spilling old toys and soiled clothing over the heap. A can of red paint had burst open, staining some of the rubbish with a vivid, congealed crimson, like dried blood.

"Fly-tipping," he said. "Honestly, if there's one crime I'd like to see harsher penalties for..."

"Not murder?"

"Most of the murders we deal with, Ivy, are done out of passion or some kind of emotion." He nodded at the heap before them. "That? That was done by a heartless, lazy, no good scumbag that deserves to be behind bars."

"Don't hold back, guv," she said, appearing shocked, to which he simply grinned pleasantly. "Shall we?"

The temperature had dropped, and George buttoned his coat

as he climbed from the car. It was a cruel reminder that even on the most blissful of summer days, darkness arrived eventually — and in full force. Ivy turned on her phone light as they walked over to the familiar officer who stood at the beginning of the footpath that led from the car park into the heart of Snipe Dales.

"Evening, guv," Maguire said as they approached. "I should've known we wouldn't get the whole weekend to relax, shouldn't I?"

"Murderers don't wait for weekdays," George replied. "What's the situation?"

"Body. Female. Byrne and Campbell are already in there with the victim. I'm securing this side, and O'Hara's securing the other end of the Country Park."

"Who found her?"

"Three kids," Maguire said, shaking his head, acknowledging the life-altering event. "Thirteen or fourteen-year-old boys, by the looks of it. They were playing in the trees and found a rolled-up carpet. When they unrolled it, she was inside."

"Christ," Ivy murmured. "What did they do?"

"Legged it. Ran all the way to the main road. Then one of them called his dad, who called us."

"Are they still around?"

"Aye. In there," he said, nodding into the gloom. "They're talking to Campbell. It was still light when we all got here," he explained.

"The blue Ford Fiesta," Ivy said, pointing a thumb over her shoulder. "Is that—"

"Hers?" He nodded solemnly. "Yes, sarge, we think so. It was here when I got here."

"Well, don't touch it," she said. "We'll have CSI go over it."

"Yes, sarge."

"Thanks, Maguire," George said, and then ventured down the path of doom.

Ivy followed close behind as they used her phone torch to

navigate the deeper puddles and muddier slip marks down the slope. Even though the day had been the first day of summer, it had been the first day of summer in England, so naturally, evidence of the week-long rains and showers still permeated the ground. Thankfully, however, much of the land was dry by now.

The path formed a near-perfect U-shape with a narrow wooden bridge at its base. They crossed the small but well-fed stream they could hear but not see, and headed uphill towards the familiar voices that spoke at an urgent but respectful volume.

"I understand that, Mr Harris, I do," came Campbell's patient tone. "But I think it's best that we talk more at the station, don't you? I doubt that your son wants to spend any more time out here than he needs to."

"Do you have any idea how that will look?" said a man wearing a full tuxedo with the bowtie undone and hanging loose around his neck. "*Me* walking into a police station? The press will have a field day."

Portable LED lights cast an unnatural glow over the scene and accentuated any pocket of darkness. George turned off the foot-path and pushed himself up the hill towards the light. Despite his language, which had suggested he was some kind of celebrity, the man Campbell was speaking to appeared no more than mildly familiar. Alongside his opulent outfit, George noticed the man's expensive watch and soiled brogues, a well-groomed beard and receding, ginger hairline with a thin fringe that did little to cover a large forehead. On closer inspection, however, he was much younger than George expected, possibly in his late thirties or early forties. It was hard to be sure under the harsh lights.

PC Byrne, Campbell's counterpart, acknowledged George and Ivy's arrival with a stoic nod.

"My priority right now, Mr Harris, is protecting your son and his friends from further psychological harm," Campbell said, glancing at the three boys.

George looked over at the teenagers who sat together on a

fallen tree trunk at the side of the path, staring at their muddy trainers. Beside the darkest-haired of the three, sat a woman who gripped his hand so tightly the whites of her knuckles shone in the gloom. She wore a thick winter coat over a pair of flannel pyjamas that told George she'd run out of the house at her son's call for help without a second's hesitation. Standing close behind with a hand on her shoulder was a middle-aged man in similar informal attire: old jeans and a bleach-stained hoody. With their stoic expressions and sunken postures, they reminded George of a Victorian family in an old sepia photograph.

"I'm sure that's what you want, too?" Campbell continued.

The tuxedoed man hesitated but then answered, "Of course it is."

"In that case," she said, "my colleague will escort you and your son to the police station, where he can make a statement."

"Is this normal, is it?" he replied. "Taking statements from minors in a police station?"

"Your son and his friends have discovered a dead body, Mr Harris. I hardly think this situation is normal in any context," she replied. "Given your son's age, we have a duty of care to ensure his well-being."

"Not to mention a duty of care to the victim," George added. "I'm sure you'll understand."

The man stood still for a second as though about to retaliate, then he spun and clicked his fingers at the widest boy of the three, who had been blessed with the broad family forehead. "Wesley, come on."

Campbell turned to the man and woman beside the remaining boys. "If you could take Louis to the station too, please, Mr and Mrs Foxon?"

"Of course," Mrs Foxon croaked, and then cleared her throat. "We'll take Oscar too," she added, glancing at the boy whose hand she wasn't clutching.

"Why?" George spoke up for the first time and stared down at the boy in the middle, the tallest of the three who hadn't moved a muscle since they'd arrived. "Are we missing some parents?"

The lad only shrugged in response. He didn't even look up.

"We called them but they didn't answer," Mr Foxon said quietly.

"Is there anybody else we can call?" George asked, to which the boy simply shook his head.

"I don't mind. He often has tea with us," the lady added helpfully.

"I'll escort them all to the station and start taking statements," Byrne said. "If that's alright with you, guv?"

"Go ahead," George said, stepping back. "My name is Detective Inspector George Larson, by the way," he added to the boys and parents with a smile. "We'll meet again in due course."

"Sorry about that, guv," Campbell said, walking over when the witnesses had dispersed. "We only got here half an hour ago and spent most of that time arguing about where to take the boys' statements. I asked Maguire and O'Hara to secure the scene from both sides and redirect any nighttime dog walkers. CSI and the FME are on their way. Nobody's been near the body since we got here."

"Good, good," George said. "And you've informed the Country Park management already?"

Campbell ran a flustered hand through her hair. "What's that, guv?"

"You informed the park management team already?" George said. "They left the gate open for us. The car park usually closes at five, doesn't it? I remember Grace and I almost got locked in once."

"We haven't informed them yet," she said slowly. "I was going to ask Ruby in the morning."

"Then why was the gate open?"

"Guv, that wasn't us." She paused and looked between him and Ivy. "Didn't you notice it on your way in?"

"Notice what, Campbell?" Ivy asked flatly.

"The yellow gate."

"What about it?"

"It's been forced open. They broke the chain and padlock," Campbell said, her face pale but eyes sharp in the moonlight. "Someone cut right through it."

CHAPTER THREE

"Detective Inspector Larson," came a familiar voice from behind George. "I was wondering if this would be one of yours."

He turned to find a gaggle of white-suited forensic investigators hiking up the path. He wasn't sure of their collective noun. A gang? A school? A murder? In the residual glow of the portable lights, they might've passed as spectres. Indeed, there was something eerie about the Country Park after nightfall. He held his hand out to the leader of the pack.

"Miss Southwell," he replied, as she shook his hand. "I'm not sure you can call it mine."

In George's eyes, Katy Southwell wasn't just the most capable and experienced member of the team, she was also the most striking. The harsh scene lights caught her electric blue eyes like opals in candlelight. Slim and of average height, she had the lean build of a runner, though George figured hours spent crouching over crime scenes and hauling boxes of equipment kept her trim.

She nodded once at Campbell and Ivy, then focused on George. "Your officer in the car park said something about a carpet?"

"Over there," Campbell said, nodding into the trees. "They found the body inside."

"Who?"

"Three teenagers. You just missed them," Campbell answered.

"We passed a police convoy on the way in," Southwell said.

"That was them. They dragged the carpet from the car park." She shook her head sadly. "They were going to use it in their den."

"So somebody dumped it?" George clarified, remembering the pile of rubbish illuminated by his headlights. "The carpet?"

"Fly-tipped by the look of it, guv."

"Pat, Jasmine," Katy announced, turning to the team behind her, from which two individuals stepped forward. "Can you make a start on that pile in the car park? We'll need the lot bagged up. DNA, fingerprints, trace evidence, do what you can."

"Will do," one of them replied, and the smaller group peeled off and retraced their steps down the path, over the bridge, and back up the hill towards Maguire.

Southwell turned back to George.

"Have you had a look?" she asked, nodding into the trees.

"Not yet," George replied. "Haven't had a chance."

"Come on then," she said and strolled fearlessly ahead, leaving him little choice but to follow at a respectful distance. "Let's see what we're dealing with."

George started after Southwell, then stopped and addressed a point he wanted dealt with as soon as possible.

"Campbell, get in touch with that boy's parents. What was his name?"

"Oscar, guv," she replied. "Oscar Wyman."

"If you can't get through to them, send an officer to the house. We need their permission to interview their son. And I want all of those boys' statements tonight, so we're ready to fact-check first thing in the morning."

"We could ask social services for an appropriate adult, guv."

"Let's not get them involved," he said. "Not yet. It rarely ends well."

"Yes, guv," she said, already pulling out her phone.

"And get some uniforms on that front gate if we can't lock it. Last thing we need is the press turning up. We'll never get rid of them."

"Guv," she called back.

George turned to the copse of trees that he had very little desire to enter. But to his surprise, Ivy picked up one of the portable lights and hurried after the forensics team, so all he had to do was follow her lead.

The boys' den wasn't far from the path, tucked deep enough into the woods to afford some privacy, but not so far that hauling junk from the car park would have been too much for three small boys.

As Ivy set down the portable light, their handiwork came into view. It was childlike in construction, rough and earnest. They had crudely hacked at branches, likely with a penknife, and lashed them together with leaf stems to form uneven walls. The leaves that had filled the spaces forming the wall were already sad and limp.

An old, faded carpet covered the ground both inside the den and out. A sagging red sofa, frayed and filthy, sat beneath the crooked arch of branches like a throne in a forgotten castle.

In front of it, still as the night, the dead woman lay, her pale and waxy complexion shining like a doll's.

"Let's establish a perimeter from here," Southwell said, motioning where she stood, "to that stump behind the sofa." As her team followed the instructions, she manoeuvred the light to scour the ground like a hunter looking for tracks. "You can see where they dropped the carpet here," she explained to George, pointing to the depressed soil beneath the edge of the carpet, "and rolled it towards the sofa. She must have tumbled out with the momentum." She bent down and sifted a handful of soil through her hands. "There are enough footprints to get a read on at least some of them, so you can corroborate the boys' stories. They were the only ones here?"

"Yes," George replied. "By the sounds of it. But until we speak to them somewhere a little more appropriate, we won't know if there was anyone else here."

Southwell shook her head.

"I can get you as accurate a footprint analysis as I can."

"Thank you."

"Meanwhile, we'll collect everything we can and, of course, collate it with any evidence found in the car park pile. I'm sure we can at least find you the carpet's manufacturer, if not some DNA. Carpet's good like that. That will give you a lead at least."

"A lead?" Ivy said. "With any luck, it would take us straight to whoever did this."

"I doubt it," George said slowly.

"What? You think he used another man's carpet to dump the body?"

"That's the problem, Ivy," George replied. "You're assuming the carpet was dumped *with the body in it*."

"What do you mean?"

"The rubbish could've been dumped here first," he explained. "*Then* someone hid the body inside the carpet. The two aren't necessarily related at all."

Ivy rubbed her forehead as though she already had a headache.

"That rubbish could have come from anywhere. This is going to be one of those investigations, isn't it?"

"I'm afraid it is," George replied gravely.

"I'll send over my report by the end of the day tomorrow," Southwell said. "For now, that's all I can do for you, George."

"It's enough. Thank you," he replied, stepping back. "We'll leave you to it until Peter gets here."

They headed back to the path, following the glow of the portable light on the path, which outlined Campbell's rigid silhouette. Southwell turned back to her team and began spewing more specific instructions concerning wide-angle shots and sterile swabs. George focused on his own tasks at hand instead.

"I'm thinking we send O'Hara over to the station," he said to Ivy. "Byrne's got three statements on his hands and at least one difficult parent. She can share the load."

"You don't think one of us should be there?"

"Not to take a few statements, no," George said. "They'll be fine."

"If you think the scene is secure enough—"

"Let's keep Maguire watching the car park, and another unit at the entrance." He checked his watch, noting the late hour. "I doubt anyone will be walking their dog at this time."

As they neared the path, a second silhouette joined Campbell's, only stouter. Whoever the newcomer was pointed a thumb over their shoulder. Against the stark light, the motion played out like a shadow show amongst the trees, and when George and Ivy stepped into the beam, he saw O'Hara pointing up the path into the heart of the Country Park.

"O'Hara, good," George said as they approached, "I was thinking you might be better off with Byrne down at the station if you don't..." He trailed off, eyeing the concern in her eyes and the twitch of her lips. He knew well enough when someone was waiting for him to finish so they could speak. "Is everything okay?"

"Yes, guv." Like Maguire, she was in full uniform. "Sorry, I didn't want to leave my post," she said, looking over her shoulder at the path that rounded a sharp corner into the night. "But there's someone you should speak to."

CHAPTER FOUR

George followed O'Hara deeper into the Country Park, and she nodded at a moonlit figure who waited further up the path.

She held up her torch to illuminate the figure, who appeared to be an older gentleman wearing a brown, woollen flat cap on a head of grey hair that seamlessly spread into his beard. He wore corduroys and an Aran jumper beneath a thin, red raincoat. Even if it had once fit, the jacket was now a few sizes too big and hung from his body like a canvas draped over a tent pole. The pockets jangled with keys and loose coins as he stood on his tiptoes to glimpse whatever he could in the light behind George and O'Hara.

"Now then," George said jovially as they approached the man. "Who do we have here?"

"Oh, hello," the old man replied in a thick local accent, his voice like soggy tissue paper, weak and wet. "Is everything okay, is it?"

"Dandy," George replied, but left it there and waited for the man to explain himself.

"Well, I live nearby, see? Saw all the police lights," he replied, while a golden-haired puppy sat timidly at his feet. "I just came to see what all the hullaballoo was about. That's all."

George eyed the puppy, then looked up at the man. "Bit late for a dog walk, isn't it, Mr..."

"Williams," the old man said, looking over George's shoulder. "Arthur Williams."

"And so far from the main road," George added.

At the shift in tone, the old man met George eye-to-eye, peering over his glasses rather than through them. "Oh, I've lived here all my life," he said with a chuckle. "Been walking these parts after dark since I were a lad."

"Well, I'm sorry to say, but it's closed for now, I'm afraid."

"Aye, *she* said," he replied, nodding at O'Hara without looking her way. "May I ask why?"

George smiled. "You may ask," he replied, "but, at the risk of sounding inhospitable, I'm afraid I can't really tell you any more than that."

He paused and eyed the old man who, he realised, was only a few years older than himself.

"Something happened, has it?" he asked. "Only, it's where we come. To walk, you know?"

George sighed.

"You say you live nearby, Mr Williams?"

The man rubbed his beard in shock.

"That's right," he said, pointing east. "Water Lane."

"Can I ask if you saw anything unusual?" George asked. "Perhaps when walking your dog, earlier?"

"Earlier?" the old man replied. "I wasn't out here earlier."

"Oh, I'm sorry. My mistake," George said and nodded at the pup. "It's just that your dog has mud in her fur, like she's been rolling around.

"He's a he," the man said. "He was playing in the garden this morning."

"Ah," George said and held the man's eye.

"If the path is closed, I suppose I should turn back," the old man said. "Find another route for... well. Best of luck."

"It's much appreciated," George said, gesturing for O'Hara to follow him back to the crime scene. "O'Hara here will take your details, of course." The man turned back briefly, and George smiled warmly. "Before you disappear."

"Of course," he replied after a moment's hesitation.

"Have a nice evening, won't you?" George added, then moved away, leaving O'Hara to deal with him.

He waited close by, studying the trees and the path, and he imagined those three boys dragging the carpet and the body. It must have taken some doing. To move a carpet alone was a challenge in itself, but add to that the weight of a limp body. They must have really wanted it for their camp.

"All done," O'Hara said, rejoining him, and they started down the path back towards Ivy and Campbell, glancing over their shoulders to check that Arthur Williams was indeed on his way home.

"Nicely done, by the way," she muttered.

"Take note," he mumbled, in the same manner a grandfather might pass on life advice. "That's how you get rid of them. A slice of information, a dash of kindness—"

"And a sprinkle of accusation?" she added with a grin.

George shrugged. "It's the only recipe I know. We didn't tell him anything the boys' parents won't have told half the village by the morning. Chances are he's harmless, but that's all we need, some nosy old so-and-so spreading rumours before our investigation's even off the ground. Best to scare them off early on," he finished with a wink.

O'Hara absorbed this advice thoughtfully.

"Do you want me to head to the station, then?"

"Yes," George said, remembering his previous intention. "I think we've got enough uniformed officers to cover all the exits. Give Byrne a hand with statements and dealing with the parents.

One of them in particular. No accusations. Just collect the facts." As they rounded the corner, he spotted the very man he had been waiting for. "We've got it from here."

"Here he is," Peter Saint said, turning away from his conversation with Ivy to grin at George. "The man of the moment."

His round face was flushed from the short climb, but he was otherwise unchanged — tall and lean, and dressed professionally with his leather doctor's bag that he never seemed to be without.

The two men shook hands as old friends and acquaintances do, which in many ways, they were. It just so happened that they never seemed to meet over a pint or a pub lunch but over a body.

"I'm happy to see you're back at work," Peter said. "Best thing for it, I say."

George translated it to something along the lines of, *Sorry about Grace, but I'm glad to see you're getting on with life.*

"Thanks, Peter," he replied, then nodded at the trees the way normal old friends might nod at a nice country pub. "Shall we?"

"Lead the way."

For the second time that evening, George navigated the loose twigs and roots that adorned the forest floor.

Saint took a respectful pause for reflection before approaching. Perhaps even the most weathered of medical examiners needed a moment before encountering death. It was odd to think that George had witnessed more death than any ordinary man should, and though his numbers were far greater than that of the average man, they paled in significance compared to a man like Peter Saint whose job it was to confirm the death, and establish where possible the cause and time of death. Although rarely would his findings be accurate enough to build a case on, they provided the forensic pathologist with a snapshot in time. The human body operates somewhere around thirty-seven degrees, therefore using Saint's temperature recording and the pathologist's alongside the elapsed time, an estimated time of death could be gauged.

Saint crouched beside the victim, and George dropped down beside him.

From first appearances, there was very little sign that anything was wrong with the woman at all, aside from her pale and waxy skin and the awkward angle at which her limbs had come to rest. There was no blood, no bruises, and no head wounds.

She was a dark-haired woman with a tangled fringe and small, hoop earrings. She appeared average in almost every way — height, build, looks. She wore a smart, white blouse that hugged her figure and tight-fitting dark jeans with brown ankle boots. A simple outfit that balanced comfort and self-care. She could have been anyone that George passed in the street on any given day, the woman at the supermarket checkout, a driving instructor, a coffee shop customer, or just another lady in the pub. Anyone at all.

"She's not been dead long," Peter mumbled, holding up her arm.

"How long?" George asked.

"Rigor mortis is setting in."

As he spoke, he methodically examined the body, moving with the practised ease and precision of a seasoned chef. He used a thermometer to check her temperature with artistic care, then held it up to the light.

"Five or six hours is my guess."

"What about the cause?"

"At a glance? Asphyxiation," he said bluntly. "Look at these little red spots in her eyes, not to mention the swelling around her nose and mouth." Saint raised the woman's chin gently. "Look here. Abrasions on the neck, along with some texture abrasions that I don't recognise. I'm leaning towards mechanical asphyxiation, but we'll know more when she's on Doctor Bell's bench." He frowned, and then sat back on his heels.

"Mechanical?"

"Hard to say for sure," he said. "The abrasions suggest something was pulled around her neck, but if that was the case, then I'd expect more bruising." He grimaced at the challenge. "It could just be the result of a struggle. Pip will be in a position to confirm it, of course." Saint ran his hands up and down the woman's limbs, like a sculptor feeling the curves of marble, respectful and precise. "Otherwise, I see no external signs of trauma at all..."

His head cocked to one side and he leaned in for a closer look. Then he straightened and cleared his throat.

"What is it?" George asked. "Have you seen something?"

"Isn't it obvious?"

George looked between his old friend and the body. Again, to his eye, there was nothing that suggested the victim might be dead at all, except for the fact she so obviously was.

"The obvious?"

"Her *chest*, George," he whispered. "Look at it."

He followed Peter's stare to the victim's chest. Across her chest, barely noticeable, was a subtle stain.

"What is that?" George asked. "Is that—?"

"Semen," Southwell said, appearing at Saint's shoulder and peering down at the victim with nothing less than regret in her eyes. "It doesn't take much imagination to work out how it got there," she said, then turned her gaze to George, who watched in real time as her expressions worked through a series of internalised emotions. "Now you just have to work out if the sick bastard did it while she was alive," she said. "Or after he murdered her."

CHAPTER FIVE

"I apologise for the setting," O'Hara began, as brightly as the fluorescent lighting that hummed above them. "I think it's best if we keep this private."

The explanation did little to ease the concern on Mr and Mrs Foxon's faces, who nudged closer to their son between them.

She pulled her notebook from her pocket, opened it to a clean page, then clicked record on the little voice recorder.

Mr Foxon, a rugby player of a man with a thick neck and bald head beneath a *Lincs Home Repairs* cap, leaned back and folded his arms over his bleach-stained hoody. Mrs Foxon, meanwhile, watched every one of O'Hara's movements with the intensity of a hovering kestrel. She eyed the way O'Hara held her pen and the way she pressed the button. She eyed the stark, white walls with the twin blue stripes that wrapped around the room.

"Is that necessary?" asked Mr Foxon, nodding at the recorder.

"Considering the severity of the situation, I think so," O'Hara replied with a reassuring smile. "It means that, with any luck, we won't need to bother you again."

Again, this did little to relieve the worried parents, whose faces remained impassive.

"Do we need a solicitor?" he asked.

"No," O'Hara replied. "You are welcome to call one of course. But for now, we are merely taking Louis's statement. He's not in any trouble at all, and had the situation been different, we would have taken it at the crime scene."

"Well, what's different about this situation?"

"Your son is under sixteen years old, which means he needs an appropriate adult present. True, we could have done this at the crime scene, but considering it was pitch dark and the boys had been through enough, we thought it would be better to bring you here where it's warm and dry and we can ensure everybody involved is looked after."

"Where you interview criminals?" came a small voice.

O'Hara turned her attention to the boy who sat nestled between his parents. He looked like a younger version of his father, thickset and thin-haired, but with his mother's large and worried eyes.

"It's where we interview all kinds of people," she said gently, even though she wasn't sure that was true. "Louis, I need you to tell me what happened today. Let's start at the beginning."

The boy looked between every responsible adult in the room, each of whom nodded, before he began his story. "I woke up," he said hesitantly, and O'Hara immediately wished she'd been more specific. "Mum made breakfast, and I played around on my Xbox for a bit. Then I went to meet the others."

O'Hara sat forward. "Where did you meet them?"

"On the bridge in the Country Park. It's where we always meet."

"Who's we?" O'Hara asked. "You, Oscar, and Wesley?"

"Yes," he said.

"Just the three of you?"

"Yes."

"What time was this? Can you remember?"

Again, Louis looked at his parents. The habit reminded

O'Hara of herself as a teenager when she couldn't find anything without help.

"He left the house about two p.m.," said Mrs Foxon. "Just after lunch."

"And you told my colleague that you live on Water Lane, is that right?"

"Yes," Mrs Foxon answered.

"Louis?"

"Yes," he confirmed.

"And how long would it take to get to the Country Park from your house, Louis? Did you walk?"

"Yeah," he said. "I cut across the fields."

"It takes about ten minutes," added Mr Foxon.

"So you met your friends at ten past two? Does that sound right?"

Louis shrugged. "Something like that."

"I'm sorry, Louis," O'Hara said, "but I need you to be as specific as possible. I know it might seem a little overcautious, but these details can really help us later on."

He nodded his understanding and squeezed his eyes closed in thought.

"We texted each other when we arrived," Louis said, looking between all the adults. "I can check the group chat, if you want?"

"That's a good idea," O'Hara said with a smile that seemed to settle the boy, if not his parents.

He pulled his phone out of his pocket and found the group chat far faster than Campbell could have. "Two twenty-three," he said.

"Do you mind if I see that, Louis?"

He hesitated for a moment, but held it up long enough for her to read the message, *I'm here. Where are you guys?* and the time tag, *14:23*. Above that message, all she could see were shared screenshots of memes and what looked like TikTok videos.

"And they arrived soon after you sent that message, did they?"

"Yeah," Louis said.

"And you met at the bridge. What did you do then?"

Louis shrugged. "We messed around for a bit."

When he didn't volunteer more information, O'Hara asked, "Like what?"

"Just walked along the river and that. There's a tree near the pool that we like to climb. We chucked some stones. Just messed about."

"And when was it that you first saw the carpet?"

"Oh, that was later. We found a pile of junk in the car park. I know we shouldn't have touched it," Louis said, glancing at his mother. "We just wanted to see what it was."

"And what was it?"

"Just a pile of old furniture and clothes and that. Mostly broken stuff. But on top, there was this red sofa."

O'Hara sat back, feigning nonchalance when she was most interested.

"So what did you do next?"

"We climbed on top of the pile," he said sheepishly, "and rolled it down."

"Louis..." his mum tutted.

"Then?" O'Hara pressed.

"Then we carried it into the park to make a den."

"Is that something you've done before?"

"Not since we were kids," he said, giving insight into how old he thought he was, even though he still looked like a child to everyone else in the room. "It was just a bit of fun."

"So you carried the sofa? Where to?"

"Down from the car park, over the bridge, up the hill, then into the trees."

"Off the right-hand side of the path?"

"Yeah."

"And then what did you do?"

"We decided to make a proper den. Wesley had a penknife,"

he said, and at this point, Mrs Foxon caught her husband's eye as urgently as if she'd grabbed his wrist, had it been in reach, but she said nothing. Louis continued, seeming not to notice. "We cut down some of the branches and tied them together to create walls."

"Tied them?" repeated O'Hara. "With what?"

"With leaf stems, willow branches, whatever we could find, really."

"Okay, and then what did you do?"

"Then we went back to the car park to see what else we could find. Like I said, it was mostly just broken furniture, but to the side, there was also a carpet."

"To the side?" O'Hara said. "Was it separate from the rest of the rubbish?"

"No, it was the same pile, just on the edge of it."

"So? What then?"

"We carried it back to the trees," Louis said. "Well, we dragged it. It was heavy."

"Why?"

Again, he shrugged. "Dunno. Just to lay it down like a floor in the den, that's all."

"Was it the only carpet there?"

"Think so, yeah. I mean, I didn't see another one."

She smiled pleasantly, coaxing him on.

"Go on."

"We dragged it all away from the car park and down the hill to the bridge."

"Louis, this is very important," O'Hara said, and he looked up to meet her eye. "What time was this?"

"I don't know. It was getting late, though. Nearly sunset. Wesley wanted to make a fire."

"So, eight-ish?"

"I don't know," he said. "Sorry. But I don't. I don't want to say the wrong thing."

"That's fine" she said. "You're doing well."

"We carried it into the trees and dumped it on the floor."

"On the *ground*," Mrs Foxon corrected him, then looked at O'Hara. "Sorry," she said. "Habit."

"Then what did you do, Louis?"

"We just sat down on the sofa. We were watching the sunset through the trees, and I told the others I'd have to leave soon. Mum had texted me. Oscar wanted to stay, but Wesley said he wanted to go home too, so we decided to unroll the carpet before we left. You know? To air it out. And then... Well. You know..."

O'Hara paused and watched the boy withdraw into himself, lowering his gaze to his lap and the fingers that picked at his cuticles.

"I'm sorry, Louis," she said. "I really am, but no, I don't know what happened. I'm going to need you to tell me."

He took a deep breath and looked at his parents. His mother nodded, her eyes full of tears, and she stroked his hair. His father placed a hand on the back of his neck; the gruff gesture seemed to strengthen Louis's resolve.

"We knelt on the floor...g-ground," Louis stuttered, "and pushed the carpet open." He looked up at O'Hara. "It *reeked*. We just figured it had been rained on. But when we opened it further, I knew something was wrong. I don't know why. I just kind of felt it. It felt wrong. Didn't feel like a carpet under my feet. Then it just kind of rolled out...well....her."

"Her?"

"The girl," he said, his voice quiet and thoughtful.

Nobody said anything, but all three adults stared at the teenager. In the dense silence, Louis felt the need to clarify.

"She was dead."

"Did you recognise the body?" O'Hara asked.

He shook his head and wiped away a tear before it had barely left his eye. "No."

"No one else was around?"

"No."

"What time did you say this was, Louis?"

"Around sunset."

More tears fell now, unstoppable tears. Too many to be wiped away before anyone noticed.

"Is that everything, officer?" asked Mr Foxon. "It's been a long day. We just want to get Louis home."

"I understand," O'Hara said, closing the notebook she hadn't written in. "We might be in touch if we have further questions, but we'll try to limit our contact."

"That's fine," he said with his hand still on the nape of his son's neck, guiding him to stand up, like a pup picked up by its neck fur.

"Where's Oscar?" Louis asked as they left the room. "Did his mum and dad come?"

"We couldn't reach them," O'Hara said. "We're still deciding what to do with him. I think my boss is keen not to start involving the authorities."

"We can take Oscar home with us," Mrs Foxon said. "It's no bother. We live just next door."

"I'll need to discuss it with my colleague," she said, "but that might be the best option, thank you. I appreciate your help," she said, shaking each of their hands in turn, "and I know my colleague feels the same." She stared across at the young man between his parents. "And as for you, Louis, I want you to know that if you suddenly remember anything, or if what you saw in any way at all begins to affect you, then you can call us, okay?" She slid a contact card across the table. "All being well, this will be the last you hear from us."

"In that case," the father said, pushing his chair back. "I look forward to not hearing from you again."

CHAPTER SIX

"I do *not* appreciate your tone, Mr Harris," Byrne said, standing to meet the man whose large forehead bulged with the single vein that ran north to south like a mountain stream. He had pulled his shirt collar looser and looser throughout the last hour, and rolled his sleeves further and further up his arms. Byrne, on the other hand, felt like the shirt on his back was unravelling by the second. "I'm going to have to ask you to calm down. Nobody is accusing anybody of anything—"

Mr Harris reeled. "That's not what it sounds like to me—"

"Well, I can't change the way you interpret the information I provide, Mr Harris."

He raised an index finger at Byrne.

"Your superior will be hearing about this."

"He'll be listening to the recording," Byrne assured him, pointing to the recorder. "I'm sure he'd like to have a word with you at some point, so, if there's anything to be discussed, he'll bring it up."

"You're treating *me* like a criminal, as well as my son."

"We are not treating anyone like a criminal," Byrne said as calmly as possible.

"You wanted his shoes and fingerprints," Mr Harris yelled. "Why's that? So you can pin it on him!"

"I guarantee you Mr Harris, that is not the case. We only took Wesley's fingerprints to eliminate the samples belonging to him. Same with his footprints." Byrne slowly sat down and addressed the young boy opposite him. "I promise you, Wesley, you are not in any trouble. Okay?"

Wesley Harris looked up and ever-so-slightly nodded. Byrne motioned for Mr Harris to take a seat, which he refused with a scoff, although he did back off to lean against the corner of the room with his arms folded like a teenager.

"Wesley, I just need you to tell me exactly what happened today. That's all."

"He's already told you, for Christ's sake." Mr Harris surged forward, and Byrne hung his head in dismay. It had been near-impossible to get two words from the boy without his father interrupting. "They met at two-thirty. They mucked around for a bit. They went to the car park. They found the sofa and the carpet, and they dragged them to their little den in the trees. What more do you need to know?"

Byrne ignored him. "Did you see anyone else in the area, Wesley?"

"I don't...I don't remember. No, I don't think so."

"Did you see who put the pile of junk in the car park?"

"No. Anyway, it was all wet, like it'd been there for hours already."

"Did anyone see you with the carpet or moving the carpet?"

Wesley shook his head. "No."

"Are you sure?"

Mr Harris threw up his arms. "He just told you, no."

"I'm talking to your son, Mr Harris, not to you right now," Byrne replied, feeling his professionalism slipping along with his patience. "Now, could you *please* take a seat?"

The silence that followed was a lull in the wind that normally precedes a storm, when the pressure drops.

"Excuse me?" Mr Harris whispered.

Byrne took a deep breath.

"Sit down, Mr Harris."

"Do you know who I am?"

"I don't think that's relevant—"

"I said," Mr Harris replied, moving forward to tower over Byrne, "do you know who I bloody-well am?"

"I don't think you want me to answer that question, Mr Harris," he replied quietly.

"Why's that then?" he asked, to which Byrne didn't reply. "Eh? Because of that rubbish in The Echo? It was fake news, you know that? I had nothing to do with—"

"No, that's not why," Byrne said, turning to look up at the man whose forehead pulsed like a pressurised pipeline.

"Why then?"

Byrne stood slowly with a grip on whatever professionalism he could muster and faced the man eye-to-eye.

"Because I have no idea who you are, Mr Harris," he said calmly. "I haven't read about you in the paper, I don't recognise your face, and I've never heard your name until this evening. You are simply a member of the public. A father of a witness whose well-being I am doing my best to protect, and right now, you are wasting my time, your son's time, and your own time."

The man opened and closed his mouth a few times in disbelief, whether at Byrne's words or the insolence of them, he couldn't be sure. Eventually, Mr Harris found the words to explain.

"I was at an event this afternoon over in Ormsby. High profile—"

"I'm not sure if that's relevant," Byrne said flatly. "This isn't about you. It's about your son, so please, for the love of God, just sit down."

And finally, Mr Harris sank into his seat, leaving Byrne to turn his attention once more to the boy, who seemed entirely unfazed by his father's outburst, as though he'd witnessed it a million times before.

Unlike his father, Byrne doubted anyone would notice a vein popping through the boy's skin. His face was full and round, much like the rest of his body.

"Wesley," Byrne started, "what did you do when you first saw the body?"

The boy gulped as though the memory alone was enough to trigger bile in his throat. "We ran," he croaked.

"Where to?"

"Back to the path, to the car park, and towards the road."

"Was the gate closed?"

Wesley looked up. "What?"

"The yellow gate," Byrne repeated, "did you have to jump over it to get to the road?"

"No," he said, confused, "it was open already. I think so anyway."

"Okay. Then what happened? You didn't see anyone or hear anything? No cars?"

"Then Louis's dad came to pick us up."

"Mr Foxon?" Byrne clarified, and Wesley nodded. "So Louis had called him, had he?"

"Yeah."

"So you must have had to wait for a bit? While Mr Foxon got ready and drove over?"

"Yeah," Wesley said, frowning. "Yeah, we waited a few minutes. It weren't long."

"Did you talk to each other while you were waiting?" Byrne asked. "About what you saw?"

"I dunno, I..." Wesley shrugged. "I can't remember."

"And what did Mr Foxon do when he got there? Did you show him the body?"

"No, we...Louis had already told him on the phone, I think, then—"

"You think?"

"No, yeah, he did tell him."

"Alright, carry on."

"He called the police, and they met us on the road. It was the Irish fella—"

"PC Maguire?"

"Yeah, him and the woman. I don't know her name."

"That's O'Hara," Byrne explained.

"Right. Well. Then we showed them to...to where she was. You know? The girl."

"Wesley," he continued, closing his notebook, "is there anything else you'd like to share with me? Anything at all?"

The boy shook his head vigorously.

"Statement concluded at eleven-forty-six p.m.," Byrne said, checking his watch, and he reached across the desk to click off the recorder. "Before you go, I do realise you hadn't intended to come to the station, but hopefully you can appreciate that we'd far rather speak to you here than in a dark forest. Our intentions were to make sure you and your friends are okay."

"Right," Wesley said. "Yeah, it's fine."

"And to get his fingerprints and shoe prints?" Mr Harris added, to which Byrne simply smiled politely.

"Where's Oscar?" Wesley asked as the three of them left the room.

"He's waiting outside for now," Byrne explained. "We're still trying to reach his parents."

Mr Harris scoffed. "Good luck with that."

Byrne turned to him. "Why?"

"Because they're wasters," he said, then clarified. "You know? Trash. You'll probably find them holed up somewhere on a bender."

"Dad—?"

"They have alcohol issues, do they?"

Again, Mr Harris laughed, as though the idea of his son's friend's family issues were mere entertainment. "And the rest," he said. "The place smells like a weed farm."

"Well," Byrne replied. "We'll continue our efforts. Thank you both. Are you okay getting home?"

"We're fine," the father said, leading his son to the door.

Byrne opened the door into the corridor and walked them to the custody suite, where he pointed Mr Harris and his son to the door. They walked away without so much as a thank you, passing Oscar on the way out, ignoring him but for a shared, worried glance between the boys. Byrne struggled to read it, though he tried to recall the perspective of a teenage boy, even if his own experience had been more than a decade ago.

Oscar watched his friend leave as though desperate to be taken home — to anyone's home. He sat barefoot on the cold, plastic chair, his trainers having been taken into evidence. The knees of his jeans were covered in mud, and his unkempt hair contained tiny scraps of dead leaves and debris. Byrne sighed and walked over to him, and as DI Larson had done to him countless times before, he sat down, crossed his legs in a George-like manner, and leaned in to meet the boy eye-to-eye.

"Where are your parents, Oscar?" he asked.

"Honestly?" The boy looked up at him with a pitiful stare. "I have no idea."

CHAPTER SEVEN

"First up," George said, turning his back on the whiteboard and the large, red question mark he'd drawn in the centre of it. "I appreciate you coming in on a Sunday and staying so late. I'll make this a quick one, just so we're ready to go first thing in the morning. Let's just lay out the basics."

He drew several legs from the question mark, allocating each element from what little they knew to each leg.

"Cause of death, by Peter Saint's account, was asphyxiation, possibly mechanical asphyxiation, likely from a bag or something over her head, but we'll need Doctor Bell's confirmation on that." He moved to another line. "Time of death, between three and four p.m.. Again, post mortem will likely give us a more accurate timing, but for the time being, that's what we're going with."

He stepped back and eyed the board. It looked rather pathetic. Until they replaced the great, red question mark in the middle, there wasn't much else to say.

"At least we know the killer's a man," Ivy offered with a shrug. "That's something to go on."

"True." George sighed. "Which means we've eliminated forty-nine per cent of the population."

"Only thirty-five million left to eliminate," she added with a grin.

"How do we know that?" Maguire asked, frowning. "That the killer's a man?"

"He left...evidence."

Maguire looked between Ivy and George as though he'd missed a memo. "What evidence?"

"A deposit," Ivy said.

"What? Like money?"

George rubbed his forehead. "No, not like money, like the kind of deposit you'd leave in a fertility clinic."

"The kind of deposit...oh," Maguire whispered, then his face contorted. "Bloody hell."

"Byrne, O'Hara, you've finished the boys' statements?" George asked, moving on.

"It's all recorded. We also sent off their fingerprints and shoes to Katy so she can factor them into the results we'll get tomorrow. No DNA without them being under caution, but they were okay with the fingerprints and shoes," O'Hara said from where she sat with her laptop resting on her lap. A large, white sheet hung from the ceiling, cutting their already limited space in half, while the back end of the incident room was decorated.

"And I just finished Wesley Harris's," Byrne replied with a yawn, then added, "Sorry."

"Long night?" George asked.

"I thought it'd never end, to be honest, guv."

"The father, was it?" he asked, and Byrne nodded with a grimace. "Thought he might be difficult."

"He said he wanted to talk to you, guv, about my, er... approach."

"Oh, I very much look forward to that conversation," George said with a grin. "Does anyone know who he is, by the way? This, Mr Harris?"

"First name Ewan," Campbell said. "I looked him up." She

turned her laptop around to show a Wikipedia article, including a photo of the man George recognised from earlier that evening. However, rather than being in a tuxedo in a dark Country Park, he was photographed wearing a crisp, light blue shirt and navy chinos beneath a linen blazer. On the lapel was an insignia of a red cross between blue and green squares, and centred with a fleur-de-lis that George recognised as the flag of Lincolnshire. "He's a local councillor. Meant to be the next Oliver Thompson, by all accounts."

"Who?" Maguire asked.

"Exactly."

"And he expected *us* to know him?"

"Delusions of grandeur," Campbell said. "Classic narcissist."

"He seemed like a regular old pompous arse to me," Byrne said.

"Well, he thinks we should know who he is, and maybe he's right," George said. "What did you find?"

"Nothing much, guv," Campbell said, clicking through notes on her laptop. "Just a quick Wikipedia search. There are the normal complaints about his policies."

"What kind of complaints?"

"Eco stuff, mostly," Campbell replied. "Putting profit before protecting the Wolds."

"Interesting," George said. "But not our priority right now. What about the other lad? Have we found his parents?"

"Oscar Wyman," Byrne said. "That's his name."

"Have we found his parents?" George repeated gently.

"Not yet, guv," O'Hara replied. "The officer we sent to their house said no one answered and there was no sign of anyone inside. They're not answering their phones either. So we sent Oscar home with the Foxons, Louis's parents."

"You don't think they might be connected to this, guv?" Maguire asked.

"What do you mean?" George asked.

"Just a bit suss, isn't it? That the lad's parents go missing on the day their son finds a dead body?"

"It's been less than four hours," he replied. "Let's not jump to conclusions yet."

"Anyway, it was pure chance that the boys found that carpet," Ivy spoke up. "Anyone could've stumbled across it."

"I'm just saying it's a coincidence," Maguire said. "And you're the one who always says you don't like coincidences, guv."

George sighed. "You're right," he said, turning back to the board. "I don't."

He wrote three names in a row: *Oscar Wyman, Louis Foxon, Wesley Harris*. Then, like a family tree, he drew two branches above each name and identified the parents: *Ewan Harris*...

George hesitated.

"Names?" he called out.

"James and Sarah Foxon," O'Hara answered.

"David and Emily Wyman," Byrne added, as George copied them to the board.

"What about Wesley Harris's mother?" He turned around to Campbell. "Does it say if the councillor is married, Campbell? On that Wikipedia article you found?"

"No, guv. I'll keep looking."

"Poor lads," O'Hara said quietly, staring at the names on the board and grabbing the team's attention. "Sorry," she added, looking around. "Maybe I'm just tired, I don't know, but interviewing Louis Foxon about what happened, his little face... I mean, it just hits different, doesn't it? When kids are involved."

"They're not kids," Ivy said. "They're thirteen."

"Well, they're sure as hell not men," George replied, leaning against a desk and rubbing his tired eyes.

"They are now," Maguire added, his thick Southern Irish accent adding a certain bluntness to his comment. "I mean, it happens to all of us, doesn't it? The day you stop being a child and become a man."

"Or a woman," Ivy added flatly.

"Aye, well, yeah, of course."

"What day was it for you then, Maguire?" she asked with a smirk. "Find a body, did you?"

"First time I kissed a girl," he said smugly and proudly. "I mean, properly kissed, you know? I was thirteen and I can remember it like it was yesterday." He sat back and smiled at the memory, then caught himself. "What about you? I mean, you know, girl-wise. Not that you kissed a...or maybe you did, which is fine, I just mean..."

"The day my dad died," Ivy said, cutting him off. "I was sixteen," she explained to the room.

"Mine was the day my sister was in her accident," Byrne said, nodding and matching her energy. "That was the first day I felt responsible. You know? Like an adult. I was seventeen."

He turned to Campbell soundlessly, who sighed and shrugged. "Honestly, I'd say I felt like a kid up until the day I joined the force. Maybe I was more sheltered than you lot. I don't know."

"Same," O'Hara said. "It wasn't until I left home, really. Maybe the first time I went grocery shopping for myself? But I was definitely sheltered. It took me a while to grow up. I'm not sure I even have yet, to be honest."

Then, as one, the team turned to George, but it was Maguire who was brave enough to ask the question on the tips of all their tongues.

"What about you, guv?"

George looked around each of them, appreciating the expectant look in their eyes. He smiled at a secret memory he chose to keep to himself.

"Perhaps that's an answer for a different day," he said. "But you're right, Maguire. Those boys had no choice. Their childhood ended today. It's our job to find out why." He turned back to the whiteboard. "The time when nobody dies..." he whispered to himself.

"What's that, guv?" Campbell asked.

He turned back to the team. "The time when nobody dies," he repeated. "It's—"

"Marguerite Duras," Byrne said. "The French writer?"

"Exactly." George smiled at the man whom he had quite clearly underestimated. The man nobody might have expected to help care for a disabled sister or recall the names of obscure French writers from memory. "She said that childhood is the time when nobody dies."

Maguire scoffed.

"What the hell's that supposed to mean? Of course, people die when we're children. My grandparents all died by the time I was eight years old."

O'Hara rolled her eyes.

"Obviously it's not literal, Dave."

"She means that childhood is a time of innocence and security," George continued. "When harsh realities seem unimaginable, or at least very distant. Don't you remember feeling invincible as a kid, Maguire? Death was something far off in your future. You knew people who died, but they were old people. Death felt distant. Like it had nothing to do with you."

"Aye, I remember," Maguire said, shrugging. "I once jumped off the garage roof because I thought I was Superman."

"Exactly," George laughed. "See, you can say that the first time you felt like a man was the first time that you kissed a girl. But I don't know if that's true. I think the first time anyone *really* feels like an adult is the first day you truly understand that you and everyone you love will die." He sighed and leaned on the desk, feeling the heaviness of the day. "It's just that most of us face that reality as a concept. Today, those boys faced it literally. It fell out of a carpet, and they looked it in the eye. I don't envy them," George said. "And I'd be surprised if that type of formative experience doesn't stay with them until the day *they* die."

He looked around the team. It was dark and eerie in the incident room. They'd only bothered to turn on a few of the desk lamps, so their sorrowful faces glowed in a shadowed, distorted light. He felt the shared dreamlike sensation that's aroused when one looks at the stars for too long, contemplates space for too long, and considers the true vastness of nothingness in which we all turn around and around.

"On that cheery note," George said, clapping loudly and startling them from their late-night musings. "Get yourselves home. We've got a lot to do in the morning."

CHAPTER EIGHT

George's home offered all the warmth and comfort a late night at work demanded. It hadn't always been that way. But since he'd fixed the heating, filled the holes in the walls, and allowed Ivy to introduce a few rugs and throws, it had become quite cosy. By the time Ivy had taken off her coat, hung it up alongside her bag, and removed her shoes with a satisfied sigh, George was already standing at the sofa with the whiskey decanter in his hand.

"Nightcap?" he asked.

Ivy eyed the temptation and gave in too easily. "Go on then," she said. "Can't say I feel relaxed enough to sleep after your little bedtime story to the team."

"You think I was too harsh?" he asked, pouring them a sleep-inducing measure.

"I think it was... philosophical," Ivy said, taking her favourite armchair. "The true tragedy that happened today wasn't three little boys losing their childhood. It was the death of an adult woman. *She* should be our priority."

"You're right, of course," George said, handing her a glass.

"We don't even know her name."

"We will, we will." He sat back, taking a long sip. "What a day," he said to the ceiling.

"I know. One minute, you're mooching around Alford, and the next, you're discussing necrophilia with your boss on the ride home," Ivy said. "At least I got a lamp out of it."

"Oh yeah, where is the monstrosity, by the way?" he asked, looking around.

"I left it in the car." She leapt up, and George groaned, wishing he hadn't said anything. "Can I borrow your keys, guv?"

"Sure, they're in my coat pocket," he said lazily, and Ivy rushed to the coat stand. "But you can keep it in the car if you like?" he called after her. "Indefinitely!"

She faked a laugh as she headed out the door.

George continued to stare at the ceiling, admiring the intricate medallion around the hanging light. It was a beautiful house. His restoration projects had taught him that much. Its builders had carefully and attentively incorporated many minor details, unlike modern houses: the Spilsby stone fireplace, the wainscoting in Ivy's room, and multiple ceiling medallions. He felt more and more recently that this might be his last home, the one in which he lived out his days as an old man. With Grace's plaque in the cemetery of St Margaret's over the road, he doubted that he'd ever be able to bring himself to move too far.

The opening and closing of the front door snapped him from his melancholy, and he turned to watch Ivy struggle through the door with the sea-shell-cum-spaceship lamp. He turned back to the ceiling with a grin. That was exactly why he'd asked her to stay, to snap him out of his grief, and remind him of what made life worth living even if it wasn't perfect.

"Guv?" she asked, walking back to her armchair.

"Yes?"

"What's this?" Ivy stood before him, holding up the scrunched-up flyer from the tearoom. He recognised the crude sketch on the front. "I found it in your coat pocket."

"Oh, nothing," he dismissed.

"Are you going to do a pottery class?"

"I thought about it." He shrugged. "Changed my mind."

"Why?" Ivy lowered herself into the seat opposite him, and George readied himself for a session of the literal armchair psychology he'd come to expect since Grace had died. "I think it's a good idea."

"I'm just not that bothered."

"I thought you were going to start living. You know, your one wild and precious life?"

"I was," he said. "I mean, I am. I just...well, learning how to make a mug isn't exactly living, is it?"

Ivy shrugged. "Isn't it? What else is there?"

George sighed. "Maybe that's the problem. I don't know."

"What about when you were a kid?"

"What *about* when I was a kid?"

"Well, was there anything you always wanted to do? Something you couldn't do until you were an adult?"

"Like what?"

Ivy sat back, thinking, then sat forward suddenly.

"Okay, like when I was a kid, I remember walking past the birthday cakes in the supermarket aisle and thinking, when I'm an adult, I'm going to buy a whole one of those and eat it all to myself. Not even on my birthday. Just one random day." She sat back and threw up her hands. "Just because I can."

George laughed.

"And how was it?"

"I don't know," she said. "I never did it."

"Why not?"

"Maybe for the same reason you won't take a pottery class." When he didn't reply, she squinted, like a real psychologist might when reading someone. "What did you want to be when you were a kid, guv? A copper?"

"God no."

"Then what?"

He puffed out a long breath of air. It was a performance. As soon as she'd asked, the answer had popped into his mind. He'd always wanted to be the same thing, ever since he'd been a little boy.

"It's stupid," he said. Ivy didn't even entertain the thought but waited silently for him to continue, until George sighed and admitted, "I wanted to be a painter."

Ivy did well to hide her incredulity. He imagined it was the last thing she had expected him to say. But she merely raised her eyebrows and sat back, pondering his response.

"Like Grace?" she asked.

George smiled. "I suppose she got there first. But no, long before I met Grace." He cleared his throat. "Do you remember the chalk painting scene in Mary Poppins?"

"When they jump into the pavement?" she said. "Of course."

"Well, I remember watching it with my sister, and it blew me away. You know, when you're a child and don't fully understand the difference between reality and stories? I thought you really could jump into paintings. Now, I was only six, you understand. But I suppose I actually thought that." He shrugged. "Right up until the day I pushed her into a painting at the National Gallery, and Mum dragged us out before security got hold of us."

Ivy laughed the kind of loud, hearty laugh he hadn't heard from her in a long time.

"She didn't fall into the painting?"

"No. She did get a nasty bruise from the frame, though." He chuckled and shook his head. "Then I grew up and joined the force," George continued. "I quickly learned the difference between reality and stories."

"And that you can't just escape into a painting?"

"I suppose. Or... I don't know. Maybe I forgot that you can. Maybe we all need a little imagination to get through life? Maybe we're doing it wrong?"

"What do you mean?"

"I mean, in a way, it *is* true, isn't it? Art does take you somewhere else." He leaned forward. "You know, I'd see it in Grace's eyes when she was really in the flow of painting. She would be lost inside it. In this other world. She would...leave." He closed his eyes and remembered his wife's focused gaze and the glaze that would separate him from whatever vision she experienced. "She would go to this whole different place. And I suppose I always wanted to know where that place was and whether I could go there too."

Ivy sat back and swirled her whiskey. "I suppose I've never thought of it like that."

George shrugged and left her to the thoughts that gathered like clouds behind her eyes. He remembered the first time he'd watched his wife paint and how he'd studied the small, changing expressions on her face, as captivated as though watching a film. He remembered the beautiful watercolour set his parents had bought him for his eighteenth birthday and how he'd never touched them because he'd met Grace by then, and was too embarrassed, or perhaps too insecure, to claim her artistic gift for himself. She'd always said that anybody can paint. But he'd been too shy to even try in front of her, like speaking a second language to a native.

"Maybe you do go somewhere," Ivy said quietly.

George rose from his memories like a diver surfacing.

He blinked at her. "What's that?"

"When you're painting," she said. "Maybe you should go to the same place you were talking about earlier?"

"Where?"

"The same place as childhood," she said, closing her eyes as though expressing a thought that brought her peace. "The place where nobody dies."

He set his empty glass down beside him and smiled warmly at her.

"I think I'll call it a night," he said, pushing himself from the chair. He stopped beside the lamp she had placed on the floor, and the pottery leaflet caught his eye. That was when he caught her in his peripheral vision, watching him curiously. He laughed to himself at the notion of him attending a pottery class and let the slip of paper fall back to the table. "Goodnight, Ivy."

CHAPTER NINE

The morning had been pleasant enough. It was a far cry from his mornings with Grace, but far more enjoyable than those mornings he had spent alone. He and Ivy had made coffee and shared toast before heading to the station in brilliant sunshine. But as he knew well enough, everything could change in a heartbeat, especially a good mood. Still, he couldn't help but groan when he recognised the man striding towards them down the first-floor corridor. George looked at Ivy, who shared his belief that their superior waited around corners just so he could detour their route to the incident room. Such was his timing.

"George, Ivy," Tim said, meeting them like a roadblock as if their meeting was by pure chance. "How were your weekends?"

"Eventful," George said, smiling to show he was at least half joking.

"Yes, well, bodies do that, don't they...?" He cleared his throat awkwardly, then bounced on the balls of his feet. "Actually, while I have you, do you have a moment? There's something I want to show you."

Detective Chief Inspector Tim Long was a notoriously serious man who, although he did his best to portray a personable demeanour, often failed at it. This morning, however, he was as giddy as a schoolboy with a new game to play, leaving George unsure of the reasons behind this excitement.

"Fine," George said. "What have you got?"

"Follow me."

Tim led them down the corridor, and instead of turning off towards his office, he led them into the incident room, which had been their original destination.

The groan of the floorboards at the doorway announced their arrival, and they entered the incident room to a chorus of good mornings, nearly all of them directed at the superior officer, with only a handful intended for either George or Ivy.

"What do you think?" Tim asked, presenting the space proudly with a sweep of his arm.

Where the white sheet had hung yesterday, now stood a glass office nestled into the back of the room. It was empty inside, but for the whiteboard that George had commandeered when he first came to the station, and a modest conference table with chairs.

"What's this?"

"It's for you, George," he said. "For your team. You said you wanted a space of your own." George tried to voice his thoughts, but they whizzed through his mind so fast and furiously, he couldn't seem to bite down on any. "I'm just sorry it took so long," Tim added sheepishly. "But, I do try to keep my promises, George. You needed somewhere discreet for your team to work. Well? Here it is."

"Thank you, Tim," George said eventually. "I must say, I'm... I'm lost for words."

"I'll leave you to settle in," Tim replied, like a landlord who had just met his new tenants. "Enjoy it."

He placed a hand on George's shoulder as he left them to it. George waited to feel the rush of air as the doors closed and for the floorboard to creak as Tim passed over them.

"Jesus, guv," Ivy said. "It's like a bloody fish tank."

She sought some kind of reaction from him, but he was lost in his thoughts. It was no secret that Tim and George went back decades, and that had George not transferred to Mablethorpe all those years ago, it very likely would have been Tim on the receiving end of a new office courtesy of George, and it would be have been George making his way back to his little private space. But ever since George's return, Tim had been somewhat aloof. Distant. It was a gut feeling that George couldn't describe in words, but put down to the difference in rank, and although the friendship remained, the new office space was no reflection of it. It was functional. It was needed for the team to operate and to discuss confidential elements of their investigations.

He and Ivy stepped into the fishbowl office and closed the door behind them, shutting out most of the noise coming from the ringing phones and chatter of the other teams in the shared incident room outside.

"Very nice," Ivy said, stroking the freshly painted white walls opposite the glass. "Very nice indeed. I guess we're officially a team now." She nodded to the door. "Do you think we've been accepted by the locals?"

"Ah, I was here long before those lot," he said with a grin as the door was opened from the outside, as Maguire stepped into the room with the rest of the team following on his heels. They moved throughout the office like tourists observing the Sistine Chapel.

"Is this ours?"

"Seems that way," George said.

"Reminds me of Wonka's glass elevator," O'Hara said.

"Whose idea was it to have glass walls?" Campbell asked with a grin, and George had to admit that his cynical side had thought the same. Despite the need for discretion, the office was designed to be looked into, that was for sure. There was no place to hide.

"Did you get this for us, guv?" Maguire asked. "Nice one."

"Just take a seat, all of you," George said. "We can show our appreciation by closing the investigation."

He wasn't sure why he felt irked. Perhaps it was Campbell's observation, the whiteness of the space, how clinical and transparent it was, like a showroom. Even his voice carried. The walls were white, the glass frames were white, and the whiteboard was white. Too white. There was too much empty space to be filled.

The team followed his instructions and set up their laptops and notebooks around the central conference table. It was a limited space, but at least they were all together. The scene reminded George of a busy family kitchen at breakfast.

"Right then," he began, his voice bouncing off the glass. "Let's get straight into it." He tapped the red question mark in the middle of the whiteboard. "Our priority today is to learn the identity of our victim. Southwell said we should have the lab results by the end of today, but I'd rather we didn't sit on our laurels. More than likely, our victim isn't even in the system. So, Ruby, I want you to look into missing persons, anyone matching the profile of our victim — middle-aged, five foot four, brown hair, brown eyes."

"Yes, guv," the civilian researcher replied with a swift flick of her mouse.

Following a bumpy start to her joining the team, Ruby now attended the office daily instead of utilising her work from home hours. She completed every task flawlessly and surpassed expectations. The only problem with such consistent hard work was that he normalised it. For her to raise the bar would be a downright miracle, and having nowhere to grow into often resulted in boredom, or worse, apathy.

"Campbell also asked you to inform the council about our activities at the Country Park," George said. "How did that go?"

"All done," Ruby replied, looking up at George through captivating eyes so dark they were almost black. "I kept it short, just the basic information. They agreed to close off that section of the park for the foreseeable future while we conduct our investigation."

"Kind of them," George said flatly.

"They also confirmed that there's no CCTV in the car park."

"Of course there isn't," Ivy mumbled. "That would be far too easy."

"I'd still like to talk to them at some point," George replied. "To find out how long fly-tipping has been a problem."

"With all due respect, guv," Maguire spoke up. "It's not the fly-tipping that's the problem. It's the dead bodies inside what's been fly-tipped."

"Not necessarily," George said, pointing his marker at the officer like a professor might challenge a student. He'd always fancied teaching criminology at a university, wearing a tweed jacket with elbow patches. Sometimes, working with younger, less experienced officers felt rather close to it. "The way I see it, we have two possible scenarios."

He turned back to the board and, in the bottom left corner, wrote down two distinct but equal possibilities.

"Number one," George began. "Somebody killed our victim, put her in the carpet, and dumped her in the car park. Number two," he said, writing as he spoke. "Somebody killed our victim, saw the carpet *already dumped* in the car park, and took the opportunity to dispose of her."

The team watched on as though George were a mathematics professor writing out an equation. He didn't know the value of X or its exponent, but he knew they needed to find a solution.

"On the information that we have so far," he continued, "we have to assume that either one of these could be just as true as the other. Therefore, I want to follow *three* lines of enquiry."

He moved to the bottom right-hand corner of the board and wrote as he spoke.

"First line of enquiry. The body of the victim," he said, writing *Body*. "Any leads from this line of enquiry will come from Southwell or Doctor Bell. That includes the murder weapon, if indeed there was one. Our second line of enquiry," he said as he wrote *Carpet Owner*. "The owner of the carpet," he explained. "They may or may not have anything to do with this, but either way, I want to find out who they are and I want to talk to them. And the *third* line of enquiry," he said. "The person who fly-tipped." George wrote *Fly-tipper*. "Again, they may or may not have anything to do with it. It may be the same person who owned the carpet. Hell, the person who owned the carpet could be the victim. Either way, we need to find the connection between these three options."

He turned back to the team.

"That's what I want you all to work on today. Ruby is on missing persons to identify our victim," he said, tapping the first line of enquiry: *Body*. "Campbell and Byrne, I want you to follow the carpet line of enquiry. Call Southwell and get the name of the carpet manufacturer. I'm sure she'll send over material results, but get that basic information for now and follow it. Find out where the carpet was manufactured and who it was sold to, if you can."

"Yes, guv," they said in unison.

"Maguire, you're on the fly-tipper," George said, pointing at the officer who looked somewhat surprised to be given an entire line of enquiry to himself. "I want you to check local cameras for any evidence of fly-tipping. Of course, we're looking for the person who specifically fly-tipped that carpet. Look for road cameras, CCTV, and dash cams from other cars in the car park. That carpet was big. You wouldn't be able to fit it in Byrne's VW Polo."

"Hey!" Byrne said, suddenly looking up. "Don't knock the Polo."

"Same with the sofa," George said, ignoring him. "Look for trucks and vans."

"Yes, guv," Maguire replied glancing at O'Hara as though a little lost without her. He'd have to get used to it. George couldn't afford to keep pairing them off, not on an investigation with so many leads.

"O'Hara," George said, "I want you to put out some information requests. Maybe someone saw someone tipping the carpet. Maybe they saw someone hanging around the area. Dog walkers are in and out of Snipe Dales every single day. I can't believe that no one saw anything. Put an information request on socials, then go talk to the locals. Knock on doors if you have to."

"Yes, guv."

"But first, I need you and Byrne to write up the boys' statements. Corroborate them. Paint me a picture as soon as I get back. Identify any differences. Ivy and I are going to speak to the Environment Agency in charge of the area. If fly-tipping is an ongoing problem, maybe they have their own leads. Maybe they know for sure who's doing it, but they can't do anything about it."

"Guv," Byrne said quietly, "there's someone you're forgetting."

George looked down at the soon-to-be detective who shared the same boyish features as the very lad they were discussing. "I haven't forgotten about him," he said, reaching for his coat. "The first thing I'm going to do before anything else is find Oscar Wyman's parents."

"Maybe that shouldn't be your priority, guv," Ivy said.

As usual, she had been straddling the space between George and the rest of the team, leaning against the new glass walls. From her position, she looked over Ruby's shoulder at her screen.

"Why not?" he said, looking between the sergeant and the researcher.

Ruby was the one to reply. "We've had an email from Southwell's team."

"And?"

She held up her phone. "We've got a name."

CHAPTER TEN

It wasn't hard to picture how the move into the new office had come about. There was little doubt it had been Tim's idea, but that was probably the extent of his involvement. He might have seconded some of the budget to the move, but he had then convinced somebody young and keen to manage the project. Somebody who was out to impress. Maybe somebody who saw the project as a way of buying into Tim's good books. Once the fit-out had been completed, he would have identified a few of the younger officers to help. Individuals who might not be as hungry as the officer in charge, but maybe a little wet behind the ears.

And one of them, George thought, had overlooked the most precious item in the office.

The whiteboard rag.

There was so little furniture in the fish bowl, which had fast become the team's nickname for the space, that had it been there, it would have stood out like a sore thumb.

Instead, George used the back of his sleeve to erase the big red question mark in the centre of the whiteboard. In its place, he wrote a name that, for now, meant only one thing. *Gemma Radford: Victim.*

"Maguire, I've a job for you," he grumbled.

"Guv?"

"Find me a new rag," he said. "You have my permission to steal one if necessary."

Maguire laughed out loud, as if he thought the comment a joke. Then his face stiffened.

"Serious?"

"Deadly," George replied.

"Can I quote you on that? You know? If I get caught?"

George underlined the name, studied it for a second then, turned to face the young Irishman.

"Don't get caught," he said, then tapped the name in case he was missing any of the team's attention. "This name," he began. "This name encapsulates a human being. As far as we're concerned, it contains an ocean of possibilities. Was she a mother, a daughter, a wife, an aunty, maybe? Employee? Sister? Lover? The list goes on."

He imagined his own name written up there in his scrawled handwriting. What would they find on him? What would they miss? Would anyone know he'd ridden the oldest, wooden roller-coaster in the world? Or, that he was mildly allergic to peppercorn sauce? Or that he'd stopped his car only that morning to let a lazy cat idle across the street? Ivy would know about the cat, but he counted the incident wouldn't even cross her mind.

"Gemma Radford could have been anybody. She could be one of us. She could have been kind, artistic, selfish, spoilt, gentle, angry, or all those things combined. The fact remains that it's our job to find out who killed her, and to do that, we need to know who she was. We're not here to judge. We're here because somebody out there knows the truth, and that somebody should be brought to justice." He took a few paces forward, and stared through the window at the various CID teams in the incident rooms outside. "All we have is a name. Gemma Radford. To us, she is devoid of characteristics and traits. She is a blank slate." He turned to face them. "Let's fill in the gaps. Let's find out who she was."

He had always enjoyed the rush of activity at the beginning of an investigation. It was a time when, in addition to those key pieces of information being sought, imaginations were pushed. In its simplest form, it was a dot-to-dot that would slowly begin to reveal an image. In its most complex form, it was a pot into which the team, witnesses, Southwell's team, the pathologist, neighbours, lovers, family members and anybody who met Gemma Radford would contribute something.

And it was down to him to interpret those ingredients.

Ruby, the only member of the team not to have been called into work on their Sunday evening, was the first to speak up.

"She's on the database," she said. "Gemma Radford, forty-two years old, arrested for vandalism in 2003 for defacing a statue of Cecil Rhodes in Oxford during student protests."

"So, she studied at Oxford University?" George asked while scribbling down the key points on the board.

"Brookes," Campbell clarified, reading from her screen. "Oxford Brookes, from 2002 to 2004."

"Who's Cecil Rhodes?" George asked. "Why do I know that name?"

"Wasn't he something to do with British imperialism in Africa?" Byrne said, clicking across his screen. "But I forget what exactly..." He paused, his eyes scanning the screen as fast as though he were on a train scanning the landscape, then read aloud, "Here we go. Cecil Rhodes expanded the British Empire across Africa in the late 1800s, establishing the countries now called Zimbabwe and Zambia. Oh, here we are," he continued, cringing. "He believed in the superiority of the Anglo-Saxon race and supported the oppression of the indigenous people, helping to establish the racial segregation that led to apartheid in South Africa." Byrne looked up at George. "Sounds like my Grandad."

"What exactly did Gemma Radford do to his statue?" George asked.

"Eggs and graffiti," she replied. "Nothing major."

"Is that all?" Maguire asked, his Irish accent coming through strong, not without a hint of menace.

"It's pretty high up," Ruby said in her defence and turned her laptop to show a statue built into the third storey of an old stone building.

"So she's political," George said, taking what he needed. "An activist of some kind, maybe?"

"She *was*, at least," Ivy agreed, leaning over Ruby's chair. "When she was a student, I mean."

"What else?" George asked.

"According to socials, it looks like she's single," Ruby said, scrolling through her feed. "Both Christmas and Valentine's Day came and went without any soppy posts about a significant other."

"Maybe she just chooses not to smear her social life all over the internet," Ivy said.

"She's pretty active otherwise. Mostly nature pics."

"According to the electoral roll, she lives with a Mr Matthew Cooper," Ruby added.

"So she wasn't single," George suggested, trying to keep up.

"Matthew Cooper. Thirty-six, works for a local security firm," Byrne said.

She shrugged. "Could be family. Her brother?"

George wrote the name *Matthew Cooper* on the board. "If he works in security, he might work shifts. If he's not home, we'll try twelve hours later," he said darkly. "What about Gemma? Where did she work?"

Again, his order triggered an immediate clicking response, and again, Ruby was the first to answer.

"Safe Haven Animal Shelter."

"I've heard of that. That's in Spilsby, isn't it?"

"*Near* Spilsby," Campbell replied before Ruby could, and not without an air of competition.

He'd noted down the main points with more of those spider legs growing from her name, as though Gemma Radford was a product they were brainstorming: *female, forty-two, student protest arrest, Oxford Brookes, single? Matthew Cooper? Animal shelter.* He couldn't help but notice all the blank space around her name, where another person in another lifetime in another job might have written the woman's hopes and dreams, her desires, favourite memories, colour, food, and aspects of nature. But George shook his head and focused on the facts. The rest was not his concern.

"Right," he said, stepping back to look at the board. "This changes things." He turned back to the team. "Ruby, focus instead on building a profile on Gemma Radford. Where did she go? What did she do? Who did she do it with? Any friends, foes, lovers, you know the drill. I want her most regular routes and the patterns of her movements. Especially this weekend. ANPR on the Ford Fiesta we saw in the car park, if that was indeed hers. If you can get access to her phone records, even better."

"Yes, guv."

"I doubt that will take you long," George said with a smile. He was well aware that he gave Ruby twice as many tasks as he might have given any other researcher. "When you're done, help the team. Check local cameras for any evidence of fly-tipping. I want to locate that carpet, where it's from, and where it went before it ended up in the car park of Snipe Dales."

"Where do you want me then, guv?" Maguire asked.

"On the road," George said. "I'm now thinking our best bet is roadside businesses. Used car sales, petrol stations, builders' yards. Anything that has a camera pointing onto the road. We're looking for trucks, vans, trailers, anything that could have carried furniture around in the last week or so. If they have any information at all, request their CCTV."

"From when, though?" Maguire asked. "We don't have a time. In the last week or so? I mean, that's an enormous window."

"You're right," George said. "It is. Take O'Hara with you. We'll need two eyes on this."

"That's not what I—"

"I know what you meant, Maguire, but we don't have a smaller window. We don't know *when* that rubbish was dumped in the car park."

"But Saint gave a time of death on the body. She died yesterday."

"But the carpet could have been there *before* she died," Ivy said, reminding him of the point she had also missed until George had pointed it out to her. "The body wasn't necessarily dumped *with* the carpet. The killer could've seen the tip and taken the chance to hide it there."

Maguire shook his head. "Jesus, that's a monumental task."

"Do what you can," George said, in what he hoped was an equal balance of authority and reassurance.

"What about the lock on the car park gate?" Campbell asked. "What if we worked out when that was broken? That might narrow it down?"

"We can't assume it was the same person who dumped the rubbish, or the same person who dumped Gemma Radford," Ivy cut in. "What we need are answers. Who dumped the rubbish? Let's eliminate them. Who did the carpet belong to? Let's eliminate them. Right now, the best chance we have of finding either of those pieces of information out is finding the van, truck or whatever on CCTV. Snipe Dales Country Park is situated between Horncastle to the west and Spilsby to the east. There's a chance that whoever dumped the rubbish travelled north to south or south to north, but it's unlikely given the nature of the roads and the size of the vehicle needed to carry a sofa, a roll of carpet and whatever else was on that rubbish pile. Therefore, roadside CCTV is our best bet, and as the guv said, that means car sales, petrol stations and builders' yards." She eyed them all, and George saw the unyielding mother in her. "Understood?"

"Understood," Byrne replied.

"She's right," George said firmly. "We can't assume anything. Not at this stage. Someone might have broken that lock for any number of reasons. Maguire, if you need a window, look at the tapes up until three p.m. on Sunday, okay?"

He didn't reply, but made a saluting gesture with his fingers.

"What about information requests, guv?" O'Hara asked. "We could have some signs put out on the road."

George paused for thought. The beginning of an investigation was usually a scramble for tiny leads, most of which would lead to dead ends but would occupy nearly ninety per cent of his resources.

"A post on our socials will be enough," he said eventually. "You can do that now before you leave. Ask for information about fly-tipping in or around the Country Park, if anybody has seen any instances of it, or even seen anybody doing it, where and when. Do *not* mention the nature of the crime," he said. "What we don't need are locals keeping you busy with speculations about their true crime theories. In fact, turn off the comments. Can you do that? Is that a thing?"

"Yes, guv," Ivy said.

"Good. Do that. People can message us directly."

"Will do," O'Hara said, opening a new tab on her laptop.

"Campbell and Byrne, stick to looking into the carpet. Go to Southwell's lab and look up the make of the carpet yourself if you have to. But I want to know who it belonged to by the end of the day."

"After I've written up the boys' statements, guv?" Byrne asked. "Or before?"

"After," he said.

"What about finding Oscar Wyman's parents?"

George hesitated, oscillating between the name Oscar Wyman

in his mind and Gemma Radford on the board. Then he met Ivy's hard stare.

"We're going to have to set that aside for now," George replied. "He's not our victim. Gemma is."

Byrne nodded slowly but didn't seem best pleased with the reply. Perhaps he saw something of himself in the boy, but George had to prioritise. That was his job.

"What about a next of kin for Gemma Radford?" he asked Ruby.

"Nothing on file, guv," she replied. "But I've got an address."

"Good, email it to me," he said, nodding at Ivy to communicate that their morning task had also changed.

"Guv," Ruby said. "In her email, Katy Southwell also mentioned the DNA found on the victim's chest."

"Go on."

"No match. No name. Sorry, guv."

"Nothing?"

Ruby shook her head. "Nothing at all."

"Right..." he said, hearing the disappointment in his voice. "Well, let's make a start then, shall we? We'll talk again this afternoon."

"Yes, guv," a few of them replied, while others rubbed their tired eyes or stared at the ceiling for some inspiration.

George headed over to the external window, taking a moment to organise his thoughts, which he often found he did best against the backdrop of a clear, crisp, blue sky.

"Guv?" Ivy walked over to him, her back against the team to offer a sliver of privacy. "What's wrong?"

"Oh, nothing," George lied.

"Guv?"

He smiled. She knew him too well.

"Something doesn't sit right, Ivy," he whispered. "Usually, suspects do everything they can to *avoid* leaving their DNA on their victim or the crime scene."

"Okay." She shrugged. "Gloves, masks, wipe-downs."

"So why would someone purposely leave their DNA on her clothing?"

She looked at him, not yet getting the point that was only just forming in George's mind.

"Heat of the moment?" she said. "Murderers aren't really known for their rationality."

"Maybe," George said, watching a blackbird flit back and forth against the blue sky like the dark thought darting through his mind. "Unless it is."

"What do you mean?"

"I mean, if it was a premeditated murder, which mechanical asphyxiation suggests it could be, then he might have left his DNA all over the victim for a much more sinister reason."

Ivy paused but failed to follow his thinking. "What reason?"

"A power play."

"With Gemma Radford?"

"No," George said, turning away from the blackbird to meet Ivy's eye. "He knows he's not on our database." He leaned on the windowsill and sighed. "We're looking for somebody with a clean record."

CHAPTER ELEVEN

"Look at that plonker," Maguire said, as he reversed into a parking space at the first petrol station on their list. He pointed at a car that had taken the first pump in the line, blocking anyone from coming in behind him.

"Plonker?" O'Hara repeated. "You've been in England too long, Dave."

"Ah, see here this eejit," Maguire said, putting on the strongest Irish accent he could muster with language stolen from his father. "Jaysus, move up there a wee bit so the rest o' us can get in, will ya? Half wit."

"That's more like it," O'Hara replied, grinning as she climbed from the car.

"Anyway, you're one to talk," he said, following. "Your accent's becoming more Lincolnshirian by the day."

She rolled her eyes.

"*Lincolnshirian*? What are you talking about? I'm Somerset through and through, I am," she said.

"Are you now?" Maguire said as they walked towards the shop. "When I first met you, it was all '*gert lush this*' and '*gert lush that*'. I haven't heard you say that in years."

"I say it all the time," she said, stopping in her tracks. "Maybe you're not listening."

"I mean, you don't even like cider. What kind of West Country girl are you?"

The little bell above the door jingled as Maguire entered the shop, and he held the door for O'Hara to catch up. She was staring at him with her mouth hanging wide open, clearly stunned by his offence. "What are you on about? Of course, I like cider."

"You didn't the other night."

"When?"

"With...what's your new bloke's name? Adam?"

"Adrian. And he's not my new bloke, he's just *a* bloke."

"Aye, well. With him," Maguire said, nodding, "I mean, a dandelion and burdock, for God's sake? It's not even alcoholic."

It wasn't the first time they'd had such a conversation about who was becoming more localised faster. It was one of those dependable forms of entertainment that anybody forced to work with another person for such lengthy periods adopts to ease the passage of time.

"So? Just because I don't have a cider one time, that means I've given up my heritage, does it?" she hushed as they approached the counter.

Maguire shrugged. "I'm just saying, I had a Guinness."

"You always have a Guinness," she muttered.

"Exactly," he finished with a grin. "And I always will."

A small woman of Asian descent looked on expectantly from behind the counter. She had watched their interaction from the door perplexed, as though watching a foreign film without subtitles.

"Hello," she said brightly.

"Now then," Maguire started, and cringed at how the quintessentially Lincolnshire greeting sounded in his own voice, and did his best to ignore O'Hara, who beamed with delight in his peripheral vision. "We're investigating an incident not far from here, and wondered if we could arrange to view your surveillance system? I noticed you have a camera that points at the road."

He got straight to the point. Unlike George and Ivy, Maguire didn't feel the need to introduce himself to every single member of the public. After all, his uniform did that for him.

The woman stared at his mouth as he spoke, as though she was lip-reading. "Camera?" she said.

"Yes. Yes, camera?"

"No, camera."

"No..." Maguire said, his patience immediately thinning. He had spent years living in England with people asking him to repeat himself or not understanding his accent, but thought those days were behind him. "We don't want to *buy* a camera. We want to *see* your cameras. You know?" He mimed what he considered to be a large truck trundling past the forecourt. "Lorry?" He then performed the classic charades depiction of a movie. "Camera?"

"Ah," she said, and the smile that formed was beautiful. But then it faded, and she shook her head. "You want DVD? Lorry DVD?"

"No, I..." he let his head fall forward, then had one last attempt. "Lorry. Passing by." He motioned a passing lorry once more. "Carrying carpet."

"Ah, carpet?"

"Yes," he said. "Yes. Carpet. Lorry. Camera."

The woman looked between him and O'Hara for one long moment. Like many women from her culture, she retained a youthful complexion. It was only now they were up close that her maturity was evident in her mannerisms and some ever so slight crow's feet. If pressed, Maguire would have placed her in her late thirties, but wouldn't have had any money on it.

"This one," she said, moving from behind the counter, waving for them to follow her to the back of the shop. But instead of leading through into a back room, she stopped beside an aisle filled with Magic Tree air fresheners, an array of window wipers, tow ropes, and...

"Jesus, Mary and..." Maguire couldn't even finish his sentence.

Slowly, she reached for a set of car mats that hung from a stainless steel hook.

"Carpet, yes," she said timidly, as though Maguire's outburst had made her suddenly doubtful.

"Listen," O'Hara said, coaxing Maguire to one side. "I'm sorry, he hasn't explained very well. Do you have CCTV? C-C-T-V," she repeated slowly and pointed to the corner of the ceiling where a dome-like camera was watching their every move.

Maguire removed himself from the interaction by walking down the crisps aisle and back towards the door, thinking that a little treat would improve his mood.

"CCTV," he heard the woman repeat back to O'Hara.

"Yes," she replied. "Cameras."

"Camera," she said. "Yes, we have."

As he reached the end of the aisle, the two women's conversation became background noise, not unlike the radio playing quietly throughout the shop. Not only had O'Hara managed to break through the language barrier, but the odds of her gloating about it later were strong. He took a deep breath and called upon a method he had learned as a child to control his frustrations. Instead of focusing on his frustration at the things he had no control over, he identified those he did have control over, such as his senses.

"It's a pop song. Don't know which one or who it's by. I smell petrol. I like the smell. I see chocolate, and crisps, and sarnies. I like them all, but I'm not paying four quid for a sarnie that looks like a two-year-old slapped it together. I see a pinboard. I see leaflets. I don't need a gardener, I'd love a cleaner. Oh, Christ, even if I wanted to try pottery, I wouldn't go to a place that thought a crude sketch of Patrick Swayze would entice me, just out of principle."

"Who are you talking to?"

"Eh?"

"You were talking to somebody?" O'Hara eyed the radio on his shoulder.

"Oh, nobody. Just muttering."

"Talking to yourself?" she said. "You were talking to yourself, Dave."

"Where's your new best mate?" he said, changing the topic as one leaflet in particular caught his eye. It was a simple flyer offering a simple service.

"She's gone to call the boss man," O'Hara said, stepping up beside him. "At least, I think that's where she's gone. Could have just gone to the loo. I don't know, if I'm honest." Maguire said nothing. He studied the flyer. "What's that?"

He passed it to her and watched for her response as she read aloud.

"House clearance and furniture removal service."

"What if whoever fly-tipped didn't fly-tip their own furniture?" Maguire said. "What if someone else paid them to do it?"

O'Hara looked up at him. "You think someone runs a business where they promise to take away their furniture and then dump it in a car park?"

"They don't promise to dump it, you half-wit," Maguire said. "The customer thinks it's being disposed of legally. The business saves a few quid."

"Yeah, and risks a hefty fine."

Maguire shrugged. "Only if they get caught. Something to think about, though, right?"

"I suppose," O'Hara said, taking a picture of the flyer with her phone.

"It's okay," came a quiet voice from the counter. She pushed open a door that led to a back office. "You come. I show you, yes?"

Maguire adopted his kindest smile, remembering his own challenges with dialect.

"Aye, that's my girl," Maguire said, and he tapped O'Hara's arm. "I told you she'd come through, eh?"

CHAPTER TWELVE

The long walk through the hospital to the mortuary was via sun-kissed, glazed corridors that belied the fact that the individual was deep inside a labyrinth, with only a few coloured lines that had been painted on the floor to guide them. It was a modern adaptation of the story of Theseus.

Architecturally, the building was of little significance, but that little detail- those glazed corridors - were a marvel, providing enough cheer that George's quest was far less arduous than it otherwise would have been.

However, instead of using the painted lines to escape the beast as Theseus used his thread, the lines would lead him directly into the lair. His Minotaur was Doctor Pippa Bell, famed throughout Lincolnshire for not only being the only forensic pathologist in the county, and therefore the most experienced and qualified, but for being an individual whose superpower was her ability to identify any weaknesses in a personality, any doubts one might hold, and any cracks in their confidence, and with nothing but razor wit and a deadly tongue, she would seek to destroy.

Theseus's Minotaur comprised the torso of a man atop the body of a bull. George's beast was nothing more than a stocky and stout young lady with a Welsh dragon tattooed across her chest, and piercings in her lip, nose, ears, and God knows where else.

"You alright, guv?" Ivy asked.

"Sorry?"

"You're quiet."

He smiled and cleared his mind of the imagery.

"Just musing," he told her.

"You were smiling."

"Was I?" he asked innocently as they neared the end of the corridor. "Are you ready?"

Ivy pouted as though genuinely considering the question and scanning her body for the usual signs of anxiety. But then she shrugged.

"As I'll ever be."

George pushed the buzzer, and the door was opened almost immediately, as if Pippa Bell had been waiting to ambush them.

She stood in the open doorway, grinning, as if daring either of them to comment on her new choice of hair colour - a bold, pea green that George had to admit, matched her eyes as if the pairing had come as a set.

"Good morning, Pip," George said as pleasantly as he could.

She reminded him of a modern-day Roald Dahl character, perhaps drawn by Quentin Blake in one of those beautifully scruffy but descriptive scenes.

"Good morning," she said brightly. "Been waiting for you, I have."

Her Welsh accent turned that otherwise featureless statement into a song.

"Raring to go, are you?" George asked as they followed her into the room.

"I am, as it goes," she replied. "Been a bit quiet lately, as it happens. Been looking forward to getting stuck into a challenge. Must be the heat."

"A bit crass, isn't it?" Ivy remarked as she pulled on a disposable gown. "I mean, she's a woman, not a specimen."

"Now, now, Ivy, we talked about this. It's a body. Nothing more than that, remember...?" Her voice trailed off, and for the first time that George could recall, the pathologist, who typically oozed confidence, sagged and sighed. "Not that your wife is, George... I just meant that... I was sorry to hear about...you know...her passing and that..."

George beamed at her.

"Who would've thought that the infamous Doctor Pippa Bell would be defeated by the topic of death? Now all I have to do is find a bar of thread."

"What's that?" she said, to which George simply laughed. "Nothing. You're alright. No offence taken."

"I just meant..." Pip continued. "Well, I was sorry to hear about it, that's all. If it's any help, I'm glad to see you back at work so soon. There's no convalescence like keeping busy, is there?"

"That's what I tell myself," George said, tying the gown behind his back. "Right then. Let's get started, shall we?"

With that, Pip shoved the insulated doors to the morgue open, and they followed her inside, immediately hit by the drop in temperature. Ivy, had been working on her ability to deal with what, even George had to admit, was one of the worst parts of the job.

As always, Pip had made the necessary preparations. Gemma Radford's body lay on a gurney in the middle of the room like the prize masterpiece in an art exhibition, partially covered by a thin blue sheet.

But what was unusual, was the man who stood at her side. He was dressed in a blue smock like Pip and sorting through the tools and implements on a stainless steel trolley.

"Andrew, this is George and Ivy," Pip said, and then presented the man with a sweep of her arm. "George, Ivy, this is Andrew. He's helping me out for a while."

"Locum?" George asked, to which the young man nodded but, given the gloves and the sterile environment, refrained from offering to shake their hands.

To George, he appeared to be in his mid-to-late twenties, early thirties at a push, and standing beside Pip, with her piercings and tattoos, he seemed quite ordinary. Vanilla.

"I'll lead," Pip muttered to him, positioning herself by the dead woman's left shoulder.

Gemma Radford looked much the same as she had the previous night. Her eyes were open, staring not at a star-filled sky or the underside of the forest canopy, but at the luminous overhead lighting, surrounded not by soil and roots and rain but by walls of white and shiny stainless steel surfaces. Her skin was pale and doll-like, her hair was tangled, and her eyes were a dark, bottomless brown.

"We're grateful you called us in early, Pip," George said as they gathered around the body. "We haven't a lot to go on with this one."

"I hope I didn't ruin your plans," she replied with unusual self-lessness.

"You did," George said. "But I'm glad. Believe me, I'd much rather be here than talking to her nearest and dearest."

"Well, I'd love to tell you it was a favour, George," she replied dryly. "We've got one coming in from Detective Chief Inspector Bloom shortly. It's going to be all hands on deck, I'm afraid. A real nasty one."

"Car accident?"

"I wasn't referring to the body," she said darkly. Then she turned her attention to Gemma Radford, seemingly compartmentalising and clapping her hands together almost happily. "Right then. Where to start?" she said. Perhaps today was a good day at work for her. George imagined that the satisfaction she felt from analysing a body might be similar to solving a puzzle, or at least finding the edges and the corners and handing it over for George to fill in the centre.

"Let's start with the basics," George said. "Cause of death?"

"I agree with Doctor Saint's report," Andrew said, flipping a sheet of paper over in a file he was holding. "Mechanical asphyxiation."

"From a bag?" Ivy asked, her voice surprisingly steady given her usual demeanour during meetings with Pip.

"Not quite. See this?" Pip said, pointing to her eyes and face. "Petechial haemorrhages. The bursting of her blood vessels from a lack of oxygen. The abrasions on her neck suggest compression, but there are no fingermarks to indicate strangulation, and there's a distinct lack of bruising, which we'd expect to see had something been forced over her head and around her neck." Pip pointed to Gemma Radford's neck and gestured for Ivy to come closer. "What do you see?"

"Marks," Ivy said quietly, and George leaned in for a look.

"A skin condition? Like eczema?"

"It's irritated skin, yes, but not from eczema. Look at the pattern." George, too, tried to get a closer look, but only Pip's trained eye could spot such an anomaly. "See? Diagonal imprints on the skin. Like a mesh-like or criss-cross pattern, see? They're faint now, but would have been quite prominent at the time."

Ivy straightened. "I'm not following."

"It's from a woven fibre," Pip explained. "Not smooth like nylon or soft like cotton. We're talking rough, coarse, a natural material."

Ivy tilted her head.

"Like burlap?"

"Exactly," Pip said. "Burlap, jute, maybe hemp. You want my guess?"

"Yes, Pip," George said. "In lieu of a definitive answer, an educated guess will have to suffice."

"A hessian sack," Pip said flatly, looking up at George. "We found a few fibres in her hair that we think match the material. Sent them to the lab, of course. But from what I can tell, that wasn't the cause of her death, but it was almost certainly an aid."

"A hessian sack?" Ivy said. "Surely she could have breathed through something like that. It's full of holes."

Pip grinned.

"Never miss a trick, do you?" she replied. "You're right, of course. My guess is that the sack was used to immobilise her, disorientate her, and stop her from fighting back. She removed enough of the blue sheet to display Gemma Radford's wrists, on which were faint red marks, barely discernible, but certainly not natural. "Her wrists were bound and the bag was put over her head. Most likely to stop her from running away."

"What makes you sure?" George asked.

"I'm not sure," she replied. "But there are no other injuries. No signs of sexual interference, for example. Why else would somebody want to immobilise her?"

"Why not just kill her? Why go to those lengths?"

"I say it as I see it," Pip said. "I'll let you decipher that little conundrum."

"So, her wrists were bound, and a sack of some description was pulled over her head? Then what?"

"Then she was suffocated," Pip said bluntly. "Could have been anything. A hand over her mouth and nose would be my guess."

"A hand?"

"Maybe," she said, looking up at Andrew, who nodded.

"It's possible," he added. "It would explain the lack of DNA or fingerprints on her skin."

"But why not just do that? Why not simply overpower her, or use a plastic bag if they were really concerned about evidence?"

"This wasn't just about murder," Pip continued. "This was degradation. Whoever did this didn't see Gemma as a person. They saw her as... I don't know what, but you saw the stain on her blouse?"

"I did, yes," George said, and the silence that followed suggested they need not describe what they were all likely thinking, but these matters had to be clear. "No signs of sexual interference, you say?"

"Nothing," she replied.

"So, he immobilised her long enough to...create that stain on her chest," George summarised. "And then he finished her off."

Pip stared down at the body. George watched her. For all the help she had given Ivy with regards to dealing with the sight of dead bodies, she appeared to truly appreciate the weight of death, and the role dignity played during the transition and the subsequent processes they were forced to follow.

Pip exhaled slowly.

"It doesn't make sense," Ivy said. "If he wanted to degrade her, by forcing her to witness what he was doing to himself, then why bother with the sack? If that's how he gets off, then surely he would want her to see what he was doing?"

"Whoever put that sack over her head was a weak man. Maybe they're deformed. Maybe he thought she might run away, and doubted his ability to catch her. Whatever the reason..." She looked back up at George, her expression one of doubtless sobriety. "He's a sick man."

CHAPTER THIRTEEN

Ivy exhaled loudly, her breath sounding loud in that huge, cold space. Pip's words had served to darken the room, thicken the atmosphere, and add teeth to the incessant frigid air.

"So we're looking for someone who owns or has access to a hessian sack?" Ivy suggested, braving the shift in the environment.

George smiled empathetically, rubbing his forehead. "I've got about fifty in the garden. They're good for storing bulbs."

"Sandbags, too," Pip suggested, "Especially these past few years with the floods we've been having."

"You can say that again," George said, remembering the recent flood that had thrown him into the deep end on his first day back in the Wolds. "What about those scratches?" He pointed to the small but bright red wounds around Gemma's throat. "Can you get us DNA from those?"

Pip shook her head. "I can try, but it's unlikely to reveal anything."

"Nothing? No fingernail analysis or—"

"No," Pip replied. "Those marks, George, are from Gemma's fingernails. She was clawing at her neck, trying to pull the sack off, I expect."

The room quietened as no doubt each person imagined the lifeless body before them, scrambling desperately for life.

"I see," he said eventually and moved on. "How about time of death?"

Pip looked up at Andrew, who once more referred to Saint's report, then nodded slowly.

"Given the reduction in body temperature, the progression of rigor mortis, and the digestive status," he said. "I'd have to agree with Doctor Saint."

It was the most Fox had said during the meeting. It was clear he was a southerner, but George was honing in on his accent, placing him from somewhere in Essex. East London at a push, but more likely Essex.

"Between three and four p.m. on Sunday afternoon?" George asked.

"I would push that out an hour either side, but yes, between three and four is the most likely window. It all depends on the conditions she was stored in."

"Stored?" Ivy repeated. "Jesus."

"We'll be talking to her next of kin shortly," George said. "Am I to assume that she suffered?" He forced a smile. "They always ask."

"A hessian sack, as you rightly pointed out," Pip started, "is full of tiny holes. Her airflow would have been restricted, and given the severity of the haemorrhaging, it's very likely the killer left her that way for some time before finishing her off."

"You mean, he watched her suffer?"

"She would have been able to breathe, but she would have endured a state of panic, if you like. Her heart rate would have been increased, and it's likely she would have been fighting to draw enough oxygen through the material."

George absorbed that description and searched for the objective facts.

"How long?"

"At least six to eight minutes," Pip replied confidently, as if she had been waiting for the question. "Maybe longer."

"That's a long time to struggle."

"Presumably, they secured the bag around her head with rope or string or something," Ivy added. "But then they removed the bag and the rope before dumping her. Why?"

"Maybe he thought it would provide a link back to him?" Andrew suggested.

"And the... deposit on her chest wouldn't?"

"Not if he's not known to the police," George said, referring to their previous conversation on the matter.

"Jesus," Ivy muttered, clearly imagining what the victim had endured, until Pip caught her eye.

"It's no way to die, Ivy," she said.

George nodded his agreement, eyeing Pip, who looked as if she had more to say.

"Pip?" he said. "What else can you give us?"

She turned to Andrew, who once more referred to his notes.

"Her blood pooling is inconsistent," he started. "Which suggests she was moved soon after death. Before livor mortis began, so within thirty to sixty minutes of death."

"She was moved," George mused, again aloud.

"We believe so, yes," Andrew said.

"To the rubbish heap, but from where?" he said, this time to Ivy.

"I can't say—" Pip started.

"But you must have an idea. Some kind of theory?" George said. "You normally do."

"It is not my job to speculate, George."

"What if I told you your insights are often helpful?" George asked. "What if I told you that we value your opinion?"

"Then I would say that you're toying with me," she replied. "Hoping to appeal to my ego, maybe? I'm not a detective, George. I'm a pathologist."

"Come on, Pip. Humour me, won't you? You're good at reading people. Give me something. Something you might have noticed. What are your instincts? Even if we can't prove it."

"I think what he's trying to say," Ivy added. "Is that we're scratching here. We have almost nothing."

Pip looked between the two detectives, then down at Gemma Radford. She hesitated. "If I were a detective..." she said cautiously.

"Yes?" George asked, stepping forward.

"If I were a detective," she said. "I would be focusing on the semen deposit on her chest and why it was left there."

"Why?"

"Because, George," she said, as though the answer was obvious, "either the killer is an idiot, or..."

"Or?"

It was as if she was deliberately teasing him, prolonging the revelation of her theory for no other purpose than her own amusement.

"Or it was purposeful," she said sighing heavily, as though fatigued from revealing her darkest thoughts. She looked up at him across Gemma Radford's body. "He thinks he's invincible."

CHAPTER FOURTEEN

Ivy always marvelled at how the landscape could transition so dramatically from the long, straight roads that cut across the Fens to the winding lanes that nuzzled their way through the Wolds, and that was so different, too, from the place she still called home, at least in her heart — the flat, coastal town of Mablethorpe.

It took time, she knew, to call a new place home, and in the back of her mind, she thought she might always consider Mablethorpe her home. Where she had met her husband, where they had bought their house, and where they had raised their children. She wondered how often they asked about her and what her husband told them, and although the stab of guilt she felt whenever they crossed her mind was ever present, the blade was dulling.

More than anything, she wondered if she had done the right thing by leaving.

George often remarked, as men of his generation often do, that time is a healer, usually in reference to his own grieving process. But the principle could be shared with her own state of affairs.

The thought of her children missing her induced far less melancholy than it might have a month ago. The idea that over the long term, they would be far better off without her, without hearing their parents bicker and row, to wake up in a house of smiles and cheer, as opposed to the underlying resentment they had endured for the past few years.

Like her children, she was adjusting to a new way of life, accepting the things she could change and those that were beyond her control.

While the expansive fields, hovering kites, and the network of interlocking dykes captured her attention, they served as a mere backdrop for her racing mind. A canvas on which her thoughts could reveal themselves as temporary pencil sketches, before being erased.

When George's phone blared from the car's speakers, they both startled.

"O'Hara," he said, pressing the green button to accept the call. "What have you got for me?"

He glanced hopefully at Ivy, but they were quickly disappointed.

"Not much, guv," she said. 'We just wanted to know if you'd heard back from Southwell?"

"Nothing yet," George said. "We're still waiting for the full report."

"Where are you now?"

"We're heading to Gemma Radford's house. Ruby sent us an address in Aswardby. Why? Where are you?"

"We're leaving the petrol station in Horncastle, which is west of the crime scene, and heading to one outside Spilsby, east of the crime scene.

"The one in Horncastle?" George said. "Why did you go back there?"

"We didn't go back," she said, shame ripe in her voice. "It was the first one we went to."

"You're joking," Ivy said dryly.

"No, sarge," O'Hara replied with equal dryness. "We just spent three hours going through seventy-two hours of barely discernible CCTV footage to find no sign of anyone who might have passed through before fly-tipping a bunch of furniture."

"No vans?" George asked.

"Oh, there were plenty of vans," she replied. "It's a main road. But we're looking for something with an open back. That carpet was longer than any van I know of, and if you want us to identify every van, then we're going to need more resources."

"You looked from Friday to Sunday?" George said, "I asked you to—"

"To look at the whole week before, guv, we know, but it's impossible, even on high speed. We sent the week's worth of recordings on to Ruby in case she can help out, but she's too busy right now. We can go further back when we're back at the station."

"At this rate, you'll be spending the whole week just looking at CCTV footage," George pointed out.

"I know, guv. But we need a smaller time window. It's a long process, by the time we've paused and analysed every potential vehicle. We need to know *when* exactly the fly-tippers were passing through."

"Well, if we knew that, O'Hara, then you wouldn't need to be looking through CCTV," Ivy said, while George resumed his usual stoic stare.

"I'm just saying," O'Hara continued, exhibiting an impressive amount of patience that Ivy doubted she would have after staring at CCTV footage for three hours. "That's why it's taking so long."

"Where are you heading now?" George asked. "Spilsby?"

"Yeah, there's a garage there that we think might be able to help. Like you said, whoever dumped all that rubbish had to come in either from the west or the east."

"You sound hopeful," George told her.

"Do I?" she laughed. "Must be the coffee."

"Alright," George said. "You're doing a good job. Let me know how you get on."

"Will do, guv."

George reached over to end the call with a stab of his finger. "We're not getting anywhere," he muttered. "We know almost nothing."

"It's always like this at the beginning," Ivy said calmly. "And you always say that."

"We usually have *something*," he argued.

"Give it time." Ivy stared at the scenery. The rolling hills, the winding lanes, and the patchwork fields. "It's funny, isn't it?"

"What is?"

"Life," she said. "I mean, we're all on a journey, aren't we?"

"Are you getting philosophical?"

"Humour me," she told him. "We're all on a journey. At some point, that journey is going to lead us into a valley, where we can't seem to find the way. Do you know what I mean?"

"Are you in a valley, Ivy?" he asked.

"No," she replied. "No, I'm halfway up the hill."

He grinned to himself.

"Is it the right hill?"

She shrugged.

"That's just it," she replied. "I won't know until I get to the top."

"Well, that's probably the maturest thing I've heard you say today," he said with a chuckle. "No, this year. It seems our roles have reversed. I'm usually the one talking *you* down from the ledge," he said, to which she laughed. "I mean it. Look at you. You were barely shaking in the morgue. You seem different, Ivy."

"Is that a bad thing?"

George shrugged and smiled as a grandfather might smile at a child.

"No, I don't think it is."

Ivy returned the smile. It seemed a good place to let the conversation slide and to allow the investigation to creep back into her thoughts.

The landscape changed as they passed through the Wolds' fringes, from a sustained single-note timbre to a graceful, swaying rhythm. If roads could dance, then those that carved a path through the rolling hills were nothing short of a waltz.

"Disgusting," Ivy whispered.

George looked between her and the summer's day beyond the window. "Disgusting?" he repeated. "Not quite how I'd describe it myself, Ivy. Stunning, maybe. Radiant even. I mean, I think it's rather beautiful on a day like—"

"I'm not talking about the scenery, guv." She rolled her eyes and nodded into the rear-view mirror. "There was a pile of rubbish back there on the side of the road."

"Oh," George said, checking his rear view mirror and slowing the car to a crawl. "I didn't notice."

"It was by that farmer's gate, out of sight. You know, the farmer will have to pay for it to be cleared, right? It's just wrong."

"I know, it's terrible." He paused and tapped the steering wheel with his fingers as though agitated by a sudden thought. "Makes you think, though, doesn't it?"

"About what?"

"Well, people are brazen enough to just fly-tip on the side of the road. Out here. I mean. Why? Why here?" His expression stiffened and his brow furrowed. "Why Snipe Dales?"

"Sorry?"

"Why the Country Park? he said, gesturing at the world around them. "Why not just do it here like someone else has?"

Ivy sat up. "I don't know."

"Snipe Dales is gated."

"Not any more, it's not."

"But, there's a car park, so the chance of witnesses..." He

paused, as if struggling to put his thoughts into a comprehensible state. "Surely there's an easier place to—"

"Stop the car!" Ivy said, leaning forward.

To his credit, George did exactly as instructed, trusting her, as no doubt she would have done for him. He slowed to a halt and pulled into the next lay by, stopping not far from a couple walking their Dalmatian, who frowned at George's erratic driving and made a show of moving into safety.

"Jesus, Ivy," he said, "what is it?"

"I want to know what they're doing," she said, eyeing the couple who stood on the other side of the farmer's gate while the Dalmatian sniffed at them through the rungs. They turned to watch as Ivy stormed from the car and ran back up the lane, with George following close behind.

It was soon clear what they were looking at — a great, distorted heap of wet cardboard boxes, two broken TVs, and numerous bin bags with jagged edges, a few of which had split and released bundles of stained clothing, children's toys, and from the smell that hit as Ivy walked closer, decaying food waste.

"Good morning," Ivy called out.

"Alright," the man said cautiously. They were what Ivy considered a typical newly retired couple, affluent with enough life in them to remain outdoorsy. They wore expensive-looking olive green jackets, and Le Chameau wellies, which Ivy knew to be more than two hundred pounds per pair.

The woman stayed back, while the man stepped forward. The dog, on the other hand, merely wagged its tail at the promise of attention from new humans.

"Everything alright?" George said when he caught up. He revealed his warrant card, and the slightly alarmed expression on the couple's worn faces faded.

"Nothing to do with you, I hope?" He pointed at the mound of rubbish.

"We're investigating fly-tipping in the area," Ivy explained, which was a sort of half-truth.

"Oh, terrible, isn't it?" the woman said, stepping past her husband and assuming control. "We live just up the road. It's been getting worse recently."

"Is that right?"

"Oh yeah, it's a real nuisance, believe me. We're just taking photos so we can shame whoever did it on social media," she said, holding up her phone. "I send them on to the council, too. Not that they do anything about it. This lot's been here for days now. And there's another pile just up the road that's been there for over a month."

"I don't suppose you've seen the individuals, have you?" George asked, to which they shook their heads.

"If I got my hands on them—" the woman started.

"If you got your hands on them, they'd probably hit you over the head, sweetheart," her husband finished for her.

"Do they go further afield?" Ivy asked. "Or is it mainly these spots?"

"Such as?"

"I don't know. Snipe Dales Country Park?"

"Oh, the Country Park. We go there quite a bit, don't we?" the woman said. "We were there this weekend. Walking Otto. It's so nice."

"You were there this weekend?" George said, with an urgency that seemed to unnerve the couple. "Can I ask when?"

"I...well, I don't know. When was it, Jack? Saturday?"

"Yeah," he confirmed, "before we went to Mum's for dinner. Saturday."

"Did you drive there?"

The man frowned but answered, "Well, yes, why? I'm sorry, but what's this about?"

"Trust me, this is very important," George said slowly, emanating his best grandfatherly aura, which often induced an element of trust. "Did you happen to park in the car park there, or were you out on the road?"

"Yes," said the man, "The car park. Had to buy a ticket, which by the way is a crime in itself—"

"Did you see anything like this in the car park?"

"Rubbish?" said the woman. "In the Country Park? No. Not there."

"No sofas or carpets?" Ivy pressed.

"I'd have taken a photo if I'd seen anything like that there," she replied. "You know? For social media and the council."

Her husband nodded in agreement. "I'm glad to say we didn't see anything of the sort. You're not saying there's more down there, are you? In the Country Park?"

"May I ask what time you were there? I'm sorry for all the questions, but we're trying to establish when the incident took place."

"About four," he replied.

"And what time did you leave?"

"Just before five, I suppose. Before the gate closed, we were one of the last ones to leave."

"You're sure about that?" George asked.

"As sure as I can be," he replied.

"One more question," George said. "Was the lock on the gate broken? I don't suppose you'd happen to notice something like that?"

"No," the woman said. "No, they were there waiting to lock it. They were waiting for us to leave; us and another couple."

"Thank you," George said sincerely. "I wonder if you'd mind us taking your details. In case we need to contact you at a later date?"

The man seemed perplexed. He looked to his wife, who shrugged.

"If it helps stop all this happening," she said.

"It would be a great help," George said, gesturing for Ivy to note down their particulars while he scrolled through his phone.

"You okay, guv?" Ivy asked as she flicked through her notepad to a clean page.

"I'm calling O'Hara," he replied with a flick of his eyebrows and a chirpy wink. "We've got ourselves a window."

CHAPTER FIFTEEN

When Maguire pulled into an empty parking spot in the second petrol station, O'Hara climbed out of the car and headed to the shop with far more urgency than she had at the first. Maguire hung back, a little awed by this renewed motivation he was witnessing.

"You alright?" she asked the young man behind the counter.

"Alright," he replied, eyeing her uniform. His tall, gangly frame and acne-scarred face suggested he couldn't have been much older than eighteen or nineteen.

"We're investigating a local incident, and wondered if you could help us."

"What?" he replied, "Me?"

"Fly-tipping," she said.

"Fly-tipping?"

"You know, when people dump rubbish in the countryside."

"Alright," he said slowly, and judging by his expression, he was more than a little bemused.

"We wondered if we could have a look at your CCTV from Saturday at five p.m. to Sunday at one p.m. I presume your system records?"

The teenager looked between them as though he only vaguely understood what was going on.

"CCTV," he repeated.

"Yes. Close-circuit television cameras."

"Right," he said again, slightly unsure of what to do, and Maguire presumed there was no script or process to follow under such circumstances. "Hold on. I'll have to ask my boss."

"Thank you," O'Hara said sweetly, and the boy pulled a phone from his pocket. Maguire took the chance to peruse the shop and perhaps subconsciously found his way to the confectionery aisle.

"Kit Kat?" he asked.

She winced. "No thanks. I'm more of a savoury girl. Anyway, shouldn't you be looking at the fruit?"

"Eh?"

She tapped her stomach while nodding at his. He peered down and sucked in his gut.

"Ah, you're probably right," he said, tossing the Kit Kat back onto the pile. He looked around the shop, his eyes immediately drawn to something beside the doors.

"Is that...?" He led her over to a pinboard where, as plain as the nose on his face, a simple, white flyer had been pinned. "Is it the same one?"

"Looks like it," she said, pulling out her phone and checking the photo she had taken before. "Yeah, it is."

"Must be popular," he mused.

"Seems so," O'Hara said, then glanced at the teenager and heard him mumbling.

"They're police. I don't know why..." the lad behind the counter said down the phone.

At Maguire's questioning expression, O'Hara strode over to the counter and held out her hand. "I can speak to him if you like."

He looked down at her hand as if contemplating whether it was a good idea.

"She said she wants to speak to you," he eventually said into the phone. He was silent as he listened to the voice on the other end, then ended the call without another word and looked up at her. "He said he'd rather not speak to you."

"Charming."

"But, it's okay. I can show you the CCTV."

She grinned at him.

"Lead the way," she said.

The teenager unlocked the door into a sad, little office with a three-by-three wall of square CCTV screens. It was the polar opposite of the fish bowl they now called their office, and Maguire imagined being confined to such a space, lunching on a soggy egg-mayo sandwich while staring at camera feeds all day.

The teenager sat down on the one chair and shook the computer mouse back and forth to wake the operating system.

"What day did you say?" he asked, clicking open a file.

"From Saturday at five p.m.," she clarified, "to Sunday at one p.m."

"You know how to work the software?"

"They're all much the same, aren't they?" she replied.

"I've got to watch the shop," he said, nodding at the door and standing up. "Space bar to start and stop, shift cursor for speed options. You can slow it down or speed it up. Whatever you want, really."

"Thank you for your help," Maguire said as the boy squeezed past him and then stopped.

"You're going to pay for that, right?" he said, nodding at the Kit Kat that Maguire had picked up, put down, and picked up again.

Maguire grinned.

"Of course," he replied, and he fished a pound coin from his pocket, then dropped it into the lad's hand. "Keep the change."

"There is no change," the boy said, then closed the door behind him. "It's a quid."

"Well, it's the thought that counts," Maguire told him, as he slipped from the room under O'Hara's scrutinising glare. "Jesus. He'll need to work on his customer service skills."

"Says you?" she replied, slotting herself into the seat.

"Let's just see what we've got," he said, leaning over her to look at the screens.

She clicked on the folder with Saturday's date and, after a few moments to familiarise herself with the software, began to play the footage that began at midnight of the day before, using the cursor to speed up the process.

"According to the guv, we're looking at anything after five p.m., apparently, some couple he met said they were at the Country Park when it was locked up."

"Narrows it down," Maguire replied, loitering over her shoulder.

"It's still going to take us ages," she sighed.

"Yeah, but while we're doing this, we're not walking the streets or standing in a field," he replied. "This is honest police work, and if they didn't come in from the west, they *have* to be on here. I mean, they've got to have dumped it sometime on Saturday night, right? Between the gates closing at five p.m. and opening again on Sunday morning at eight-thirty? Otherwise, why would they have broken the lock?"

"You know how it is. We can't assume anything. Someone else could've broken the lock, someone with nothing to do with the fly-tipping."

He stretched his neck and groaned. "It's obvious, though, isn't it?"

"It might be obvious, but we need to evidence it," she said, to which he gave a little laugh.

"This job is ridiculous sometimes, right? Jumping through hoops to prove what everyone already knows, all so some lawyer can't claim plausible deniability. Seriously, it's like the law works for the criminals and against us."

"That *is* the job, Dave," she said.

They sat in silence for a while watching the fast, silent movie that reminded O'Hara of old black and white footage where everyone, including the horses, seemed to speed walk. Cars zipped in and out of the petrol station at high speed, while others whizzed by in a blur. They had to pay attention to every movement, occasionally jumping back and pausing the tape to focus on a specific vehicle.

Nearly an hour had passed when O'Hara shifted in the seat, circling her feet to restore some circulation in her legs.

"My God," Maguire groaned, while she remained fixated on the tape, her fingers hovering over the space bar. "I've watched more interesting grass growing—"

"Stop!" O'Hara said, tapping hard. "What's that?" She skipped backwards a few frames.

"Documentaries..." Maguire finished his joke. "And *that* is a Vauxhall Corsa. It's barely big enough to fit a week's worth of shopping in, let alone—"

"No, not *in* the garage," she said. "On the road behind it. Look."

She pointed at the grainy screen where there was a grainy image of a grainy truck against a grainy background. It hadn't pulled into the petrol station, but had idled by.

"It's an open back truck," she muttered to herself, searching for the zoom function. "What is that on the back?" she said, pointing to the load it carried.

"Can you zoom in?" he asked.

She looked down at the keyboard. "I'm trying to," she said, but instead she dragged the monitor towards her, pressing her nose against the screen.

"That's one way of doing it," Maguire muttered.

"Now I might be mistaken," she said, leaning back and blinking to restore her vision, "but I'd swear on my job that *that*..." She prodded the screen and sat back. "is our truck."

CHAPTER SIXTEEN

"A red sofa?" George repeated, staring through the windscreen at the narrow, tree-lined road ahead. To his right stood a low hedgerow, beyond which was a huge field of rape that resembled a watercolour painting, and to his left stood the kind of picture-book cottage the Lincolnshire Wolds was famous for.

Despite the distractions, George stared into space.

"Yes, guv," Maguire said. "Just like the one the kids used in their den."

"You're sure it's the same one?" Ivy asked.

"We can't say for certain, no, but we requested the footage to be sent to Ruby to confirm. We're hoping we can get one of the tech guys to sharpen the image a bit."

"What time does it pass the petrol station?" George asked.

"Sunday morning. Two-forty-eight a.m.".

"Which means whoever it was would've reached the Country Park just before three a.m."

"Yes, guv."

George scratched at his stubble, putting the reminder of his need to shave to one side. "Have you sent Ruby the number plate?"

"No, guv. It's not clear enough."

"What do you mean?"

"I mean, the CCTV is old. Very old. Very grainy. Anyway, it's in the back of the shot, driving past. It's too far away to see."

"Great," mumbled George. "What kind of truck is it, at least?"

"A flatbed Ford Transit."

"See what Ruby can do with that information," he said. "There'll be a ton of those out this way, but check if any local owners are on record."

"Yes, guv."

"And see if you can find any other cameras between that petrol station and the Country Park. I want to know for certain that's where he was going. Actually, come to think of it, when she gets the footage, ask Ruby to check for a return journey. With any luck, the truck will be empty and she'll have a clearer view of the number plate."

"Yes, guv."

"We'll meet you back at the station later," he said. "What are Byrne and Campbell up to?"

"You told them to follow up on the carpet, guv. Last I heard, Southwell's team found a sticker or some kind of identifier."

George glanced at Ivy, who seemed mildly pleased at the news, yet less than hopeful it would lead anywhere.

"Well, let's see where that takes us, shall we?" he said. "Okay, I'll see you back at the station."

"Will do, guv," Maguire replied, but he didn't end the call.

"Maguire?"

"I just wanted to say good luck, guv..." he hesitated for a moment. "I don't envy you."

It was George's turn to hesitate, before he replied.

"I'm not sure if luck is the right word, but thank you."

He looked up at the house again. The quaint little cottage that was about to receive a sinister makeover. It was probably the one part of the job that sat above their previous task on the scale of most-dreaded responsibilities. He delayed the moment when he would have to get out of the car and tell somebody that their loved one had died, slowly and very likely quite painfully.

"You realise what this means, don't you?" he asked Ivy.

"It means that Gemma Radford was killed thirteen hours *after* the fly-tipper dumped the rubbish in the Country Park," she replied.

George nodded and sighed. The answer didn't bring much relief. It only confused matters further. In fact, just as Pip had done, the news unravelled most of their existing assumptions.

"Doesn't change what we have to do next, though, does it?" he said.

"Do you want me to take the lead on this one, guv?" Ivy asked from the passenger seat.

It was as if she thought he had grown more sensitive since Grace's death. Perhaps she was worried that the task before them would stir painful memories. But the truth was, it wouldn't. Grace had died in his arms. Nobody had been forced to inform him, or wonder how best to phrase the news. He had seen it with his own eyes. He had held her when she had slipped into whatever came next.

"No," he said quietly. "No, I've got it."

"As you like," Ivy said, and she climbed from the car doing what she could to help by moving into action.

They passed through a white garden gate and up the garden path. He stopped only to admire the thriving vegetable garden to the side of the path, identifying the various vegetables and herbs that flourished there in the sun.

Eventually, George knocked on the door. Two raps and they waited for the sound of footsteps from inside. Of someone, perhaps hoping for their loved one to announce they had lost their keys. Of someone doing something they had done a thousand times before, not knowing that, this time, their world would be turned upside down.

But nobody answered.

George knocked again. He and Ivy waited patiently on the doorstep, and when nobody answered a second time, he saw Ivy's shoulders slump in his peripheral.

"Maybe he's at work, guv. We should try the phone number for him."

But George stepped forward to try again. If Grace hadn't died in his arms, if someone *had* been tasked with breaking the news, and if that someone had called him on the phone instead of looking him in the eye when announcing the loss of the most important person in the world, he would never have forgiven them. He knocked a third time, much harder than before, and placed his ear to the door to listen for movement.

"What's that?" he asked, beckoning her to do the same. She pressed her ear to the door, facing him, and adopted a similar expression to his own.

"Smoke alarm?"

He sniffed at the air, then slammed his palm against the wood.

"Anyone home?" he yelled.

"Stand back, guv," Ivy said, stepping back to stamp her foot into the door.

Over the years, George had seen her wear anything from smart trainers to flat sandals to work, and was grateful that, for whatever reason, today she had opted for a pair of heavy, black boots. He wasn't sure his brogues would've done the trick, even if they might, his hip certainly wouldn't have been up to the job.

It took Ivy five attempts before the door eventually gave, and when it did, she burst into the house without a second thought, heading straight towards the smoke. George followed more cautiously. The source of the fire, however, seemed somewhat innocuous. He peered along the hallway as she stepped into view, using a towel to carry a smoking pot from the stove, which she tossed into the sink and doused with water before swinging the cloth at the screaming alarm on the ceiling. George coughed through the smoke and opened the back door as wide as it would go.

The smoke stung at his eyes, and he held his handkerchief over his face to breathe through, as he stepped over to the old butler sink and peered down at what appeared to be a cremated pile of charred baked beans.

He caught Ivy's eye, just as the burst of fresh air worked its charm and the alarm switched off. They waited a moment, his head cocked to one side as he listened for movement.

"Anyone home?" he called out.

Ivy shook her head and shrugged.

Despite the smoke, the house had a warm and cosy feel, and although the rooms that they had seen so far had been empty, they mirrored Gemma Radford's appearance - clean, well-presented, and cared for. It was evident that she was somebody who took care of herself, and the home reflected her values, with references to her love of nature and animals in the form of lake-side paintings, framed pet photos, and huge potted plants occupying every available corner.

They re-entered the hallway, noting the narrow staircase and one door, which was closed.

He waited for Ivy to signal that she was ready, and slowly, George nudged the door open to reveal nothing short of an absolute mess. Empty beer cans had fallen from the coffee table onto a cream rug, and a hand-rolled cigarette in the ashtray had burned down to almost nothing.

But it wasn't the beer or the stench of stale cigarettes that caught their attention. It was the man who lay face down on the sofa as naked as the day he was born.

Ivy marched through the room and shoved the bay windows open, and despite the cool breeze that circled the room, still the man didn't stir.

George stepped over to the couch, looked down at him, and assured himself that the man was breathing.

From what he could tell, the man appeared to be of average height and build, with longer-than-average, greasy hair tied back in a ponytail. To complement the mass of hair on his head, he maintained a thick goatee beard, although to call it maintained was a stretch of the imagination.

Along with the grubby jeans and off-white shirt that were serving as a pillow, he reminded George of a dishevelled cowboy. All he needed was the bolo tie.

Ivy, who had clearly had enough of the charade, stepped on one of his empty cans, and slowly the man stirred, as though he had a positive association with the noise of beer cans being crushed.

He opened his eyes as a newborn might first glance at the world, reached up and scratched his chin before rolling onto his back, where his eyes widened and he frowned at the two strangers in his living room. The sight did not seem to shock him. He looked more confused than alarmed.

He made no attempt to cover himself. If anything, he seemed rather pleased to be exposing himself to Ivy, at least, until she presented her warrant card.

"My name is Detective Sergeant Hart," she said. "This is my colleague, Detective Inspector Larson." The man looked Ivy up and down, a smirk developing on his face. "We presume you are Matthew Cooper?"

He seemed a little surprised that they knew his name, but kept his cool.

"That's right," he said, stretching his arms above his head, completely unabashed. He reached over to the coffee table, shook each can until he found one that still contained beer, then downed its remnants before settling back into position. "Did Gemma let you in?"

"I think we need a word," George said. "About Gemma."

CHAPTER SEVENTEEN

Miller & Son Carpets was as old-fashioned a shop as Campbell had ever seen. If the hand-painted, cursive font signage above the shop front hadn't been vintage enough, the tagline beneath it, *Carpeting Lincolnshire since 1923*, proved its heritage.

The casement-styled windows were dusty, and piled with stacks of folded carpet samples, and to top it all off, a brass bell rang above their heads when she and Byrne stepped inside.

The shop's air was an asthmatic's nightmare, thin and dusty with an underlying chemical taste that clung to the back of Campbell's throat. Yet, despite the unsavoury entrance, she couldn't deny the old place's charm. From the forest green walls and oak-panelled decor to the warm lighting reminiscent of candlelight, it felt like stepping back in time. Rolls of carpets surrounded them, each looking like a handwoven tapestry, heavy and thick with a quality and care so often neglected in modern furnishings. The man behind the wooden counter wore a rustic, leather apron that proved to Campbell that they were truly leaning into the old-fashioned, personalised shopping experience.

He welcomed them with warm eyes and a genuine smile beneath his thick beard. "Help you?" he said, eyeing their uniforms as they approached. "Are you looking for something for the house or the station?"

"Neither, sadly," Campbell replied, ignoring the joke. She lowered her voice so that the handful of customers in the shop wouldn't hear. "We're investigating an incident that took place over the weekend."

"Okay?" he said, sounding unsure of where she was leading him.

"It involved one of your carpets," Byrne added.

"One of ours?"

"We were able to identify the distributor as this shop, and we were hoping you could identify the buyer for us."

"How do you know it's one of ours?" he asked cautiously.

"The label stamped on the underside," Campbell explained. "It shows the name of your shop, alongside this address."

"I see."

He didn't ask about the incident. Perhaps he wasn't curious. Perhaps he'd rather not know the details or, maybe he already knew them.

"There was also what we believe to be a batch number. We wondered if you could identify it for us?"

"It's possible," he replied, grabbing a pen and paper. "What's the number?"

Byrne checked his emails and read out the number that Southwell had sent through.

"13254A-1967." The man quickly wrote down the numbers as Byrne spoke, then rubbed his forehead with the end of the pen. "Something wrong?"

"No, not wrong exactly," the man said slowly. He turned the paper around. "See these first numbers? That's a regional identifier. The letter is from our batch sub-group. And see these four numbers here after the dash?" he asked, pointing to the last four digits. "That's the manufacturing date."

"The date it was made," Campbell said.

"Yeah," the man said, grimacing. "Look, something that old would have been during my granddad's time. If anyone kept decades-old records of sales, it would have been him. But I doubt my old man would have kept them after we digitalised. Sorry."

"Could you check?" she asked. "Sorry if it's a pain."

He glanced between the pair, most likely considering the time and effort against the possibility that the other customers would buy something. "I'll have to check the computer out back," he said. "I'll see what I can do."

"I appreciate it," Campbell said. "Thank you."

After quickly checking on his other customers, Mr Miller disappeared along the long, narrow corridor lined with velvet curtains to the back of the shop.

"This is a waste of time," Byrne muttered as soon as the man was beyond earshot. "He's not going to have access to paper records of a carpet bought fifty-eight years ago, and frankly, he's a madman if he does." He leaned on the counter and mindlessly opened the carpet sample book in front of him. "If I were the guv, I wouldn't have bothered. We should be finding Oscar Wyman's parents and asking them where they were."

"Good thing you're not in charge then, eh?" she replied, watching him flick through the samples. "The guv knows what he's doing. We have to cover every lead, every line of enquiry. For the CPS, if nothing else."

"Well, with any luck, we'll be out of these uniforms soon. The other two can do all this."

"Speaking of which, have you started studying?"

"For what?" he replied distractedly, stroking a particularly fluffy carpet sample.

"What do you think?" she said, getting nervous. "The exams?"

Byrne turned to face her, and his face dropped.

"We have to study?"

"*Yes*, Liam," she said, scanning his face in disbelief. "My god, we have the NIE in six weeks."

"The what?"

"The National Investigators' Exam," she whispered in shock. "Liam, this is serious. You've got to brush up on criminal law, investigation techniques, ethics, forensics, not to mention legal procedures and policies. This isn't a GCSE English exam you can just...." Her voice faded as a grin developed on his face. She turned back to the counter, her face burning hot. "You're messing with me."

"It's too easy," he laughed, nudging her playfully. "Come on, of course I've started. Read all the books, even downloaded some practice exams, didn't I?" he said proudly. "Why? You looking for a study buddy?"

"No, thanks," she replied.

"Shame. I could use your help, to be honest." She scanned his face for signs of the dry humour she'd missed last time. "I'm serious," he said. "The NIE stuff isn't so bad, but it's the ICIC I can't get my head around."

She turned to face him. "What?"

"The Initial Crime Investigators' Course, or something," he said. "It's the second assessment we have to—"

"I know what it is, Liam," she said, rolling her eyes. "I just mean...wow, you're serious about this, aren't you? You've started revising for that already?"

Byrne shrugged. "Of course. Look, the guv took a chance on me, more than once. This is my chance. I know it is." He looked down at her. "Why? Haven't you started yet?"

Campbell's blood ran cold. "Well, I...there hasn't been much—"

"Saturday afternoon. My place. Bring your books. And snacks," he added with a grin, eyeing the shop owner, who was heading back towards the counter carrying nothing but a grim expression. "I'm prone to a caramel digestive myself."

CHAPTER EIGHTEEN

"That was Byrne," Ivy said, holding up her phone and dropping it back in her pocket. "The carpet shop was a dead end. It was sold decades ago, and there are no paper records of it."

"It was a long shot," George replied, looking around the living room, keeping an ear out for the sound of teaspoons on teacups coming from the kitchen. "It didn't exactly look new."

"Would've been nice, though, wouldn't it?" she said, leaning back. "If we'd got a credit card transaction for the carpet leading us to an address, leading us to—"

"To what?" George pushed. "The killer? Not necessarily. Probably not, in fact. If he was smart, which I think he is, he would have used somebody else's carpet."

"I think you're giving him too much credit, guv. People panic. We both know that. They don't think straight."

"I think you're not giving him enough credit, Ivy," he said, hushing as the sound of footsteps sounded along the hall.

"Here we go," came a voice, and Cooper re-entered the room with two hot mugs in one hand and one in the other. He set them down on the coffee table and returned to his spot on the sofa, looking more than a little sheepish. "Thanks for the erm..." he nodded at the door. "The kitchen, you know?"

"It's nothing," George replied gently.

George and Ivy had opted for the less comfortable armchairs that had not been in contact with either Mr Cooper's bare backside or his genitals.

He was fully dressed now, at least, in his blue jeans and a beer-stained white shirt, and he had even run some cold water over his face. The smell of stale alcohol however, still lingered in the air, not least because the beer cans still lay strewn around the carpet.

"Now what's this about?" he asked. "She's alright, isn't she?"

"Before we begin, I just want to understand your relationship with her," George began slowly. "Is she your girlfriend, partner? Or were you simply living here?"

"My missus, I suppose," he said, taking a sip of tea and wincing at the heat of it. "My girlfriend," he clarified when he saw George's questioning look.

"Did you notice that she didn't come home last night?"

"Oh, that's nothing unusual," he said, placing his cup down and leaning back into the sofa with a chuckle. "She does that. She'll have tied herself to a tree somewhere, or she'll be out helping a badger cross the road or something. Either that or she's gone on the piss."

He laughed, but in the serious silence that followed, Cooper's smile faded into a worried realisation.

George briefly met Ivy's eye and then sat forward.

"I'm very sorry to tell you, Matthew," he said, firm enough not to incite delusions of hope, but gentle enough to soften the blow. "We found Gemma's body last night in Snipe Dales Country Park."

"What?" he said, looking between them as if they were about to tell him they were pulling his leg.

"I'm very sorry to be the one to tell you."

Cooper rose to his feet, and George imagined that a shot of

adrenaline had just coursed through his body. He cleared his throat.

"This is a joke, right?" he asked, then, when George shook his head, he paced back and forth, clawing at his hair in despair.

"Sit down, Matthew, please," he said.

"No. No, I need to process this—"

"Matthew, there's something else you need to know."

"What?" he asked, pausing his pacing briefly enough to look him in the eye. "You just told me Gemma's dead. How can it possibly be any worse than that? Eh? Answer me? What can possibly be worse?"

It was one of those moments that George called upon every ounce of patience and empathy he could muster.

"Please," he said, and gestured at the sofa.

George's calm disposition seemed to break through the wall Cooper had developed. Slowly, he lowered himself onto the sofa, clinging to the arm for balance. Only when he was seated did George continue. He took a breath, held Cooper's gaze, and then spoke.

"We believe she was murdered, Matthew."

"What?"

"We believe it happened over the weekend."

"She didn't *die* then, did she?" he spat, his voice breaking.

"Sorry?"

"You said she died. She didn't die," he said, his voice venturing into a childlike whine. "Who would do that? Who would hurt her, and..." He looked at Ivy for a moment, then at George. "How? Can I ask how? Is that allowed?"

Matthew Cooper looked rough. His hands shook, beads of sweat had formed on his arms and neck, as well as his forehead, and his eyes were red and bloodshot, whether from the news or the drink, George couldn't be sure, though he guessed it was likely a combination of both. George had had some late nights in his day, a few whiskies too many, a few sleepless nights even, but he couldn't imagine ever having to deal with news like this in such a state.

"I'd like to know a little more about her, if I may," George said.

"You didn't answer my question," he replied, dropping his head into his hands. "Oh, God. Is it bad? It is, isn't it?"

"And I will," George said. "I promise, we'll share everything we can. But, right now, our primary objective is to find out who did this to her."

Slowly, Cooper nodded.

"Was Gemma politically active, Matthew?" George asked. "Was she doing something like that yesterday?"

"What?"

"You said you thought she was out helping a badger or tied to a tree, and we know that she had similar interests at university."

"It was just a joke," he said, rubbing his face with his hands.

"But is she? An activist, I mean?"

"Well, yeah," he moaned, dropping his hands. "I mean, she loves that stuff, kicking up a fuss, protesting, signing petitions."

"What kinds of protests?"

"I don't bloody know, do I? Eco stuff," he threw out. "Wind farms, animal rights. Whatever happens to be the latest thing to moan about."

"Wind farms," George repeated. "As in, she was for or against them?"

Cooper didn't reply at first. He just held George's gaze for what seemed like an eternity.

"Is that what you came to ask me? If Gemma was for or against wind farms?"

"I just meant—"

"Why aren't you out there doing something?" he said, standing up again, a victim to the ebbs and flows of his massive chemical imbalance. "You said she was murdered? Eh? Then who the hell did it?"

"Please sit down, Mr Cooper," George said, an instruction the man followed reluctantly. "I'm asking if you know what Gemma was doing on Sunday?"

He scratched at his beard as if he might pull the tiny hairs from his skin.

"She was out with a friend for lunch," he said eventually.

"What friend?"

"Sophie or Jenny or someone. One of them. I don't know."

"Well, we're going to need you to remember, Matthew. It's important."

"Jenny, I think. I..." He faded out as though the realisation about what had happened kept hitting him in waves, knocking the wind out of him, unable to speak. He rapped his head with his knuckles, then took a deep breath. "I can text her and ask?" he said, peering up at them through his fingers.

"That would be helpful."

They watched him wipe his nose on his sleeve, type a text on his phone, and then press send.

"So it didn't alarm you?" George continued. "When Gemma didn't contact you all day yesterday?"

"I didn't...I wasn't...I was at the pub, alright? I'm not her bloody keeper," he spat. "We're not like that. She does her thing, I do my thing. It's casual."

"But you live together?" Ivy pointed out.

"Yeah, so? I moved in a few months ago. She's fine with it."

"I didn't say she wasn't," Ivy replied flatly.

The leering sneer he'd worn had dissolved into a derisive snarl, but she'd seen it all before, and George was confident Ivy could handle the transformation of a stranger objectifying her, then turning on her in a matter of minutes.

"What time did you go to the pub, Matthew?" George asked.

"What?" he replied, tearing his focus from Ivy.

"What time did you go to the pub?"

"About midday," he said slowly.

"Until when?"

He shrugged.

"Closing, I think. I don't know."

"You don't remember?"

"I was drunk," he said flatly.

"And when did Gemma leave the house?"

But Matthew was distracted by the chiming of his phone on the armrest. He picked it up, read the message, and held it up to them. "It was Jenny, yeah. Gemma was with her yesterday."

"Good. I'm going to need Jenny's number."

"Whatever," he said, opening the contact and passing the phone to Ivy to copy down. "She dropped me off at the pub. I don't know what she did after that."

"In her car?" George clarified.

Matthew shot him a dry look. "No, she gave me a piggyback."

"What pub were you at yesterday, Matthew?"

"The George and Dragon. It's just down the road," he said nonchalantly. Then his slow, alcohol-laden brain cells caught up with the reality of the situation. "Wait, you don't think I had anything to do with this, do you?"

"It's our duty to—"

"That's why you're here, isn't it?" he said, standing for a third and final time. "You're accusing me of—"

"We're not accusing you of anything, Matthew," George said calmly, then paused. "But I will need to speak with you again. So perhaps it's best if you stay local."

"Whatever," he replied.

"One more thing," George said. "Gemma's parents. Are you able to share their details? It might be a good idea for us to speak with them before they find out through some other means."

"Good luck with that," he replied. "She doesn't speak about them. Never has."

George nodded. If the parents were out there, Ruby would find them.

"Can I offer some advice?" he said, then waited for Cooper's glowing eyes to traverse the room and settle on his. "Get yourself sober. The next few weeks will be very difficult."

"Yes, Dad," Cooper replied.

"Do you have somebody who can sit with you? A friend, or...I don't know, a parent?"

"I'll be fine."

"We can send somebody if you feel you need it. They can help you through the investigation. They'll answer any questions you have—"

"I said, I'm fine," Cooper spat, then realised how unnecessary his rudeness had been and looked away.

"We'll be in touch," George said. "We'll arrange for you to see her."

Cooper said nothing. He checked the cans for a drink, found a winner, then sat back as if they weren't even there and they hadn't just delivered the worst news possible.

That's how they left him, staring into space, processing his grief and hangover in one long, sickening headache.

As soon as they were back in the car, Ivy pulled out her phone and got to work. She found the contact Matthew had given her and placed the call on loudspeaker. It rang with the might of an organ filling a cathedral, echoing forcefully in the solemn silence.

Quickly enough, a sharp, panicked voice answered.

"Gemma? Is that you?"

"No, I'm sorry, it's not," Ivy said. "Is this Jennifer MacFadyen?"

"Sorry?"

"Matthew Cooper gave us your number?"

"Us?"

"My name is Detective Sergeant Hart. I'm with Lincolnshire Police."

"You're what? You're with the police?"

"You're a friend of Gemma Radford's?" Ivy said. "Is that right?

"Yes, I am. Do you know where she is?" came the panicked voice. "Is she alright? She's not answering her phone."

Ivy looked up at George, and he saw the dread in her eyes.

"Have you heard from Matthew, Jennifer?"

"What? Yeah, he just texted me. What's this about?"

"He asked if you were with Gemma yesterday?"

"Yes. Look, can you please just tell me what's going on?" she said. "Is Gemma okay?"

Ivy closed her eyes, as though distancing herself from the pain she was about to inflict. "I'm sorry to tell you," she said, her voice detached and cold, as though she'd gone to her own inner space of self-preservation. "Gemma was found dead last night in Snipe Dales Country Park."

The silence that followed was worse than any cry of denial or scream of dismay. It was the silence that follows a tragedy, an explosion, or the switching off of a flatlining heart monitor.

"Jenny?"

"I'm here," she whispered.

"What time did you and Gemma meet yesterday?" Ivy asked.

"I didn't meet Gemma yesterday." Her voice matched the same detached tone as Ivy's, the tone of self-preservation, of delayed, debilitating grief.

"Sorry?"

"I just told Matthew I met with her," she said. "I lied."

"Why?"

"Because she asked me to." Jenny sighed. "She told me that whenever Matthew asks if I was with her, I should say yes. But I'm not even in the country. I'm in Tenerife with my husband. I can send you my flight details if you want. We left on Thursday."

"Why would she ask you to lie?"

"I don't know. I just assumed she was cheating on him. You've met him, right?"

Ivy narrowed her eyes.

"When did this start?"

"A few months ago. She never gave me the details, I swear. She just said it mattered."

"What mattered?" Ivy pressed.

Jennifer hesitated, and George glanced at the house, at the man who stood at the bay window of the living room, watching them through a narrow slit in the curtains, his face pale, and his eyes dull.

"She just said that..." Jennifer lowered her voice, as though she, too, could see him in the window. "She said that Matthew couldn't find out where she was. Nobody could know."

CHAPTER NINETEEN

"I can't work miracles, Maguire," Ruby said to the Irishman breathing down her neck. They formed an obtuse triangle at the end of the conference table, and seeing as Ruby was the only one of the team not required to leave the office, she had claimed the best space. With Ruby at her laptop, O'Hara at one shoulder, and Maguire at the other, the three pored over the footage from the petrol station.

"Can't you just zoom in?" he asked.

"If I could—"

"It's the red sofa, isn't it?" he said, prodding at the screen so its pixels flared angrily. "Because I told the guv it was, and if I have to go back to another bloody petrol—"

"Give the woman some space, Dave," O'Hara said, pulling him back by his vest. "My God, let her do her job."

"Thank you," Ruby said, turning her chair to face them both, forcing Maguire to take another step back. "Look, pixels don't work like they do in the movies," she explained. "You can't just zoom into a blurry piece of footage and it'll suddenly become clear as day. The fact that the video is so pixelated means the original data is at its limit, and there's nothing I or anyone can do to make it clearer. What we see is what we get."

"So you can't identify the number plate?" Maguire asked.

"No," Ruby said, "I can't. The best I can do is identify the truck, which should help you narrow down the potential owners."

"Okay," O'Hara said slowly. "And how do you suggest we do that?"

"Maybe she's a car enthusiast in her spare time," Maguire joked.

"Don't even begin to question what I do in my spare time," Ruby said with a chuckle. "But, as it happens, I know somebody who might be able to help."

She nodded through the glass at an officer from another team, who was leaning back in his chair, twirling a pen in his fingers.

"Griffiths?" Maguire said.

"Three years in Traffic Police before transferring to CID," Ruby explained which earned her a questioning stare from both Maguire and O'Hara.

"How d'you know that?" he asked.

"I looked him up."

"When? You've only just been given the task?"

"Oh, I get it," O'Hara said, grinning. "You like him."

"What?" Maguire said. "Griffiths?"

"You're not exactly an oil painting," O'Hara told him.

"Can we not..." Ruby said, her dark skin flushing even darker.

"Well, anyway. Just because he was in traffic doesn't make him a vehicle database," Maguire told her.

"No, but it makes him a darn sight more qualified than us," she replied. "Or I could venture down the alternative route."

"Which is?"

"Call Lincoln HQ. Ask them to send a specialist."

"Who would more than likely tell us the same thing he does," O'Hara cut in. "Do it. Let's get him in."

She tapped on the glass, which raised a few heads from

members of various teams, and O'Hara pointed at Griffiths. Eventually, Griffiths caught on that people were trying to get his attention and glanced over his shoulder. Maguire shuddered to imagine what he must have thought, seeing three people inside a glass box waving at him like lunatics.

He had one of those ageless, boyish faces that seemed immune to the relentless forces of time, gravity, or the job that seemed to affect Maguire's own body. A sprinkling of grey hairs brought out the grey-blue of his eyes, and he wore a combination of chequered shirt and plain tie that could have been a set from a supermarket.

"Griffiths?" O'Hara said, shaking his hand. "I'm—"

"I know who you are."

"Oh," she said.

"You're O'Hara," he replied, then worked his way around the room. "You're Dave Maguire, and you're Ruby."

"I didn't realise we were so famous."

"You were pulled from the rota to work in major crimes. Things like that tend to get noticed," he said. "Besides, you now have an aquarium for an office."

"I suppose, when you put it like that."

"Anyway," he said. "What can I do for you?"

"I'm sorry," O'Hara said. "But, I'm getting negative vibes. There's no jealousy here, is there?"

"Jealousy? Why would there be jealousy?"

"You know? One minute we're pounding the beat, the next we're in this team. While you get pulled from traffic—"

"I transferred," he said. "There's a difference. And no, there's no jealousy. I'm just busy."

"Twiddling your pen?"

"Look, do you need help or not?"

"Okay, okay," Ruby said, holding her hands up. "Apologies, this was my idea. I knew you'd been in traffic and wondered if you could help us identify a vehicle."

"What am I, a bloody database?"

"Told you," Maguire said.

"You're experienced," O'Hara told him. "We just need to know what vehicle we're dealing with so that we can filter through local ownership records. Can you help us?"

He looked around at them all in turn, then settled his gaze on Ruby, whose cheeks were still flushed.

"Alright. No promises."

"An opinion based on experience is all we need," Maguire said. "We won't hold you to it."

"Okay," he said with a shrug. "Let's take a look."

Ruby turned her screen for him to see."

"The footage is blurry, but we think it's a flatbed Ford Transit," she explained.

"If it is, then you're looking at a thousand or more in Lincolnshire alone," he said, leaning over for a better look.

"I was hoping you could maybe narrow it down to a model, or a year, or something."

"Can I?" he asked, referring to the mouse and keyboard.

"Be my guest," Ruby said, pushing herself away from the desk.

"Yeah, thought so," he muttered to himself after a minute or so.

"Thought what?" Maguire asked.

He straightened and nodded to himself.

"See the headlights?" he said. "They're not rectangular like the early models, and the indicator light is integrated into the design, which suggests later than 2014, when Transits had a big facelift. But Ford integrated LED lighting in 2019, which I don't believe this model has, judging by the shape of the cab."

Maguire cleared his throat somewhat insecurely. "Okay...so?"

"So my guess is that this is a model made sometime between 2014 and 2019. I'd lean towards the 2015 model," Owen said, standing to his full height again.

"Well, that was easy," O'Hara said happily.

"Hold on," he said.

He navigated to a web browser and ran a search for *Ford Transit, 2015, white*.

The page filled with images of old Transit vans and he refined his search to include, *flatbed*.

Again, they were presented with a page filled with images, and Griffiths squinted at them, comparing them to the image in the video.

He adjusted his search terms to 2016, studied the results, and then straightened.

"There," he said. "I was wrong. It's the 2016 model. There's not much difference, but the styling has been upgraded."

"Sure?"

"As sure as I can be." He shoved his hands into his pockets. "Anything else?"

Ruby resumed control of her keyboard and mouse, avoiding eye contact with him.

"I think we're good, thank you," O'Hara said. "You have a good eye for detail. Your wife must be very lucky."

"Right," he said, a little unsure of how to respond.

"Is that what she calls you, is it?" she asked. "Griffiths?"

"It's Owen," he said. "And I'm not married."

"Well, Owen. If we need any more...advice of the vehicular nature, I'm sure Ruby will be in touch."

He eyed Ruby, who again refused to meet him eye-to-eye, feigning interest in her computer screen.

"Alright," he said, backing out of the door. "No worries."

He lingered at the door for a moment, eyeing Ruby with curiosity. Then smiled at O'Hara politely before leaving them to it.

O'Hara watched him return to his seat through the glass. He sat, picked up his pen, and glanced over his shoulder at Ruby once more, saw O'Hara watching him, and then got back to work.

"Well, he's a cutie," O'Hara said.

"Easy there," Maguire said horrified. "What about Adam?"

"It's Adrian," she laughed. "And what about him? I just said he was cute, that's all. Reminds me of Adam Scott."

Maguire scoffed. "Who?"

"God, don't you watch anything decent on TV?"

"Not that rubbish, no," he answered. "By the time I get home from this place, I need humour."

"Anyway..." O'Hara said, rolling her eyes. "Owen *is* a cutie, but I wasn't talking about for me." O'Hara looked over at Ruby, whose brown skin was a deep shade of rosewood.

"We're colleagues," she mumbled. "I don't get involved with colleagues."

O'Hara shrugged.

"So were me and Adrian. Before I joined the force," she clarified. "When I was in data entry for a hot second."

"Yeah, well," Ruby said, turning back to her trusty, non-complicated, non-heartbreaking screen. "I'm not interested, and even if I were, there's not much time for all that in this job, is there?"

"For all what?"

"Boyfriends, husbands, family. I mean, look at Ivy."

"Lots of people get divorced," O'Hara said. "Doesn't mean anyone who works for the force can't have a healthy home life."

"No, of course not," Maguire said dryly. "Just those working in Major Crimes, specifically in this station."

"I mean, that's why they broke up, isn't it?" Ruby asked. "Because she moved here? Because she put the job first? Is that right?"

"It is right," O'Hara said, "but that was their choice. You don't *have* to put the job first."

"I'm not sure we get much of a choice."

"True," Maguire sighed. "I thought we were actually going to get the weekend off yesterday. We ended up here until midnight."

Ruby smiled at the screen.

"It's worth it though, isn't it?"

"Yeah." Maguire grinned back. "I have to admit, I had my reservations before, but I do love it. It's addictive, right?"

"You love it, do you?" O'Hara asked.

"Yeah, the adrenaline, the pressure, the stakes. Makes it all worth it. I mean, we're working on murder investigations. I always thought I'd be stuck doing boring stuff. It's more exciting than doing what they do out there, isn't it?"

"I bet they get to switch off when they get home," Ruby added, which left them with something to ponder.

She returned to clicking through the stilled, blurry footage, making a note of the lights as well as Owen's analysis, and writing down the models he'd identified.

"What's that?" Maguire said over her shoulder.

"What's what?" Ruby replied.

"*That*," he said, leaning past her to poke the screen.

"That's what they call a petrol tank, Maguire," she replied, sardonically.

"I know, but look, what's that dark patch beneath it?" He pulled her screen closer, and like a mother protecting her child, she slapped his hand away. "*Look*," he insisted.

She squinted at the screen, identifying a shadowy mark on the petrol filler flap.

"That's a dent, that is," Maguire said, standing straight.

"No, it's just the light," Ruby countered, sounding unsure of herself. "Isn't it?"

"Wanna bet?" he said, running to the door and yanking it open. "Owen!"

Through the glass, O'Hara watched as Owen Griffiths turned in his seat, as if he'd been waiting to be called back.

"What?"

"Got a sec, fella? We need your expertise," Maguire called, and he grinned at O'Hara. "Or rather, Ruby does."

CHAPTER TWENTY

"You sure about this, guv?" Ivy asked as George pulled up outside a semi-detached property on Water Lane, where each house backed onto the expansive fields that eventually bled into Snipe Dales Country Park.

A few twitching curtains suggested their presence hadn't gone unnoticed.

"What do you mean?" he replied.

"I mean, is this really our priority right now?" Ivy said. "Shouldn't we be following up on the evidence instead of returning to infamously unreliable leads?"

"Without Southwell's report, we don't have any evidence. Nothing concrete, anyway."

"We have video evidence of the fly-tipper transporting the rubbish. All we need is that truck's number plate. That *could* lead us straight to the killer."

"Unlikely, Ivy," he said. "Not now we know the rubbish was dumped long before Gemma was killed."

"So what, somebody drove to Snipe Dales on a whim, spotted the carpet, and thought, perfect, I'll just hide the body I've been storing in my boot there? Easy!"

"That's exactly my point. The timeline doesn't make sense. It needs tidying."

"Well, then let's tidy it," she replied, not frustrated but firm. "Let's get the tech guys from Lincoln HQ on it."

"Ruby's on it," George told her.

"I just—"

"Look at the witness statements Byrne and O'Hara sent through Ivy," he said, holding up the email on his phone. "They're inconsistent."

"They're exactly the same, guv."

"They're inconsistent with reality," he grumbled. "You're telling me those boys didn't see a single other person all day yesterday? When they spent the entire day in a popular Country Park? Tosh."

"Tosh?" Ivy whistled. "Wow, you are serious, aren't you?"

He smiled, releasing the tension.

"Look, I know you want to focus on Gemma Radford instead of the boys. She's our victim. I get it. But something tells me they're more involved than they're letting on. These statements, Ivy, something's not adding up."

"Snipe Dales is a massive Country Park. It rained all morning, and the boys were busy mucking around building a den. It's hardly surprising that they didn't see anyone else."

"Ivy, I—"

"Alright, alright," she said. "I've said my piece, guv. I know not to fight your instincts."

He grinned at her.

"Good."

"Good?" she replied over the car's roof. "Good?"

"I'd prefer it if we were on the same side on this one," he said. "I get it. I really do, and do you know what? You're right. We *should* be looking into Gemma Radford's personal life, but we can't even find a next of kin, so until we can progress that line of enquiry, we're progressing this. It's got to be done at some point, and the sooner the better in my opinion."

"She doesn't have one," Ivy said.

"Who doesn't have what?"

"Gemma Radford," she said. "She has no next of kin. Ruby emailed earlier."

"Did she?" he said, checking his phone. The message was one of four unread emails.

"Both parents are dead. No siblings," he read aloud. "Brilliant. So, the best we have is a naked alcoholic. Do you want to go back and see him?"

She dropped her head onto her arm, which in turn rested on the car roof, then she straightened, defeated.

"No," she said, relenting. "No, you're right, as always."

They walked the few steps to the green front door that matched the adjoining house, as though they had once been part of an old estate.

George pushed a trailing lobelia that hung from a basket to one side and knocked twice on the door. It was quickly answered by Mrs Foxon, whose face dropped into utter dismay at the sight of George and Ivy as though she'd hoped the previous night's interaction had been nothing less than a bad dream. From the sound of the radio and sizzling behind her, George imagined they were trying to establish some sort of normality.

"I'm sorry to disturb you, Mrs Foxon," he said. "Do you remember us?"

"How could I forget?" she said quietly. "Mr Larson, wasn't it?"

"That's right," he replied with a smile. "Is Louis home?"

"I...yes. Your colleague suggested we keep him home today so we can keep an eye on him."

"We need to follow up with him about his statement."

"He only gave it to you yesterday."

"That's right. We have further questions."

"Already?"

"Mrs Foxon," George began slowly and quietly in case they were being overheard, "the events that took place yesterday, as I'm sure you can appreciate, are serious. So yes, we are working as fast as possible to make progress, and while I respect your privacy and appreciate your family's cooperation, Louis's statement remains a vital part of our investigation." He let that sink in, then added, "May we come in? Please?"

At this, she opened the door silently, still processing, no doubt, how her life had changed so drastically in less than twenty-four hours. "Second door on the right," she mumbled. "He's in the kitchen."

George nodded, needing only to follow his nose towards the tempting aroma of fried bacon. Louis Foxon and Oscar Wyman sat at a rustic kitchen table, while Mr Foxon was at the range, tending to the bacon. The man shared a worried glance with his wife, who had stepped in behind them, but chose not to offer an argument and nodded once by way of a greeting.

"Inspector Larson," he said, nodding down at the pan. "Do you want one?"

George's stomach groaned in plea. There were few things in life he enjoyed more than a bacon butty, but the timing was far from ideal.

"Thanks, but no," he said. "We just need a word with your son."

"Right," Foxon replied. "Mind if I stay?"

"I'd prefer it if you did," George replied, looking back at his wife. "Both of you, in fact."

"Sit down, sit down," Mr Foxon said, pointing to the table with his spatula, where Oscar Wyman peered up at them hopefully.

"Have you heard from your parents, Oscar?" George asked, to which the boy shook his head.

"He's fine here," Mrs Foxon said. "He's always round here, anyway. Aren't you, Oscar?"

He nodded, but said nothing.

"I need to have a little chat with Louis, Oscar," George started. "The thing is, the law dictates that, should I feel the need to question a minor, either their parents or an appropriate adult needs to be present."

"We can be his appropriate adults," Mr Foxon said. "If it helps, I mean."

George shook his head.

"No, as much as I'm grateful for the offer of help, I can't allow it. Ideally, we need to speak to his mum and dad. Has there been nothing from them at all?"

Mr Foxon smiled sadly, and George addressed his wife.

"Is there somewhere Oscar could go while we speak to Louis?" he asked. "What I'm trying to avoid is having your son's statement influenced by Oscar, and vice versa. I'm trying to maintain credibility."

"I suppose he could go upstairs to Louis's room," she said, turning to the boy in question. "Do you want to do that, Oscar?"

"It won't be for long," George told him.

"Okay," Oscar replied quietly.

"Why don't you take your sandwich?" Mrs Foxon said. "I'll give you a shout when we're done."

He left the table and ventured upstairs without a look back.

"Is he alright?" George asked, to which Mrs Foxon shrugged.

"He's fine. They're both fine. I think he's more worried about his parents than... you know?"

The table, much like the rest of the house, seemed cosy and welcoming, with a soft, linen runner and a vase of fresh daisies in the middle. He imagined Mrs Foxon lighting the many small, mismatched candles that were scattered along the runner to bathe the happy family in a warm glow during suppertime.

George took the seat opposite Louis, who was already halfway through his breakfast. Louis's mother came to sit next to him, while his father turned off the stove and faced the table, wiping his hands on a tea towel. Ivy remained in the doorway, leaning against the frame with a wide-angle view of the room, presumably so as not to crowd the lad.

"Louis, I've been reading through the statement you gave to my colleague yesterday," George started, and when the boy didn't reply, he continued. "I just need to clarify a few things, if I may." The boy blinked and swallowed, but said nothing. "You see, I'm struggling with the fact that you spent nearly all day in the Country Park, yet didn't see anybody."

"Well, I never," the boy replied, looking across at his mum. "I didn't."

"It's alright," George said. "You're not in any trouble. But you saw nobody, nobody at all?"

Louis glanced at his dad, a worried look pulling the corners of his eyes down and the edges of his mouth up.

"I don't remember," he mumbled.

"Not even a dog walker?" he asked. "Or a runner? Lots of people go there, especially on a Sunday."

"I don't know."

"No other kids playing?"

"I—"

"No family picnics?"

"We—"

"Or someone out for a hike?"

Again, he looked to his parents before answering.

"Maybe there were *some* people about."

"Okay." George smiled. "What kind of people?"

"Some people walking their dogs. But it had been raining all morning," he insisted. "It weren't busy."

George smiled, hoping to ease the boy's nerves.

"Did you see anyone in the car park, Louis?"

The boy shook his head.

"Did anybody see you near the pile of rubbish?"

"No."

"But you did see some cars parked up, surely?"

"Some, but I don't know which ones. I didn't take any notice."

"That's understandable," George said. "We tend not to question those things that seem insignificant, do we? Our eyes seem to...I don't know, wash over them. It's perfectly natural."

Louis shrugged, and George gave him a friendly smile.

"Where did you see dog walkers, then?"

"Eh?"

"You said you saw some people walking their dogs. Where was that?"

"I think...well, on the path."

"The path by the trees?"

"Yeah."

"Did they talk to you?"

"I...no, they just left us alone."

George leaned back. The quick-fire questioning wasn't his favourite technique. On one hand, it had worked. Louis's statement had evolved from having seen nobody all day to seeing at least one dog walker and some cars. On the other hand, it had left the lad guarded.

George stretched his back, as though sharing the boy's weariness. He spoke slowly, hoping to reassure the lad.

"I wonder if you would do something for me, Louis?"

"What?" he replied tentatively.

"I want you to close your eyes."

"Eh?"

"Close your eyes. It's okay. Trust me."

At this, the boy panicked, which was entirely understandable. He looked at his parents, as embarrassed as if he'd been asked to strip. But George simply closed his eyes as an example, and when he opened them again, Louis had mirrored his expression.

"That's it," George said softly. "Take a few deep breaths and relax, alright?"

The boy did as he was asked.

"I want you to imagine you're in the Country Park," George said, watching the boy's eyelids twitch. "Just like you were on Sunday. You're walking through the park with Wesley and Oscar. Tell me what you see."

Louis swallowed, and then took a deep breath as though inhaling the air.

"Trees," he started slowly.

"That's good," George told him. "What does the ground look like?"

"Muddy," Louis replied.

"Wet or dry?" George pressed.

"Both," came the reply.

"And the sky?" George asked, doing his best to keep the questions slow and steady.

"Erm, clouds? Grey ones passing over and the sun coming through. There's grass, too, and water. We're playing by the stream."

"Good, good," George said. "And do you see anyone walking around?"

"Not really."

"No?"

"Maybe a family in the distance."

"No one on their own?"

"No, it's raining."

"Okay," George sighed. "Now, Louis, I want you to tell me what happened on Sunday, but I want you to tell me it in reverse order, okay? So let's start at the end of the day."

Louis's face crinkled, but he kept his eyes closed. "You mean, with the woman...?"

"No," George said softly. "It's okay. We don't have to relive that. Let's start with when you sat looking at the sunset. That's what it says in your statement. That was a nice moment, wasn't it?"

"Yeah, I suppose."

"So you're watching the sunset with Wesley and Oscar. Take me backwards from that moment. Imagine it like a video in rewind."

"This is ridiculous—" Mrs Foxon started, but was cut off when George raised his hand to beg a few moments more.

Louis frowned at the task, as though it took all of his intellect to do so. "Well, I guess, the sun was going...up?"

George smiled. "Good."

"I saw my mum's text and stood up from the sofa. It stank a bit."

"Good, very good," he encouraged.

"Wesley and Oscar were...talking," the boy said, picking up momentum. "Wesley threw something. A stick."

"A stick?"

"It was meant for the dog?" Louis said.

"What dog is that?"

"The old man's..." he stopped mid-sentence and closed his eyes.

"What dog?" George asked. "What old man?"

Louis's eyes snapped open.

"Hey, that's not fair," Mr Foxon said, stepping forward. "You tricked him."

"Mr Foxon—"

"You hypnotised him or something. You've confused him."

"It's a cognitive technique," Ivy said flatly. "It makes it harder for Louis's memory to *assume* what happened next through linear thinking."

"Actually, I learned it as a way to remember where I left my keys," he said to Louis, hoping to raise a smile. "I was always losing them. But it also helps in cases like this."

"Like what?"

"Cases when trauma might affect somebody's memory. You see, when we deal with trauma, our minds can block access to our memory, if that makes sense? There's nothing untoward about it, I can assure you."

George focused on the boy. "Tell me about the man and the dog, Louis."

"H-he didn't mean to..." Louis stammered. "He was just mucking around."

"Who? Who was mucking around?"

But Louis didn't reply. He stared wide-eyed at his mother, and for the first time, she put the gravity of the situation before the potential upset of her own child, taking accountability as the parent of a witness.

"Tell the truth, honey," she said quietly. "You're doing well."

Only then did Louis turn to George, defeated.

"Wesley," he said. "Wesley did it."

CHAPTER TWENTY-ONE

The first thought Ivy had as they neared Bluewater Manor via a seemingly endless driveway was how two neighbouring houses could be so vastly different. The Harris household, which they were approaching, was only half a mile up the road, yet seemed to belong in another world, let alone another street.

While the Foxons' property had been charming and homely, the Harris's could have been from a scene in a Bram Stoker novel. It comprised countless dormers jutting from the various pitched roofs, and more chimneys than anybody could ever need. The entire lower half had been claimed by climbing ivy, as though the owners had deliberately sought to hide the natural stone. It was, without question, an impressive building, designed to make a statement.

George found space to park on the ample forecourt, and although he refrained from commenting on the grandeur, he must have been thinking what she was. They climbed from the car in silence, absorbing the beautifully detailed mouldings and arches, as was no doubt the builder's intention.

"It's so quiet," Ivy whispered. "You can't even hear the main road."

"I'd rather hear the road and have a couple of million quid in my pocket than the other way around," George added, peering around for signs of life.

Even the manicured grounds were still, as though the flowers and plants were immune to the whims of the wind, and the tree-tops were untouched by the breeze.

Then they saw him - a gangly, grey-haired man who backed into view, with some kind of weed sprayer strapped to his back. He was working his way along the gravel path that encircled the house.

"Good afternoon," George called over with a wave, and the man's head snapped around, as if startled. He returned the wave and fiddled with the sprayer until the jet of liquid slowed to a stop.

He eyed them curiously for a moment, as if waiting for them to say something.

"Hello there. We're looking for Mr Harris," George called out.

"Wouldn't park there," came the reply, and he gestured at the spray. "This stuff'll strip that back to bare metal if the wind gets hold of it."

"Is he around?" George pressed. "Mr Harris? Can we speak to him?" He raised his warrant card. "We're with Lincolnshire Police."

He eyed them both, perhaps in a new light, then shrugged.

"Best knock on the door," he replied. "Not my doing."

He returned to his gardening, as if the goings-on of his employer were beyond his duties.

"Let's leave him to it, eh?" George suggested, and he started towards the main entrance.

They climbed the five flagstone steps and assessed the huge double doors. The old wooden porch creaked in the wind, and Ivy shivered dramatically, imagining the scene of many a movie, where a passerby's car breaks down and seeks shelter for the night.

George knocked twice, using the large brass knocker, then stepped back, and they were greeted by the sound of a woman singing what Ivy thought were church hymns. The singing stopped, and the door opened to reveal a woman who Ivy summarised in her mind as weathered, petite, and mature, with flushed cheeks that gave the impression she had just come in from the cold, despite the warm day. Accordingly, she wore a thick, woollen cardigan over a knee-length winter dress and thick tights. Her deep, grey eyes reminded Ivy of an overcast lake, and her thick, grey hair was held in place by impressive intertwined Celtic-style braids.

"Hello," George said, breaking the silence. "I wonder if you could help. We're looking for Mr Harris. Ewan Harris?"

"Oh, I'm afraid now's not a good time," she said, and was likely about to start explaining why now wasn't a good time when George stopped her.

"To be more accurate, we'd like a word with his son. Wesley Harris. Is he home?" He let his warrant card fall open again. "I'm Detective Inspector Larson."

She nodded solemnly, taking it all in.

"I see," she said, her voice deep and her accent unmistakably Scottish. "You'd better come in, dears." They followed her shuffling footsteps into a grand hallway, where gold-framed paintings filled oak panels, and a broad, wooden staircase commanded the room. "Terrible news," she said. "That poor woman, I don't know what the world's coming to. Have you found him yet? Suppose he's scarpered, has he?"

George smiled politely.

"We're doing our best."

"Well, if you need to talk to Wesley, I can certainly..." She paused, tilting her head like a kestrel sensing a shift in the wind. From the deeper recesses of the house, a door slammed. "Oh dear."

"Is that them?" a voice roared, male and gruff. "What the bloody hell do they want now?"

From what George assumed to be a corridor beneath the staircase emerged Ewan Harris, whose ginger hair was in a wispy disarray that rivalled his flushed cheeks.

"I knew you'd be back," he started as soon as he saw them. "It's not enough to keep him until midnight, is it?" he yelled. "Now you want to bother him again. After what he's seen?"

George remained as impassive as ever.

"We have a few follow-up questions, Mr Harris."

"Do you know how this looks?" Ewan said, throwing out a furious arm. "For the neighbours to see you lot coming down the drive?"

"There's no reason for anybody to know we're—"

"I can't deal with this right now," he said, his voice breaking with fatigue. "I have too much to do."

The woman who had answered the door stepped up and placed a motherly hand on his arm.

"I'll take them to Wesley, shall I? You get on now, okay, Ewie?"

To Ivy's surprise, Ewan gripped her fingers and turned to her lovingly.

"Could you deal with it for me, Janet?"

"Of course, dear." She gave his face a tender stroke with a light and friendly slap at the end of it.

"Thank you," he said, kissing her hand, throwing one last glare at Ivy and George, and pointing at them. "Five minutes. That's all you're getting."

"That should be fine," George told him, as he skulked back to wherever he'd come from. The woman watched him leave sorrowfully with a hand on her heart.

"Would you follow me?" she asked, starting towards the stairs.

"Janet, is it?" George said, holding out his hand as they climbed. "I don't believe we've been properly introduced. I'm Detective Inspector George Larson."

"Oh, yes," she said, shaking it. "Sorry about that. It's just a very stressful time for him. He works so hard."

"Of course," he said. "Wesley went through a lot yesterday. It must be very difficult."

"Aye, yes, that too."

"What is it that he's busy with?" Ivy asked. "Ewan, I mean. Is it work?"

"Oh well, you know how it is. Working with the public, I'm sure. They're always getting at you about something, eh?" She shook her head. "Ewie has a lot going on, bless his heart."

"Yes, bless Ewie," Ivy muttered.

"It's harassment, is what it is, what those lot do."

"What lot?" George asked.

"Those lot on Facebook and whatever else," she said, her small fists clenched. "These online hate groups, they're always getting at him. I'm fair scunnered with it."

George grinned at the use of the old Scottish phrase.

"I hope it's not rude to ask," he said, "but you don't sound like you're from around here?"

"Oh no," she chuckled, her anger easing. "Not at all. My husband and I moved from Inverness. Forty-odd years ago now, would you believe? When Ewie was just a wee boy."

"Your husband?"

"Aye, you might have seen him outside."

"Ewan?"

"No, no," she chuckled again, as though easily humoured. "My husband, John. He works on the grounds, and I manage the house."

"Oh, I see."

"Aye," she said, like an old grandmother. "We were ready to go when Ewie's parents died. Practically begged us to stay. To be honest, I've no idea what we'd have done or where we'd have gone. Kept a roof over our head, he did. Heart of gold."

"What do you manage?" George asked. "If you don't mind me asking?"

"Oh, pretty much everything you see. I cook, clean, take care of Wesley, and then there's the guests, of course."

"Guests? Is it some kind of hotel?"

She chuckled heartily.

"No, but there's always somebody about - politicians, members of the community, even journalists every now and again, and so forth. I make them feel at home, make sure they're fed, and..." she leaned close and winked, "well liquored if the occasion calls for it," she said with a laugh. "Ewie's very, very busy. Hard worker, that boy. So it's best if I take care of what I can."

"I see."

"And your husband?"

"Ah, he looks after the grounds. Very proud, he is, too. Does all sorts. The gardens, the lawns. Do you know he's past retirement, and he's still fit enough to decorate the old stables, changing them into a games room for Wesley. Ewan said he should get someone in, but no, John wouldn't have that. There's always something to do. He's doing the games room, he's to build something for the bins—"

"For the bins?"

"Foxes," she explained. "Make a terrible mess, they do. And that's on top of keeping the gardens nice."

"Well, I dare say Mr Harris is very lucky to have you both," George remarked. "It's not often we come across a house with staff. I rather like it."

"Oh, we're not staff," she said. "We're more like family."

"Well, like I said. I hope he shows his appreciation."

"With everything coming up next year, he needs all the help he can get."

"Next year?"

Janet stopped at the top of the broad staircase, turning to look down at them. Her expression was a mix of surprise and theatrical delight.

"You haven't heard?"

George glanced at Ivy, who gave the faintest shrug.

"Heard what?"

Janet's smile widened into something akin to pride.

"Our Ewie's running in the by-election," she said, as if it were common knowledge, as if the very idea of not knowing bordered on absurd. Her eyes glowed with pride, her posture swelling like a lioness presenting her prize cub. "All being well, he'll be our next MP," she told them. "Imagine that?"

CHAPTER TWENTY-TWO

The first-floor corridor flanked the north-facing wall, allowing scant light through the large sash windows and casting a gloom over the rich and dusty mahoganies and oaks. The mood that the poor light created was only exacerbated by the heavy crimson drapes and the deep green walls.

Unlike the Foxons' home, there were no candid family photographs atop bureaus or cabinets and no family portraits on the walls, save for one of a much younger Wesley and Ewan Harris alongside a woman Ivy failed to recognise.

Her hair was lush and blonde, her skin appeared to shine, and unlike the males in the image, her smile radiated from the frame.

"Can I ask you something, Janet?" George started, adding to Ivy's sense that there was some kind of rapport developing between him and the lovely housekeeper. "Where's Wesley's mother? Is Ewan married?"

"He *was*," she said sadly, and for a moment it looked as if she might add to that, but offered nothing more.

"He's not anymore?"

She sighed heavily.

"Her name was Georgina."

"Oh, I'm so sorry," he said, blushing. "I've put my foot in it—"

"Oh no, no. No, she left him. Poor Wesley was just a wee boy. Heaven knows where she is now. I mean, how you could abandon a wee bairn like that, I have no idea."

"It beggars belief," George added, to which she smiled pleasantly.

"Some of us just aren't cut out for motherhood, I suppose," she replied. "It's just a shame they find out too late."

"Do you have children of your own?" Ivy asked, wondering if that judgement had been earned.

"No," Janet answered flatly. "But I raised Wesley as my own, as I did Ewan, come to think of it."

"Well, they were lucky to have you," Ivy told her, forcing a smile.

Janet smiled back. "That's very nice of you to say so, dear."

Ivy met George's eye, conveying his appreciation that she hadn't unravelled his rapport with the woman. If Janet thought of herself as the equivalent of the Harris boys' mother, then she would make a good ally.

"Forgive me," he started, "but if you don't know where Georgina is, then how do you know she's not..."

"Dead?" Janet laughed. "Oh, believe me, Mr..."

"Inspector," he said. "Inspector Larson."

"Well, Inspector Larson, abandoning her family was a deliberate choice. We still hear from her from time to time. She'll send a Happy Birthday or Merry Christmas text here and there. You know? Wishing the bairn well. I'm not sure if that's a good thing. Upsets him more than anything, if I'm being honest. But what can I do?"

She led them to a large oak door that looked like it had been rescued from an abbey during the Reformation, and knocked sharply.

"Wesley, dear, the detectives are here to see you," she said, and her commitment to those old-fashioned terms of endearment reminded Ivy of the woman she'd once counted calling George *sweetie* five times in a single sentence. "Wesley? Are you there, dear?"

Another ten seconds or so passed before they heard his gruff response. "Yeah?"

She turned the old wrought iron handle and led them into Wesley's bedroom, which was the size of Ivy's first flat when she had left home. But where she had fit an entire kitchen, bathroom, living-dining and bedroom area, the boy had a gaming corner, work desk, wardrobe, and an ensuite, all centred by a super king sized bed at the end of which was a pile of wrapped presents, some of which were yet to be opened.

Wesley Harris leaned against the headboard, still dressed in his pyjamas, his laptop closed and resting on his thighs.

"Good afternoon, Wesley," George said, as Ivy's eyes adjusted to a deeper shade of gloom. Janet strode across the room and tugged open the heavy drapes, allowing the sunlight to billow into the room, illuminating the circling columns of dust the ensuing breeze had stirred. "How are you today?"

Wesley shrugged.

Janet sat at the foot of his bed.

"Sit up, dear," she told him, and he followed her instructions with obvious reluctance. "And answer the question. Come on. Where are your manners?"

"I'm fine, thank you," he muttered, almost robotically. "Thank you for asking."

The response clearly lacked sincerity, but at least he was talking.

"We have something to ask you about yesterday," George started. "The woman you saw, the one in the carpet—"

"The dead one," he said flatly.

"Yes," George said. "I was wondering, have you ever seen her before?"

Wesley shrugged. Then, at a sharp look from Janet, he said, "What do you mean?"

"I mean, have you ever seen her out walking, maybe? Did you recognise her at all?"

"No," he said sullenly.

"Okay," George said. "Thank you. I do have another question. Did you see anybody else out and about that day?"

He shrugged. "Not really. It was raining. I told this to the woman."

"To my colleague, Constable O'Hara?"

"Yeah. Her."

"So you didn't see anyone out walking their dog that day?"

"I told you, no," he said, his voice building momentum to the kind of outburst they'd witnessed from his father less than ten minutes ago.

"What about the man you threw a stick at?"

At this, Wesley gaped for a few seconds and avoided looking at the disappointment evident on Janet's face.

"I didn't—"

"We know that you did, Wesley."

"It were an accident."

"*Was*," Janet said sharply.

"It *was* an accident."

"You didn't mean to throw the stick?" Ivy asked flatly. "Seems a strange mistake to make."

"I was just playing with his dog," Wesley said.

"We heard it was a very big stick, Wesley," George said calmly. "The kind of stick that could have hurt somebody."

"More like a branch, we heard, didn't we, guv?" Ivy said.

"That's right, Wesley. More of a branch. Why did you throw it?"

"Because he was a nosy, old codger," Wesley spat. "He was bothering us for no reason. We weren't doing anybody any harm."

"What were you doing, then?"

"We were just building our den."

"So, he saw you with the carpet, did he?"

"He...I...yeah, I guess."

"Why didn't you tell us this before?"

"I forgot."

"You forgot?" George said. "Or you didn't want to get in trouble for harassing someone?"

"*He* was harassing *us*!"

"Oh? What did he say to you? Was he aggressive?"

"He told us to leave the carpet alone. That it was rubbish and might have glass or something in it. The idiot."

"*Wesley,*" Janet scolded, her tone motherly and harsher than Ivy thought her capable.

"Well, he was! Couldn't even control his dog. It was jumping all over the place. More like a rat than a dog. Like, it had a perm, for God's sake—"

"Wait, wait," George said, halting the boy's derogatory tirade. "Slow down." He stepped into the new light that shone through the arched window, his face steeped in realisation. "I need you to think hard, Wesley. I need you to tell me what this man looked like."

CHAPTER TWENTY-THREE

Staring at the mess on the whiteboard, George felt like one of those home organisers he'd once caught Ivy watching on Instagram. The plan had been to take the chaotic sprawl of information before him and sort it into lists. He hoped to hold each piece of information in his mind and make a decision on its significance, creating a priority list.

But so thin was the information, and so fresh was the investigation that his hopes were dashed before he'd begun. The long and short of it was that he couldn't bear to relinquish any of it yet.

He turned to face the team, feeling the swell of pride in his chest. Here they were in their office, each one of them hard at work. It hadn't been that long ago that Ivy had to corral and hush their chitter chatter.

Ruby and O'Hara were tapping away on their laptops, Byrne and Campbell frowned over a notebook as though collaborating on a particularly tricky crossword, while Maguire studied his laptop screen with his face so close, he was very nearly in the image.

Ivy was in her usual position, to one side of the room, her

attention divided between anticipating George's next move and her emails.

"I know it's getting late," he started, waiting for each of them to look up, "but I want to sleep on what we have. We've received Southwell's report, so Ivy will update us as we go along. Let's start with our lines of enquiry." He gestured at the board and narrated. "The body, the fly-tipper, the carpet. Let's start with the carpet. Byrne, Campbell?"

"Sure, guv," Byrne started, closing his notebook. "We found diddly."

"I was hoping for a few more details."

"The carpet's label led us to a shop called Miller and Son Carpets. We spoke to the owner, who told us the carpet was manufactured in 1967, further back than their records reach."

"So it's a dead end?"

"Pretty much, yeah."

"Ivy, what was Southwell's analysis of the carpet?" George asked.

But she shook her head.

"*Nothing?*"

"No, guv," she said, her face grim. "The carpet sample contained limited traces of DNA, but overwhelmingly Gemma Radford's. Nothing else we could follow. She says the carpet's probably been bleached, but she'll take other samples from other parts of the carpet and try those." She rubbed her brow, feeling the lack of evidence as much as George was. "She did at least find DNA from the rest of the dumped material," Ivy said, moving on. "In particular, the sofa."

"But that doesn't make sense," Campbell said. "Why would someone bleach the carpet when it was dumped *before* Gemma was killed?"

O'Hara shrugged. "Maybe the killer knew he was going to use that carpet to dump her body."

"What, so he bleached a carpet, left it overnight on a pile of junk *with* his DNA on, in preparation for the murder he planned to commit the next day?" Campbell scoffed. "That's ridiculous."

"Maybe he wanted to throw us off," Byrne said.

"Well, it's working," she observed.

"Is there a lead on the sofa DNA, Ivy?" George asked.

"Yes, as it happens." Ivy checked Southwell's printed report. "A Steven Corbyn. He's got form, but nothing major. Did a three-month stint in HMP Lincoln a few years back."

"What did he do?" Maguire asked. "Post something on social media?"

"Theft," Ivy said. "He's what we call a recidivist."

"No wonder we've got an overcrowding problem," he mumbled.

"His DNA accounts for more than fifty per cent of the samples found on the sofa," Ivy continued. "She's excluded the others as guests as the samples were so small."

"Good," George said. "That's something to go on." He turned to Byrne. "And how did it go with the couple Ivy and I bumped into? What were their names?"

"Thea Drake and Jack Jennings," he replied.

"Did you call them?"

"*I* did," Campbell cut in. "They were polite enough. I think they realised it was about something more serious than fly-tipping."

"Statement?"

"Yep, and they'd be happy to testify."

"I thought they'd be keen," he replied. "Keep them warm. We might need them later down the line."

"According to them, the rubbish pile wasn't there when they left the Country Park just before five p.m. on Saturday evening."

"Direct messages from our post on socials confirm that, by the way, guv," Ivy said. "I've been checking. A few people said the rubbish wasn't there on Saturday, but others say they saw it on Sunday."

"Did anyone see anything useful? Anything suspicious?"

"No, guv, but to be honest, there was a limited amount of feedback. But loads of people commented on it. It clearly riled the community."

"Okay, well, that leads us nicely to our second line of enquiry," George moved on. "Maguire, O'Hara, tell us about the CCTV." He tapped the section of the board that held a printed screenshot of the petrol station footage, its time stamp highlighted in red: *02:48*. Someone — he assumed Ruby, judging by the neat handwriting — had drawn an arrow from the headlights and written, *2014-2019 Model Flatbed Ford Transit*. "What are we looking at here?"

"A 2014 to 2019 Model Flatbed Ford Transit," Maguire said. "Most likely a 2016 model."

"I can read that much."

"It's from a petrol station just outside Spilsby. The truck drove past at two forty-eight on Sunday morning with a red sofa on the back, among other stuff. We believe that to be the truck that fly-tipped the carpet."

"Which means the stuff was dumped about three a.m."

"Yes, guv."

Byrne squinted at the photo. "I can't see the carpet."

"I can't see much at all," Campbell agreed.

"The carpet must be buried beneath, but look." Maguire stood up and pointed. "*That's* the red sofa. You can even see the stains. We found something else, guv." He gestured to the board. "Can I?"

"By all means." George stepped back, pleased to see Maguire getting involved.

"*Here,*" Maguire continued, stabbing the printed screenshot.

"What is that?" Byrne asked, again squinting.

"It's a dent, we think."

Byrne shrugged. "It looks like a shadow."

"It's a dent. Owen confirmed it."

"Who's Owen?" George asked, to which O'Hara beamed childishly.

"Ruby's friend."

"Owen Griffiths, and he's not my friend. He's CID. Transferred from traffic, guv," she corrected quickly and professionally.

"The important thing is, it's an identifier," Maguire said. "There're more than a thousand Flatbed Ford Transits in Lincolnshire alone." He tapped the board. "But I'll bet only one of them has a dent like this."

"Whatever happened to a number plate?" Campbell asked.

"We can't see it," Maguire said.

"Did you try zooming in?"

He rolled his eyes.

"Now, why didn't we think of that?"

"Just asking, that's all."

"You can't just zoom in and it'll magically become clear. What we see is what we get," he said, and George caught Ruby smiling as though enjoying a private joke.

"DC Griffiths also gave us a model, guv," she said. "From the headlights, he identified it as a 2014 to 2019 model, most likely a 2016 model, which I narrowed down to forty-odd registered trucks in the Wolds."

"Forty?" George said, surprised.

She shrugged.

"It's better than a hundred."

"So we just need to find one of the forty with a dent near its diesel filler flap?"

"Yes, guv."

"Great," George said, unsure whether this was a useful lead or not. He tapped the third and final line of enquiry. "Body," he said, "I guess that's my update." He rubbed his forehead with the end of the marker. "Pip agreed with Saint's time of death as between three and four p.m. on Sunday afternoon. Worst case, it's an hour either side of that. She also confirmed the cause of death as mechanical asphyxiation. But she also confirmed that a hessian sack was used to restrain and disorientate Gemma Radford, which in turn narrows down our suspects to—"

"Everyone in Lincolnshire," Campbell muttered.

George sighed.

"That's what I said."

"Any sign of... you know?" Maguire started, then shied from the topic.

"You can say it," Ruby said. "Sexual abuse."

"Well, she's got a fella, doesn't she? This Matthew Cooper?"

"No and yes," Ivy said dryly. "No sign of sexual activity of any kind, and yes, she had a boyfriend. We met him."

"What's he like?" O'Hara asked.

"A dream," she replied with a straight face. "We caught him starkers on the sofa, buried in empty beer cans, almost burning the house down with a saucepan of baked beans."

"What a catch," Ruby added.

"He said Gemma Radford left the house yesterday at eleven a.m.," George spoke up. "She dropped him at the pub, then met a friend, Jennifer MacFadyen, for lunch. His alibi is that he was at the pub all day. We'll need to follow that up. I don't trust him one bit."

"What about the friend?" Campbell asked. "Have you spoken to her?"

"Yes."

"And?"

"Jennifer wasn't with Gemma," Ivy explained.

"And you believe her?" Campbell frowned. "Is she a suspect?"

"Jennifer MacFadyen isn't even in the country," Ivy said firmly. "We confirmed her flight records. She's been in Tenerife with her husband since Thursday."

"So she lied to Matthew?" Campbell asked.

"Yes."

"Why?"

"Because Gemma asked her to. She requested that Jenny tell Matthew she'd been with Gemma if Matthew ever asked."

"So where *was* Gemma?" Maguire asked the team. "Before she died?"

At this, they all turned to Ruby, who looked up from her screen only when feeling all the weight of all eyes in the room.

"I have no idea," she sighed, shaking her head. "Sorry, guv."

"I'm sure you tried your best," George replied with a tired smile.

"ANPR isn't so easy out here, as you know. The roads between Gemma's house and Snipe Dales don't have any cameras, and as you know, mobile phone towers out there are few and far between. It would have helped if she had made a call or used her phone, but she hadn't done any of that since she was at home on Sunday morning before leaving the house. The last text she sent was to Jennifer, and the last one she received was from two days before. She used Facebook, but the phone company can't pinpoint her exact whereabouts."

"Anything else?"

"She received photos of some more fly tipping, would you believe? *Not* the one from the Country Park," she added quickly. "From an unknown number. But there were a load more photos like that."

"Probably from one of her activist friends showing the latest addition to the problem," George said.

"Exactly, guv. That was my thinking," she replied.

"So we don't know where Gemma Radford was, or where she was going?" Campbell clarified.

"Great," Maguire said, slumping in his seat.

"We know something," Ivy said, displaying her newfound optimism. "Her friend Jenny was sure about one important thing." She paused and looked around the room with a certain, sharp stare. "Maybe something that explains why Gemma was secretive. Because the last thing Gemma Radford wanted was for Matthew Cooper to know where she was."

"She was up to something?" Maguire suggested.

"I think so," she replied. "But it's not what you're all thinking."

CHAPTER TWENTY-FOUR

The team processed this information in thoughtful silence. The most obvious answer to Ivy's revelation rode a wave of cool air, raising goosebumps on arms and prickling the soft down on tense napes. Campbell voiced what they were all thinking.

"So Gemma Radford was having an affair," she stated.

"No," Ivy countered, ready for someone to point out the assumed answer. "Not necessarily."

"Come on, sarge," Maguire said. "It's always an affair."

"No, we always *assume* it's an affair."

"Yeah, because it usually is—"

"There's no sign of sexual activity," Ivy said, cutting him off.

"So?"

"So if Gemma was having an affair with the man she met on Sunday morning, why didn't they have sex?"

Campbell frowned. "What do you mean?"

"I mean, she drops her boyfriend off at the pub, and then meets her lover. Then what? They enjoy a nice stroll through the Country Park?"

"Affairs aren't always randy rendezvous in hotel rooms or

sordid encounters in the backs of cars," O'Hara said. "They can be more emotional than that."

"Or maybe they were going to do it after their walk," Maguire replied.

O'Hara shrugged.

"Yeah, or that."

"I would imagine that, given the outcome, sex wasn't the main objective of the meet."

"It *is* usually the boyfriend," Campbell added, "and if not the boyfriend, then the lover."

Byrne nodded his agreement. "And without going into detail, the killer obviously felt sexually attracted to her."

"Speaking of which, did Southwell mention the semen on Gemma's chest in her report?" George re-entered the conversation, steering them back to the tiny nuggets of information the report promised.

"She identified the DNA, guv, yes," Ivy replied. "But there's no match on the database," she added, shutting down Byrne's theory.

"So what does that mean?" asked Maguire.

"It means there's no match, and we're no closer," Ivy said sternly. "If you're looking for some kind of positive, then we could rule out every man who hasn't provided the police with a DNA sample. How's that?"

"Let's stay objective, shall we. Let's not match the chest sample up with the killer, just yet."

"I think it's a given, guv," Maguire added, his face contorted in disgust.

"I just think we would do well to keep an open mind," George replied. "Now, is there anything I've missed?"

"Footprint analysis came back negative," Ivy replied. "The mud in the immediate area was at the top of the hill, therefore, it was dry. The path *through* the Country Park at the bottom of the hill, however, which we know was wet, is a main thoroughfare. It's like Piccadilly Circus, guv. There's no way of identifying which prints were made on the Sunday. They could have been there for days."

"I suppose it was always a long shot," George replied. "Anything else? What about her car? Was it hers?"

"It was. No signs of struggle, though. Nothing untoward at all," she summarised, reading through the notes. "They're running DNA analysis, but that will take a while given how much stuff was in that rubbish pile."

"Anything else?"

Ivy scanned Southwell's report, then tossed it onto a nearby table.

"That good, eh?" George said, sensing a few of the team waiting to put forward counter-arguments. "Look, let's put the victim's potential affair aside for a moment."

"Blind speculation isn't going to help us, you mean?"

"No, no," he said. "Now I'm all for blind speculation. God knows it's all we have to go on most of the time. However, in this instance, I want to explore motives. I wonder if it might unlock new avenues."

Ivy rubbed at her forehead, but held her tongue.

"Okay," she said. "Okay, let's give it a go."

"Isn't it, follow the evidence, not, follow the motive, guv?" Byrne asked. "Isn't that what you always say?"

"Yes, Byrne," Ivy said pointedly. "It is."

"And where is that referenced?" George asked.

"In the Code of Practice for the Criminal Justice System, and the NCA Operational Procedures guidelines, guv."

"Nice try. Those aren't references." He pointed at Byrne with his pen. "Those are suggested procedures. Guidelines, if you will, and although I'd be remiss in suggesting you ignore them, I should warn you that, if you used those *guidelines* to steer you through every investigation you're ever faced with, you're going to see slow progress."

"Eh?"

"You'll be doing the Justice Secretary a favour, though," George continued. "As I understand it, we're running out of prison cells."

"What are you saying, guv?"

"I'm saying that, yes, respect the *guidelines*, but don't close off any other angles. Use everything around you. *Speculate*, if need be," he said, pointing at Ivy to reference his earlier conversation. "Create hypotheses, even if it's only to draw a line through a suspect's name rather than beneath it. Think big, alright?"

"Right," Maguire said. "Think big."

"So, in lieu of any game-changing evidence, we're going to explore motives." He pulled the cap from his marker. "Suspects. Who have we got?"

"Well, there's Matthew Cooper," Campbell began. "His girl-friend was having an affair."

"Potentially," Ivy corrected her.

"Okay, she was *potentially* having an affair."

"To be honest, I'd have him at the top of the list," Ivy said. "The man's a creep. How's that for speculation, guv?"

"Either way, Gemma was lying to him," George replied, as he wrote *Matthew Cooper* on the board. "Who else?"

"Steven Corbyn. The man who owned the sofa," Maguire suggested.

"He's based on evidence, not suspicion," George said dryly, adding the name to the board. "Does he have a link to Gemma Radford?"

"Not that we know of," Ruby said. "I need to look into him."

George nodded gratefully.

"Arthur Williams," Ivy said.

Campbell checked her notebook frantically. "Who?"

"The old man from the crime scene?" O'Hara asked. "The nosy one?"

George clicked. "Exactly."

"What's he got to do with this?" Byrne asked.

"Ivy?" George said. "Do you want to update them?"

She sighed and uncrossed her arms.

"We spoke to the boys this afternoon. We found their statements... what was the phrase?"

George grinned. "Inconsistent with reality."

"Yeah, that was it. Well, it turns out we were right. They'd been lying."

"No, they weren't lying, they just omitted a part of the story."

"They lied, then?" Maguire said, to which George shook his head.

"It could have been a result of the trauma they'd been through."

"Trauma? They didn't look traumatised."

"Okay," George said, snapping the lid on the pen. "You're driving down the street. It's a busy high street. The traffic is slow, so you're in second gear, let's say. You're gazing out of the window and you spy a nice shirt in a shop window, there's a huge discount on at the travel agents in the next window—"

"Travel what?" Byrne said.

"They used to be a thing," Ivy told him, then nodded for George to continue.

"Two hundred yards later, a woman steps into the road with a pushchair. You swerve to miss the baby, but you knock an old man to the ground. Moments later, the car behind crashes into you and your airbags go off."

"Jesus, I'm having a bad day," Maguire said.

"Before you know it," George continued, "the local bobbies are pulling you from the car, they've got you on the ground with your arms behind your back. Your head is turned to one side, and you can see somebody is performing CPR on the old man. You're dragged to your feet, where an officer steps in front of you, stares you in the eye, and reads you your rights."

"Christ," Maguire said, to which George nodded.

"What colour was the shirt?"

"Eh?"

"What colour was the shirt?"

"I...I don't know—"

"Where was the last-minute holiday deal to?"

"Sorry?"

"Was it all inclusive?"

Maguire grinned. He closed his eyes for a moment and then nodded his acceptance.

"Alright, alright. I get it."

"Yeah, and so would any prosecution lawyer worth his or her salt," George replied. "If the boys omitted to tell us a particular fact, regardless if we believe them or not, we have to take it at face value." He glanced at Ivy, gesturing that she could pick up where she left off.

"The boys came across Arthur Williams on Sunday afternoon, not long before they discovered Gemma Radford's body. He'd told them off for playing with the rubbish and said it could be dangerous. And in return, they threw a tree branch at him."

"Wesley Harris threw the branch," George clarified.

"And that makes him a suspect, does it?" Campbell asked.

"No, but it does mean that Arthur Williams lied to us, and that's one we do not have to take at face value. When I spoke to him at the crime scene, he explicitly said he hadn't been to the Country Park earlier that day."

"Maybe he was just embarrassed that he'd been harassed by some little kids," Byrne offered.

"Wesley Harris is not a little kid," Ivy pointed out. "None of them are."

"Either way, he chose to lie," George said. "And if he *was* embarrassed, why would he return to the scene?"

"That's not necessarily suspicious, though, is it?" O'Hara asked. "I mean, he was just walking his dog."

"Of course it's suspicious," Campbell said. "He could have been returning to the murder scene."

"What kind of idiot would return to the scene of a murder?" Maguire asked. "You'd hunker down and stay out of the way until it all blows over."

"Tell that to Ted Bundy, Ian Brady, the Zodiac Killer," Ivy said. "All of whom returned to the scenes of their murders. Often, more than once. The Green River Killer returned to nearly all of his victims."

"Why?"

"Often, it's to relive the moment," George said. "Others, like Ian Huntley, for example, volunteered to help with the search. He wanted to be close to the investigation. He was even interviewed on the news, saying how appalling the incident was."

"That's sick," Maguire spat.

"So, Arthur Williams..." George said, moving on.

"Wait," Campbell spoke up before George could write anything, and he slowly turned to the visibly divided constable. "Look, I'm not saying he's not a suspect, but just think about it. Put yourself in his shoes. You see three young men carrying a heavy carpet into the woods. When you ask them about it, they tell you to bugger off. They throw stuff at you. Then a few hours later, the area is full of police cars and flashing lights."

"You think he suspected them?" Ivy asked.

"I think it's fair that he'd be curious, that's all."

"Guv?" They'd all watched Campbell speak, but none more earnestly than Byrne.

"What if..." he said slowly, a thought developing like storm clouds behind his eyes. "I mean, how do you know that they aren't?"

"Who?"

"The boys."

"Aren't what, Byrne?" Ivy said.

"Suspects." A quiet descended on the room, like that which

accompanies a snowfall. "I mean, we're basing this whole thing on their accounts of what happened. They've already lied to us."

"Potentially," Ivy said.

"Right. But, what if their stories are totally fabricated? If the boys were at the Country Park all day, maybe they *did* come across Gemma Radford. Maybe one thing led to another...and things got out of hand. Then they made up the carpet story using the rubbish from the car park as...I don't know...props."

A quiet followed as they all processed Byrne's theory, a theory that George had considered, but had set to one side, and it was interesting to see one of the younger members of the team voicing it.

George recalled the boys he'd visited only that afternoon, one halfway through a bacon sandwich, the other in his pyjamas on his bed.

The thought of their hands being responsible for Gemma Radford's death was nothing short of sickening.

"According to Pip," George said slowly, "Gemma Radford had the hessian sack, or a similar material, pulled over her head to disorientate her. The bag was tied off, and a hand was clamped over her mouth." He eyed the young officer who had dared to raise the question. "One, where's the bag? A search of the immediate area was carried out. Was anything found?"

He looked to Ivy for a response.

"If anything was found, I'd have told you."

"Right," he continued. "Tell me, Byrne. Do you think those boys are capable of that? And if they are, then wouldn't they have the foresight to hide the bag?"

Byrne swallowed hard and took a breath.

"It's been thirty-two years since the murder of James Bulger," he said simply. "We know what kids are capable of."

"Anyway," Ivy said, her voice thick, no doubt, with the realisation that they were considering three boys only a few years older than her own son as murderers. "You said it yourself, guv, as of last night, those boys are no longer boys." She took a deep breath, a sort of existential sigh at the tragedy of humanity. "I don't think we can rule anybody out at this stage."

The four constables, Byrne, Maguire, Campbell, and O'Hara, looked between George and Ivy for guidance.

Eventually, George nodded.

"I agree. If anything, we'll need to rule them out," he said. "We believe Gemma Radford was lying to Matthew Cooper. About what, we don't know, but there's a motive there that needs following up on. Have somebody check The George and Dragon, his local pub. He said he was there all day."

Ivy made a note of the task.

"Ruby, find a link between Stephen Corbyn and Gemma Radford. Without that, we have no chance of developing a motive, but we will still need to talk to him, so find us his details, please."

"Guv," she replied.

"What about the boys?" Maguire asked. "What could have possibly driven them to murder Gemma Radford?"

"There's the million-pound question," he replied. "The short answer is that I don't know."

"I can ask Katy Southwell if a hessian sack or anything similar was found in the rubbish," Ruby said. "They went through the lot, didn't they? And the search wouldn't have covered that. It was cordoned off as evidence."

"Good. Yes, do that," George said, checking his watch. "Let's sleep on it. Get some creative distance, as they say."

"You okay, guv?" Ivy asked, perhaps sensing the shift in his demeanour.

"I'm fine," he said, feigning a smile and studying Byrne. "But something like this needs serious consideration."

"Something like what, guv?" Maguire asked.

"Something like this," he replied. "Pursuing three teenage boys as suspects in a murder investigation." He shook his head. "If

I'm honest, though, I'm less concerned about the boys than I am the missing parents."

"You think they could be involved?"

He shrugged, unwilling to commit either way.

"Let's increase our efforts into finding them," he said. "They've had long enough now, and if they're not involved, then they have some serious questions to answer."

CHAPTER TWENTY-FIVE

Even though the vote for who should cook dinner had been a fifty-fifty tie, George pulled rank. Cooking was something he'd been enjoying more since Grace's passing, and had moved onto trying some of her old recipes, perhaps subliminally hoping to be close to her, as though taste was a portal to the past or might stir a fond memory.

Tonight, it was beef wellington, which had been the main course at their wedding. Even reading Grace's barely legible handwriting in the margins of an old cookbook had enabled a connection. The woman had painted what he would class as masterpieces, yet she couldn't write for toffee.

One particular side note of hers had recommended preparing the meat the day before and leaving it in the fridge overnight, but there was no time for any fuss.

The recipe also described how to make the pastry, but there were boxes of the stuff in the supermarkets these days, which saved a lot of fuss, and considering it was just flour and other odds and sods, how much of a difference could it really make?

Proudly, he slid a well-presented serving in front of Ivy,

complete with a few honey-glazed carrots, a dollop of mash, and some runner beans.

Ivy didn't even look up from her phone, even when she set it down beside the plate, and blindly collected her cutlery.

George took his usual seat, opposite her, wondering if family meals had been a large part of the Hart household before she had left, and what they must have been like.

"You know, having dinner with you is one of my favourite parts of the day," he said.

She didn't look up, but replied distractedly.

"Yeah?"

"I think it's the fine conversation," he muttered, stabbing at a runner bean. "You know? The quality time." She said nothing, and judging by her focused expression, the words hadn't even resonated. "Ivy?"

"Guv?" she said, suddenly looking up. Then, as though shaking herself from a fugue state, she pushed the phone away. "God, I'm so sorry!"

"That's okay—"

"No, it's not. I'm so rude. Sorry, guv." She cut into the puff pastry, where the knife met immediate resistance, forcing her to apply a little more vigour. Eventually, she placed a forkful of pastry and beef into her mouth and chewed. Then she chewed some more, averting her eyes to the kitchen behind George. "This is... good," she said.

"Maybe I should have stuck with a soup or something."

"No, no. Honest, guv. It's good. A little tougher than I was expecting, but the flavours are there."

He smiled at her manners, however late they were, and collected his own cutlery.

"Was I interrupting you?" he asked, nodding at the phone with a grin while his knife met a similar resistance to that which Ivy's had.

"Oh, it's nothing," she said, but immediately picked her phone back up, buying her time to chew another morsel of beef. "See, I was just thinking about what the housekeeper said, remember? About Ewan Harris being criticised online?"

"Okay?" he replied, coaxing her on.

"I searched for his name on Facebook. It turns out there's a whole group about him."

"A group?"

"Yeah, a Facebook group. It's like a private space for people. You know, like a celebrity fan club, or I don't know, a football team, or a village. I'll bet this place has one."

"Bagendersby does not have a fan club," George laughed. "I might not be a millennial, but I know that much."

"It's not a fan club," she told him, and she tapped away on her phone. "Here you go. Bagenderby." She turned the phone for him to see. "It's a residents thing. A place where they can discuss local events and whatnot. Or maybe somebody has a piece of furniture they no longer want. They can tell their neighbours about it before selling it."

"Oh, like a lamp?"

"Yes, like a..." she caught on to what he was referring to, and her disappointment was evident in her expression.

"Should I be on there? Do I need a Facebook for that?"

She laughed, but at what he couldn't tell.

"Do you have any plans to attend a local club or a quiz night?" she asked.

"Lord, no," he said.

"What about local affairs? Are you interested?"

"I prefer to keep myself to myself, really," he admitted.

"Well, then you don't need...you don't need a Facebook account."

"Oh, well," he said, reaching for his water to help his food down. "That's good then, isn't it?"

"Ewan Harris, however," she continued, "has garnered quite a bit of interest from the locals."

"In Bagenderby?"

"No, from across the area. Although, to be fair, there are some people standing up for him, too. Not everyone's against him."

"Is it a fair split?" George asked.

"No. A resounding no," she replied. "Not from what I've seen, anyway. I found all sorts of local groups talking about him. There's your usual hobby groups, book clubs, and such, but most of them are for environmental advocacy, at least the ones that mention Ewan Harris multiple times." What on earth that all meant was beyond George. Why a book club would be talking about Ewan Harris beggared belief, but her enthusiasm was alluring, and he smiled politely while she scrolled through the groups, narrating as she progressed through the list. "Say No to Wind Farms. Save our Water Voles. Stop Fly-Tipping in Lincolnshire..."

"Oh, now there's a turn up," he said, finding himself interested.

She grinned. "That's the one I was just looking at. It's brilliant."

"Brilliant?"

"The drama, guv. It's something else."

He leaned over to have a look. "How so?"

"Some members are more active than others," she said. "And by active, I mean *active*. Almost obsessed. They post ten, twelve times a day, sometimes."

George startled. "About what? How do they find the time?"

"About the state of the area, what's becoming of it."

"The state of the area?" George repeated, incredulous. "It's glorious."

"They say otherwise, what with the wind farms, the increased traffic, the demise of nature, and of course, fly tipping. Most people blame—"

"Ewan Harris?"

"Exactly."

"But why *him*?" George asked. "Why not blame the council at large?"

"Well, don't quote me on this," she said, holding up the phone. "*This* isn't a reputable source, and I don't want to spread misinformation."

"But?"

"But, allegedly, he's the one actively blocking new policies. From what I can see, he pushed for a new wind farm in the migration path of some kind of bird. He..." She paused to read the information she quoted back to George. "He wants to cut public transport funding and push motorisation. He wants housing developments given the green light in protected areas of the Wolds."

"Don't tell me, except in the immediate area surrounding Snipe Dales Country Park?"

"Got it in one, guv," she said.

George set his knife and fork down and sat back.

"Of course he doesn't. That's where he lives. It'll mean more congestion, more noise, fewer doctors' appointments and school places."

"That's what people are saying. He's selfish, basically. Putting his own needs before the community's and, more importantly, the environment's."

George picked up a runner bean with his fingers and chewed while he gave it some thought.

"Sounds like he'll go far in politics."

They ate in silence for a minute or so, although the temptation to reach for her phone was evident in Ivy's body language.

"I noticed you brought the lamp in from the car," he said, trying a carrot, if anything, to give his teeth a rest.

"I'm still looking for the right place for it."

"Oh?" he replied, not willing to commit to his opinion, knowing that it would look better in the boot of her car. He was considering a gentler response when Ivy's phone gave off a loud ping.

"Oh, here we go," she said, gazing at the screen, practically salivating at the news. "Thea Drake just posted something."

"Thea who?"

"The woman we met earlier," she told him. "You know, at the fly-tipping site."

"Oh, okay," he replied. "Does she say anything nice?" Again, Ivy was lost in cyberspace somewhere. "Is it relevant to the investigation, Ivy?"

"What?" she said, glancing between him and the screen as if the distraction was a nuisance. "Of course it is. What else would it be about?"

George shrugged.

"It's human nature to enjoy a bit of gossip, but over dinner?"

"Gossip?" She laughed. "That's not what this is."

"Isn't it?"

"No, it's...it's research," she said. "I'm studying the nuanced social dynamics of the locals and noting their concerns. It relates to Ewan Harris, therefore it relates to the investigation."

George shrugged. "I didn't realise Ewan Harris was a suspect."

"He's not. He's just interesting."

"He's interesting?"

"He makes an interesting read," she corrected. "Anyway, it's my community now, isn't it? I live in the Wolds. I'm a Woldsonian...a Woldite?"

"A Woldonian?" George suggested.

"I really do think it can help the investigation. Look." Again, she turned the screen his way. "That's Thea Drake, the woman we met earlier, and *that's* the photo she took of the rubbish."

George looked at the photo and recognised the farmer's gate, the pile of rubbish behind it, and a blurry Dalmatian's wagging tail in the foreground.

"Hold on," he said with a sudden thought. "Can you do searches on that thing?"

"What's that?" Ivy asked, taking back the phone, already distracted by the next post.

"Can you search for names in the club?"

"The group, you mean?"

"Whatever. Can you?"

"Well, yeah. If they're part of it."

"Try Wyman," he said.

"Wyman? Oscar Wyman's parents?" she asked, as though surprised this was his first go-to. He nodded. "Emily, was it?"

"And David."

"They're not in the fly-tipping group," she said, tapping away. After half a minute, she added, "I think I found their profiles, though." She frowned. "Nothing posted recently. But I can keep checking."

"Try Arthur Williams."

"Who?"

"The old man at the crime scene," he said. "He seems like the kind of nosy old so-and-so who might get involved in local hoo-hars." George looked up and grimaced. "No offence."

She typed, then scrolled, and pulled a few thoughtful faces along the way. "Maybe you are a millennial, guv. He's in the group. He hasn't posted much. Looks like he mostly just comments on other people's posts." She read a little more, scrolled some more, and thought some more. "One thing is for sure, he's definitely part of the anti-Ewan Harris club, though."

"There's a club called that?"

"They're groups, guv," she said. "And no, there's not. But he's here calling Harris all sorts of things."

"What kind of things?" George asked.

"Nothing I'd care to repeat, guv. Not at the dinner table, anyway."

"I didn't realise we were actually eating. I thought these were just ornaments. Like your lamp monstrosity."

She gave him another disappointed look, not too dissimilar to those Grace used to give him.

"It's not a monstrosity. It's pretty."

"Fine." He waved it off. "What about Gemma Radford?"

"What about her?"

"Is she on there? She was active, wasn't she? Helped badgers cross the road and all that."

He tried another mouthful of the wellington, hoping the first try had been unlucky.

It wasn't.

Ivy typed and waited, then her face glowed with a dopamine rush.

"You really are a millennial."

"She's in there?"

"And she's active. Nothing too recent, but her last post got a lot of likes about..."

"Likes?"

She descended into the online abyss through the six-inch by three-inch screen, like stepping through a portal into a world where conversation is banished.

"Ivy?"

"Oh, guv," she said, her eyes widening. "You're not going to believe this."

CHAPTER TWENTY-SIX

The one thing George appreciated most about the fishbowl was that when he closed its door, the noise from the incident room was shut out, like they had entered a vacuum. Since he and Ivy had transferred from their small coastal station, which had been closed down due to cutbacks, he'd grown accustomed to the incessant ringing of phones, squeaking chairs, whirring printers, and the loud banter that CID shared, but he'd never appreciated it.

When he stared at the whiteboard, envisioning alternative timelines and scenarios, and the consequences of each, he needed peace. To understand motives, he needed to put himself there, like a fly on the wall. He needed to empathise, and for that, printers, phones, and banter, no matter how playful, was not conducive.

"Right," he said, turning to the team. "I hope you all had a good night's sleep, because today..." He jabbed at the board with an index finger. "Is going to place us firmly in the Gulf Stream. It's going to dictate where this investigation takes us."

"I thought you wanted to explore motives, guv?" Maguire said.

"Oh, I do. I also want to cross names off." He pointed to the board again. "Now, do all these names make sense to everyone?"

"Matthew Cooper," Campbell read aloud first. "Gemma Radford's boyfriend, who—"

"We found naked on her couch, yes," George finished. "Next?"

"Steven Corbyn," Byrne said next. "The bloke whose DNA is all over the red sofa, but not on the victim."

"Good," he said.

"Arthur Williams," O'Hara spoke up. "The dog walker we met on Sunday night, who we now know the boys had a serious altercation with."

"Just one boy, by all accounts," George said. "But good."

"And the three boys," Ruby said. "Wesley, Louis, and Oscar."

"Good. And the last one?" George said, pointing to the seventh and final name on the board. "Anyone?"

"Move Right?" Maguire read slowly. "Who's that?"

"Not who, what?" Ivy corrected.

Maguire grimaced. "What?"

"It's a company," George explained. "One word. MoveRight. They're our latest addition. Ivy, care to explain?"

Ivy stepped forward, filling the space between George at the whiteboard and the team at the table.

"Last night, I was doing some research into public opinion groups in the local area," she explained, avoiding George's pointed stare. "Notably, people aren't happy about the fly-tipping. During my search, I found something that Gemma Radford posted a couple of weeks ago. She accused a house clearance company of dumping people's trash in the countryside to save on recycling fees."

"MoveRight?" Campbell clarified.

"Exactly."

"MoveRight..." O'Hara was mumbling. "MoveRight. I know that name."

"Did Gemma Radford have evidence to support that claim?" Byrne asked, to which Ivy shook her head.

"No. She claimed to have seen it happen though."

"And people believed her?"

"Overwhelmingly so. They called for a boycott in the comments. There was even a petition."

"So, what? She cancelled them?" O'Hara asked.

"Pretty much."

"Has she posted about it since?" Byrne asked.

"No, it seems her efforts worked," Ivy said. "She's also very vocal against Ewan Harris but hasn't posted in a while. Her last post just said, '*Something big coming. Stay tuned. Still gathering evidence.*'"

"And you think that could be about MoveRight?" O'Hara asked. "Now she has a video or something?"

"Possibly," Ivy said.

"Well, what about Harris?" Campbell pointed out.

"What about him?"

"Well, she's complaining about him, too, right? Doesn't that give him as much motivation as MoveRight?"

"They're all after Harris," George spoke up. "It's all part of being a politician. Water off a duck's back. He can't go after every member of the public who criticises him. He wouldn't have a constituency to speak up for. Gemma Radford's targeted attack on MoveRight is different. She singles them out. It affects their business. They *can't* deal with it. Clearly."

"Clearly?" Campbell asked.

"We couldn't find any online presence at all," Ivy explained. "Someone in the comments said they've deleted all their profiles, website, everything. Looks like they stopped advertising completely."

"Gemma Radford could have been planning to cancel another company, too," Byrne pointed out. "Maybe they offed her before she could."

"That's a lot of maybes," George said.

"I'm speculating," he replied with a grin, which George ignored politely.

"I want to speak to the owner of MoveRight. I want to know exactly how Gemma Radford's attack affected their business. Ruby?"

"Leave it with me," she replied, making a note of the task.

"MoveRight…" O'Hara mumbled again. "Is it just me?"

"No, I know it, too," Maguire replied.

They all stared at the board, waiting for something to click. In the end, it was Maguire who clicked his fingers then slammed his hand down on the desk, excitedly.

"Their flyer!" He clicked his fingers at O'Hara. "You took a photo. In the petrol station."

"Here," she said, handing her phone to George with the photo on the screen. "They were advertising at the petrol stations. I mean, the leaflets look a bit dated, but if you went out of business, you wouldn't go around taking them all down, would you?"

George looked down at the phone, and then up at Maguire.

"Good work," he said sincerely, handing it to Ruby.

"And an address," Ruby said. "They're still registered."

"Send it to Ivy," he said. "We'll pay them a visit."

"You're going to speak to the boss, guv?" Byrne asked.

"Not empty-handed, I'm not," he said, turning to frown at the board. "Find me something to work with."

"What about the boys?" Campbell asked. "How do we strike *their* names off?"

It was interesting that she had picked up on George's reluctance to pursue them as lines of enquiry.

"We eliminate them, I suppose," he said.

"How do we do that?"

He shrugged.

"Evidence. The same as any other suspect. Fingerprints, DNA." He glanced across at Ivy. "Is there anything in Southwell's report that suggests that any of the boy's fingerprints or DNA were on the body?"

"If there was, their names would be at the top of that list, guv," she replied.

"Do we have their DNA?" he asked, turning to Maguire and Campbell. "Did we take it when they came in?"

"We took their fingerprints and shoes to identify any rogue prints at the crime scene. They were witnesses, guv," Campbell said, her tone more than a little defensive. "We can't take their DNA unless they're under arrest and cautioned."

"Witnesses who had been close to the body," he said. "They can volunteer it."

"They were three scared little boys who'd discovered a dead body, guv," Maguire cut in, defending his colleague.

"It's okay," he said. "You did the right thing."

"According to Southwell's report," Ivy said, breaking the tension, "her team found various DNA samples on various parts of Gemma Radford's body—"

"Various parts?"

"Her arms, guv," she said. "And her clothing. Most likely spit or hair from the struggle."

"Or from people she'd spoken to," Maguire suggested, which earned him a few nods of agreement.

"Why don't we get DNA samples from each of the suspects?" Campbell suggested.

"No," George said. "No, you're right. We can't get anyone's DNA until we have a better reason to do so."

"I thought we could ask them to volunteer it. Same applies to the other names on the board, guv."

"Oh, okay, and what do you think will happen when we knock on the right person's door and ask them nicely for a DNA swab, just to eliminate them?"

"They'd run a mile?" Byrne said.

"A thousand miles," George replied. "No. Yes, good idea. But not yet. Not until we have something. Everything every one of you is saying is right, one hundred per cent right. But we simply must do these things in the right order. We can't go scaring people off. Who knows what they'd do? We know that whoever did this is likely to react emotionally. Who's to say they won't do something similar to someone else?"

"Like who?"

"I don't know? Maybe somebody saw them? Maybe they *think* somebody saw them? What if the old man is guilty? The boys saw him. They can even place him at the scene. What if something happened to one of them? Could you live with that?"

"I suppose, when you put it like that," Campbell agreed quietly.

"That's the only way *to* put it," he said. "Look, I...I adore how enthused everyone in this room is. Honestly, it brings me so much joy to see it. Every idea that has been voiced this morning has been spot on. You have brilliant minds. What's lacking, through no fault of your own, is experience. That's where I come in. I need to channel those ideas into an investigation that not only delivers results, but keeps those people out there..." He pointed to the window emphatically. "Safe. Not only that, but I need to ensure that nobody is dragged up in front of the ACC on a career-ending charge. Okay?"

A silence ensued, and for a brief moment, he thought his little speech had done more damage than good.

"Yeah, I get it," Maguire said, looking around the room for support, which followed a few seconds later.

"Yeah, alright," Campbell agreed. "We'll take your lead."

Ivy's eyebrows raised in respect, but she kept her praise to herself.

"Good," he said. "Good, so moving on. Let's go through MMO for each name." He tapped the board. "In chess terms, we're going from positional strategy to piece-by-piece play, alright?" At the lack of response and the blank looks on their faces, he elaborated. "I want to look at individuals rather than lines of enquiry."

"Oh," Maguire said. "You mean like man-to-man instead of zone defending?"

George shrugged.

"More of an attack than a defence, but sure."

"Can we skip the sports metaphors?" Ivy said flatly. "They're alienating."

"I wouldn't call chess a sport, to be fair, Sarge," Byrne replied.

"Forget the metaphor," George said, waving his marker. "You get my point. Now let's start with Matthew Cooper."

"Motive, Gemma was lying to him about where she was. Possibly an affair," Maguire began. "Means, absolutely. He just needed access to a hessian sack, and their relationship suggests he was into her enough to do what the killer did. Opportunity? Well, depends on the alibi."

"Good," George said, updating the grid as Maguire spoke. "Ivy, who's looking into his alibi?"

"Not assigned yet, guv."

"Maguire? O'Hara? Follow it up. Go to The George and Dragon in Hagworthingham. That's where he claims to have been all of Sunday."

"Yes, guv."

"Now. Steve Corbyn?"

The team remained silent, perhaps demotivated by the lack of connection to the victim.

"Motive, we don't know," George answered himself. "Means, the same as everyone else. Opportunity, we don't know." He rubbed his head and sighed. "Ivy, you and I will go and see him. How about Arthur Williams?"

Again, the team stayed silent until Byrne was brave enough to express the obvious.

"We've got nothing on him except he was in the area at the

right time, and returned to the scene, so that's opportunity, but not much else."

"Could an old man overpower the victim?" Byrne asked. "She was young and fit."

"So, we're saying he lacks means?" George asked.

"Possibly. I don't want to judge, but if three little boys scared him off by lobbing a stick at him..."

"True. Let's get him crossed off."

"Williams and Gemma Radford are in the same anti-fly-tipping Facebook group," Ivy offered lamely, holding up her phone. It pinged with a notification, and she immediately turned her attention to it.

"Yes, but didn't you say they were in agreement over their dislike for Ewan Harris?" George asked, and she looked up from her phone briefly. "If we consider that a connection, half the county would be a suspect."

"We'll need a bigger whiteboard," Maguire said, but the joke fell flat, and George pressed on.

"Right, Ivy and I will go and see Steve Corbyn. Maguire, O'Hara, you cover Matthew Cooper's alibi. That should allow us to cross at least two names off. Let's make that a focus. Ruby, can you look into MoveRight. Do some digging. See what you find."

"Yep," she agreed.

"Byrne and Campbell..." George eyed the names on the board, running his gaze up and down them until he could no longer ignore the majority group. "Make a start on the boys, will you?"

"Guv?"

"I want Oscar Wyman's statement. I want to see if it matches the other two, or if there's some other little nugget they failed to share."

"Right," Byrne said, a little confused.

"Don't we need his parents for that?"

"And therein lies the task," George told him. "Find them."

"How the...?" Byrne started. "They're not home. They've no jobs to speak of. We've checked."

"Be a *detective*, Byrne," George said, grinning. "Detect. Follow those guidelines. If everyone was at home all the time, our job would be a lot easier, wouldn't it? Come on. Think big, remember? Talk to neighbours, check ANPR. Treat them like missing persons, if you—"

"Guv?" Ivy called out, bringing his motivational speech to a halt. She stepped forward, holding her phone before her like a grenade in the palm of her hand. "I might be able to help with that."

CHAPTER TWENTY-SEVEN

The fields rolled by in an endless panorama of lush greens and vivid yellows, stitched together with thorny hedgerows that offered the abundant wildlife a place to thrive, or deep dykes for the fertile land to drain.

The scenery was a pleasant distraction for Campbell. She glanced across at Byrne, who drove with one lightly browned arm resting on the open window, as though he was on his day off, heading to the coast for some fresh air and relaxation.

It had been less than a year since they had transferred to DI Larson's team, and already Byrne was a changed man. From the slightly awkward young man he had been, who had used wit to mask his lack of confidence, he was developing into somebody she wouldn't be embarrassed about being with. He had joined a gym and took a healthy pride in his appearance. Not that she would date a colleague, but if circumstances were different, then perhaps.

She shook the thought from her mind, slightly nauseated. It would be like dating a brother or a cousin.

"You okay?" he asked, perhaps sensing she was thinking about him.

"Eh?"

"You were staring."

"Was I?"

He checked the road and glanced her way again.

"What are you thinking?"

"I'd much rather know what you're thinking," she replied, turning his question around.

"Me? I was wondering how long it's been since I was here."

"Skegness?"

"Yeah. Used to come all the time when we were kids."

"Liam, we were here a couple of months ago. Literally, a matter of weeks."

"I mean to the beach," he replied calmly. "You know, to see the sea."

"You haven't been to the beach since you were a kid?"

"I've been to *a* beach. I've been to Greece and Spain and that, but to Skeggy Beach, no."

"Skeg-vegas?"

"Yeah," he replied, as though he accepted it wasn't paradise, but did have some charm. "A bag of chips, a bit of people watching. Love it."

"Well, I hate to put a dampener on your little dreamworld, Liam, but we're not here to play on the arcades." She glanced down at the sat nav, noting their destination was a mere four minutes away. "It's going to be busy. You know that, right? Families, kids, dogs—"

"You're not anti-family, are you?"

"No, I'm anti lots of families. I don't like crowds of people."

"You're a copper."

"I know, but that doesn't mean I enjoy crowds. I didn't join up so I can spend my days amongst screaming kids, barking dogs, and drunk parents."

"Ah," he said. "I see."

"What's that supposed to mean?"

"Nothing."

"No, go on."

"It just means that kids scream, dogs bark, and—"

"Parents get drunk?"

"Sometimes," he said.

"And that is my point," she told him. "We're going an hour out of our way to track down two people who can't look after their child properly."

"That's just police work, isn't it?" Byrne muttered. "Sounds to me like you're just jealous that it isn't you getting drunk."

"So, going to the carpet shop was a waste of time, but this isn't?"

"A waste of time? No," he said. "I always wanted to look for Oscar's parents. Said so from the start. Now we are. I think this is the right thing to do."

"You feel bad for him," Campbell said. It was an observation, not a question.

"Yeah, I do feel bad for the kid. His two friends had parents there to support them, and he had no one. People think child abuse only counts when it's assault, you know? But neglect, even emotional neglect, can be just as damaging. That kind of thing stays with you."

"I remember, a few years ago, I responded to a call from a neighbour about a crying baby and barking dog coming from a house," she said, the details coming back to her as fresh as if it happened a week before. "We knocked over and over again, but there was no answer, so we kicked our way inside. The house was freezing, lights off, rubbish and dirty dishes everywhere, dog mess in the kitchen. You know the like."

Byrne groaned in recognition. In their line of work, the scene was so familiar it painted itself.

"Yeah, been there, done that."

"We went upstairs and found this tiny baby, couldn't have been more than four weeks old, beneath a thin blanket. The mum came home a bit later and was absolutely mortified to find us."

"As they all are," he said sardonically.

"No, she was genuinely distressed. She'd gone out for a job interview in a betting shop or something, and her sister hadn't shown up to babysit. It wasn't violent or malicious, but technically, it was neglect."

"Exactly," Byrne said. "And look, I'm not saying I was neglected growing up, of course, I wasn't. My parents did their best. But I..." He grimaced and looked out the window, as though deciding whether to share something so personal. "I had a younger sister, and she needed them more than I did."

"Your sister?" Campbell asked.

"Yeah. Molly, her name is."

"I didn't know. Why didn't I know that?"

"Ah, I don't really like to talk about it. She's had MS since she was a little girl. Needs full-time care."

"That's terrible."

"Yeah, it is. But she has a routine. I mean, when you live with something like that for so long, you learn to adapt, right? Mum and dad know what they're doing."

"Do you resent that?"

"The attention she needed? No, of course not. I just found that if I did everything quietly and by myself, that was the best way I could help Molly. You know? So my parents could focus on her."

"Wow," Campbell said quietly. "You have depth? That's two things I've learned about you in..." she checked her watch, "an hour."

"We've all got stories," he told her, as he turned into the caravan park, pulled up to the small kiosk alongside a barrier, and lowered his window.

"Good morning," he said to the middle-aged, sour-mouthed woman behind the glass. "I wonder if you can help us. We're looking for David and Emily Wyman. We believe they're staying here. Can you tell me which caravan they're in?"

"I'm not sure if I can—" she started, eyeing the liveried car.

"If it helps, we're not here to cause a scene," Campbell said, unable to stop herself from leaning across and getting involved. "It's concerning their son, that's all."

The woman sighed and turned to the computer. "Who was it, again?"

"David and Emily Wyman," Byrne said slowly.

"Hundred and sixteen," she replied, then recognised Byrne's apologetic expression. "Second right, first left, then follow the road round. It's up there on the right. Keep your speed below five miles an hour, and observe the one-ways."

"Easy," Byrne said brightly, as the barrier rose. He grinned at Campbell. "You get that?"

"Did you?"

"I'm sure it'll become clear," he said, entering the maze.

It was as though the person who'd designed the caravan park held a grudge against straight lines. Identical caravans formed identical corridors that looped back on themselves, with very few defining features between them. Any signage came in the form of a tiny, wooden plaque half-eroded by the salty sea air.

"There!" Campbell said, after more than five minutes of them taking several turns, both left and right. She pointed to a small sign that had been kicked or driven over. "One hundred to one hundred and twenty."

Caravan 116 was, on the surface, at least, much like any of the other caravans — a white, oblong with a wooden terrace. But where neighbouring holiday homeowners had created homes from home, the owners of caravan 116 had used thin, bohemian scarves as curtains, and instead of walking the rubbish to the communal bins, the occupants of 116 had created a collection of bin bags on the grass at the foot of the steps, serving only to attract hungry wasps.

The door was answered by a middle-aged couple, and before anybody had even uttered a single word of greeting or introduction, the pungent scent of incense burners billowed from the caravan.

David Wyman had pulled his long, grey hair into a low ponytail that trailed down the back of his beige tunic, and like his wife, he wore a bone-bead necklace around his neck with loose-fitting faded jeans. His wife, Emily, wore a patchwork, hand-knit cardigan in hues of umbers and ambers that complemented her naturally red hair.

"Yes?" she asked, as her husband threw a limp arm over her shoulder and eyed their uniforms suspiciously.

"Emily and David Wyman?" Byrne asked.

"Is there a problem?" the husband answered.

"I'm PC Byrne, and this is PC Campbell. We're here about your son, Oscar."

"Oscar? What about him? What's he done?"

"Actually, it might be better if we came inside."

"What's he done?" Emily asked, making it clear that nobody was going anywhere until she had an answer. Reluctantly, Campbell provided a summarised version of events.

"He's not in any trouble—"

"What's he done?" she said, a little sharper this time.

"He and his friends discovered a body on Sunday evening. We've been trying to contact you."

"A body?" the husband said. "What do you mean, a body?"

Byrne checked to make sure they weren't being overheard.

"As in, a dead body, sir," he said.

"Jesus," the father muttered to himself. "Who was it?"

"It's probably more practical to direct your concerns at your child, Mr Wyman," Campbell told him. "Who, it seems, you left home alone."

"Christ," the mother said, closing her eyes as if all her worst nightmares had come true. "You want to know what we're doing, don't you?"

"I don't, but social services might."

"Oh for God's..." her voice trailed off, and her eyes welled. She sighed heavily and looked at her husband with regret. "Look, is he okay?"

"He's fine," Campbell said. "Hasn't a clue where you are, but he's fine. I'd love to be a fly on the wall when you tell him all about the little holiday you've been having while he was home alone. A thirteen-year-old boy."

"It's not a holiday."

"No?" Byrne said, making a show of looking around them. "You're staying in a holiday park, but it's not a holiday?"

"It's a digital detox," she said, by way of an explanation.

"A what?"

"A digital detox. I knew you wouldn't understand."

"No, we don't," Campbell said.

"We just wanted to get away from the world for a few days."

"That pretty much defines a holiday."

"From technology," she stated, as if there was a difference. "We thought he'd be okay. He normally is."

The last part of the statement was something Campbell hadn't needed to hear.

"Do you know how we found you, Mrs Wyman?"

"Oscar?" she said hopefully, to which Campbell shook her head.

"Facebook," she said. "You know? That *technology* company? You shared what a nice holiday you were having."

"I think we should come in?" Byrne suggested.

"Hold on, hold on," Emily said, holding a hand up. "Look, I'm sorry, but what is it you want from us?"

"What?" Byrne said, his voice rising in pitch. "Your son and his friends discovered a dead body. He's traumatised. He needs his mum and dad."

"He's being dramatic," David said.

"Okay, okay," Campbell cut in, doing her best to keep her cool. "Let me put this in a context you might understand, seeing as neglecting your child hasn't resonated."

"We don't neglect him—"

"Based on the body your son discovered, we are now undertaking a murder investigation. Murder, Mr Wyman. A murder investigation."

"What does that have to do with Oscar? You don't think he—"

"We've been unable to take his statement without your permission. We could, of course, assign an appropriate adult courtesy of social services, but the likelihood is that Oscar won't be at home when you return from your little getaway. He'll be in a home somewhere. With strangers. So far, we've elected not to go down that route on the basis that it will not be beneficial in any way, shape, or form for Oscar's well-being. Is that clear enough?"

"Well, can't we just give you permission?" Emily asked.

"You need to be present while he's questioned, Mrs Wyman. We need you to come with us to the station."

"We're on a break," Emily said, placing a hand low on her husband's waist. "Can't it just wait 'til we're home?"

"You left your son alone," Campbell said. "He's a minor."

"We left him some money. He knows how to take care of himself."

"He's *thirteen years old*."

"So what?" David shrugged. "My parents left me at home when I was that age. He's got his friends next door. He's fine."

"You haven't answered his calls?" Byrne asked.

"It's a *digital detox*," Emily replied, her tone infuriatingly soft, as if they might suddenly appreciate the benefits.

"Look, your son needs you right now," Byrne said. "Either you come with us, or I'll make the call, and he'll be in the care of social services. By rights, he should be in care already."

"Where is he?" she asked. "Is he at home?"

Campbell wanted to tell her that he'd been taken to an emergency care home, if nothing more than to gauge her response.

"He's with Louis Foxon's parents."

"Oh, he'll be fine, then. They're lovely."

Campbell had to look away. She found solace in Byrne, who stared in disbelief at the couple but said nothing.

"We can give you five minutes to pack your things," Campbell told them, and she started down the wooden steps, but stopped when they showed no sign of moving.

"And he's obliged to do this, is he?" David asked.

"Excuse me?"

"Oscar. He's obliged to provide a statement to you lot?"

Byrne hesitated. "Well..."

"No," Campbell answered. "He has a moral duty to assist us in our enquiries."

"A moral duty?" he scoffed. "So he's under no obligation to?"

Campbell studied his expression, wondering what planet he was on.

"He's a witness, not a suspect," she said, to which he nodded knowingly. "Although it's a murder investigation. He hasn't been ruled out."

"Well thank God he's not a suspect," he said. "We'll check out tomorrow morning. Can you tell them we'll pick him up around ten?"

"No," Campbell said. "No, I bloody well can't."

CHAPTER TWENTY-EIGHT

"Bloody hell!" Ivy said as soon as they drew up outside Steven Corbyn's house. "Well, is he suspected of fly-tipping, or is he a victim of it?"

George laughed.

"I've seen worse," he told her.

Broken furniture and home appliances littered the front garden, creating a scene not unlike that which they had seen at the Country Park or by the farmer's gate.

"It's a shame, though," she continued. "The house itself is quite nice, and it's not like this is a dodgy area."

"No, it's a lovely place to live. I knew somebody who lived here once."

"Did he move on?" she asked, as they climbed from the car.

"Yes, the last I heard, he moved to the Isle of Wight."

"Nice. Alright for some."

"Yes, he downsized. Got himself a little one-bed place, if I recall," George continued. "You know? Open plan, no garden to care for."

"No garden?"

"There isn't much privacy, either," he remarked, waiting for her to fall in. "People are always peering through the window."

"Eh?"

He grinned at her. Considering the incredible intelligence she demonstrated nearly every single day, she could sometimes miss the obvious.

"It's a little noisy at night, too."

"Right?" she said slowly, not following, but clearly sensing she was missing something.

"You know? All the junkies crying out."

He smiled again, and she rolled her eyes.

"You mean, you nicked somebody from around here, and now he's serving time?"

"HMP Isle of Wight," he said. "You won't find that on Rightmove."

The neighbourhood was on the outskirts of Partney, which George deemed to be a very respectable, and family-oriented area.

"Hold on," she said, taking a closer look at the smattering of discarded items. "I just want to see something."

"Like a red sofa?"

She checked behind her to make sure she wasn't being overheard.

"Hessian sack?" she said.

"Ah, yes," he said, letting Ivy be the one to get her hands dirty. But while he was waiting, an old estate car approached, slowed, and then parked in front of his car.

"You alright?" the driver asked, his accent local and his gaze curious. "Looking for something?"

"Steven Corbyn?" George asked which caught his intrigue.

"Yeah?"

Discreetly, George presented his warrant card.

"My name is Detective Inspector Larson. This is my colleague

Detective Sergeant Hart," George said, looking around. "Can we talk inside?"

"Do we need to?" he replied, his intrigue fading and the beginnings of an attitude showing itself.

"Unless you want the neighbours to hear what we have to say," George told him. "Personally, I'd opt for privacy."

Corbyn gestured at the mess that constituted his front garden. "Don't tell me, somebody complained? Who was it? The old dear up the road?" He glanced across at Ivy. "Oi, do you mind?"

George refrained from dignifying his response with one of his own.

"Having a clear out, are you?"

Corbyn recognised he wasn't going to get an answer until he began to comply.

"I'm going into business, if you must know," he said proudly, arranging the nearest of the bin bags into a neater pile. "Been clearing out the junk room, turning it into a home office, you know?"

"What kind of business?"

"Resale," he replied, straightening to face them properly. "Vintage clothing and that."

"Bric-a-brac?"

"No, vintage clothing. Genuine stuff."

"There's a market for that, is there?"

"There's a market for everything if you know how to get it."

"And this is all from that one room, is it?" George asked, spotting a bookshelf, a smashed mirror, and a single broken drawer amongst the chaos.

"Ah, no, ended up going through the entire attic, didn't I? You know what it's like. A job you think'll take a day turns into a week."

"Right," George said, recognising the issue through several of his own projects.

"It's my ADHD, see. Once I get started on a job, I get a bit side-tracked."

"I see," George said, gauging the man as somebody who, as far as he could tell, felt more than comfortable talking to a police officer. "And how are you planning on getting rid of everything?"

"Most of it I take to the tip," he said, shrugging. He pointed to his car. "Whatever I can fit in the car. You know, how it is. Bit-by-bit."

"And the rest of it? The stuff you can't fit in the car?"

"Well, I sold a few bits."

"And you dumped the rest, did you?"

At the incessant questioning, Corbyn looked up. Only then did reality seem to hit him. He looked George and Ivy up and down slowly.

"What's all this about?"

"Could you answer the question, Mr Corbyn?"

"Why?"

"All right, we'll get straight to it, Mr Corbyn," George said, stepping forward. "A piece of furniture we believe belongs, or belonged to you was recently found at a crime scene."

Steven Corbyn's small, dark eyes widened, a surprising amount, like the unfurling leaf of a touch-me-not.

"What type of crime scene?" he whispered, his voice rising. "What type of furniture? What are you on about?"

"It's a live investigation," George said flatly. "Very serious."

"Very serious?" He ran a hand through his short, bristly hair. "I...I'm not following—"

"Where were you on Sunday afternoon, Mr Corbyn?"

"I was..." He laughed, a short, wide-eyed laugh one performs when unsure what other noise to make. "Am I being arrested here? Is that what this is?"

"If you could answer the question," George said, as Ivy joined them, shaking her head to signal no joy in the search for anything hessian.

"I can't," he said quietly. "I can't just...tell you. I don't even know you."

"I would strongly suggest you give that some thought, Mr Corbyn. You are, as of now, linked to a serious incident, and quite strongly, I might add."

"What are you talking about? How am I linked? The furniture? What furniture? You can't just turn up here and—"

"A red sofa," George said, and for a fleeting moment, there was recognition in Corbyn's eyes. "Now, look at this from my point of view. We discovered a body not far from here—"

"A what?"

"Amongst a pile of rubbish that had been fly-tipped."

"You cannot be—"

"Your DNA, Mr Corbyn, was the primary sample found on one of those items."

"A body? Murder? You think I—"

"We came here to discuss the matter calmly, and we discover that you are in the process of...how did you phrase it? Having a clear-out?"

"Well, yeah...but—"

"When I asked where you were on Sunday, you refused to give me a suitable answer."

"Well, yeah, but—"

"So, unless you have a good explanation, I'm going to ask you to accompany us to the station, so we can get to the bottom of this. You do understand that, don't you?"

"I'm being arrested?"

"I always prefer to keep things amicable where I can," George assured him with as pleasant a smile as he could muster.

"You mean, you don't have anything on me," he said. "If you had anything on me that would stick, you'd have nicked me."

"A civilised discussion, Mr Corbyn. That's all I'm asking for."

"No," he said. "No, I'm not going to a police station. I've done nothing wrong."

"I'm giving you the opportunity to eliminate yourself from our enquiries, Mr Corbyn. Believe me, it gives me no pleasure in making an arrest, and I rarely do so lightly."

"You've got nothing on me."

"We've got your DNA all over the crime scene, Mr Corbyn," Ivy cut in. "There's a ninety-nine-point-nine, nine, nine, per cent chance of it being accurate." She kicked idly at a bin bag near her feet. "Makes me wonder what's in here."

Her kick must have off-balanced the bag, and slowly, it tipped over, spilling the topmost of its contents onto the driveway.

"Oh, for God's sake—" Corbyn started, as Ivy bent to collect something from the ground. She straightened, holding an empty bleach bottle up for them both to see.

"What?" he said, but instead of giving him an answer, she looked knowingly at George.

"Anyway, how did you get my DNA..." his voice trailed off as he worked the answer out for himself.

"The cons of being a con," George explained.

"Ex-con," Corbyn corrected him. "Listen, I know I did wrong. I know I wasn't exactly kosher. But I'm making a new go of it. I'm going legit."

"Well, that's great," George said. "Honestly, I commend you. If that's true, then I fully support your efforts. But right now, I have a list of people I need to either eliminate from my enquiry, or charge, and you are on that list. So you can either come with us, or—"

"I'm not coming," he said. "I've done nothing wrong. I'm just trying to make something work."

"In that case," George said, stepping to one side so Ivy could step up, pulling the handcuffs from her belt. "Steven Corbyn, I am arresting you on suspicion of the murder of Gemma Radford. You do not have to say anything, but it may harm your defence if you do not mention, when questioned, something which you later rely on in court. Anything you do say may be given in evidence."

"Who? Who did you say?"

Ivy pulled Corbyn's hands behind his back and handcuffed his wrists, and although exasperated, he offered no resistance.

"Do you understand?" George asked.

"Not really," Steve exhaled croakily. "Honestly, I just came home to move on with my life, and then this happens."

"Do you understand the charges?" George rephrased.

"I...yes, I do," he replied, shaking his head as if seeking some sense of it all. "What did you say her name was?"

"Radford," George told him, as Ivy made the call for a unit to come and collect Corbyn. "Gemma Radford."

George led him to the side of the house, out of sight of the neighbours.

"Gemma Radford," he said slowly, as if the name was familiar, but only distantly.

"There's still time," George told him. "If you can prove where you were on Sunday, then we can make this far easier." Corbyn shook his head vigorously, as if in utter denial. "You know her, don't you?"

George moved into Corbyn's vacant line of sight, until he had his attention.

"I swear to you," he said, meeting George's stare with eyes as dark and sharp as a raven's. "I *swear* to God...please. I have no idea who Gemma Radford is."

"On their way," Ivy called out, staying near the road to flag the car down.

George returned his attention to Corbyn, who, despite his previous entanglements with the law and brazen exterior, let loose a tear that trickled down his cheek and broke when it met his beard growth.

"I hope you're right about that," George told him quietly. "For your sake, I hope you're right."

CHAPTER TWENTY-NINE

The George and Dragon was a classic English pub with a classic English pub name, and Maguire beamed broadly as he and O'Hara climbed from the car.

"What are you grinning about?" O'Hara asked.

"Eh?"

"Come on, you look like a teenage boy who just had his first..."

"What?" he asked. "First, what? Come on, PC PC."

"PC PC?"

"Police Constable Politically Correct," he said, tugging his notepad and pen out. "Come on. What do I look like? It better not be obscene. I'll go straight to HR when we're back."

"Girlfriend," she told him. "You look like a teenage boy who just got his first girlfriend."

"You bloody liar," he snarled playfully. "That was *not* what you was going to say."

"Of course it was. What did you think I was going to say?" she asked. "Oh, come on. You didn't think I was going to make a lewd or inappropriate comment, did you?"

"Yeah, right," he grumbled. "If you really want to know why I was smiling..." He stopped and presented the pub with both arms, but stopped short of giving a '*ta-daaa*'.

"It's a pub," she said.

"I know. But look at it."

"What?" she asked. "What am I looking at?"

"The pub," he told her. "It's bloody gorgeous, is it not?"

"I suppose—"

"You know, when you're in town, there's a pub on every corner. You go from bar to bar, from pub to pub, and you don't really pay a blind bit of notice to them," he said. "You just go in, have a drink or six, then move on to the next one."

"Well, you might, but—"

"But out here? Out here, it's not like that at all. Out here, you get one pub every few miles or so, and they're all like this. Absolutely stunning."

"I get the impression you're quite chuffed at this particular assignment."

"Oh, come on. How often does your boss say, right you two. Off to the pub, wid ya. Go on, now. And don't come back until you've been. It's brilliant."

"You also realise that it's..." O'Hara checked her watch briefly. "Ten past eleven in the morning, and we won't finish until five, if we're lucky."

"Well, aye, but—"

"You also realise that if, and I mean if, if you order a sneaky drink while I'm in the loos, I'll know, and you know how you called me PC PC, just now, yeah?"

"Yeah?"

"Well, this particular PC PC has a nose like a bloodhound. She'll be on the phone to the boss's boss before your glass leaves the bar."

"Right," he said. "Got it."

"Eejit."

"Hey now! You don't get to call me the eejit. I'm the paddy. If anyone's going to call anyone else an eejit, it'll be me, right?"

"Come on," she said, and she started towards the door, and he followed.

"I mean it. You don't hear me giving it all *'alright my lover'* do you?" he said, doing his best to mimic her West Country accent.

She turned at the door and raised a finger at him.

"I don't talk like that. I've never spoken like that, and nobody I know talks like that."

"Alright, alright," he said with a laugh. Then, as she turned and pushed into the pub, he added a little suffix just to twist the blade. "My lover."

"Not open yet," the barman called with his back to the door. He was hunched over a laptop behind the bar with his mobile phone in his hand.

"We're not looking for a drink," O'Hara said, and there must have been something in her tone or accent that caught his attention, and he eyed them in the mirror behind the bar before turning.

"Now then," he said. He rested his thick, tattooed forearms on the bar and ran his warm, brown eyes over them both. "Didn't think you lot could drink on duty."

"We were hoping to speak to the landlord," Campbell continued.

"You found him," he replied, checking his watch. "But you'll have to be quick, because you're about to lose him, again."

"Matthew Cooper," O'Hara said. "Know him?"

"Cooper?" he said, shaking his head. "Not that I know of."

"He calls this place his local," Maguire added.

"So do half the people in a five-mile radius," he replied. "What does he drink?"

Maguire shook his head and looked to O'Hara.

"Warm Stella?" he offered.

"We don't serve warm Stella."

"He's a drinker," Maguire said. "Heavy. Lives with his girl-friend on Water Lane."

The landlord pondered the loose description, closed his laptop, and leaned against the bar behind him.

"There's a Matty?" he said. "I don't know his last name."

"Here on Sunday?"

"Yeah, as it happens," the man said. He snatched a piece of till roll from where it had been pinned to the wall and laid it on the bar before them. Then he ran a finger down the list of drinks.

"What's this?" O'Hara asked.

"His tab," Maguire said, which the landlord confirmed by sucking in a deep breath.

"That's one day? What's the total?" O'Hara said.

"Hundred and thirty quid," the landlord replied.

"All day sesh, then?" Maguire said.

"First round ordered at five past twelve. He was keen."

"What time do you open?" O'Hara asked.

"Twelve," he replied. "On a Sunday."

"Last drink?"

"Quarter past ten," he said.

"Christ, ten hours of drinking?"

"I know,' Maguire said. "What happened? He fell at the last hurdle."

"What?" O'Hara said in disbelief.

"Well, he missed the last forty-five minutes."

"He drank for ten hours straight," O'Hara said, then turned to the landlord. "Can I see that?"

He slid the till receipt across to her.

"What?" Maguire asked.

"I want to see something," she said, checking the drinks, line by line, and eventually she passed it back to him.

"What?" Maguire said.

"I was just seeing if he could have left at some point and come back, but he literally ordered drinks at every hour, sometimes more."

"Matty wouldn't leave," The landlord said. "When he's on a sesh, he doesn't stop, and believe me, he was on one."

"So, how would he have got home?"

The landlord shrugged.

"He could have ponced a lift from someone. He could have walked. Who knows. *He* probably doesn't even know."

"Hold on," Maguire said. "You just said he was definitely on a sesh."

"Yeah?"

"But before then, you said you don't know what time he got here."

"S'right. I was out in the morning. Got back in the afternoon and took care of the bar while my staff had their breaks."

"And then what did you do?"

"Had a drink," he said. "With my customers. It's allowed, you know."

"With Matthew Cooper?" Maguire asked, to which the landlord simply laughed.

"What?"

"I don't drink with drunks," he said. "I don't mind them coming in if they're no trouble, but I don't drink with them."

"It might have been easier if you'd just told us that," O'Hara said.

"It might have been easier if you'd asked," he replied, but his argument fell on deaf ears and was countered with a practised look. "Alright, alright. He got drunk as hell, love. Is that what you want to hear?"

"Any trouble?" Maguire asked.

"Not at first, no," the landlord replied. "Come nine o'clock-ish, he started to flag. Gave him a few warnings, you know? As you do."

"But?"

The landlord sucked in another lungful of air.

"But, he gave me no option," he said. "Punters were leaving. He was causing a scene, and this is a decent pub. People don't come here to listen to a drunk making a scene."

"You kicked him out."

"Bloody right," the landlord replied.

"What about his girlfriend?" Maguire asked. "Gemma Radford? Know her?"

"Yeah," the barman said, leaning again on the counter to give them his full attention. "She's alright. She's been around here long before he was."

"See her often?"

"No," he said. "No, she doesn't drink much, and she definitely doesn't come here with him."

"Why's that?"

"Like I said, he's a drunk. Not much fun to be around. Or to be seen with."

"Do you have CCTV?" O'Hara asked, and Maguire inwardly groaned. The last thing he wanted was to sift through more hours of footage.

"One behind the bar, one round the back, and one outside in the car park," he said. "Listen, I've got to be somewhere. Can I ask what this is about?"

"No," she said apologetically. "But if I could ask one more favour?"

"You want to see the footage?"

"From twelve until ten on Sunday, please."

He made no attempt to hide his displeasure, but clearly recognised the urgency.

"It's on the laptop," he said, dragging it over. While he worked, he looked up at O'Hara. "Gemma alright, is she?"

"Why would you ask that?"

"No reason," he explained. "But you know? She's a good lass. He's a loser. Shame to see him drag her down, is all."

"Are the two of you close?" Maguire asked.

"She's been coming here since she could get a fake ID, mate."

"But you wouldn't consider yourself friends?"

"No, I wouldn't say we were good friends, no," the barman said, his eyebrows coming together in worry. "Why? She's okay, isn't she?"

The man seemed genuine. The pub was well-presented, warm, friendly, and just the type of place he could enjoy a session, and on any other occasion, he could have enjoyed a chat with the land-lord. He seemed a good, honest man.

But there were lines that simply couldn't be crossed.

"We just need to see those recordings," he answered, and the landlord understood the message.

"Want me to leave you to it?" he asked.

"Ten minutes?" Maguire suggested, and he nodded a friendly '*no problem*'. Only when the landlord had left them to it and O'Hara was breezing through the footage, did Maguire continue. "I read once that, on average, one person's death has an effect on close to fifty people. Fifty people?"

"Is that right?" O'Hara replied,

"Makes you think, eh?" he said. "How often do we have to deal with it at a surface level, and how many people have to deal with it far closer. Puts it into perspective, right?"

O'Hara didn't comment. She busied herself with the screen.

"Still, I don't think I'd change now. Not now, we've got this chance," he said, and again she was silent. "What about you? You in this for the long haul?" O'Hara refused to look at him. "O'Hara?"

"Sorry?" she said.

"In this for the long haul, are you? You know? The team, and that."

She took her finger off the scroll button and exhaled long and hard, puffing her cheeks.

"Actually, I don't know."

"Eh?"

"I don't know."

"You don't know what? If you're in it for the long haul, or… Are you not enjoying it?"

O'Hara shrugged. "Sometimes I miss patrolling the high street on a Friday night."

"You're kidding me?"

"Don't you?"

"Not in the slightest," he said, to which she gave a little laugh and returned her attention to scrolling through the footage. "Sophie? Talk to me. Come on. It's me."

"Let's just do this, alright?" she said, and for a moment, he thought she was actually going to look at him, but her face stiffened, and her eyes narrowed.

"What?" he said.

"It's him," she replied, scrolling back a little. "Watch this."

They watched as the other punters stood at the bar ordering drinks, and spoke politely to Cooper before escaping as soon as they could. Then, without warning, he rose from his barstool, headed straight for the door, and disappeared outside.

"Where did he go?" O'Hara asked, looking up at the bar, where the landlord stood in the doorway, reaching for his keys.

"Sorry?"

"Cooper left halfway through the day. He just walked out the door. Where did he go?"

He was about to say something when his attention was turned to something behind them.

"Why don't you ask him yourself?" he answered, and he nodded to that very same door behind them, where Matthew Cooper was framed in the midday sun.

"You going to serve him?" Maguire asked.

"He owes me money," the landlord replied. "Hardly likely to chuck him out until then, am I?"

"Good, keep it that way," Maguire said, and he closed the

laptop, slid it back across the bar, and tugged on O'Hara's arm for them to leave."

"What are you doing?" she hissed.

"Thank you, sir," he called back to the landlord, nudging her past an intrigued Cooper and a couple who had entered behind him. "We'll be in touch regarding the erm... the incident."

He coaxed O'Hara into the car park, where she turned on him.

"What the bloody hell are you doing?" she said. "His alibi has a hole in it. He's right there."

"He's an alcoholic in a pub," Maguire replied. "He's not going anywhere. Phone the guv. Let him make the call."

CHAPTER THIRTY

Slumped in the chair opposite George, Steven Corbyn was calm and distant, absent-mindedly picking at a crusty stain on his cuff.

Ivy hit the button to initiate the recording, and the loud and lengthy buzz that followed roused him from his dreamlike state. She announced the time, date, and location, before handing over to George to begin the introductions.

"Conducting the interview will be myself, DI George Larson, along with DS Ivy Hart." He looked across the table, his eyebrows raised expectantly.

"Er... Steven Corbyn."

"Thank you, Mr Corbyn. For the record, you have opted not to have a solicitor present, Mr Corbyn, and you have refused your right to legal representation provided by us. It's not too late to change your mind."

"I have no idea what's going on," he laughed. "I wouldn't even know what to say to help him defend me. One thing I do know is that I haven't done a bloody thing."

"Very well," George said. "Do you understand the charges against you?"

"You said something about a sofa."

"Alright. Let's start from the beginning," George said. "Steven Corbyn, you have been arrested on suspicion of the murder of Gemma Radford. You do not have to say anything, but it may harm your defence if you do not mention, when questioned, something that you later rely on in court. Anything you do say may be given in evidence. Is that clear enough?"

Corbyn stared, not with malice, but as though he was trying to understand George. Eventually, he nodded.

"For the recording, please?" Ivy cut in.

"Yes," he said. "Yes, it's clear."

"Good," George said. "So, let's move on, shall we?" He pulled the folder towards him. Until now, it had sat like a flat, sinister centrepiece, from which he removed a photograph and slid it across the table to Steven. The photo had been taken under the portable scene lights' harsh glow, and even without context, it had an eerie feel. "For the recording, I'm showing Mr Corbyn evidence number HC005. Do you recognise the sofa in this image, Steven?"

Steven looked between the photo and George and Ivy as though checking that the question was indeed for him, and then said, "I think so. I had one similar. Could be any sofa though, right?"

"So, to clarify, you had a sofa like the one shown in the image?"

"Yeah. Yeah, I did."

"And where is that sofa now?"

"I don't know."

"You misplaced it?"

"I got rid of it," he said. "Chucked it out, but that don't mean that that one's mine, does it?"

It was a fair point easily disproved but fair. George slid a second photo from the folder.

"What about this?" he asked, turning it for Corbyn to see. "For the recording, I'm now showing Mr Corbyn evidence number HC009."

"It's a wardrobe," he replied.

"Your wardrobe?"

"Could be?"

"Have you ever owned a wardrobe like this? Does it look like a wardrobe you once owned?"

He shrugged.

"Yeah, I suppose."

"And where is that wardrobe now?"

Again, he shrugged.

"Got rid of it."

"You got rid of it?"

"Yeah."

"At the same time as the sofa?"

"Well, yeah. I had a clear-out. I told you."

"You seem to have a lot of clear-outs, Mr Corbyn. When we arrived at your home today, you were in the middle of yet another one."

"What do you want me to say? I had some stuff to get rid of, so I got rid of it."

"When exactly did you get rid of the sofa and the wardrobe, Mr Corbyn?"

"What?"

George opened the folder and began sliding more photos across to him.

"At the same time as this bedside table, an old lamp, and a coat stand? Are these all yours?" George asked. "For the benefit of the recording, I am showing Mr Corbyn evidence numbers HC010, 013, and 019." He stared across the table at Corbyn. "You've probably guessed by the numbering that we have other images of other items. I thought these would be enough to jog your memory, but I can get more if you need convincing." He turned to Ivy. "Would you?"

Corbyn sat back in his seat and held his hands up.

"Alright. Alright, they're mine. They *were* mine, I should say.

"Thank you," George said, sliding the images to one side to make room for another, the final image he wanted to present, which he pushed into place. "How about this? For the recording, Mr Corbyn is viewing evidence number HC002."

Corbyn frowned, his brow furrowed, his eyes narrowed, and he pursed his lips in thought.

Eventually, he shook his head.

"No," he said.

"No, what?"

"No," he said. "S'not mine."

"The carpet?"

"Yeah, never seen it before," he said. "

"So, the bedside table, lamp, sofa—"

"Yeah, they were mine," he said. "I'll freely admit they were mine. But that weren't." He pointed to the image. "You said you had my DNA on the sofa, right?"

"That's correct," George replied.

"And the carpet?"

George grimaced inwardly.

"We're still running tests. As you can appreciate, it's a significant size and appears to have been cleaned."

"So, no then?" he said. "None of my DNA on the carpet?"

"Our lab has reported the carpet had potentially been bleached," Ivy added. "To remove any residual evidence."

"I see," he replied.

"I also discovered an empty bleach bottle in one of the bin bags outside your home, Mr Corbyn," she said. "From your latest clear out?"

"I was having a clear-out, of course, there's an empty bleach bottle. Besides, you shouldn't have gone through that without a warrant, surely?"

"Oh, the bag wasn't tied," she told him. "It was just there in plain sight. You saw me nudge it with my boot."

"Is there any part of your statement you'd like to change, Mr Corbyn?" George asked.

"What? No. No, this is ludicrous. Of course, there's a bleach bottle. I had a clear-out. I cleaned, didn't I?"

"Have you ever been to Snipe Dales Country Park?" George asked, changing tack.

"Where?"

"Snipe Dales Country Park, it's just outside Horncastle. Five or ten minutes drive."

"I've heard of it, but I've never been. Haven't got a dog, have I?"

"You weren't there last Sunday?" George asked.

"What? No, I told you. I was..." He stopped before he said too much. "No. I wasn't."

George eyed Ivy, who offered little more than a hint of uncertainty. "Do you have a truck, Mr Corbyn?"

"A what? A truck? No. Why on earth would I have a truck?"

"Do you have access to one? A friend, or...I don't know, a business perhaps?"

"No," he said. "You saw my car at my house."

"And we've checked the DVLA database," George said. "The only vehicle registered to you is indeed the car we saw, but we all know how useful vehicles can be borrowed, or loaned."

"No," he stated again. "I have not got, nor do I have access to, a truck, a van, or a lorry."

"So, these clear-outs you seem to enjoy so much. Did you use your car for them?"

"What?"

"How did you get rid of everything? I mean, surely you couldn't have fit the sofa in your car. On the roof, maybe—"

"I hired a firm, didn't I? To take the bigger bits," he said.

"Like the sofa and the wardrobe?"

"Yes," he said.

"And the carpet?"

He stared at George, unblinking.

"The carpet is not mine."

George studied his face for any sign of deceit, but found none, which wasn't unusual for a recidivist.

"That must have been expensive?"

"Not really. Cheaper than a skip anyway."

"And do you remember who you used? Or was it just somebody you know? A favour?"

"No, it was a firm. Found a leaflet in the local chippy."

"How much did they charge?"

"What?"

"I just wondered how much a firm like that would charge to remove such a lot of rubbish."

He shook his head.

"I don't recall," he said.

"It was last week," Ivy said. "Surely you can remember how much you paid a company to remove all that? They would have been at your home for at least an hour."

"A lot's happened since last week."

"And I presume you checked to ensure they were certified?"

"Certified? His driving licence, you mean?"

"No, I'm referring to the licence required to remove any unwanted items and dispose of them at the correct recycling facility."

He shook his head.

"I just wanted shot of them, love. Christ, I even helped load the truck. Just a few little bits, you know? He had a dodgy arm, the fella. Said he'd done his shoulder in the previous week loading a cabinet by himself."

"Oh, so you can remember that he hurt himself loading a cabinet during a previous job, but you can't remember how much you paid?"

He sighed.

"Alright, alright. It was fifty quid to get rid of the lot."

"Cash?"

"Yes, of course, cash."

"And what day was this?"

"Sorry?"

"What day was it when the furniture was removed?"

"I don't know. It was last week."

"You can't remember which day it was?"

"Sunday. It was Sunday."

"You're sure?"

"Positive," he said. "I had to leave them to it. I was off..." He paused again. "I was off out."

"I see," George said. "Sundays are your thing, are they?"

"Sorry?"

"Well, for some reason, you're reluctant to tell us where you were this Sunday, presumably for the same reason you're hesitant about telling us where you were off to last Sunday. Is there something we should know about?"

"No," he said.

"No, meetings with anybody?"

"What? Like who?"

"Gemma Radford?" George said flatly, to which Corbyn closed his eyes to calm his nerves. "Where were you on Sunday afternoon, Mr Corbyn?"

"I told you, I'd rather not say, and I don't know any Gemma bloody Radford."

"I don't know if you fully understand the severity of the situation—"

"Look, I know what you're getting at, okay?" Corbyn burst out, tapping his foot as the reality of it all must have hit home. "I know what you're trying to pin on me."

"Pin on you?"

"I know that fly-tipping is a problem right now. It's very topical and everything. But I don't do that, okay? Someone got rid of it for me. Fella in his truck. I told you. I got his number from a leaflet in the chippy."

"I'm sorry to tell you, Mr Corbyn, but the situation is far more severe than that."

"What are you talking about?"

"You have been arrested for murder. Do you understand what that means?"

"I thought you just meant…" His words drifted away, as though Corbyn wasn't sure what George had meant, or how he remembered interpreting the situation.

"A young woman's body was found inside this carpet, Mr Corbyn," George said, stabbing the photo with his finger. "A carpet found amongst a pile of rubbish that you freely admit belongs to you. A carpet that has been bleached, and again, we find an empty bottle of bleach amongst the rubbish in your front garden." The blood drained from Corbyn's face, and though his dark skin didn't pale, something in his face seemed to hollow — like the air had been sucked from inside, and the light in his eyes had been snuffed. "We know that Gemma Radford was killed around three p.m. on Sunday afternoon. If you cannot tell us where you were, then I'm afraid I have little option but to detain you."

"What?" he whispered.

"Your DNA is all over this furniture," George said, pointing at the photo of the junk. "And this is where she was found. Now, can you please tell us where you were on Sunday afternoon?"

The silence that followed was as long and drawn-out as a summertime sunset across the rolling Wolds.

"It's private," he said eventually.

"Very well, you leave me no option," George began. "Steven Corbyn, I am charging you with—"

"Okay, wait, wait, wait," he said, his voice high and panicked. He rubbed his face hard, so that his cheeks turned a sharp, rosewood hue. He took a deep breath. "Look, I'm still on licence, alright."

"Okay?"

"And there are certain conditions of my bail," he explained.

George sat forward. Something told him that if Steven Corbyn was not guilty of the murder of Gemma Radford, he was certainly guilty of something. "What conditions?"

"I can't drink," he said. "I'm not allowed any alcohol, whatsoever."

"Okay, so?"

Corbyn stared through him.

"I'm an alcoholic," he said quietly. "Do you know how hard it is for me on the outside?"

"I'm still not following. Are you saying you were at the pub—"

"No. God, no," he said. "I have to go to these meetings once a week."

"On Sundays?"

Steven picked at his cuticles. "Look, I'm not proud of it. But I don't want to go back inside. I'm trying to turn my life around. It's just that...every now and then, I slip up, right?"

"You drink?"

Corbyn stared at the recorder, as if unwilling to voice his response for fear of it being used against him to prove he had broken his bail terms. But George read all he needed from the silence.

"You all talk about your compulsions in this group, do you?"

"Yeah," he said.

"And, Mr Corbyn, would it be fair to say that, despite your best intentions, and honestly, I can see how you're trying to turn your life around, but is it fair to say that you might have missed one or two of these meetings?"

Corbyn said nothing, but bit down on his lower lip.

George gave Ivy the nod, if nothing but to confirm what he hoped she was thinking.

"Do you know what, Mr Corbyn?"

"What?" he said.

"I believe you," George said, and Corbyn's disposition shifted in a heartbeat.

"Sorry?"

"I believe you," he repeated. "I believe you truly are a troubled soul, doing what you can to make a life for yourself. You've fallen in the past, and you've got back up. You'll fall again, too. We all do. But keep getting back up, Steven. As long as you keep getting back up, you'll make it."

"So, what? I can go?"

"Not just yet," George told him. "But soon. I just need a few more details."

"Like what?"

"Like someone who can corroborate your story."

"Ah, for God's—"

"Like the name of the business on the flyer in your local chippy," George continued.

"What?"

"The name of the business you paid fifty pounds in cash to, for them to remove your unwanted furniture."

"I don't..."

"Oh, come on, Steven," George said, and he leaned forward. "You were doing so well. Don't spoil it now, eh? Don't lose my trust." He leaned in close so that the two men were eye to eye. "Because, believe me, we're going to be checking your alibi. If I have to come looking for you again, if you break that trust that I'm affording you, a little Sunday drink will be the least of your worries."

CHAPTER THIRTY-ONE

It was a short drive from the police station to the address in Horncastle that Ruby had provided. George would have appreciated a longer journey, finding that the tangled lanes that meandered through the area often helped to untangle his thoughts. Instead, he perused the charming storefronts and idly observed the shoppers while settling his racing mind.

"Thank you for your time," Ivy said, ending the call in the seat beside him and tapping her phone against her thigh in thought. She turned to George. "Corbyn wasn't lying. The therapy group confirmed that he is a registered member and has missed two sessions recently."

"What are your thoughts?" he asked, keen for another viewpoint.

"Well, it's enough to charge him, guv," she said.

"But?"

"I think that every time we squeeze him, we get a little bit more. If we proceed with charges, he'll stop talking, and developing a case against him will be nigh on impossible."

"You think he has more juice to be squeezed?"

"I do," she said. "What about you?

"Me? Oh, I believe him."

"Seriously?"

"Yes," he said. "Is that so hard to believe?"

"He can't prove where he was on Sunday, guv."

"He was in a pub somewhere," George explained. "And if we take action to prove that, then we'll have to submit that evidence along with our final reports to the CPS."

"And he'll be back inside," Ivy finished.

"An innocent man who is doing his best to turn his life around, back behind bars, and for what?"

"So the evidence means nothing," she said eventually. "DNA means nothing."

"No, the evidence means everything," he replied. "The evidence, along with Corbyn's statement, tells us that the carpet was not a part of the original deposit, which stands to reason, as there was no match between the DNA on the sofa and those samples found on the body, and to date, we have found no direct link between Gemma Radford and Corbyn."

"Well, that sucks," she said.

"No," he countered. "No, we just struck a name off our list," he said with a smile. "We're closing in."

"This is it," she said, pointing at a small business unit on the edge of town.

George pulled the car up beside an old flat-bed Transit, and Ivy gave him a promising look. In a few moments, they were both circling the truck like sharks. George peered in through the window, while Ivy dropped to a crouch beside the door.

The wall that encircled the little business park, which was little more than a few tired warehouses and a cracked concrete apron, had been claimed by roving ivy that no doubt masked a thousand sins and a few decades of graffiti. Signs had been installed on the wall, every fifty feet or so, claiming that the area was monitored by CCTV, courtesy of Admiral Security. The signs had been designed to resemble official government signage, but in all practicality, meant little more than the local council was paying a private business for a few cameras and the odd patrol, and stood no greater chance of achieving a conviction should a theft be recorded. Even if the security patrol stumbled upon a robbery in progress, they would have no powers to apprehend the individual, if they did take action, they would likely be more liable for prosecution than the real villain. Such was the modern world, when criminals enjoyed far greater privileges than law-abiding citizens.

"Here we go," Ivy said, vying for a better view of a small defect in the bodywork. In reality, the dent was subtle and looked not unlike a shadow. He watched her fingers graze its uneven surface. But it was, without doubt, a defining feature.

"What the bloody hell do you think you're doing?" came a voice from behind them.

George turned to find a man striding towards them, rolling his sleeves up, with a sneer on his face. It was a combination of body language and facial expressions that officers become accustomed to fairly quickly, and those who failed to, found themselves in compromising and challenging situations. The man was practically salivating at the idea of tearing limbs from George's old and frail torso.

That is, until George revealed his warrant card, letting the little leather wallet fall open just at the right time.

"DI Larson, Lincolnshire Police," he said cordially. "Is this your truck, sir?"

The man took a breath as the adrenaline wound down, and he seemed almost relieved at not making a huge mistake, but said nothing.

"This is my colleague, Detective Sergeant Hart. Can I ask who you are, sir?"

"No," he said roughly. "But you can tell me what you're doing with my truck?"

"So it is yours?"

"It is, yeah."

"So that would make you Thomas Ingram. Is that correct?"

"I asked you, what do you want?"

"Do you happen to know a woman called Gemma Radford?"

His shoulders slumped, and he seemed to deflate at the mention of the name. His head rolled around on his neck like he was a children's toy and would snap upright if George pulled the string protruding from his behind.

"Oh Christ," he said. "Is that what this is about?"

"I'll take that as a yes, then, shall I?"

"Gemma bloody Radford?"

"I'm quite sure that's not her middle name—"

"She sent you, did she? I knew this would come back to haunt me. I bloody knew it."

Ivy rose from where she was crouched, and George waved for her to stand back. He waited for Ingram to compose himself so they could resume what George was finding to be a thrilling and revealing conversation.

"So?" Ingram said. "What did she say?"

"Actually, she hasn't said much."

"Get about a bit, do you?" Ivy asked.

"What?"

"You know? House clearances and whatnot. You must get around a fair bit."

"A decent amount. Local mainly."

"And is that all you do? Rubbish disposal, house clearances?"

"I assume all this is leading to something," Ingram replied, ignoring the line of questioning. "Because, if it is, then I wish you'd just come out and say it."

"Okay," George said. "We have CCTV evidence of your truck transporting a pile of furniture through Spilsby at two forty-eight on Sunday morning."

"Is that a crime?"

"That same furniture was later found fly-tipped in Snipe Dales Country Park."

"The same furniture, yeah?"

"*We* think so," Ivy said.

"Well, I don't," he replied. "You've got CCTV, have you?"

Ivy nodded while George remained solemn, still making a decision about the man.

"Do you think we could see your licence?"

"Driving licence?" he asked. "It's at home."

"Waste carrier's licence," George corrected him.

"What?"

"You know, the ticket you need to enter a recycling facility. Only licensed businesses can dispose of waste, which I'm assuming you are."

"Well, you know how it is. These things get waylaid."

"Oh, so you've lost it, have you?"

"Well...not lost. Mislaid more like. It'll be around somewhere. Probably with my paperwork."

"As I understand it, you can't even drive into a recycling facility without one," George said, doing his best to appear perplexed as he looked towards Ivy. "Is that right?"

"S'right, guv," she said. "Won't even lift the barrier until you show it. Not worth their while to turn a blind eye. The Environment Agency will be all over them like a rash. Not good for business, guv. Not with social media the way it is."

"Yeah? Lucky I haven't needed to then," Ingram replied, as if he had them covered at every turn and knew their next moves.

"So, how come we have CCTV evidence of your truck moving a load of old furniture?"

"I told you, I never fly-tipped nothing."

"So presumably you disposed of the furniture in the correct fashion," George said. "And the fly-tipping we discovered must belong to somebody else? Which is it, Mr Ingram? Either you disposed of said furniture correctly, but without a ticket, in which case I'd love to know which facility it was, or you just dumped it in the first place you deemed suitable. Which one?"

He looked between them, his confidence waning.

"What makes you think it was *my* truck? My number plates need a good wipe after all that rain. There's no way a camera would pick them up."

"Which, I might add, is a traffic offence," Ivy added.

"Am I being nicked for it?" he asked, glancing over his shoulder at the old business unit behind him. "I'll need to lock up if I am."

"Not yet, you're not," George told him.

"Well, you've had all you're going to get from me, then," he said, folding his beefy arms in protest. "No comment."

"You do understand that you are not under arrest, Mr Ingram?" George asked. "We're simply trying to gain a better understanding of your business. Our colleague found your business flyer in a petrol station outside of Spilsby, the same petrol station, in fact, in which we found the CCTV."

"Well, it's not like I can do any online marketing, is it?" he replied, rubbing his forehead in defeat.

"Why's that?"

He waved his hand at the rest of the street, or perhaps the rest of the world. "Because there's a witch hunt against me. They close me down the moment I try."

"Who?"

"*Them*," he spat, the paranoia ripe in his voice. "The locals. Not to my face, of course. No, no. Don't have the stones for that, do they? But online. I've had to shut my Facebook page down. Do you know how long it took to build up all them followers? All those little village groups? Done me up like a kipper, she has."

"Who has?"

"Radford," he said. "Who d'ya think? Bleeding pictures of old crap on the side of the road, fridges in forests, you name it. If it ain't supposed to be there, then she assumed it's me what dumped it."

"Assumed?" George said. "Past tense?"

"Eh?" he said, and George let it go.

"So, you've had to resort to leaving leaflets in local petrol stations and chip shops to drum up a bit of business, have you?"

"What choice do I have, other than to sell the truck and sign on?"

"And that's how Steven Corbyn contacted you, is it?"

"Who?"

"Steven Corbyn," he repeated slowly. "He's a customer of yours."

"Where were you on Sunday afternoon?" Ivy asked, adding a little pressure.

"I was on a job," he said.

"What job?"

"A local one," he said. "Just some old girl wanted the contents of her husband's shed cleared out. He died. Lucky bastard."

"And what did you do with it?" Ivy asked, to which he grinned and jabbed a thumb over his shoulder.

"It's in there, darling. Get yourself a warrant, and you come and have a look. I'll even get my boy to make you a cup of tea,"

"You store the goods?" George asked.

"Yeah, course. Some of it's alright, you know? I don't just tip the lot. Some of the wood can be reclaimed, plenty of old furniture places in Horncastle want something to restore."

"Right," George said, suddenly seeing the missing link. "And you dump the rest, do you?"

"Yeah."

"And if you can't find your ticket?"

"It's around somewhere," he replied.

"Fly-tip it?" Ivy asked.

"Not my style," he replied.

"So, Gemma Radford was wrong, was she? There wasn't a scrap of truth in those things she said about you online?"

He opened his mouth to speak, but held his tongue long enough to divert their attention.

"See, that's the trouble with the world now. One person says something, right or wrong, and all the sheep follow. Can't think for themselves, can they?"

"I didn't say I believed her—"

"It doesn't matter if you believe what she says or not,' he spat. "What matters is the fact that you lot go with the majority, don't you? You blow around in the breeze, people pleasing. Haven't got your own principles to follow. You just follow the path of least resistance."

"All that's very interesting, I'm sure," George told him. "Personally, I couldn't care less how you make your money. I don't agree with fly-tipping, but is it my job to police it?" He shook his head. "No. No, it's not."

Ingram looked bemused. He looked to each of them for an answer.

"So, what's all this about?" he said. "What the bloody hell are you wasting my time for?"

"Well, we're here about the mess that...somebody, I'm not saying who, left in the Country Park on Sunday morning."

Again, he looked bemused.

"But you just said—"

"I have it on good authority, Mr Ingram, that you collected a pile of furniture, including a red sofa, from a nearby property last Sunday."

"What—?"

"You then stored the rubbish in your unit, I imagine," George continued. "You pulled out the bits you thought you might be able to resell, and in the early hours of Sunday morning, you loaded your truck up with the sofa, and anything else you wanted to get rid of, and you dumped it in Snipe Dales Country Park. Look, I'm not about to arrest you for fly-tipping. Frankly, I've got more important things to worry about."

"Like what?"

"Like the body that was found in the carpet, alongside the sofa, the bedside table, the lamp—"

"The what?" Ingram said, cutting him off.

"The body," George said, matter-of-factly. "It was inside the roll of carpet. Fell out when three young boys tried to make a camp with it."

He searched for a reaction, but found only surprise.

"Who?" Ingram said slowly, his lips barely moving.

"Just three lads. You know what boys are like—"

"No, who did you find?" he asked, as if he already knew the answer. "The body."

"Gemma Radford," George said. "Your number one fan."

The news hit him as if George had just announced the death of his sainted mother. He squeezed his eyes closed and let his head fall back. Finally, he stared up at the sky.

"Is there anything you care to say, Mr Ingram?" Ivy asked, and in that posture, he shook his head.

"No," he croaked, perhaps sensing the gravity of the discussion.

"We *know* it was your truck, Mr Ingram," George started. "We know where you got the furniture from, and now we know why it took a week to dump it. We know there was ongoing drama between Gemma Radford and yourself, and we know that the outcome of that drama was a severe loss of earnings for you. We have a motive. We have the means. We have the opportunity." He stepped in closer, so he could lower his voice. "All we need from you is a statement."

Ivy held her phone up for George to see a call coming in from Maguire, and he nodded for her to take it.

"Come on, Mr Ingram. You're running out of places to hide," he said.

Many men under such circumstances might have shed a tear, knowing the game was up. Others might have fought on, perhaps retaliating with an insult or two - nothing that would harm anything softer than an ego, and even then for only a few minutes.

But Ingram's brow furrowed. He opened his eyes, and his head snapped upright.

"You've got me," he said, holding his hands out, wrists together. "Everything you just said was true." George caught the shift in Ivy's demeanour in the corner of his eye. She stiffened, readying herself to take action. "I took that furniture the Sunday before last. Grubby fella. Lives in a bomb site with toot all over his garden." He pulled an expression, indicating he was thinking hard. "Corbyn. That's his name, right? I was suffering with my shoulder, so he helped me load up."

"That's correct," George said quietly.

"And yeah, I kept it all here. Bugger all worth keeping, though. Sofa was covered in God knows what, the lamps didn't work, and the furniture was rotten. It was filth."

"So you dumped it?"

"Yeah," he said. "Yeah, I dumped it."

"Because you don't have a licence?"

"Yes," he said again. "Because I don't have a licence."

"So everything Gemma Radford said about you was true, and you were just sore that somebody had the guts to call you out on it."

"Something like that," he said, after a short pause for reflection. "But I'll tell you one thing you're wrong about."

"Go on," George said.

"I didn't dump a sodding carpet," Ingram replied, a smug sneer spreading across his face. "And if you don't believe me, look up there."

He pointed to the post at the entrance to the little business park, atop which was a CCTV camera that captured every vehicle going in and out.

"If that can prove you weren't carrying a carpet, Mr Ingram,"

George said. "Then I'll be the first to strike a line through your name rather than under it. That is, if the camera is working."

"Oh, I know it's working," he said.

"How?"

"Because that camera there," he started, "is what Gemma Radford used to destroy my business."

"Sorry?" Ivy said as she returned, pocketing her phone. "Gemma Radford had access to that camera?"

"I'm not following," George said, to which Ingram shrugged.

"I don't know how," he said. "But the image she shared online was from that camera." His grin was broad and that of a winner. "I take it I won't need to lock up then?"

CHAPTER THIRTY-TWO

When George and Ivy entered the George and Dragon, they edged through the lunchtime rush and took places on either side of the tall, long-haired man at the bar, who sleeved the remnants of his beer from his lips. He eyed them in the mirror behind the bar, recognised their faces, then dropped his head into his hands.

"What do you want?" he grumbled through his fingers.

"What do you fancy, Ivy?" George asked, ignoring the question. "Red wine?"

She shook her head. "Diet Coke for me. Cheers, guv."

"Diet Coke and half a lager shandy, thanks," he ordered from the barman, who nodded at them as though he'd expected their arrival. The wait was brief but tense, and lasted until their drinks had been placed before them. Ivy sipped at her drink, which reminded her of long winter evenings in the pub with Jamie.

Matthew Cooper rubbed his face and turned to face George with a sigh. "I asked what you wanted?"

"What?" George said, appearing perplexed. "Can't we have a drink in a local pub?"

"I've answered all your questions."

"Well," George replied. "Not really. You see, while I'm doing my best to take into consideration the tragic loss you've just suffered, and believe me, I am, I'm also tasked with getting to the bottom of Gemma's murder, Matthew."

"And yet, here you are with a beer," Cooper replied, to which George offered little remorse.

"One of the first things we do at the beginning of an investigation like this is to understand what the victim, in this instance, Gemma, was doing. Where she was, who she was with, and her mental state, if you like."

"Her mental state?"

"What she was thinking? Had she been distracted, busy, or excited about something? You know? How was she?"

"Gemma was...Gemma," he replied. "If I thought she was...off, somehow, then I'd have said so. But she weren't."

"That's what I thought," George told him, taking a sip of his shandy. "Alongside that, we seek to understand those closest to the victim. Not for the purpose of pointing any fingers mind, but to ensure that before we take the investigation wider, we're confident that her nearest and dearest were not involved in any way."

"Yeah? So, what? You want to know where I was. I've told you where I was."

"Ah, yes. You did, and if it helps, I can confirm that we know that you were in here for most of the day."

"Most?"

George grimaced.

"You popped out."

"Hold on. How the..." He looked up at the barman and then across at Ivy. "Is that what those two coppers were doing in here?"

"They were doing their jobs, Matthew—"

"Rich?" he called across the bar to the barman. "Oy, Rich. You been talking to the old bill about me?"

"Unless you want us to take this conversation elsewhere, Matthew, I think you should refrain from drawing attention to yourself," George warned. "Let's not make a scene, eh?"

But Cooper ignored him entirely and stood from his bar stool to lean over the bar.

"Oy, Rich. Answer me. You been talking to plod about me?"

The barman, who in Ivy's opinion was doing a sterling job of maintaining a professional outlook, finished pouring a pint of ale and slid it towards the customer, who eyed the threesome curiously, then sloped off to find a table.

"You need to wind your neck in, Matty," Rich said quietly but firmly. He walked over to them, leaned on the bar opposite Cooper and spoke clearly. "You're one outburst away from being barred. I suggest you drink your drink. Talk to your mates, then f—"

"You have, haven't you? Who else was in here on Sunday?"

"Actually, Matthew, I think you'll find that it wasn't Richard," Ivy cut in.

"Eh?"

Ivy pointed to the little camera mounted above the bar, and Cooper gave a loud sigh.

"Those two coppers in here earlier?" he said.

"Those two coppers indeed," she replied, and gestured that the barman could return to his duties. "You should be grateful that one of them had the sense to call us before they dragged you back to the station."

"Drag me? What? Why?"

"You left the building, Matthew," George said, "for a very specific period of time. Coincidently, at the very time we believe Gemma died."

He was silent. He stared at his pint, turning it in his hands, which he then wiped on his jeans.

"That was when she..." he started, then stopped and cleared his throat. "It was then, was it?"

"We believe so," George said softly.

"You think I did it, then?" he asked, his voice almost boyish. "You think I'm capable of that, do you?"

"It might surprise you to learn that I still need convincing," George said, and judging by Cooper's expression, he *was* surprised. "But if I were you, I wouldn't take that to mean that I admire you. I empathise, of course. That goes without saying. You've just lost somebody close to you. You deserve empathy, sympathy, and any other nouns you want to throw in there. But not admire. In fact, after the way in which we first met, it astounds me that somebody like Gemma was even with you."

"Don't judge me," he muttered. "You don't know what I've been through."

"What did Gemma see in you?" he asked quietly. "That's what I was wondering. Everyone seems to think you're worthless; the barman, Gemma's best friend. So why did Gemma stay with you? Why did she invite you into her home?"

"I don't know," he said quietly.

"Do you want to know my theory?" He looked up at George, like a patient seeking clarity from a therapist. "Initially, I thought that Gemma had a thing for strays. For neglected animals like you. She hoped she could take you in, get you back on your feet, then release you back into the world, a better man."

"And now," he asked, a tear winding its way down his cheek.

"Now, I think I know the real reason," George said. "But, hey. We're getting ahead of ourselves. We want to know all about this little trip out you made on Sunday."

"Where did you go when you left the pub on Sunday afternoon, Matthew?" Ivy asked for clarity and to cut through the emotion George had, quite masterfully, built.

Whatever Cooper muttered was too quiet for Ivy to make sense of.

"Speak louder, Matthew," she said, in the way she might scold Theo for mumbling.

He took a deep breath and repeated, "I was with someone."

"You were with someone?"

"Another woman," he said, and George pulled a look of utter distaste and disappointment.

"Who?"

"Nobody special," he replied. "She's a bit of an old slag, if you want to know the truth."

"Where?" Ivy asked. "You told us that Gemma dropped you off, and by all accounts, you were in no fit state to drive anywhere yourself." He grinned at her, and she swallowed the nausea induced by his yellowing teeth and foul breath. "Our colleagues saw the CCTV footage from that camera, Matthew," she said, pointing up at the camera again. "You were sitting right here, drinking, then you finished your pint, stumbled across the floor, and went outside. Where did you meet her?"

"That camera there, yeah?" he asked, to which Ivy nodded, as if there were any more cameras inside that could have been in the frame. "You want to check the other one?"

At this, the barman stopped what he was doing and listened.

"What other camera?" George asked.

"The one round the back," Cooper explained coolly.

Ivy turned to Richard, who was staring at Cooper in disgust.

"Is there another camera around the back?" she asked.

The barman's top lip pulled back, revealing a row of clean white teeth.

"You dirty—"

"Right up against his front door," Cooper continued, grinning. "While he was in here, giving it all the Billy big b—"

"As much as it pains me to say it," George cut in, before any profanities were ejaculated into the conversation. "Can we see this video?"

"Out," Richard said, no longer keeping his voice low and professional. "I want *him* out. Now!"

"Hold on, hold on," George said, doing his best to calm matters down." He held his hands up to appease Richard. "Let's just...let's just get to the bottom of this, shall we? Then, when we're done, you can do as you wish." Richard said nothing, and didn't, for one second, remove his eyes from Cooper's joy-filled stare. "I'll take another shandy," George said. "And another Diet Coke, please." He fished a ten-pound note from his wallet and slid it across the bar.

"Not for me, guv," Ivy said.

"You don't have to drink it," George muttered.

"Mine's a lager," Cooper said, grinning.

"Yours is going to be a warm cup of water in a warm and sticky police cell if you keep going like that, Matthew," George warned. "And you'll think yourself lucky you get even that."

Richard placed the drinks down, avoiding Cooper's taunting stare.

"I'll have somebody call you for the footage," George assured him. "I don't think we need to see it right here, right now."

"Who was it?" Ivy asked, and eventually Cooper turned his grin on her. "Who did you meet? Come on. You know full well we're going to have to speak to her."

"You'll see who she is," he said, leaning towards her. "When you watch me banging on her against his front door. I'll bet you're looking forward to that." His gaze wandered to Ivy's naval, then worked its way back up, slowly, as if he was recording every detail.

"What about Gemma?" Ivy asked. "Why would you do that?"

"I don't think that's any of our— George started.

"A man's got to do what a man's got to do," Cooper said, cutting him off, daring Ivy to respond.

"And what about her? Was *she* doing what she had to do?"

"Ivy," George warned, but she held a hand up to stop him.

"No, guv. I want to hear it. What's good for the goose is good for the gander, and all that."

"You what?" Cooper said.

"Oh, sorry. I thought you knew," she replied.

"Ivy, this is not the time—"

"Knew what?" Cooper snapped.

"About Gemma, and what she was doing on Sunday."

He shook his head in disbelief and even gave a little laugh.

"She was with Jenny. What are you on about?"

"Is that what she told you?"

"What?"

"We've spoken to Jenny," Ivy told him, savouring the new pain the man before her was experiencing, like she was twisting a blade deep into his heart. "She says she wasn't with Gemma on Sunday afternoon. She thinks Gemma was with a man."

Matthew shook his head. "There's no way she would—"

"I mean, she was a pretty girl. She must have had opportunities all the time."

"You bitch."

"And I mean, she obviously wasn't with you for the sex, was she?" It was Ivy's turn to lean in close. "You're forgetting. I've seen you naked." She waggled her little finger, winked, and returned his winning grin.

"What are you saying?"

"Do you really need me to spell it out?" Ivy asked, still holding her little finger up.

"So why was she with me? What do you know? What are you saying?"

"She's referring to your job, Matthew," George said, and he glared at Ivy as a warning.

"My job?"

"You work for a security firm, is that right?"

"Yeah, so?"

"A security guard?"

"Not really. I'm a CCTV operator."

"And you monitor the premises of certain businesses, do you?"

"No, I monitor the council's security network."

"For Admiral Security?"

"Yeah, of course. They've got the contract."

"From home?"

"Well, yeah. It's not like the old days, is it? Don't have to be on site to look at the cameras. I can see them all from my laptop. Why? What's this got to do with Gemma?"

"Oh, it's got everything to do with Gemma," George replied. "And I hate to say this, but it's likely the reason she let you move into her house."

"What?"

"Would she have had access to your laptop?"

"What? Well, yeah. I suppose."

"And did you ever see her using your laptop?"

"All the time, but she wouldn't have looked at the cameras. It's work stuff. She might have bought something on Amazon, or something. I don't know."

"And you monitored her activity on your laptop?" George asked.

"What? No, course I never. She's my...she *was* my girlfriend." He spoke that last sentence slowly and thoughtfully, as if doubtful of how true it now was.

"You let her use your laptop without supervision?"

"She wasn't a child," Cooper said. "Didn't need a bloody password to access the internet, did she." He sank the remnants of his beer and thought twice about ordering another, knowing the answer would have been resoundingly negative. "Anyway, she spent most of her time in her office. I wouldn't have known what she was looking at."

"In her what?" Ivy asked.

"Her office," he repeated, as if she was intellectually challenged. "The spare room."

George whipped Cooper's jacket from the back of his seat and thrust it into his chest.

"What? What are you doing?"

"You're coming with us," he said, stepping aside to give Cooper room to exit his stool. "I want to see this office of hers."

CHAPTER THIRTY-THREE

Compared to their previous visit, Gemma Radford's home was in perfect order. There were no beer cans or ashtrays in the living room, and more importantly, there was no smoke coming from the kitchen. The place even smelled nice.

"You've been busy," George said.

"Yeah, well," he replied. "Funny what guilt does, eh? Always hated the place a mess, she did. Didn't seem right, that's all." He eyed George sadly, and then gestured up the stairs. "It's this way."

They followed, and George admired the old cottage. Gemma Radford had clearly invested a lot of time and energy into maintaining the house, somehow creating a modern home while retaining the original features. Where some might have knocked walls down to create open living, she had created warm spaces that were so very clearly loved.

"It's in here," Cooper said, pushing open one of four doors, stepping back to allow them to enter.

The room was mid-sized, large enough for a double bed but not much else, or a single bed with a wardrobe and a dresser. Gemma Radford had opted for a large desk with an old wooden chair and an armchair in the corner. Floral wallpaper adorned the walls, which could have been a carryover from the previous owner, and something she hadn't got around to changing. But it worked, adding its own charm to the little room. There were no pictures on the walls or ornaments on the window ledge. Only a three-foot by two-foot pinboard fixed to the wall above the desk.

"I'll leave you to it," Cooper said from the doorway.

"No wait,' George said, halting him. "How often was she in here?"

"Gemma?" he said with a shrug. "Every night. Slept in the armchair more often than not. It's a recliner."

"And you?"

"In the bed," he said. "Like I told you. She wasn't much interested in... you know? She wasn't like that. I suppose, now I know why."

"So, what did she do in here?" Again, he shrugged. "You don't know? You didn't ever come in and sit with her?"

"Oh no," he said. "No, no, no. I'm not allowed in here."

George eyed him and the way he seemed to loiter in the doorway.

"You never came in here?"

"It's *her* space," he told them.

"And you respected that, did you?"

"What choice did I have? The way she explained it was that she'd let me live here and let me share her bed, although we rarely shared it. But this was her space. She needed somewhere to call her own."

Ivy gave a little sideways nod as if to say, 'that's fair enough', and she gestured at a laptop on the desk.

"Might be useful." She opened the lid, and they were presented with the option to enter a password.

"Have someone come and collect it," he told her, then looked up at Cooper. "Unless you know the password?"

Cooper shook his head.

"Wouldn't have a clue."

"She didn't have a particular phrase, or a date maybe?"

"Not as far as I know."

"Her parents died. Maybe a date relating to them?"

"Honestly, I've told you what I know."

"What is all this, guv?" Ivy said, studying the pinboard. "Photos of rubbish. Fly-tipping, I'll bet."

"What about that?" George asked, referring to a document with a ring mark from a cup near the top. "East Lindsey solar farm. The potential positive effects on the local economy through reduced reliance on fossil fuels and increased employment."

"Sounds like whoever worked on that had a creative mind," Ivy said. "What about the negative effects on the landscape, the wildlife, and farming?"

"That was Gemma's argument," Cooper said. "She used to say that once they started developing in the Wolds, it would snowball. She said it happened in the greenbelt around London. They put this protection in place to preserve wildlife and nature and whatever, but then as soon as one person starts building, there's no argument against anybody else doing it."

"Sounds fair to me," George replied, pointing at another document pinned beside it. "What about this one? Reclaiming unused farmland for the greater good. A proposal to help local unused farmland give back to the community."

"Solar farms? Ivy said. "I don't even have to read that one to know what it's going to say. Farmland is sold off to pay inheritance tax, and the only people able to buy it are wealthy power companies, or the government."

"I thought you lot were supposed to be impartial?" Cooper said.

"We are," George added, with more than a little warning in his tone.

"We're human," Ivy added, dismissing any notions that she shouldn't have an opinion, and steering them back to the board. "What about this?"

George leaned in and peered at the document she was indicating, which had been pinned prominently in the dead centre of the board.

She caught his attention, her eyebrows raised in question.

"Look familiar?"

"That's the Country Park," he said, tracing the outline of the map before them, and then fingering a stamp mark in bright red ink. "But this is interesting."

CHAPTER THIRTY-FOUR

To any passing dog walkers, the six of them must have looked like a lost hiking group or even a ritualistic cult standing in a tight circle in the middle of a meadow on the very edge of the Country Park. George stood at the head, already questioning wearing his long jacket and soiled brogues.

As usual, Ivy positioned herself somewhere between him and the team, watching Maguire swat a persistent horsefly. The rest of them. Byrne, Campbell, and O'Hara savoured the warm, cloud-free sunlight in peace as the early evening chill set in. Although summer had undoubtedly arrived, it was still only fifteen degrees — a true English summer.

Seeing the place in the light of day, she understood why Wesley Harris, Oscar Wyman, and Louis Foxon had chosen Snipe Dales as their playground. It was the perfect place to explore their boyhood, with the exciting trickle of water nearby, an abundance of trees to climb, and long-grass meadows in which they could burn off that prepubescent energy.

"Thank you for joining us," George said. "I wanted to give you all a quick update before we begin."

"Begin what, guv?" Maguire asked, taking a violent swing at the horsefly.

George smiled politely, but didn't reply.

"Campbell, Byrne, how did it go with the Wymans?"

Byrne shook his head sadly. "They don't seem to give a monkey's, guv. I told them what happened to their son, that Oscar needs their help, but they just can't seem to get their heads around how important this is."

"You told them we're running a murder investigation, here?" Ivy asked. "And that their son is involved?"

"Yes, sarge."

"And they don't care?"

"They said they'll be back tomorrow and we can talk to them then."

"Can't we do something, guv?" Ivy asked.

Campbell shook her head sadly.

"Surely they have a responsibility to be with their son?" she asked.

"Is it even legal for him to be left on his own?" O'Hara added.

They all turned to George, who met each of their stares and shook his head with a similar sadness to Byrne.

"A parent is not legally required to act as a witness. The boy needs an appropriate adult, yes, but maybe it's time to ask the Foxons for their help."

"But the Wymans are his parents. One of *them* should be his appropriate adult."

"They *should*, yes," George said simply.

"What about Oscar being left on his own?" Byrne asked.

"There's no legal age for a child to be left alone, so long as they're mature and responsible enough to handle an emergency."

"But he's a child," Campbell scoffed. "Can't we call social services?"

"We can," George replied calmly. "But they're unlikely to act on it unless something goes wrong, and besides, who knows what course of action might follow that? We could trigger the lad's demise. Social services take him away, and then what? His entire life is turned upside down." He shook his head. "I'm not keen on changing lives. Not when it's out of our remit."

"And if the boy burns his house down?" Byrne asked.

"It's not a perfect solution, I freely admit," George told him. "But we can't police the world, and we can't foresee the future."

The team grew silent, contemplating the loopholes of the system that allowed vulnerable children to slip through the cracks, even in plain sight, even under the watchful eyes of the law.

Byrne kicked at a tuft of grass.

"So, we just wait then, do we?" he said.

George waited until Byrne looked him in the eye, the officer who, amongst the long grass, and with the low sun highlighting the tips of his hair, looked more like a boy than any of them."

"They're back tomorrow," he said, then turned his attention elsewhere. "O'Hara, do you want to update the rest of the team about Matthew Cooper?"

She straightened when all eyes moved onto her.

"I can tell you what we know, guv. We talked to the barman at the pub, who showed us CCTV footage from inside the bar. Cooper got there early and sat on a bar stool for most of the day."

"*Most* of the day?" Byrne asked.

"He left for less than an hour."

"Let me guess..." Campbell started.

"The exact time Gemma was killed, yeah," O'Hara finished.

"Alright," George said, clapping his hands before they organised a manhunt. "We paid him a visit at the pub, and I think we made quite the impression, isn't that right, Ivy?"

He gave her the type of look a parent might give to shame their child.

"Yes, guv."

"And long story short, he gave us an alibi for that period. Ruby has looked into it for us. He's in the clear."

"He told you where he went?" Campbell asked.

"Yes, but I think that's all we need to—"

"Where was he?" Maguire asked, clearly sensing George was avoiding the topic.

"Out the back," Ivy said, to avoid George's embarrassment.

"What do you mean?"

"He was with another woman. It's okay, you'll learn about that type of thing, one day."

"Okay..." O'Hara said, confusion etched on her innocent face.

"So he was cheating on Gemma?" Byrne asked.

"It looks like it," George said. "But that's not the point—"

"So, how did Ruby confirm it? Have you spoken to the other lass?" Maguire asked.

"We have video evidence," George said. "Of his...alibi."

O'Hara grimaced. "Video evidence?"

"Security camera around the back," Ivy said with a grin.

"Oh, God."

"The important thing is that we can strike a line through his name," George said. "As we can with Steven Corbyn."

Maguire whistled.

"You said you wanted to cross some people off, guv," he said. "We've only the boys and the old man left, and I don't see a motive for any one of them."

"And Thomas Ingram," Ivy reminded him. "Don't forget him."

"Yes," George said darkly. "Don't forget about that little gem."

"So *he's* why we're here?" Maguire asked

"Not exactly," George said cryptically, and the Irishman turned his head to the skies, clearly confused. "See, it transpires that Gemma Radford did in fact destroy Ingram's business. He's still operating, but any digital presence has been tainted by remarks from Gemma Radford, and other like-minded individuals."

"How?"

"Video and photographic evidence of his fly-tipping practice," Ivy told him.

"Evidence?"

"There's a camera near his business unit. That camera is owned by the council, but monitored by a private security firm."

"Admiral?" Campbell said, and George smiled at the speed at which she had connected the dots.

"Very good, Campbell," he said, and left the space open for her to justify that claim.

"Cooper works for Admiral."

"Give that officer a star," George said. "His job is, I suppose, the modern equivalent of a security guard. But instead of patrolling buildings, or monitoring the cameras from inside, he does so on his laptop, very probably with a can of beer in his hand, from the comfort of his own home."

"Or Gemma Radford's home," O'Hara cut in again. "That's how she got the evidence of Ingram's fly-tipping? She accessed his laptop."

"And that's how we know that Ingram did in fact collect the furniture from Steven Corbyn's house. Alas, he did not have a roll of carpet on his truck. The camera is mounted up high. It's a top-down view. As clear as day."

"So Ingram resorted to old-school local marketing techniques?" Byrne said, to which George nodded. "And continues to fly-tip?"

"Yes, thank you," he replied. "I'm happy to pass on that information to the relevant team once, and only once, a suspect has been apprehended, charged, tried, and sentenced."

"Right," Maguire said, clearly doing his best to follow. So, we're here because...?"

"Because Gemma Radford accessed Cooper's laptop," George

said. "She was with him for that very purpose. Thomas Ingram is just one of her targets. One of many. She was using the council's CCTV system to support her own little activist projects."

"Jesus," Maguire replied. "What, and she...you know...slept with him, for that?"

"I doubt there was much sleeping with anybody going on," Ivy added. "Hence, Cooper's little romance behind the pub. What we do know is that Gemma Radford took his laptop into her office at times."

"Her office?"

"Her spare room," George said. "And before you ask, yes, Cooper showed us, and yes, it's exactly how you might imagine it to look."

"Pictures of badgers crossing the street, guv?" Byrne suggested.

"There were all kinds of photographs," he replied. "She clearly felt strongly about many causes. Animal welfare being just one, yes. Gaza, the environment, wind farms, solar farms, fly-tipping, you name it. All of which were entirely unrelated to Snipe Dales Country Park..." he paused, waiting for their curiosities to waken. "Except one."

He looked across to Ivy for her to continue.

"We found a map," she said.

"A map?" Maguire said. "Of this place?"

Ivy nodded at him.

"Beside it, we found an archaeological proposal. An archaeological proposal for *this* very meadow." She stamped the ground for emphasis. "It had been rejected."

"Why?" Campbell asked.

"That's exactly what Gemma Radford wanted to know," George said, taking out a piece of paper from his folder and holding it up for the team. It showed a map of the area with a circle around the meadow in which they stood. With his finger, George traced Gemma's handwriting: *REJECTED! WHY?*

"Well, who rejected it?" Byrne asked.

"We don't know," Ivy said. "We called the archaeologists involved in the application, and they just said the local council rejected it with no reason given. They're in the process of resubmitting."

"So that's why we're here?" he asked. "Come on. We're dying to know."

George grinned, if not at his lack of self-control, but at his enthusiasm.

"We are going to search from here..." He pointed to the point on the map close to where they were standing, then at the path fifty metres away. "To here. Which, in reality, is from that path over there," he said, pointing into the distance. "To that line of trees," he finished, gesturing to the row of trees at the edge of the meadow.

"Search for what, guv?" Byrne asked.

"Honestly," George said, folding the paper back into his pocket. "I'm not sure. But I think that this is where Gemma was on Sunday afternoon, and whatever *she* was looking for, that's what *we* need to be looking for."

How do we know that this map and the whole archaeological thing, was why she was here?" O'Hara asked.

"Two reasons," George said. "Firstly, it's the only one of her little activist projects that directly involved the Country Park. Secondly, because of where it was placed on her wall."

"Sorry? Where it was placed?"

"Dead centre," he told her. "With space all around it, ready for her to add more information as and when she got it."

"Surely she must have had more?"

"You'd think so, wouldn't you?" he replied. "And if she did have more, would she have pinned it to the wall for somebody like Matthew Cooper to see?"

"Was there really nothing else?" Maguire asked. "No photos, no...I don't know, people?"

"We've had a uniformed officer collect her laptop. Hopefully, one of the tech team can get into it. We might be lucky, but I don't intend to wait for an answer." He looked around the team, and the seriousness of his stare caught even Maguire's attention. "Because I have a feeling that whatever it was she was looking for," he said, bringing the briefing to an end. "She found it."

CHAPTER THIRTY-FIVE

"I don't even know what we're looking for," Byrne said, as they scoured the perimeter of the meadow. He stared into the sky above. "What if it's some kind of crop circle?"

"What are you going on about?" Campbell asked.

"Crop circles," he said again. "Come on, we know she was a bit of a nutter. What if she thought there was something odd going on? We shouldn't be walking around down here. We should just send a drone up, or a chopper or something. You know? Looking for marks on the ground, or something. Bird's eye view, and all that."

"A helicopter?"

"Well, I don't know. All I know is that my bloody hay fever is kicking off like you wouldn't believe. Feels like I've got broken glass in my eyeballs. I could be staring right at whatever it is we're supposed to be looking for, and I wouldn't know, because my eyes are on fire."

"Mate, she was an activist, not a bloody alien, and if you think the force would commission a bloody helicopter to search a field when they have people like you and me, you are deluded."

"Right," he said.

"I hope that chatter means you've found something," the guv called out, and Byrne gave him the thumbs up.

"Just a stick, guv," Byrne called back.

"Well, keep looking," he replied. "Heads down, eyes peeled."

"Eyes burning, more like," Byrne grumbled. "I mean, what if she was just planning a protest to save a vole nest?"

"A what?"

"You know? Like a small mouse. Lives in the fields."

"I suppose it's something, and it would explain why the archaeological dig was rejected," Campbell replied. "If there is evidence of voles out here, and a dig was going to disturb them, I suppose it would be rejected."

"So why was she bothered about it? She's on the side of the wildlife?"

"She was," Campbell corrected him.

"Right. You know what I mean. She won, surely? Why challenge it?"

Campbell stopped for a moment and stared at him.

"Are you going to shut up at all during this search?"

"I just want to know," he said.

"We all want to know Liam. And do you know how we find out?"

"We search, yeah, yeah. I just...I just want a bloody clue."

"Another stick?" The guv called out.

"No, it's just a vole," Byrne called back, then muttered under his breath. "A dead one. Ravaged by plague-ridden badgers."

"TB," Campbell corrected him.

"Eh?"

"TB," she said. "Badgers carry TB, not the plague."

"Same thing."

"Well, no. Not really. One is a disease carried by rats that infects the lymph node in humans, the other is a bacteria that infects our lungs. They're quite different."

"Jesus, she's a doctor now."

"I'm just saying that if you're going to be facetious, at least get your facts straight."

"Alright, alright," he said, and they moved on in silence, swishing through the long grass, stopping on occasion when something caught their eye, and then moving on with that familiar pang of disappointment.

"So, who rejected it?"

She closed her eyes and counted to ten, taking deep breaths to calm her nerves.

"What?"

"Who rejected it? The proposal, I mean."

"The people who run the Country Park, I suppose. The council? I mean, they own all this land. Don't they?"

"I suppose," he said. "What would an archaeological firm want out here anyway?" he asked.

She stopped in her tracks. "You're joking, aren't you?"

"No, I'm not joking."

"Lincolnshire is abundant in archaeological treasures," she said, and continued walking. Her voice had become high and bright in the way it did when she talked about things that excited her. "There's historical stuff all over the place."

"Like what?"

"Like flint tools, Anglo-Saxon settlements, Roman mosaics, coins, pottery, even medieval villages. It's all here."

"You were a doctor a minute ago," he said. "Now you're Tony bloody Robinson."

"And there's Caistor just up the road," she continued.

"Who?"

"Caistor," she said, rolling her eyes. "It's an old Roman town."

"Is that Roman?" Byrne said, mooching on with his hands in his pockets. "I never knew that." He wandered on for a little while, scrolling through his phone while he walked. "So, would the Country Park make money if the archaeologists found something? Surely it's in their interest to let them dig here?"

Campbell shrugged.

"Depends if they find anything," she said. "I mean, it's unlikely they'd find human remains. But artefacts...maybe? I don't think they could sell it, but the Park could apply for heritage funding, which would help tourism."

"Well then, they've nothing to lose?"

"Apart from some big holes in the ground? Not really."

"And some homeless voles," Byrne added, and she had to laugh. "So what do they have to hide?"

"We don't know they *are* hiding anything," she said. "All we know is that a dig was rejected."

He turned the phone for her to see, checking to make sure the guv wasn't watching.

"What's that?" she asked, stepping closer for a better look. "It's pictures from a dig?"

"Yeah, here somewhere," he said. "In the Country Park."

"I don't get it."

"They've already dug here," he said. "This was in 2012."

"So?"

"So, they approved a dig before."

"Yeah, in 2012, when I'm pretty certain environmentalists had less of a voice."

"That's not the point," he said. "They dug here before. What if it's something to do with that? What if..." his voice trailed off.

"What if what?" she asked.

"I don't know. I had it. It was on the tip of my tongue."

"You think it's about the previous archaeological dig?"

"No, I don't think anything. It was just an idea," he said. "I mean, we know she stands up for things like the environment, animals, and anything like that, right?"

"Right?"

"So, what would be the negative connotations associated with another dig? What happened during the first dig that she was trying to stop from happening again?"

"Not homeless voles?"

"No, not homeless voles, though I'm sure they'd have been a few," he said. "I don't know. Diggers and dumpers driving over the place?"

"Hardly Greta Thunburg worthy is it?"

"Alright then. What about the rubbish they'd create? They'd not only destroy the land and animal homes, but rubbish."

"I think you're trying to make a square peg fit a round hole," she told him. "What do you think about the old man?"

"The one the boys lobbed a stick at? I don't know. Seems a bit suspect, if you ask me."

"Yeah, same. Ruby can't find a link between him and Gemma Radford, though."

"Does there need to be a link?" he asked. "I mean, let's say the guv is right, and Gemma Radford was out here on some kind of animal welfare project, and then the old man comes along, sees a young woman on her own. Pretty. Distracted. Not really focusing on her surroundings. It doesn't take much of an imagination to put the pieces together, does it?"

"Where did he get the hessian sack from?" she asked. "If he was out walking his dog, why would he be carrying a sack?"

"He might not have been walking his dog. Not the first time, at least. He could have been out feeding the birds or the badgers," Byrne replied. "Or the voles." He grinned at his own joke, but something he had said resonated and he must have recognised the look on Campbell's face. "What?"

"The badgers," she said. "Everyone knows the damage they do to local wildlife."

"Do they?"

"Yes. Well, you can't really blame the badgers. It's our fault. We build houses everywhere, forcing the wildlife into smaller and smaller pockets. Then we put a ban on culling the badgers, which means that their numbers grow which, in turn, means their prey suffers."

"And their prey is?"

"Hedgehogs," she said. "They're declining in numbers. Bumblebees."

"Bumblebees?"

"It's true," she said. "They nest in the ground."

"Bees do not nest in the ground."

"They do," she said. "Specifically in loose soil, or compost, or I don't know, anything like that."

"I did not know that," he said, not for the first time that day. "Okay, so, what's your idea?"

"He was out killing them, or poisoning them, or something. Maybe he carried his poison in a hessian sack, and when Gemma Radford caught him and started giving him gyp about it, he turned on her. He might not have meant to kill her, and almost certainly didn't set out to, but we both know how these things can escalate."

"Yeah, one minute you're enjoying a walk in the country park, and next minute you've pulled a bag over some poor girl's head and she's dead. What about the semen on her chest?"

Campbell grimaced.

"I didn't say I had all the answers. It's just a hypothesis. I'm trying to work out why the old man would have done it. Maybe he runs a hedgehog sanctuary, or something."

She moved across to the tree line and peered down into the forest.

"What's up?" he asked, following her gaze.

"I'm looking for a badger set. If we find evidence of poisoning, then maybe there's something to follow."

"Or..." Byrne said, leading her into another version of events. "The old man is anti-hedgehog and bumblebees, or pro-badger, or something."

"He was feeding them?" she said, as if the idea was somehow more absurd than her own."

"Well, I don't know," he replied, throwing his arms into the air.

"I honestly don't know what we're looking for. I mean, the old man is the most obvious lead to follow, and he has to have a reason for being out here, and there had to have been some kind of reason for him and Gemma to have had some kind of altercation."

He marched off a few steps, then turned and started a new thread.

"Alright, forget the old man. The boys," he said. "Maybe Gemma was out here looking into the archaeological thing, and caught boys doing something. I don't know, putting fireworks down a badger hole." She studied him, from his face down to his feet, and then slowly she stepped back. "Or catching voles," he continued. "You know what boys are like. They..." He caught the expression on her face, and with nothing but her eyes, she led his gaze down to his feet.

His head snapped upright, and his eyes widened.

"Jesus," he said, and they both turned to the fields. "Guv!"

From around forty metres away, DI Larson looked up from where he was sifting through the tall grass.

"What is it?" he yelled. "Another vole hole?"

"If it is," Campbell replied. "Then it's a bloody big vole."

CHAPTER THIRTY-SIX

What had been, only an hour beforehand, a serene meadow merging with a wild and ancient forest, was now a buzzing crime scene.

The bird song that had filled the evening air had given way to the hum of man, whose long shadows streaked across the tall grass. It was poetic, George thought, that mankind's endless pursuit of destroying the earth, now cast a shadow of nature's beauty.

"You okay, guv?" Ivy asked.

"Yes," he replied. "Yes, yes. I'm fine. Just...I'm just keen to get going, that's all."

"Southwell wants to speak to you," she said, leading the way to the eastern edge of the meadow. "She said you should see something."

He turned from that little pocket of serenity he had sought and eyed her.

"Is it?"

"We think so," she said, leading the way.

The CSI team were huddled around the four-foot patch of

dirt Byrne and Campbell had discovered, and as they neared, Southwell saw them and stood.

"What have we got?" George asked, to which Southwell simply held up a clear evidence bag containing what appeared to be little more than a scrap of blue fabric.

"It's from a coat, we think," Southwell said, nodding. "That's our guess. A thick piece of wool. Kashmir maybe. We think *that*..." She pointed to some imperceptible clue. "We think that this tiny thread was once connected to a button."

"Is that the only clothing you found?" George asked.

"We're taking it slowly," she replied.

"Any idea how long it's been there?"

"A while. Wool might withstand the elements better than other fabrics, but it will still break down like everything else."

"Define 'a while'," George said. "How long do you think it's been here?"

She studied the hole, like an expert appraising an artefact. "From the taphonomic changes, we're looking at significant degradation. Once we've fully analysed the texture and breakdown, I'll be able to confirm it. But from experience?" She nodded, sure of herself. "I'd say more than two years, less than ten. It's hard to say. I would have thought that, given the extent of the degradation, the soil would have compacted over that time."

George looked over at the hole. How anyone might read so much from a pile of soil was anyone's guess. "Human remains?" he asked.

"Remains, yes. As to whether or not they're human, we'll have to wait and see."

"Gut?"

"Hard to say. We found two small bones. Possibly phalanges, carpal, or sesamoid bones, if they're human. The collagen is mostly degraded, and brittle, which is consistent with our time estimate, but I'm not a medical doctor. My knowledge is a little too broad to give you anything concrete."

"We have clothing and bones," Ivy said.

"I agree, it's easy to assume, but—"

"But we could work with the idea that they *are* human bones, and whoever it was, was wearing that jacket?"

"Between us? Absolutely. But you'll have to wait—"

"For your full report," George said. "Yes, I know how it works."

"I understand it's frustrating," Southwell said.

"We only just got your last report," Ivy said dryly.

George rubbed his forehead.

"We can only hope that it brings us more leads than the last one did."

"It's good to know that our hard work is appreciated," Southwell replied, her tone carrying more than a little frost.

"Again, should the bones prove to be human," George cut in, "are we able to identify them?"

"DNA?" she asked. "I would hope so." She took a deep breath, as if assembling her response in a cohesive manner. "Bone marrow carries DNA. If you or I were to drop down dead right now, our DNA could be extracted with little to no fuss. However, the environment in which the bones are stored has a significant effect on how reliable that DNA sample is. For example, the soil acidity, whether or not predators have got to them—"

"Predators?"

"The marrow," she explained. "What dog doesn't enjoy digging the marrow from a fat, juicy bone?"

"I see," George said. "But you mentioned the soil. You said it should be more compacted."

"Yes, you'd think so, wouldn't you? Again, we're running tests, but from what I can see, this isn't an old burial site."

"Define old," Ivy said.

"Years," she replied.

"So, what? Months? Weeks?"

"Could be less than that," Southwell replied. "The soil was

relatively loose, and there's very little grass growing this close to the trees. We're taking soil samples inside the hole at regular depths, which we'll compare to samples from another hole nearby. That should, if I'm right, tell us if the soil has been recently disturbed. Think of a pack of playing cards. You take out all the hearts and you stack them up in order. That's what the soil beneath our feet looks like. If you dig a hole here and fill it in again, you're basically shuffling the deck."

"Until some kind of normality is established, I presume?" George asked. "Which could take years."

"Exactly, the bugs and critters need time to do their thing. To burrow and feed, and excrete. The soil will never match its surroundings one hundred per cent, but given long enough, it'll resemble it."

"So, if that hole was dug in the last week or so...?

"Our tests will show vastly different results," Southwell replied. She relaxed a little, sensing that any technical questions they had had been asked. "What's your hypothesis? Am I right in assuming this is linked to the woman in the carpet?"

"We think so," George said. "At least, we're hoping. Otherwise, all we've done is open a large can of worms and made ourselves even busier."

"Have you entertained the idea that this was her?"

"Sorry?"

"What was her name?"

"Gemma Radford," Ivy said, her brow furrowing as what Southwell said started to permeate.

"When we were here a few days ago, you wondered what she was doing here. I mean, I don't want to overstep the mark here, but I'm just stating the obvious."

"That Gemma Radford dug this hole? Where's the spade?" Ivy asked.

"The killer took it," she replied. "Maybe he threw it in the woods? Tossed it in the river?"

"Christ," George said, then shook his head to clear his mind. "So, let me just summarise, before we run away with a mad idea. We have a hole that you think was recently dug, in which there are some bones that you believe could be human. However, you feel that the bones are older than the hole?"

"That's about the size of it," Southwell said. "Off record, of course. We'll need to run some tests."

"So, if whoever this was was nothing more than a bag of bones, Gemma Radford could have carried it?"

"I'd say so," Southwell said. "I mean, we don't even know if we'll find any more bones. The team is still digging, but even if we find all two hundred and six, which I very much doubt we will, a human skeleton, minus the organs, fats, muscles, and sinews, weighs about ten or twelve kilos, if I recall correctly from my old uni days."

"What's that in old money?"

"Twenty-two pounds, give or take," she replied, rocking her head from side to side to suggest it was a finger-in-the-air type of response.

George stared at Ivy, searching for some kind of sign that he was on the right track.

"Gemma Radford lied to her boyfriend about where she was going and who she was meeting. She could have come here. She could have carried a bag of old bones from her car and buried them here. It's plausible," he said.

"Yes, it's plausible," Ivy said, thoughtfully. "And the sack, in which she carried said bones, could also have been hessian."

CHAPTER THIRTY-SEVEN

"I don't buy it," Maguire said when George had relayed the new theory to the team. "Why would someone wrap her up in a carpet if they had a ready-made grave available?"

They had moved from the grave site and were huddled in the country park car park, where George had intended to develop a plan of attack for the following morning before setting them free for the evening.

A pigeon pecked at crumbs on the ground beside Byrne and Campbell's car, no doubt scavenging for crumbs from the protein bars the young officer seemed to live off.

"Currently," George said, "we are not treating this as a primary theory."

"I didn't realise we were categorising theories, guv," Ivy said.

"I'm not sure we have much choice," he replied. "It's been a solid day. We've achieved great things. At least three men's names struck from our list on day three. We should be proud. That's progress."

"We're still no closer, guv," Byrne said.

"No," he replied. "No, we're not, and if you're looking to apply a distance-based analogy then we're skirting around the fringes, seeking a way in, and today we've ascertained that three of the potential routes are dead ends. There are more roads in, of course, but we need some fog to clear in order to find them, and with that, I'd like to leave something with you all. Something to consider during your evenings."

"Guv?" O'Hara said coaxing him on.

"Maguire was right. Why would somebody elect to dispose of Gemma Radford's body in a carpet when, as Maguire stated, there was a ready-made grave five minutes from where we stand?" The statement, perhaps due to George's tone or phrasing, seemed to settle this time. The team considered it in silence. "I'd also like you to consider this. Our investigation so far has proved that Steven Corbyn could not have been complicit, and in the same vein, Thomas Ingram, and, though it pains me to say it, Matthew Cooper. We've learned that Thomas Ingram was not carrying a roll of carpet when he set out to dump his load over there." He pointed to the spot on the far side of the car park where the pile of rubbish had been. "Which means we're missing something," he said. "That carpet *must* have been delivered *after* the rest of the rubbish."

"It can't have," Maguire said. "We checked the CCTV in both directions."

"Could have been an enclosed van," Ivy added. How many vans did you see?"

"Jesus, hundreds," he said. "We can't possibly—"

"No," George said. "No, it would be a complete waste of resources to ask you to. But there may come a time when we need to prove that a vehicle in particular passed by one of those petrol stations, so be mindful."

"Guv," Maguire said, by way of acknowledgement.

"I'd also like you to consider Gemma Radford's reason for being here. We know it was planned, as she clearly lied to her boyfriend. Who was she meeting, if she was meeting anybody? Where did she go beforehand, if indeed she did go somewhere?"

"The pay and display parking ticket was an all-day ticket," Ivy said. "Southwell's team found it when they checked her car."

"Anything else inside that concerns us?"

"If you're asking if there was a spade and a hessian sack in the boot, then no," she replied. "The DNA was mainly hers, as you'd expect. Nothing really of note. If there was, then I'd have told you."

"Thank you," he replied. "So, that leaves us with three foggy roads to navigate. The first is that Gemma Radford came here to work on one of her activist projects, probably relating to the archaeological dig. But, there is a chance, a small chance, that she came to bury the bones that Byrne and Campbell discovered. That's a detail we'll need to flesh out if the bones are fresh enough to give us any usable DNA results. Whatever her reason for being here, she was subsequently killed and wrapped in a carpet that somebody entirely separate from all of this dumped *after* Ingram dumped Corbyn's furniture." He left a few seconds space for the team to put those facts straight in their heads. "The second was that Gemma Radford was brought here *in* the carpet, and again, dumped some time after Thomas Ingram had dumped Corbyn's furniture."

"Her car was here," O'Hara said.

"Yes, it was," he replied. "But we found no car keys on her person. Is it such a stretch of the imagination that the car was moved here some time after she had been killed?"

"But there was no indication that anybody had driven it."

"And if you were to move a car that belonged to somebody you had, for whatever reason, murdered, what lengths would you go to?"

"Gloves," she said, to which George nodded.

"The second option is a far simpler version of events and, in my experience, simple is usually the way to go. It does, however, indicate that the individual we seek is far more calculating than the suspect in option one, who, by all accounts, panicked and hid her in the first place they found."

"Alright," Maguire started. "Alright, but it doesn't answer the question, guv. I mean, let's say we're looking at option one. Gemma Radford comes here, and for whatever reason, is burying the remains of somebody—"

"Or digging them up," Campbell added.

"Right, or digging them up. Why then would somebody dump her body in a carpet five hundred metres away from a ready-made grave?"

"Because they panicked," George said. "I just told you that."

"Yeah, but...sorry, maybe I'm not articulating myself very well."

"You're articulating yourself just fine," George told him. "What you lack is empathy and imagination."

"Oh?"

George studied him, then glanced around at the rest of the team to make sure he had their attention.

"This is something you would all benefit from," he said, refocusing on Maguire. "What we do is based on facts. Data. Information that we gather. Yet, as we all know, to get to those facts, we often find ourselves coming up with ideas of what might have transpired. Were they having an affair? Who were they with? We fill in those blanks with possibilities, and then prove those possibilities right or wrong. That's how we move forward and how we get to the truth, by proving our ideas right or wrong."

"Right, I get it," Maguire said.

"But often," George continued, with the crux of his speech still to come. "We must empathise. We must picture the scene. We have to close our eyes to life's distractions, to whatever is going on around us, and *be* there. We have to *become* that person. In this instance, it's a young woman, fit and healthy, and driven by a passion to protect the underdog, be that animals, the environment, or whatever it was. We need to picture her parking right there," he said, pointing at the parking spot where they had discovered her car. "We need to imagine," he said, tapping his temple with an index finger, "her walking through the forest, along that path. Maybe with a sack and a little shovel. We need to envisage her on her knees when somebody sees her. What would she do? This fit and agile young woman? What would she do?"

"Depends who it was that found her," Campbell said.

"Right," George said, pointing at her and clicking his fingers in excitement. "So, picture somebody. Picture the old man. Run that through your mind. Let it play like an old film. Rewind it if you have to. Then run it again, but this time it's the boys who find her. How would she react then? Rewind it further, and she isn't carrying a hessian sack and a shovel, she's just off to meet somebody. The affair, maybe? Somebody to do with the archaeological dig. Picture them all. Watch the movies over and over. Experience them all from Gemma Radford's point of view. Change just one detail each time. Just one. See how it plays out. If the old man discovered her by the hole, what would she have done?"

"If she was committing a crime, and she knew it, then she would have run, surely."

"In which case, why did she have to die?"

"Depends," she said.

"And could a man in his autumn years catch up with a young and healthy woman?"

"S'pose not," O'Hara said.

"Well, in my head, that's how she got here. She ran. She was scared. Scared of being caught doing something wrong, or scared of who found her, I don't know. But she ran here, and that's why she was wrapped in the carpet over there, and not dumped in the hole five hundred metres from here."

"What if she wasn't burying the bones but had discovered them?" he asked. "The old man discovers her. Why does she have to die?"

"Because *he* put the bones there in the first place?" Maguire suggested.

"Good," George said. "Do you see what I mean, now? Do you see what we have to do? Not every answer we're looking for is written in the data. Sometimes we need to put ourselves in that world, as awful as it is. That's our job."

"And the third?" Maguire asked.

"Sorry?" George asked, not following.

"You said there were three roads in. Three foggy roads."

"Ah. Yes. Well, we have to consider the idea that neither of those options is right. We have to remember that there's always another way."

"And what is it that way? Any ideas?"

"The third road," he started, clearing his mind after delivering a much heavier speech than he had anticipated, "is the foggiest of them all." He spoke quietly, grabbing their attention with his grave synopsis. "And if I'm honest, Maguire, right now I can't even see the entrance."

"Well, if *you* can't see it, guv, how the hell are we—"

"But I can tell you this," he added, before Maguire's negativity dragged the motivation down. "The road through the fog lies with either the old man or the boys, and if neither of those lead us anywhere, then I'm afraid that third road will be our only option. And if it comes to that, then God helps us, that's all I can say."

CHAPTER THIRTY-EIGHT

Less than five minutes from the country park, George slowed the car, then pulled to a stop outside a particular house.

Ivy, roused from her thoughts by the unannounced stop, looked about the car, then at George, clearly hoping for a clue.

"Something wrong?" she asked.

"No," he replied, staring out of the window. "Well, unless you count one dead body, potentially two, and..."

"And what, guv?"

"The fog," he replied, referring to the analogy that had carried them through the team briefing. He turned to her. "We've two roads left," he said. "Let's venture down one, shall we?"

"What now?" she said, looking at her watch. "It's late, guv."

"I know, I know," he replied, reaching for the door handle. "But let's face it, we'll only go home and speculate. Why not venture down the path now?" He shoved the door open, and she met him over the car roof with an inquisitive stare. "I don't know about you, but I am done speculating for one day." Her lack of enthusiasm was as evident in her eyes as if she had remained in the car with her arms folded, like a teenager. "Am I missing something?"

"No, guv," she said, the frown softening into something like an apology. "It's just..."

"What?"

"Well, sometimes I wonder why we've got four bloody PCs, when we seem to do most of the legwork."

"I prefer to call it jaw work," he replied, which raised a smile, however brief. "We'll save the legwork for the younger lot. Trust me. Tomorrow, I want them out first thing. In the morning, I want somebody down at Gemma's workplace. Have we got the details, by the way?"

"Ruby has them," she replied.

"Right. I also want them chasing the boys."

"You somehow made that sound quite sinister, guv."

"You know what I mean. Something's missing," he said. "I want someone to talk to the Wymans and the Foxons. We know, well, we think we know what happened prior to the boys discovering Gemma Radford's body, but what happened afterwards?"

"They ran out to the road, I think," she said. "They met one of the parents there."

"Who happened to be nearby?"

"Well, they're only five minutes away, guv."

"Still. Let's take a deep dive, shall we?" he told her. "Or rather, let's have the team take a deep dive. Open it up. Search for the cracks and pull them apart."

"Right," she said. "And us?"

"Gemma Radford," he replied. "I think we've exhausted any low-hanging fruit. The clock is ticking." He tapped his watch to illustrate his point. "It's time we delved deeper into who she was. What was she up to in that final week? Who did she speak to?"

"We've put the requests for information in, guv. Phone company, bank—"

"Push harder," he said. "Or if you prefer, have Ruby push harder. In fact, do that. Tell her to lean on them. We're looking for GPS data. Where did she go?"

"That should keep her busy," Ivy replied.

"And then there's Southwell. What happened with the tests on the carpet? She said she was going to take more samples."

"I'll chase her," she said. "Although I imagine we've toyed with her schedule somewhat."

"Chase her," he told her. "Not now. In the morning. But when you speak to her, push for answers. Are those bones human?"

"Well, she said she thought they were—"

"I want definitive answers, Ivy," he said. "Ideally, I'd like a yes, they are human and the owner's name. Someone we can link to Gemma Radford or to…to whoever. If they *are* human bones, then it's highly likely that the two incidents are linked. Let's have timelines. When did they die? Were they reported missing? We can use that. We can look at missing persons. We can build bridges instead of hitting dead ends."

"Even in the fog, guv?" she said, making light of the analogy.

"To lift us over the fog," he replied curtly, but with a smile. "Come on. Let's get this little dead end dealt with, shall we?"

He shoved off the car and started down the footpath. The cottage was generously proportioned, yet carried enough of that country charm for it to feel cosy. George imagined it had, over time, been extended at several points, but with enough sympathy to its original pedigree for those additions to seem as authentic as the old front door.

"God, what is it about this street?" Ivy asked, looking up and down the empty road.

The door swung open lazily, and the homeowner, wearing a grey chequered dressing gown and loafer slippers, stared into the dusk at them.

George held his warrant card up for the man to see.

"Evening Arthur," he said. "Remember me?"

"*What on earth?*" he said, tugging the gown's belt around his waist. "Do you have any idea what time it is?"

"Oh, you know how it is," George replied. "Strike while the iron's hot and all that."

"And is it?"

"Hot? No," George admitted. "To be honest, we're just getting the fire stoked. I wonder if we might come in for a few minutes. We won't take up too much of your time. Just a few questions to help us move things along."

"I'm sorry, but what is this about? It's late."

"It's not really a conversation for the doorstep," George assured him, and offered him a well-practised smile that very few people could say no to.

Reluctantly, Williams stepped aside.

"Come on, then," he said. "I suppose you'll want tea."

"You've been watching too many crime dramas," Ivy told him as she followed George in. "We're more coffee people."

"Not for me," George added. "It's just a quick in and out."

Williams closed the door and ushered them through to a warm and stuffy lounge with the faint aroma of wet dog in the air. The place was clean and tidy, and much like George's home, the furniture was an eclectic mix: an old writing bureau, a walnut dresser, and a three-piece suite that could have been bought in the seventies. The dog watched them from his bed between the armchair and one of the sofas, and following a command from Williams' hand, he lay his head back down.

Atop the bureau were a few framed photographs of a much younger Arthur Williams with a woman in one photo, in a uniform in another, and with what appeared to be grandchildren in another. It was hard not to imagine the family as depicted in the image, during happier times, when his wife was alive.

A slight burn formed at the back of George's eyes, and he felt an odd connection to the man. They were kindred of sorts, although George's pain was still fresh.

The chink of ice in a glass brought George back to the now.

"So?" Williams said as he sipped at either a brandy or a scotch.

George had fully intended to apply pressure, perhaps setting his gentler tones to one side and pressing for detail. Detail was the key. Detail was where the answers were. The right detail would lift the fog.

"You served," George said, that gentler tone of his shining through.

"RAF," Williams replied. "Thirty odd years."

"Miss it?"

"The routine," he said. "The fellas, too."

There were a hundred different routes that George could have taken. Where was he stationed? What did he do? Did he see active duty?

"We're following up on the discussion we had on Sunday," he said, opting for a more direct path. "Just trying to match your statement with those we've had from others."

"I see," he replied, settling on the arm of the nearest sofa. "Reading between the lines, you're unable to do that."

George smiled in response, his eyes wandering back over to the photos.

"Your wife?" he asked, gesturing at the central photograph. Another officer might have picked it up. Somebody who didn't know. Didn't understand. Couldn't empathise.

"June," he replied, and whatever aggression had been loitering in the background faded into the dark rings around his eyes. "She was lovely."

"I'm sure she was," George told him, and despite every instinct in his body telling him to move on, he stayed on the topic. "I lost my wife, too."

Williams said nothing at first. His body language shifted, his shoulders slumped, and he held the glass in both hands on his lap.

"Recent, was it?" Again, George smiled in response. Had he opened his mouth to speak, he was unsure of what might have come out, and he certainly would have had no control over the pitch. "It gets easier," Williams continued. "You never forget, but you do...you do become numb to it."

"I'm not there yet," George replied, and he glanced at Ivy, who stood awkwardly to one side.

"I knew a few men once upon a time. Ex-forces, you know? Two of them had lost a leg each, and one had lost an arm."

"I see where you're going," George cut in.

"What I'm trying to say is that, yes, life is..." He drank while he thought of the right thing to say to deliver his point. "It's easier, it's better, and life is richer with them. But you *can* go on. You *can* forge a future for yourself without them."

"That's a nice way of putting it," George told him, to which Williams gave a little laugh.

"I've had a decade to think about it," he said. "And I do, you know? I never stop thinking about her. Still talk to her, if truth be told, but don't tell anyone. I'm still in possession of my faculties, wouldn't want people to think of me as that mad old man."

"You mean, like three boys you happened across in the country park?" George said, seeing the way in, and Williams' demeanour shifted in a heartbeat. "Why didn't you tell us, Arthur? Why didn't you tell us about the boys?"

"I..." he started, sighed, and drank a little more. "I don't know."

"You *were* in Snipe Dales on Sunday afternoon, weren't you? You saw those three boys moving a carpet. You even told them off."

"Yes," he said. "And did they tell you what they did?"

"They threw a stick for your dog?"

"For my dog," he scoffed. "Believe that, and you'll believe anything."

Williams's exasperated expression transformed into something more akin to depletion, but he showed no trace of regret for his actions.

"I need some help here, Arthur," George continued. "Why lie

about it? Why did you tell us you were at home on Sunday afternoon?"

Williams stood and moved across to the dresser, from which he sought the bottle and gave himself a top up, offering the bottle to George, who declined politely with a wave of his hand. Once poured, he dropped to a crouch beside the dog and lovingly stroked his forehead.

"He belonged to my sister, you know?"

"The dog?"

Williams nodded.

"Took him in when she died. Turns out he's not bad company. Not exactly the missing limb I was looking for, but..."

"More of a prosthetic?" George suggested, and Williams smiled at the comparison.

"There's something missing in today's generation, you know?" he said, shoving himself to his feet and returning to his perch. "I tell you, these kids don't know how good they have it. I served my country, you know? My father served, too. As did his dad, and his before that. That's what you did, isn't it? You did your bit, and before you did, you respected those who had. No respect, these days. None at all."

George could almost see the memories forming behind his eyes.

"You're preaching to the choir," George replied, who had a few stories that would probably shock even the old man.

"I stayed up for forty hours, you know? More than once. No sleep, in the freezing rain and howling wind. I've seen things no young lad should ever have to see." Williams leaned forward, as though sharing a secret.

"For what it's worth, there are those who are grateful. We're still out there."

"So when some young thug throws a stick at me..." he drank again.

"Arthur, if it's a matter of pride, I understand," George told him. "I don't know when it happens, but at some point in your life, you stop being invincible, don't you?" Williams looked up at him, biting down on his lower lip. "If they asked me to patrol the high street now, I think I'd go back to bed," George joked, shaking his head. "Those days are long gone." He paused for a moment to let the mood settle. "But this isn't about your pride, Arthur. Nor mine, come to think of it. It's about a young woman who lost her life. It's about paving the way for us to do our jobs, so that whoever was responsible sees justice." He moved closer to Williams, but refrained from placing a hand on his shoulder. "It's about doing your bit."

"I see," Williams said, using the dog as a distraction to his embarrassment.

"Her name was Gemma Radford," Ivy said. "Local girl."

Williams seemed to stiffen at the mention of her name - not through recognition, but perhaps at how the name made her more human, made her loved. The old man stared into his glass.

"Never heard of her."

"That surprises me," Ivy continued. "I think she was quite well known."

"Oh?"

"Yes, she was quite active. Did a lot for the local area. Wildlife causes and the like."

"I don't really get about—"

"You might have seen her out and about."

Williams shook his head.

"Like I said, I—"

"What about social media, Arthur?" she pressed. "Do you use it much?"

"Well, not really—"

"You don't follow any local groups?" George asked.

"Like what?"

"Oh, you know. The village group? Maybe you keep an eye on what's going on."

"What's going on?"

"Yes, you know, environmental debates, political groups, local people advocating for changes."

"No," he said defensively. "Should I be? I'm not one for computers."

"So you haven't commented on a Facebook post relating to fly-tipping in the area?" Ivy said, and George was grateful it was her going in hard. "Specifically, a post from Gemma Radford."

His eyes widened, and he shook his head, as if the whole thing was a misunderstanding.

"Oh, that? For God's sake," he said. "I don't know what I'm doing on there half the time. Yes, yes, I remember now."

"So you are active on Facebook?"

"Oh, I wouldn't call myself active," he replied. "In any sense of the word. Maybe I'll see that someone has written something I agree with, and I'll press the *like* button. That doesn't mean I know who they are. I just...I don't know. I just like to show my support, that's all."

"Arthur, if I may," George added, hoping to bring the heat down a few degrees. "I don't doubt that these websites and apps we're almost forced to use these days can be challenging. I'd be a hypocrite if I said otherwise."

"Well, I'm glad we got that ironed out," Williams started, but George hadn't finished.

"But, if you could look at this from our point of view for a moment. It doesn't alter the fact that, whether willingly or not, you have now straddled the truth on more than one occasion."

"Well, I'm not sure that's a fair assessment—"

"Just level with me, Arthur," he said. "That's all I ask. Did you know, or at least know of, Gemma Radford?" he asked.

"No, I don't, or at least, I didn't."

"The particular post that you engaged with was criticising Ewan Harris for his stance on fly-tipping," Ivy said. "You're aware of who he is, I'm sure."

He shrugged.

"It's hard *not* to know who he is," Williams replied.

"Do you agree with the policies he's put forward?"

"Listen, I've nothing against the man. I don't like the man's politics, but who am I to have an opinion? It's not my world anymore, is it? It's for the likes of you," he said, nodding at Ivy. "The younger lot. The next generation. Is that a crime? Is it a crime to support a local cause? You can't really lock me up for having an opinion, can you?"

From the far side of the room, Ivy's eyebrows rose and fell, as if to suggest that particular question was an entirely different debate.

"No. No, it's not," George replied. "But your responses, or lack of forthcoming information, I should say, could be construed as obstructing the course of justice."

"Excuse me? Sorry, but am I in some sort of bother, here?"

"No," George told him. "No, I'm doing my best to steer you onto the right track, that's all."

"You just said I was obstructing the course of justice. I'm just an old man, Inspector—"

"It's nothing," George told him. "You've nothing to worry about in that regard. It's one of those crimes that I prefer to call *frowned upon,* given the circumstances."

"I explained why I didn't tell you about the boys."

"I just need you to level with me," George said, and for the first time, he settled into one of the chairs, as if planting a flag in the dirt. "Why don't we start from the beginning, eh?"

CHAPTER THIRTY-NINE

"So that's it?" Ivy asked. "That's all that happened?"

"That's all that happened." Williams shrugged. "I took the dog for his afternoon walk, had my little interaction with the lads, then I went home."

"The same route you take every day?"

"Yes," he said, beginning to slur. "Out the back gate, across the field, around the country park, and back again."

"And the boys, where were they?"

"I told you, near the path to the car park."

"No, I mean, where on the path? What were their positions?"

Williams sighed loudly. "The chubby and the dark-haired ones were carrying the carpet up the hill, and the tall, skinny one was waiting at the top. Then they carried it into the trees."

"Did you recognise them?"

He scoffed. "I've seen them before, but you know what it's like these days. Nobody even says good morning any more, do they? And I daren't. Everyone's so bloody sensitive these days, aren't they? You never know if somebody's going to go for you."

"I'm afraid that's a sign of the times, Arthur," George added. "So, what prompted you to get involved? Why not just walk on, if, as you say, you never know if somebody's going to go for you? Why tell them off? Why not just walk on, or call somebody?"

"Because I care," he said passionately. "I don't want to see the place covered in all sorts of crap." He held an index finger up to accentuate his point. "There's only one reason why we've got places like Snipe Dales," he said. "The locals. People like me. People who care. People who don't want to see this place turned into a... I don't know, a shopping centre or more bleeding housing."

"The country is short of housing," George said. "But thankfully we're protected around here."

"Protected, my backside," he muttered. "Once that Harris bloke gets in, you watch. We'll have bleeding solar farms and wind farms, and every type of farm except the ones that put food on the table, that's what. And do you think it'll be for the greater good? No, course it won't. He couldn't give a monkey's about the environment. He's doing it for votes."

"Virtue signalling?" Ivy said.

"If that's what you want to call it," he replied. "In my day, we called it lying. Deception. Greed. That's what it is."

"If we could get back to your interaction with the boys," George said. "What exactly did you say to them?"

"Well, I don't recall my exact words," he started.

"The gist will be fine," George told him, sensing that his language might not be appropriate.

"I asked them what the bloody hell they were doing," he said.

"And what did they have to say?"

"The polite version? They told me to leave them alone. Then the big lad picked up a stick and threw it at me."

"Not for the dog?"

"For the dog? It was twice the size of him. Scared Otto to hell, it did. Poor little sod."

"And did you retaliate, Arthur?" Ivy asked.

"No. No, I know better than that. I got hold of the dog and we got out of there."

"Out of the country park, or just the immediate area?"

"The country park. I wasn't going to hang around after that," he said, looking at George. "Shakes you up a bit, you know?"

"Did you see anyone on the way back?"

"Not a soul," he said. "It had been raining all morning. No one was around."

"What about after the fact? Did you tell anyone about the incident? Friends? Neighbours?"

"I've already told you what I think of the neighbours."

"What then? What did you do for the rest of the afternoon?"

"We stayed at home. I looked after the dog. I was shaken up, you know? Bloody scared stiff if I'm being honest." He drank again then nursed his glass, running his thumb over the mouldings in the crystal. "Bit later, I saw the blue lights, you know? Thought it might have been those boys. Bloody knew they were up to no good, I did. That's when I met you, and well, I suppose you know the rest."

"Why not stay at home like everyone else?" Ivy asked, to which the old man pulled a bitter expression.

"I know what you expect me to say. You expect me to say something like it was because I thought the boys might be in trouble," he said, frowning. "That maybe they'd cut themselves or found a needle, and that I was concerned."

"But you're not going to say that," Ivy asked.

"No," he said. "No, if you want the truth, I went because I hoped it *was* them. I hoped they'd bloody well hurt themselves. Maybe that would teach them a lesson. There. That's why I went." He sipped his drink. "Not the sweet old man you thought I was, am I?"

"I didn't think that," Ivy replied.

"Our opinions have no bearing, Arthur," he replied. "We're

not here to judge. In fact, I think that's enough for today. I'd like to thank you for your time. You've been more than generous."

"My reasons for going back might not be what you wanted to hear," Williams said as he stood to see them out. "But if it gives you a slightly more rounded view of me, I was glad they weren't hurt. I mean it. Yes, they need a firm hand, and maybe a little accident or two might give them the reality slap they need, but deep down, I was glad. I know they're just kids and... well, times have changed, haven't they?"

It wasn't until they were crossing the threshold that George spoke the words he'd been leading up to.

"There is one more thing," he added, turning to face the old man. "If I discover any more flaws in your statement, Arthur, I'll have little option but to take this further." He held the old man's gaze. "I hope that's clear enough."

Arthur Williams stared beyond George into the evening outside.

"This country has gone to the dogs," he said eventually, as George was halfway up the path.

"Excuse me?" George said.

"You heard me. Kids run riot, bloody fly-tipping, and now the police, the people who are supposed to have our backs, become offended."

"I'm not *offended*, I—"

"You're all the same," he spat, the drink perhaps getting the better of his judgement. "You're allowing this country to fall apart. More interested in arresting an old man, aren't you?"

"I think we should leave it there, before you say something you regret," George said, starting to turn away again.

"You should be taking care of people like me. People like *my sister,* forced into a care home in her last days by her useless, scrounging kids, because no one cares about family values anymore." He threw an arm out, pointing up the street. "Then you've got scumbags like Ewan Harris doing whatever they please—"

"If you have an issue with Mr Harris's politics, then perhaps this isn't the best forum," Ivy said.

"I'm not talking about his politics," he said. "I'm talking about the man. I'm talking about his values. We need a family man speaking up for us. Someone who understands us."

"Harris *was* married," Ivy said slowly, trying to understand. "He has a child. How is he not a family man? And I'm sorry, but I fail to see what this has to do with us. Perhaps you should talk to your Facebook friends."

Her final comment seemed to drive her point home. Williams sneered, which George put down to the drink.

"You want my advice?" Williams said, leaning towards and jabbing a finger their way. "Stop worrying about old men like me, and start worrying about people like him."

CHAPTER FORTY

Bagenderby was pitch dark by the time Ivy and George arrived home. That thought hung in Ivy's mind. Not the part about it being pitch dark, but about the reference to home. Up until a few months ago, home had been a three–bed-end-of-terrace house in a coastal town that tourists flocked to during the summer months. Home had been toys scattered across carpets, soiled dinner plates on the breakfast bar, and where the draining board was rarely, if ever, devoid of cutlery, glasses, and saucepans, drip-drying.

Now, that four-letter word meant something vastly different. Home meant a bed in a room in a house that she didn't own. It meant a kettle in a kitchen that she had no control over, and where she dared not suggest keeping the coffee in a cupboard nearer the kettle, for fear of upsetting the status quo.

From that viewpoint, it wasn't a home. It was merely a bed in a room in her boss's house.

"Here we go," he said, finally finding the keyhole in the dark. He switched on the lamp by the front door and set his keys down. "Home at last, eh?"

It was as if he had read her mind.

She said nothing, and instead bent to switch on her new lamp, if only to see how well it illuminated the room. She stood back to admire her purchase.

"Is that where that's living, is it?" he asked, clearly not as enthused as her.

"I thought so," she said, kicking the cord into the corner. "I think it goes well with the cabinet. Like a contrast. It really brings out the purple fringe, don't you think?"

"Shame about the cable," George replied. "It would be nice to walk in without breaking my neck."

"What about by the bookcase?" she said, pointing further into the room. "It should go nicely with the—"

"How about in your room?" George suggested. "Might be nice for you to have a lamp in there."

Ivy's stomach dropped. His choice of words hinted at a suggestion, but his leading tone said otherwise.

"Alright," she said. "If that's what you want." He walked to the drinks cabinet, and perhaps subconsciously swayed by Arthur Williams, poured himself a measure of scotch. That single act spoke volumes. For the entire time Ivy had been staying with him, not once had he forgotten to offer her a drink.

"Guv?"

"Mmmm," he replied, taking a long sip of his drink, but keeping his back to her.

"I was just wondering what you're thinking about."

"What am I thinking?" he asked, and this time he turned to look at her, although his expression did little to welcome conversation.

"I just..." she faltered. "Would you rather be on your own?"

His tense shoulders sank, and like Williams had, he perched on the arm of a nearby chair.

"I told you that you're welcome," he told her.

"I know, it's just...well, it's just that I don't always feel it. I don't always feel like...well, it's not that I don't feel welcome, but more, you have better things to think about. More important things and that if I weren't around, then maybe you could have a clearer mind."

The softness in his eyes that followed told a story. One that he'd likely lived a hundred times before. With Grace. With somebody he actually wanted to share his space with.

"It's a curse that comes with the job," he explained. "You know that as well as me. It's not a job you can leave in the office. If it was then, maybe you'd still be with your own family."

"Thanks, guv," she said, "nothing like being kicked when you're down."

"I can't apologise for speaking the truth," he said. "And I won't. I'm sorry, I just can't, but that doesn't mean I'm not on your side. Nobody understands the pressure on us better than... well, *us*." He sipped at his drink before resting it in his lap, just as Williams had. "Grace used to say the same thing, you know? She used to ask what I was thinking. '*Where is your head at?*' she used to say. Sometimes she wouldn't say anything at all, which was often worse," he said. "Her body language, her silence. Far more potent than words."

Ivy idled across the room and poured her own drink. She raised the glass in toast, testing the water, and graciously, he followed suit.

"To never switching off."

"To never switching off," he said. "And to Grace."

He watched her, perhaps waiting for her to add, 'To Jamie.' But that was never going to happen.

"She stuck with me. Despite those silences and those times when I would come home in body only, my mind buried in whatever investigation I was working on. She stuck with me. That's how you know they're a good one. That's how you know they're worth fighting for. That's how you know where you should be."

"I don't have that luxury," she replied.

"No? You don't think you could go back to Jamie? You don't think you could make it work?"

"I doubt he'd have me even if I wanted to," she replied.

"We had our ups and downs," George explained. "Everyone does. That's what makes you stronger as a couple. It's the ups that get you through the downs, and it's the downs that make you appreciate the ups."

"Do you think those bones are related?" she asked.

"Wow," he said, with a laugh. "You need to work on your avoidance tactics."

"Do you?" she asked.

"Do *you*?" he countered.

"I think they have to be. I can't see Gemma Radford burying them, but I can understand how somebody as tenacious as her could find them. I totally see her having an inclination about them, and going for it."

"Which means that whoever killed her, likely put the bones there in the first place," he said. "Why don't you talk to him?"

"Who?" she asked.

"Jamie."

"Oh, come on, guv—"

"It's a suggestion," he said. "He's your husband. You're missing your children growing up—"

"That's his choice," she said.

"Is it?" He eyed her, his gaze somehow boring into her. "Well, maybe you're right." He finished his drink and set his glass down on the side, ready to clean in the morning. "Maybe you should just give up on them. Maybe you shouldn't fight."

"What if he isn't worth fighting for?" she asked. "I mean, what if he really doesn't want me there?"

"I don't know," he replied, as he wandered over to the stairs. "Why not take him a peace offering and see how he reacts?" He smiled warmly at her perplexed expression, then glanced at the lamp before leaving her with a knowing wink. "Goodnight, Ivy."

CHAPTER FORTY-ONE

George's driving was infuriatingly slow-steady, but slow, leaving Ivy plenty of time to catch up on her emails.

"Pippa Bell has been in touch," she said.

"Oh?"

"It looks like Katy Southwell's team have delivered her the bones."

"And?" he asked. "And what does the good Doctor tell us?"

"Human, guv," Ivy told him.

"Well, I don't think there was really any doubt, was there?"

"Not just that," Ivy said. "The bones were delivered in an evidence box."

"Standard practice—"

"No, guv," she said. "They were contained in a sack, and the sack was in the box."

George's mouth fell open, but no words followed at first. And then a single word summarised his thoughts.

"Hessian?"

"Hessian," she said, watching the muscles in his face twitch, contort, contract and expand. "They're looking into the DNA."

"Why don't you tell me what you're thinking?" he asked, eventually. "What does this tell you?"

"It increases the odds of the bones being linked to Gemma Radford's murder," she said. "But, those bones are old. It would be almost impossible to evidence that exact sack being used to aid Gemma Radford's murder."

"No, I agree," he said. "It's not like our killer could have emptied the bones to use the sack, more like he had, or has, several of those sacks. Any identifiers? Any branding or labels? Manufacturers often brand them—"

"Nothing," she said. "Just a plain old generic hessian sack."

"And why do you think he, presuming it is a he, used those sacks?" he asked.

"Because he has them in great supply?"

"Maybe," George said. "But I'm leaning towards another reason. Several reasons in fact. First of all, due to the fabric nature, there is very little chance of them retaining fingerprints, unlike a plastic bag, for example."

"True," she said. "DNA maybe?"

"No, he's too careful for that," George continued. "But I think the primary reason he chose to use hessian sacks is the very same reason that gardeners use them. They are strong, durable, natural, and above all, they provide airflow so that potatoes or other vegetables don't sweat and rot."

"And so that body parts can decompose?"

"Which suggests something else, entirely," he said. "You may fit a full set of human bones into one of those sacks, but you wouldn't fit an entire human inside?"

"What are you saying?"

He grinned to himself, but seemed unsure.

"I think I'm going to mull that one over for a while."

"Guv," she started. "About last night. I've been thinking about what you said—"

"Actually, I've been thinking about what *you* said, Ivy," George interrupted, still staring ahead.

"Last night?"

"No, at the beginning of the investigation? You were right. Sometimes we're so busy thinking about suspects, witnesses, motives, and whatever, that we lose focus of the actual victim. Gemma Radford. Who she really was." He turned to her, his gaze gentle but unwavering. "So let's just focus on Gemma today, shall we?"

The message was abundantly clear. Home was home, and work was work.

"Alright, guv," she said, swallowing. "Yeah."

Having broken free of the winding lanes, the road towards Horncastle was long and fairly straight, an easy drive slowed only by speed limits protecting the villages that dotted the way. Ivy stared out the passenger window as hedgerows and fields streaked by, a blur of green like paint dragged across glass...suddenly broken by a flash of blue and white.

She turned in her seat and just caught sight of an old mattress tucked beside a farmer's gate.

"Did you see that?" she asked, turning back to see two more interruptions of white amongst the sea of green. "Slow down. There's another one." George eased off the accelerator as they passed two fridges amid a heap of broken furniture and torn bin bags strewn across the roadside. "They weren't there yesterday, were they?" she asked.

"I don't think so," George said, watching the fly-tipped pile grow smaller in the rear-view mirror.

"Well, either Thomas Ingram is a very busy man, or this problem is much bigger than we thought."

Ivy sat back, welcoming the distraction from her and George's home life. Her mind kept turning over the image of the rubbish. They drove on in silence, yet their thoughts were no doubt entwined.

"Who has two fridges?" she asked slowly.

George glanced at her. "Sorry?"

She sat up straight, her body realising something before her mind caught up.

"Who owns two fridges to throw away?" she said. "I mean, you get a new fridge, what? Every ten years? You don't keep the old one all that time, do you? And what house in the UK has two fridges at one time?"

"What's your point?"

"My point is, you get rid of one fridge at a time."

"Okay..."

"And that last pile," she said, pointing a thumb over her shoulder, "had two fridges. I'm sure of it."

George shuffled in his seat.

"Maybe it's a popular...spot," he said, his voice slowing, no doubt the same thought was developing in his mind as that which Ivy was nurturing.

"The carpet was added," she said. "Take that last pile. All it takes is for one lazy scumbag to start a pile, and everyone jumps on the bandwagon."

"Not everyone, Ivy. Most of us are respectable."

"You know what I mean. The carpet had to have been added."

"But we surmised that," he said.

"And now we know," she replied. "The only way we're going to know who dropped that carpet there is to have the team locate every van that passed the petrol stations to the East and West of the country park."

"Too much," he said.

"I know. It's just...it's so bloody infuriating."

"Not really," he said. "We'll find them another way, and when we do, we'll use the footage from those petrol station cameras to prove they were in the area at the right time. It's not a lost cause."

"Even then," she continued. "We'd have to prove that Gemma was in the carpet when it was dumped."

"Ah," he said, grinning. "Remember what I said to the team yesterday? About our options?"

"Option one being that Gemma drove there, and the killer dumped her in the carpet he found, and option two being that she was taken there with the carpet, and her car was moved afterwards?"

"That's right. I'm going with option one."

"You're ruling option two out?"

"No, I'm prioritising my resources," he replied. "We exhaust the possibilities that she drove herself to the country park, and only when we have no further avenues to follow in that scenario, do we move onto option two. I laid in bed thinking about it last night. We simply don't have the manpower to pursue both lines of enquiry."

"Can't we ask for more?"

"Not likely," George replied. "I'm still gearing up to request a coffee machine in our new office. Me requesting more beating hearts and thumping minds would probably knock Detective Superintendent Long off his chair. I'd have to rouse him back to reality with smelling salts."

"So we focus on her driving herself there?"

"For the time being," he said. "We laser in on what we have before us. We visualise it, take the most logical and plausible scenario, and drill down. When we hit a dead end, we pull back and drill into the next scenario. One of those avenues has a light at the end of it."

"Are you seeing how many analogies you can use in a single investigation, guv?"

"I'm trying to make sense of what I can only describe as *a complete mess*," he said. "Just focus. Ingram dumped Corbyn's furniture. We know that, and when this is all over, we'll pass that little nugget on to the right team. We assume that the carpet was dumped after Ingram had started the pile. What does that tell you?" She shook her head and considered the piles they had just passed. "All it takes is for one person to start the pile," George added, coaxing her on.

"Whoever dumped the carpet had to know that the pile was there?"

"There we go," he said. "Now, you mentioned a van or a truck having to pass either the Horncastle petrol station or the Spilsby petrol station, but that's not entirely true, is it?"

"They could live closer," she said, to which he simply grinned. "Jesus. They could—"

"Walk their dog there?" he suggested. "Or they could have, I don't know, collected their son from there who might spend his days at the country park with his friends."

"Now we're getting somewhere," George said. "What we need to do is establish if our killer dumped the carpet or not. We know that Gemma Radford was murdered between 3 p.m. and 4 p.m. on the Sunday. The CCTV footage of Ingram's truck suggests he dumped the rubbish on Saturday night or early Sunday morning, which can't be proved, of course, but does help us eliminate Ingram. But, it also means that if he did dump the rubbish during the night, then to find whoever dumped the carpet, we're looking for a local who visited the country park anytime Sunday morning or early afternoon. My guess would be the early morning, as dumping a carpet would likely draw unwanted attention."

"Not necessarily, guv," she said, recalling the heap of old furniture in the trees near the car park. "If it was an enclosed van, then they could have backed into the spot and opened the rear doors up. It wouldn't have been too hard for them to drag the carpet into the trees without being seen. They'd have to keep an eye out, of course, but it's plausible."

"Ha, it's working then, is it?" George replied.

"Guv?"

"You're picturing the scene play out," he said with a wry smile. "And your conclusion?"

"My conclusion is that..." She assembled the elements in the right order. "Ingram dumped the first load. A local spots the rubbish, maybe while walking their dog or…"

A thought struck her, and she sought answers from her phone. "Ivy?"

"Hold on," she said, scrolling through Facebook. "There. Here it is." She held the phone up for him to see, and he glanced, but wasn't one to take his eyes off the road for too long.

"You'll have to narrate," he told her.

"It's a Facebook group," she said. "There's a picture of the rubbish Ingram dropped, posted at 12:15 on Sunday afternoon."

"Is the carpet there?"

"No," she said. "Not that I can see."

"Who posted it?"

She read the poster's name and dropped the phone to her lap.

"Oh God," she said, sighing.

"Ivy?"

"Gemma Radford," she said. "Gemma Radford took the photo and posted it on Facebook."

"What? Why have we only just seen this?"

"I don't know," she replied. "I don't know. We've been so bloody preoccupied with everything else, and there are dozens of these groups. We'd need somebody on social media full time to go through them all."

"Okay, okay," George said. "We can't change the past. Don't worry. Let's just work with the facts. We now know for certain that Gemma arrived at the country park of her own accord. She arrived before the carpet had been dumped."

"Yeah, and she was at the country park for at least three hours before she died."

"And she was at the country park for at least three hours before she died," he repeated, agreeing with her. He glanced at Ivy. "What the bloody hell was she doing for three hours?"

"Looking for a bag of old bones?" Ivy suggested.

"We don't know for certain she knew about the bones," he

replied. "All we do know is that she was curious as to why the dig was rejected."

"Suspicious, you mean?"

"Let's start with curious," he said, "until we have a finger to point that curiosity at."

"So, she was investigating why the archaeological dig was rejected?" Ivy countered. "What if she got too close to finding out?"

"Three hours," he said to himself. "Three hours in a country park with no dog to walk. It rained, too. Can't have been pleasant."

"And during that time, somebody came along in a van and dumped the carpet," Ivy said.

"Okay," George continued, and Ivy had the impression they were sharing a vision of sorts. "Okay, Gemma Radford is seeking answers. She gets too close to understanding. She's caught, or found near the bones. Maybe she's recognised?"

"And she's chased," George said, nodding along.

"Right. She's chased. He catches her in the car park, or near it, at least. There were no car keys on her body, so maybe he caught her fumbling to get into her car to make her escape."

"Right, and the boys said there was nobody about. The killer grabbed her, pulled a sack over her head..."

"Hold on. What sack?" she asked. "Why would he have another sack with him?"

"Aha," he said, one step ahead of her. "Now you see my conundrum."

CHAPTER FORTY-TWO

From first impressions, the iron gates that stood before them seemed imposing, almost like a Victorian workhouse or an orphanage.

The sign read *Safe Haven Animal Shelter* but offered little in the way of warmth. There were no little dog or cat outlines or painted paw prints-just those four words in New Times Roman font to provide visitors and guests with the knowledge that they had arrived in the correct place.

There were six red-brick buildings, and from where O'Hara was standing, each was marked with a sign as bland as that on the main gate depicting their purpose, such as *Reception, Kennels, Yard, Store,* and so on.

Across the car park, they watched a young couple walking together, adoring the tiny ball of fluff in the woman's arms.

"Look at them," she said. "So happy. People live such different lives, don't they?"

"Different to us? I suppose they do. I'd hope they do, anyway," Maguire replied, climbing out of the car. "The world would be a cynical place if they didn't." She caught him following her gaze. "Have a pet, did you?" he asked as they walked towards the shelter. "As a kid, I mean. Did you have a wee cat or something?"

"Dogs. We had dogs," she replied. "My parents always said they'd never get a new one when the old one died, but they always did. They could never go for long without one."

Maguire smiled. "What kind of dogs?"

"Labradors. Always Labradors," she said, as memories of their ruffled ears and long walks across Clifton Downs came flooding back. "Any colour. Black, golden, chocolate. They just rotated," she added with a laugh.

"But you never had one as an adult?"

"It never seemed possible with the job. And I doubt there's one in my future." She peered across at him. "Adrian is more of a cat man."

"I thought you weren't that serious with him?" Maguire frowned. "I thought he was just *a* bloke?"

O'Hara shrugged.

"We'll see."

"Fine, so why don't you get a cat?" he asked.

"Because," she sighed, "if I had a cat, I would just resent it not being a dog."

Maguire laughed. "Fair enough."

"What about you? Did you ever have pets?"

He made a disgusted face. "Never. Dirty, needy, smelly things that bother you as soon as you get home from a long day and demand your attention? Couldn't think of anything worse. No, thank you." O'Hara didn't reply. "Probably why I'm single, too, come to think of it."

Gravel crunched underfoot as they followed the narrow path leading up to the shelter's reception. A low chorus of barking began before the building even came into full view, as if the dogs inside had already caught wind of their scents.

The structure itself was plain and practical, with sun-faded signage above the entrance reading, *Adopt, Don't Shop.*

"Preaching to the choir, aren't they?" Maguire pointed out.

The air thickened with the scent of dogs and disinfectant, and was alive with the sounds of barking, panting, and the occasional yowl.

Inside, it wasn't too dissimilar to the visitor's area in a prison. Steel cages rattled somewhere in the distance, and the inmates taunted each other, winding each other up into a frenzy. A young man in hiking boots struggled to lead a tangle of leashes past them and out the front door, and behind the reception desk a frizzy-haired woman eyed their uniforms curiously.

"Good morning," she said.

"Morning," O'Hara said, taking the lead. "We're looking for somebody in charge. A manager, or...I'm sorry, I'm not sure of the hierarchy here."

"You can talk to me," she said. "I'm the manager. Charlotte Hudson."

She slid a card across the desk and waited for some kind of explanation.

"It's concerning a colleague of yours. A Gemma Radford?"

"Oh yes, Gemma. I'm afraid she's not in today, though," she replied. "Hasn't been in for a couple of days."

"We're not here to talk *to* Gemma," O'Hara clarified. "We need to talk to you *about* Gemma."

"Oh? What about her? Is she in some kind of trouble?"

"You haven't heard, then?" Maguire asked, to which the woman's inquisitive stare became slightly concerned.

"No," she replied, sliding a pile of paperwork from one side of the desk to the other so she could lean on her elbows. "What am I supposed to have heard?"

"We thought that Matthew Cooper might have been in touch with you."

Only then did the receptionist stop what she was doing and look at them properly.

"Why would someone have been in touch with us?" she asked.

O'Hara took in the chaos, the mound of paperwork, the barking dogs, the lack of staff and made a judgment call. They had to find out eventually. If Matthew Cooper was too busy in the pub to handle the practicalities of Gemma's death, then she would have to do it herself.

"Is there somewhere we could speak privately, Charlotte?" she asked.

"I'm afraid I can't leave the front desk, but it's okay. Nobody's here." She eyed them both. "Are you going to tell me what's going on here?"

"I'm sorry to tell you this," O'Hara started. "But Gemma's body was discovered on Sunday afternoon."

She watched as Charlotte processed the news, shaking her head a little in denial, but eventually succumbing to the truth.

"She's dead?"

"I'm afraid so," Maguire said. "We're conducting the investigation into her death."

"An investigation? Why would..." her voice trailed off as she answered her own question. "You mean, she was—"

"We are treating her death as suspicious, Miss Hudson."

"We hadn't heard from her," she said. "We just thought..." Charlotte trailed off, as though she'd already forgotten how they'd justified Gemma's absence, as though her judgement and guilt now consumed her mind.

"Is there somewhere quiet we can speak, Charlotte?" O'Hara asked

"Yeah..." she said, and in a pang of clear-mindedness, she placed a sign on the counter with trembling hands: *Be right back. Just stepped out for a paws*. "Follow me."

She led them along a corridor to the left of the reception desk that only added to O'Hara's comparison to a prison, with cells on either side of a narrow walkway, and the prisoners hurling abuse at the guards. Only one dog, a red-coated Irish setter, remained calm, peering up at them with large, glistening eyes.

"Hey, buddy?" Maguire said, crouching to face it. "What's your name then?"

"That's Maggie," Charlotte told him, watching the dog lick his knuckles. "She likes you." She waited a moment, then coaxed him away. "Shall we?"

"Sorry," he said, standing and pulling his eyes away. "Coming."

"When was the last time you saw Gemma?" O'Hara asked as Charlotte led them into a waiting room at the end of the corridor, where the smell of wet dog was pungent, and most likely permanent.

"She left here on Friday evening," Charlotte replied.

"And you expected her back in on Monday?"

Charlotte swallowed, her eyes welling. "Yes."

"Did you hear from her over the weekend at all?"

"No, but that wasn't unusual," Charlotte said. "Don't get me wrong, we all get on, but we're not close. Not like that."

"Did Gemma tell you what she was planning to do that weekend? Is that the sort of thing she might have shared?"

"I think I asked her when we were closing up on Friday," Charlotte said, frowning, trying to grasp at a memory she probably never thought would be important to remember. "I think she mentioned going for a walk."

"Did she say where?"

"No. No, it was just small talk. I was just being polite."

"Was Gemma well-liked at work?" Maguire asked, to which Charlotte smiled sadly.

"Everyone loved Gemma, the staff, the customers, the dogs. The dogs, especially. She was a natural with them. She was made for the job."

O'Hara leaned forward.

"Why?"

"She was patient. She was... empathetic and caring," Charlotte started, her eyes glazing as she remembered her colleague. "Like she understood what the dogs had been through and felt their pain. Not everyone can handle that. It takes a certain somebody. But she was strong. She never shied away from hard work, cleaning the kennels, handling waste, or whatever needed to be done. And she *cared*. She really did care. Deeply. If a dog needs to be euthanised, she'd be there, steady and quiet, until the end. She wouldn't let it go alone."

O'Hara swallowed her emotions. She only hoped her colleagues would speak so highly of her if the time ever came.

"We understand that Gemma was interested in wildlife protection and conservation," she said. "She was part of various activist groups. Did she ever talk about that with you?"

"Oh yes," Charlotte laughed. "She loved to go on about all that. Always riled about something. It's not that I don't agree, don't get me wrong. It's just, well, I never knew how she had the energy to care so much about it. It's enough to just get through the day here."

"Did she ever mention anyone particular? A member of one of those groups?"

Charlotte shook her head, thinking. "No, she didn't talk about anyone in particular. Just the problems in general. We're all pretty busy here. There's not a lot of time for chatting."

"And you're sure Gemma didn't come to work any time during the weekend? You're open during the weekend, aren't you?"

"Yes, but I was here all weekend, and I'm sure she didn't come in. Not even for a visit."

"Have you ever met her boyfriend, Matthew Cooper?" Maguire asked.

Charlotte sighed sadly.

"To be honest with you, I didn't even know she had a boyfriend."

"Oh?" "O'Hara said. "That's odd, isn't it?"

"Not really," she replied. "Everyone has a private life, don't they?" She smiled warmly at them both. "Listen, no matter how hard life seems, when you walk through those doors..." she pointed back the way they had come, "it's all overshadowed. Most of these dogs will be euthanised. What you're seeing here today is their last days, especially the older ones. The puppies are usually fine, we rehomed one this morning. But more often than not, the dogs we care for are in their winter years. We give them love, and that's all we can do."

"It must be challenging," O'Hara said. "We face similar issues."

"So you'll understand then?"

"No," O'Hara said. "No, we talk. We have to. You have to know the person you work with is human. You have to speak about the normal things in life. If we didn't, well, we'd go a bit mad."

The woman shrugged.

"Gemma was a passionate woman. You could see that in the way that she worked. The way she cared for the dogs. And yes, when she discussed local problems, those things that were important to her. She talked about the things she cared about."

"But not Matthew Cooper? Not her boyfriend?"

"No," Charlotte replied. "Makes me a bit sad. To think that I never knew her as I thought I did."

"Surely, if she spoke about those matters close to her heart, she would have mentioned Matthew?"

"I'm just saying," Charlotte said. "She talked about her passions. More than that. She *did* something about it. That's rare these days, isn't it? Someone who doesn't just complain about life but tries to make a difference?" She shook her head, still processing the news. "Look, I know that she would do anything for these dogs. She wouldn't let one die alone. She had to be there, even though she came out in tears every single time. And if she was willing to endure the pain of watching a helpless animal die, just to offer it comfort in its final moments..." Charlotte brushed away a tear. "Well, then, I can only imagine what she might have done for the people she loves. Gemma Radford was a good person. No, not just good. She was a bloody saint."

CHAPTER FORTY-THREE

"Good morning," George said as he approached the man behind the desk. "We're looking for a Ben Holloway?"

In his forest-green fleece and cargo trousers, the man seemed somewhat out of place in an office, and would have been more at home outside, which, judging by the state of his desk, he likely was.

They shook hands firmly, the man's rough thumbs scratching George's skin.

"You found him," he said.

"Ah, well, that was easier than I'd imagined," George told him, presenting his warrant card. "Detective Inspector Larson and this is my colleague, Detective Sergeant Hart."

Ivy shook the man's hand, and slightly unnerved, the man offered them seats, then shifted some paperwork to one side so he could sit and lean on his desk.

The office was small and modestly furnished with a pine desk, pine chairs, and walls decorated with posters of local maps and wildlife species, including intricate drawings, diagrams, and their Latin names.

"Thank you," George continued, focusing his attention on the dark eyes framed by a mass of thick, unkempt hair that hung over much of Holloway's face. "I'm sure you're aware by now of the incidents over at Snipe Dales Country Park."

"News travels fast," Holloway replied. "Naturally, we're keen to work alongside your teams. Snipe Dales is a protected area, as I'm sure you're aware."

"I'm sensing an undertone," George replied, studying the man's expression for an indication of his thoughts.

"Snipe Dales is a wildlife habitat, and, well, not to put too fine a point on it, your team haven't demonstrated much understanding of how preservation works."

"I'm sure they've been careful, Mr Holloway," George replied, matching his tone. "But this is a murder enquiry, and while we respect the area, we do have to do our jobs."

"Did you know that it's a crime to disturb a badger set?" Holloway said. "What am I saying? Of course you do—"

"We haven't touched a badger set. Why would we?"

"You don't really have to touch them to disturb them. But digging a hole in close proximity can be enough to alarm them." He watched them both, and then settled on George. "Your team dug a hole on the edge of the forest, twelve feet from an established badger set."

"Well, if that's the case, then it was an oversight—"

"There's also a police cordon tied to trees further in the forest. Just left there, flapping around in the breeze. Plastic tape. Plastic?"

"Again, I'll see to it that—"

"None of this looks particularly good, Inspector," Holloway continued. "And it's certainly not good for the wildlife. I dread to think of the fuss locals would make if a deer or a badger is found to have choked on some plastic tape that the police just left lying around."

"I think that's a bit far-fetched—"

"Whilst I don't want to hinder your progress, I do think that perhaps any further activity should be agreed, somehow."

"Red tape?" Ivy said.

"Ivy, leave it—"

"No, guv. Sorry," she said, focusing on Holloway. "At least one young lady has died. Do you have any idea of the bureaucracy we have to deal with through the police force alone? How many hoops we have to jump through just to get our jobs done? How do you think it would look when we fail to gain a conviction, and our press release suggests that, due to the local Environment Agency, we were unable to investigate in a timely manner?"

"I'm sorry, but I don't see the need—"

"No, because there is no need," Ivy said. "We came here with the best intentions, and if you want to spout the law at us, then you should know that Snipe Dales may be protected, but it's publicly owned land. That means that we must be allowed to do our jobs, and any attempt to hinder our investigation will be seen as obstruction."

"I see," he said.

"Perhaps we should start again?" George suggested, offering Ivy a look he hoped would both thank her for her input and request that she calm down. He focused on Holloway again. "I can't do anything about the hole near the badger set, but I can ensure that no trace of our presence is left behind when we're finished."

"That would be appreciated," Holloway said.

"In short, the sooner we sort this out, the sooner you can have your country park back."

"Again, that would be appreciated."

George sat back in his chair and folded one leg over the other, hoping to put the man behind the desk at ease.

"I used to go there with my wife, you know?" George said with a smile, establishing a common ground. "It's a beautiful place."

Holloway smiled back, or at least his beard moved.

"We think so."

"How long have you managed it?" George asked.

"Five years," he said proudly. "Give or take."

"Five years? Oh, you must be very familiar with its history?"

"That's the beauty of places like Snipe Dales, Inspector," he replied. "There is no history. Aside from the footpaths, the toilets, and the car park, it is exactly as nature intended."

"I was thinking more recent history," George said. "In particular, the various archaeological searches that have taken place in the last decade?"

"Ah, yes. There's been quite a few." He leaned forward. "You know, they found a Neolithic hand axe there once."

"I didn't," George said. "But that explains why the teams would want to return."

"Sorry?"

"The archaeologists," George told him. "They recently requested a revisit."

Holloway's brow furrowed, and he began flicking through various folders.

"That's news to me."

"Perhaps the request was lost in that pile of paperwork," Ivy said, to which George offered her another warning glare.

"Is it something you could have missed?" he asked.

"No," he replied, leaving his paperwork for another time. "It just might not have reached me yet. You're not the only ones who suffer with red tape."

He smiled smugly at Ivy, who shook her head, but bit her tongue.

"Are you aware of recent complaints about fly-tipping in the area?" George started, to which Holloway laughed.

"Am I aware?" He rubbed his beard. "It has been the bane of my existence."

"Oh? How so?"

"I receive multiple calls every week complaining about fly-tipping, Inspector. It's a bloody endemic."

"They complain to you?"

"Of course," he said simply. "People like to inform us. I expect they think we have the resources to prosecute every instance."

"You have that power?"

"We have the power, not the resources."

"We're more alike than you might think," George joked, but neither Holloway nor Ivy saw the humour. "How long has it been a problem?"

"The fly-tipping?" he asked, his beard rising again. "Or the informing us about the fly-tipping?"

George saw a man who had to deal with members of the public just like he did, knowing full well the trouble it caused.

"Both."

Holloway sighed and scratched his mass of hair.

"Fly-tipping has always been a problem, and is one that will only get worse as the population increases and respect for our countryside diminishes. It's cultural."

"Along with good manners and values," George added, to which Holloway nodded his agreement.

"Of course, there's the pollution from old fridge freezers, loss of wildlife habitat, the safety hazard to wildlife, and the financial cost of clearing it up. So, yes, it's getting worse. Hence the increase in complaints."

"Why is it getting worse?" Ivy asked.

"We can't say exactly. Cost of living, people can't afford the tip fees, or a lack of recycling facilities." Holloway spoke articulately, as though comfortable educating a room of people. "The fact is that we need more affordable waste management solutions, better enforcement, and greater public awareness. If we aren't going to get the resources we need to deal with the problems, then the public needs to be empowered."

"That's a dangerous proposition," George said.

"It's a dangerous problem," Holloway countered, and as much as George could have continued to prove that solution unfeasible, it was not the reason for their visit.

"Are you aware that the lock on your car park gate has been broken?" George asked, as Holloway nodded. "You're aware of this?"

"On Saturday night, yes," he said. "And that's the council's remit, though you wouldn't think it. Why on earth people would report a broken padlock to the Environment Agency is beyond me."

"Is that the first time?"

"No, sadly not. It's happened a few times. We had a problem with a certain travelling community a few years back."

"And before that? No fly-tipping inside the park?"

He shook his head.

"People had dumped on the outskirts of the park. You know, out on the road, but not *in* the car park itself. But it's quiet at night, and when the gates are closed, it's secluded. Ideal territory for them, I suppose."

George glanced at Ivy, then back at Holloway, who saw the shared look and waited patiently for George to explain it.

"Have you heard of a company called MoveRight, Mr Holloway?"

The man's face darkened, his bushy eyebrows coming together in a scowl. "I've heard of them, yes. They've been publicly accused of dumping on our land. You think they did this?"

"We can't confirm it," George said. "Yet."

"Is there anything you have in place?" Ivy asked. "To prevent fly-tipping in the country park?"

"No offence," Holloway said gently, "but you sound just like the people who ring me to complain every day. I don't know what more they expect me to do. I can't magic up a budget for CCTV, and even if we were allocated funds, we'd need more power and more cabling, which would involve trenches and a whole upheaval that none of us really wants. Better to cut the head off the snake, that's their idea."

"Whose idea?"

"The local council's. They're the ones who are meant to clean it up," Holloway said, hearing his voice rise and making an effort to lower it. "That's the problem. The people inform us, and we inform the council. We're the middleman taking all the flak."

"Oh, so you informed them, did you?"

"I've got them on speed dial," he replied, raising his mobile phone to support his statement. "As soon as the barrage of calls came through on Sunday morning, we did what we always do."

"And what's that?"

"We complained to our local councillor."

"Who's your local councillor?" Ivy asked, perhaps sensing George's intrigue.

"Hold on," he said, before Holloway could answer. "You report all instances of fly-tipping to the local council, correct?"

"Yes, of course, I—"

"And may I just take a step back a bit? The request for the archaeological dig. You said it might not have reached you yet, in which case I assume there's a process to be followed."

"That's right," he said. "The request is put in front of the parish committee, who then approach the council—"

"The council?"

"Yes. If they're in agreement, then it goes through us, so we can work alongside the team to ensure—"

"I need a name," George said. "Who's the local councillor that would be responsible for these incidents?"

Holloway shook his head, as if the answer was common knowledge.

"You should know the answer to that one, Inspector," Holloway said. "It's Harris. Ewan Harris."

CHAPTER FORTY-FOUR

The coin turned in the air before Byrne's eyes. Beyond it, through the passenger window, two houses dominated the view. But inside the car, the spinning coin would determine the rest of his day.

It fell, as the law of gravity dictated, and landed in Campbell's open palm. She balled a fist and slapped it down onto her other hand, keeping it covered while they agreed terms.

"Hippies or happies?" she asked.

He studied her grin, and she watched in anticipation of his answer.

"Heads," he said. "If it's heads, I get the happies."

"Heads you get the happies," she repeated, slowly revealing the coin.

And then that grin of hers broadened as the tails side came into view. He let his fall back onto the headrest. "It's hippies for you, I'm afraid."

"Alright," he said. "Alright, I'll take the Wyman's, you take the Foxons, but if you hear screaming, you'd better come running."

"You're not scared, are you?"

He shoved the door open and started to climb out, but paused long enough to explain. "They won't be my screams," he said.

He could see why the two boys had become best friends. It was the kind of street that defied modern times, where kids could still pop next door to their mate's house to ask if they wanted to play football in the middle of the road or build a den in the nearby country park.

"Meet you back here in half an hour?" he called out, as they each approached their respective houses.

"Let's hope they're not home," she said.

"They said they'd be back this morning," Byrne started, eyeing the windows for movement. "If they're not back yet, I'll drive back to Skegness and drag them here myself."

"Just keep your head," Campbell warned quietly.

He turned to meet her concerned gaze. "What's that supposed to mean?"

"I mean, don't let them bother you," she said. "They just have a different parenting style, that's all."

"They don't *have* a parenting style," he muttered. "Some people should never be parents."

"Well, thankfully, the government doesn't control that part of our lives, just yet."

"Yet," he replied.

The house was similar to the caravan in Skegness, with sandalwood incense spiralling out of the open windows, wind chimes clanging, and prayer flags tied to the crab apple tree in the front garden. The scene was a picture of peace. Even the door knocker had been fashioned from brass to resemble a chubby laughing Buddha.

He banged on the door with his fist, ignoring the symbol of peace, and before long, the sound of bare feet slapping on a wooden floor came.

The look on David Wyman's face when he recognised Byrne was one of inevitable disappointment.

"Ah, it's you," he said, to which Byrne simply forced a smile. "Well, come on in, then. Let's get this over with."

He wore a similar outfit to the one he had worn the previous day, a beige tunic over which his long, grey ponytail dangled down its back. Byrne followed him inside, inwardly remarking that he had got further than they had at the caravan.

"Is that him, darling?" Emily Wyman called from the kitchen.

"Yes, it is," David replied as they walked through the open-plan living room to the kitchen.

Byrne looked out the sink window at the garden with open views across to Snipe Dales Country Park.

"We expected you at the crack of dawn, PC..."

"Byrne."

"That's right. Where's the other one?"

"Solving a crime," he replied curtly, cutting the line of questioning off to maintain control.

"Well, you should know that after careful consideration and much deliberation," Emily said from beside the kitchen worktop, "we feel that we should let you interview our son, but only as a witness."

"That's all we ask," he said flatly.

"Byrne?" David said, as if to himself. "You know that's an Irish name, don't you?"

"My parents mentioned it."

"Some say it comes from *bran*, meaning raven, but I always connected it to *brón*, meaning sorrow. Seems more appropriate, don't you think?"

"I've never really given it—"

"Are you in tune with your Celtic heritage, Officer Byrne?"

Byrne held his breath, counting to ten in his mind, then offered an end to that particular question.

"No," he said flatly. "My family has lived in Lincolnshire for generations. I'm as much a local as you."

"I see." David looked disheartened, but Byrne was in no mood to indulge in the man's reaching conversation when he was there to discuss his child's recent trauma.

"I'm afraid there was a miscommunication," Emily explained, pouring a glass of orange juice that she carried over to the kitchen table, where she stopped and looked up at the door. "Oh, hello dear."

Byrne turned to find Oscar Wyman staring at him, wide-eyed.

"Hello, Oscar," he said. "How are you bearing up?"

The boy shrugged and leaned on the doorframe, immersing himself in his oversized hoody.

"See," his mother continued. "I thought David had left the note for Oscar telling him where we'd gone, and David thought I had." She laughed weakly. "It was a harmless mistake, and the Foxons are lovely. They're very good neighbours."

"I see," Byrne said, not wanting to make a deal out of it.

"So, there's really no need to take that any further," Emily pressed. "He's fine. Look at him. He's a fit young lad."

Byrne said nothing and instead drew a chair from the table, which he offered to Oscar.

"Take a seat, Oscar," he said, pulling a chair out opposite. "I just need to go over a few things with you."

"Maybe we should have some tea?" David suggested. "Emily?"

"Tea would be good," Byrne replied, while Oscar took the seat with obvious trepidation.

"Green, rose and lavender, or nettle?"

"Sorry?"

"Tea," Emily said. "Green, rose lavender, or—"

"Yorkshire," he replied hopefully. "White, no sugar. Thank you."

Emily shared a worried look with her husband, and Oscar laughed to himself.

"We don't really do caffeine," Emily explained with a sweet smile.

"It's fine. I'm not that thirsty, anyway," he replied and nodded at Oscar. "Mind if we crack on?"

Emily carried two herbal teas to the table, and was joined by

David. The two sat as spectators, each toying with their teabags to expedite the brewing process.

Oscar sat alone, but seemed unfazed.

"Oscar," Byrne started, "you know why I'm here, don't you?"

"To take my statement," he said, then sipped at his orange juice nervously.

"That's right. You're not in any trouble. We just need to record your version of what happened on Sunday afternoon. I imagine something like that is still pretty clear in your mind, eh?"

"Hard to forget," the boy said, and Byrne nodded knowingly.

"Why don't you start from the beginning?" he asked, and the boy looked between his parents and didn't reply. "What time did you meet your friends?"

"Twenty past two," Oscar replied, no doubt having already thought his answers through.

"And what did you do together?" he asked

Oscar shrugged. "Just messed about. We went down to the stream for a bit."

"What's at the stream?"

Oscar's eyes widened, as if the answer was obvious.

"Water?" he said.

"You played in the water?"

"Yeah. Just chucking stones, and that. Getting each other wet, you know?"

"Ah, right," Byrne said. "Yeah, I remember doing that. Who won?"

"Won? Nobody won. We were just messing about."

"And after that?" Byrne asked. "Where did you go then?"

"I don't know, we just... we just walked, I suppose."

"Where to?"

"Nowhere in particular. Ended up at the car park."

"The car park?"

"Yeah. That's when we saw the sofa and that."

"And?"

"And then someone had the idea to make a den with the sofa."

"Who had the idea?"

"I don't know," he said. "But it seemed like a good idea."

"How so?"

"Well...." he looked to his parents, who offered encouraging smiles, albeit from a distance. "We've built camps before, but never one with a sofa. It just seemed like a good idea to have somewhere to sit."

"And that's what you did, is it? You took the sofa and built a camp?"

"Yeah. It came out pretty good, so we went back to see what else we could find. I remember Louis said it would be good to have a little table so we could put our feet up."

"But?"

"But we saw the carpet, so we took that." He took another sip of his drink, then toyed with the glass. Byrne gave him time to develop his thoughts. To put the events in order. To let the emotions he experienced emerge through words. "It was heavy," he started. "Really heavy. We had to stop, and Louis was shouting at us."

"You and Wesley?"

"Yeah," he said. "The uphill bit was the hardest. Ended up dragging it. We didn't know. If we'd known, then..." He stopped. There was nothing more he could have said that would have added any weight to his statement.

"I dare say it was a bit of a surprise," Byrne offered, to get him going again. "When you unrolled the carpet, I mean."

"She just rolled out," he said, his voice high but quiet. "I thought it was a joke at first. I thought Louis might have... I don't know, but it didn't really click. You know? Like it wasn't real."

Byrne sat back. So far, Oscar's story was perfectly consistent with the others. He had even omitted the part about the old man, suggesting they had discussed it and come to an agreement.

Maybe Campbell had been right, he thought. Maybe chasing

after the Wymans and expecting a revelation from Oscar's statement had been a mistake.

"What happened then?"

"We legged it," he said with a shrug.

"Where to?"

"The road."

"What route did you take?"

Oscar closed his eyes tightly, as though remembering, or perhaps trying not to remember too much. "We ran down the hill to the path, then turned left, up into the car park, then up the track to the main road. That's where we called Louis's dad to come pick us up."

"Why Louis's dad?"

"What do you mean?"

"I mean, why not *your* dad or Wesley's dad?"

"Well, I didn't know if you'd be home," Oscar said, with a worried glance at his father. "And neither of us had Wesley's dad's number."

"Neither of you?"

"No, none of us."

"No," Byrne said, shuffling in his chair. "You just said that *neither* of you had his number, not *none* of you. As in, there were only two of you?"

"Yeah," he said, frowning, "Louis and me. So when Louis's dad got there, he called the police and we—"

"Hold on, hold on. Back up a second," Byrne said, sounding more like George than he cared to admit. He leaned forward, his mind racing, reminding himself to trust his instincts. "What do you mean, you and Louis?"

The colour left Oscar's face.

"Yeah," he said.

"Where was Wesley?" Byrne asked, but Oscar said nothing. He just stared at his drink. "Oscar, where was Wesley when you were running?"

"I thought he was behind us somewhere," he said. "He's...he's bigger, you know?"

"And was he?" Byrne asked. "Was he behind you?"

CHAPTER FORTY-FIVE

"So the boys called you at eight forty-five," Campbell asked.

She sat on the plush cream sofa in the Foxons' living room, a cup of tea in one hand and a plate full of custard creams on the table before her.

Her hosts had forced both upon her when she'd sat down, as though their reaction to yet another police officer in their house was to pile her with treats. They'd sent Louis upstairs, but judging by the occasional creak of a floorboard outside, she guessed that he was listening from the stairs.

"That's right," Mr Foxon said. He had ditched the bleach-stained hoody for a smart jumper over a blue, chequered shirt, as though he'd been about to leave for work when Campbell had knocked.

"And what time did you arrive at the country park?"

He looked at his wife, who nodded supportively as he said, "Must've been about eight-fifty. I pulled on some shoes and went straight over. It's only up the road."

"It's a three-minute drive," Mrs Foxon added, squeezing his hand.

"And when did you call the police?"

Mr Foxon exhaled. "It couldn't have been more than two minutes after I got there."

Campbell nodded and finally took a sip of tea as she considered her next question and a change of tack.

"How did you feel, Mr Foxon when your son called to tell you what happened?"

"Well, he didn't tell me. Not on the phone, anyway. He just said they needed to be picked up."

"How did he sound?"

Mr Foxon puffed his cheeks in thought.

"Scared, I suppose," he said simply. "Like a kid. I mean, I know he still is a kid, but like when he was a little boy." His voice took on that thickness that accompanied a swelling of the throat. His wife dabbed her eyes as if in support. "Like when he'd had a nightmare and would come into our room."

Campbell felt for the man and tried to empathise. She wasn't a mother and had no plan to become one anytime soon, but she could imagine the dread a parent must feel when they realise they can no longer protect their child from the horrors of the world.

"When you arrived," she said, "that's when they told you, is it?"

"That's right."

"What did they say, exactly?"

"I erm...I can't remember what he said exactly. They were all over the place. Trying to talk over each other."

"So clearly worked up about something?"

"Well, yes. Of course."

"But, how did that feel?"

He looked at her blankly.

"Well, it's every parent's nightmare, isn't it? I knew something was wrong when they called. I mean, I'm sure you've received calls like that in your time. Their voice changes. It's like they regress. I could hear it in Louis' voice on the phone, and when I got there, I could see it on his face, like he'd seen a monster."

"So you pulled up on the side of the road?"

"Yes, I pulled up by the gate."

"And they were there already?"

"They were down the road a bit, but yeah. To be honest," he said with a slight laugh, "I got the fright of my life when I saw them."

Campbell smiled back. "Why?"

"I mean, it was getting dark. Middle of nowhere, no street lights, no cars. And I see these two boys sprinting down the road to meet me. I thought someone was behind them. Chasing them, you know?"

"*Two* boys running towards you?"

She frowned at the man who likely thought the hardest part of the interview was over.

"Yeah," he said. "Oscar and Louis."

"Only them?" she asked, and the Foxons looked at each other, picking up on the urgency in her voice. "Where was Wesley?"

"Well, he...he came after."

"What do you mean?"

"Well, he's a bit slower than the others, isn't he? He's a bigger lad."

"How long after?"

Mr Foxon shrugged. "About ten minutes. Fifteen at the most."

"*Ten minutes?*" Campbell repeated, failing to hide the judgment in her voice. It was a detail he'd failed to mention. One that could make all the difference. "He's not that big a lad, Mr Foxon. It wouldn't take him ten minutes longer than the other boys to run to you."

"I just...didn't think about it," he said, staring at his wife, hoping for some support.

"Did he say where he'd been?"

"No, he was just..."

"What?" Campbell asked, her patience thin.

"Out of breath, I suppose," he said. "He'd just run from the car park to the road," Mr Foxon said, growing more and more defensive. "Where are you going with this?" he asked, as Campbell stood and placed her full mug of tea on the coffee table.

"Excuse me a moment," she said, heading for the door. "I need to discuss this with my colleague."

"What's the problem?" Mr Foxon called out. "I mean, what does it matter?"

"Oh, Mr. Foxon," Campbell said, stopping at the door where her gaze drifted past him, drawn to the young man sitting on the stairs, peering through the spindles, his shame unmistakable. "Believe me. It matters a great deal."

CHAPTER FORTY-SIX

The floorboard at the incident room door protested at George's weight, much as Grace used to. Although her protests were often far more subtle and usually involved a lack of pudding that evening, or her forgetting to bake a cake for the weekend. The floorboard had very little concern for his feelings, and its groan alerted most of the CID officers to his arrival.

He marched past the other teams, nodding a greeting here and there, and pushed open the door to their new fishbowl office, seeing two fewer people than he'd expected for the scheduled meeting.

O'Hara looked up at him, most likely judging his mood.

"Where are Byrne and Campbell?" he asked.

"Interviewing the Wymans and the Foxons, guv," O'Hara said. "I haven't heard from them."

"Right," he said, sliding his folder onto his new desk.

"I thought Sergeant Hart was with you," she said, tentatively.

"She's in the custody suite," he said, moving to the whiteboard where he snatched up a pen and wrote a single name in the middle of it, a name they could no longer ignore.

"Oh," O'Hara said, acting as the voice for the team. "Something we ought to know, guv?"

Leaving the name hanging there like a bad smell, George pulled up a chair and sat with them at the central table.

"On our way to work today, Ivy and I saw another fly-tipped pile of rubbish on the roadside," he began, and they leaned in closer to listen. "Someone had dumped two fridges." Unlike with Ivy, this image failed to elicit anything other than perplexity from the team. "Why would someone dump two fridges?" he asked the table.

It was like they didn't quite understand the question, but Ruby was the first to put forward her most logical guess.

"People keep things in the garage for years, don't they? Waiting for the day they'll sort it out and throw it away?" she said. "So if I were paying someone to clean my house, I'd give them everything I'd accumulated in the last twenty years."

"Okay," George said. "Well, *we* came to a different conclusion."

"Two fridges..." O'Hara said slowly. "From two different people."

"Exactly."

"What am I missing?" Maguire asked. "I thought we'd established that."

"Well, we empathised. We took it further," George said. "All it takes is for one person to start a pile. Somebody drives past, sees it, and then remembers that fridge they've had in their garage for years. The fridge that, by rights, ought to be taken to the recycling centre, but let's face it, who has time for that?"

"Okay..." Maguire said. "I'm with you."

"The carpet was almost certainly not a part of the original pile."

The team sat back, not really understanding where he was leading them.

"I thought we knew that," O'Hara said. "We cleared Ingram and Corbyn."

"Yes, and we left it there. We didn't take it further," he continued. "We assumed that whoever owned the carpet had driven past either the Spilsby petrol station or the Horncastle petrol station, and that to identify them, we'd have to identify, locate, and examine every van that passed in the time frame."

"Hundreds," Maguire said.

"Which would take days or weeks, even," George agreed.

"But, why would two separate people choose to dump rubbish in the same place?"

"You're saying that whoever dumped the carpet *saw* the rubbish and figured they had a carpet to get rid of?"

"Exactly," he said. "And who would have seen the rubbish that Ingram left?"

"Dog walkers," Ruby suggested.

"Precisely," he said. "Locals."

"People who live between the petrol stations and who frequent the country park," Maguire said, finally falling in, and George slammed his hand down.

"Point one," he said. "We're closing in." He reached for his folder from his desk and opened it on the table so they could all see a specific document. "This is the map that we found in Gemma Radford's office." He used a pen to highlight a specific area. "This is the country park car park, and this little area here is where the rubbish was dumped."

"Right," Maguire said, nodding along, until slowly his nods became sideways shakes. "So...?"

"A van could reverse into any of these parking spots, and assuming the car park was quiet—"

"It was raining," Ruby said. "So it's unlikely to have been busy."

"Good, which means that our carpet owner could have opened the back doors and dragged a carpet out in relative privacy.

Nobody would have been any the wiser. The only other car we know was there was Gemma Radford's, and we believe that she was somewhere near the makeshift grave hundreds of metres away."

"How do we know she was there?"

"Because she posted a photo in one of those groups. Ivy has it," he said, hoping they wouldn't ask for details. "Which means that our carpet was dumped while Gemma was there. She very likely wasn't taken there in the carpet. She drove there."

"So the carpet is a dead end?" Maguire said.

"We're establishing a timeline," George said. "I don't want to rule anything out, and so far, all of this has been speculation. Now we have facts. We have data. Now we know that it wasn't just people who had visited the country park who would have known about the rubbish pile. It could be anyone who lives between those two petrol stations."

"Because of social media?" O'Hara asked.

"Because of social media, and also..." he teased. "Because we now know that those images were sent to the local Environment Agency responsible for the park."

"Sorry?"

"Somebody sees an instance of fly-tipping," he started. "They take a photo and post it on one of those Facebook groups. From there, somebody reports it to the Environment Agency," George explained, "who then pass that information onto the local councillor to deal with."

"The local councillor?"

"The local councillor, who we believe also denied the archaeological team access to the park."

"Ewan Harris?" O'Hara said, pointing at the board. "Ewan Harris denied the dig?"

"We think so," he said.

"So Ewan Harris knew the rubbish pile was there *before* the carpet was dumped?"

"That's our working theory, yes," George said, gaining more belief in the idea now that he had verbalised it. "Therefore, I want to talk through his MMO."

"Everyone has access to an old hessian sack. My dad probably has a few knocking about," O'Hara started, double-checking Pip's pathology report. "That's the means, surely?"

"That's not going to stand up in court," George said. "We need a definitive confirmation that Harris has them. Let's get warrants in place. Ruby?"

"Guv," she said, and George looked to O'Hara for her to continue.

"Opportunity," he said, prompting her.

"Ewan Harris's house is a good few hundred metres from the country park," Ruby added. "But all this land here..." she gestured at the map, indicating the area to the edge of the country park. "This all belongs to him."

"He owns all that?" Maguire said in disbelief.

"Twenty-something acres," Ruby explained. "Looks like he's given a lot of it over to nature and woodland so it pretty much merges with the country park."

"How's that for opportunity?" O'Hara asked.

"That all depends on his alibi," he replied. "Motive?"

"Judging by Gemma's Facebook posts, it's pretty clear she didn't like him."

"I don't think that sentiment was unique to Gemma Radford," Ruby said from behind her open laptop. "But she was fairly vocal about him. Chances are that he held a grudge."

"Is that a motive, guv?" Maguire jumped in. "Can we evidence that?"

"No," he replied. "Not yet, we can't, and if we can't evidence the fact that she had upset him somehow, or even threatened his career or his family, then we don't have anywhere near enough to warrant murder. There has to be a consequence. There has to be something on him. She must have had something on him, and whatever that is, we need to find it." He settled back in his chair. They had come so far, but it was the gaps, the details that would make or break the investigation, and they were severely lacking. "What if Gemma stood out from the crowd?" he asked, remembering Gemma Radford's spare room and the extent of her research. "What if she was more than just another angry member of the public? What if she was obsessed with Harris? Stalking him, even?"

"Was she obsessed with him, guv?" O'Hara asked. "Did Matthew Cooper mention him?"

"I think it's very possible," he replied. "He didn't mention her name, but the language he used..." He pondered that thought for a moment.

"It's possible she was the obsessive type. She was certainly tenacious and forthright. We spoke to a colleague at the animal shelter who would probably support that," Maguire said.

"But she *hated* him," Ruby said, turning around her laptop to show a list of Gemma's recent Facebook posts — one after another, criticising Harris's policies and personality. "This wasn't just a general dislike. She loathed him. There has to be something in here."

"Okay, somebody, go through the posts and see what you can find. Let's start with his alibi, shall we?"

"He said he was at some fancy do, guv," Maguire said. "I mean, he was in a tux, so..."

"Look into it," George told him. "And we all know what these people are like. They cover for each other. Talk to more than one person. Did the event take place, and if it did, was Harris there? If he was, when did he arrive, when did he leave, and did he pop out? Have his alibi, alibied. I'm not leaving him any wiggle room, okay?" Through the glass, he watched Ivy make her way through the incident room, so he closed his folder, stood just as she entered the room, and loitered near the door.

Maguire watched with interest.

"How are those calls going?" George asked, and the young officer hurriedly picked up his phone. "Message Sergeant Hart when you have the details. Same with everyone else. I need a steady stream of information."

He turned back to Ivy.

"Ready?" he asked, to which she gave a single nod.

"Where you off to, guv?" Maguire asked. "I mean, if we're allowed to ask, that is."

"I'm done speculating," he said. "Ruby, call Katy Southwell. Tell her she's about to receive some DNA samples. I need them turned around now. Not this evening, not tomorrow, and not next week. I need them now."

"He's downstairs?" Maguire said. "You've nicked Harris already? What happened to empathising and picturing the scene, and all that... fluffy stuff?"

"Oh, I empathised," George replied, as he glanced around the room. "I imagined and I used the data we have." He winked at the young Irishman. "And then I nicked him." He strode towards Ivy, who held the door open for him, and he called back over his shoulder. "I need those answers, people. Now, please! We've got one shot at this."

CHAPTER FORTY-SEVEN

The two of them stood facing the interview room door like boxers before a fight, outwardly composed but with a surge of adrenaline rushing through their bodies. Beyond the door was a ring of sorts, a place of immense challenge and judgement, with the underlying possibility of defeat.

George turned to the young woman at his side. "I know what you're thinking," he said.

Ivy took a deep breath.

"Do you? Well, if you can read my thoughts, then I can only apologise. I'm afraid some of them are a bit obscene."

"You're thinking that we've brought him in too early."

"Maybe," she replied. "But, I'm guessing you have a plan, guv." She studied his expression. "At least, I'm hoping you have a plan."

"Present the facts, respect his legal rights, and implicate peace," George replied.

"Okay, that's the guidelines," she said. "What's the reality?"

He laughed once and smiled at how astute she could be.

"Present the facts, hope the team come through, and hope he breaks."

"That's more like it."

George nodded at the door, inviting the sergeant to take the first step, which she did without hesitation and made her way to the seat beside the recorder, where she immediately prepared it to start.

"Where's my boy?" Ewan Harris started focusing on him like a soaring kite eyeing a field mouse.

George took the seat opposite him and shuffled through his papers while Ivy announced the date and time, then introduced those present before handing over to George.

"I said, where's my boy?" Harris repeated. "Where's Wesley?"

George skimmed through the file prepared by Campbell and Ruby as he spoke.

"Before we begin, Mr Harris, I should remind you that you are entitled to legal representation if you feel you need it—"

"Are you listening? I asked you where my boy is—"

"If you do not have access to legal representation or the means to provide your own, then we can arrange a duty solicitor."

He stared at the man before him, who eventually relented and shook his head.

"There's no need," he replied. "We'll be out of here before you know it, and you, you will be finished Inspector Larson."

"And I should also remind you that you are under arrest on suspicion of murder. You do not have to say anything. But it may harm your defence if you do not mention, when questioned, something which you later rely on in court. Anything you do say may be given in evidence. Do you understand?"

"I do," he said, his nostrils flaring. "Now, I've answered your questions, so please, for the love of God, tell me where my boy is?"

"In addition to your arrest, we have also arrested your son, Wesley—"

"I know, I was there—"

"I understand you would like to act as his appropriate adult, but due to your own circumstances, I cannot allow this. It would create a conflict of interest."

"He has no one else," Harris replied. "Besides, if you lot are going to start accusing him, then I want to be there."

"That's understandable," George replied. "However, as I have explained—"

"He's got nobody else."

"In that case, Sergeant Hart here will make the necessary arrangements. We can have somebody from social services here in under half an hour, usually."

"Social services?"

"Now," George said. "We've a lot to get through, so—"

"What do you want with him, anyway? He's just a lad."

"Once we've spoken to him, we can share the details, but only if you are proven not guilty. I'm sure you can understand—"

"He's a boy," Harris said. "He's just a boy. What's he in for?"

"Suspicion of conspiracy to murder," Ivy said.

"Conspiracy? What?" He gave the word some thought. "And you have me on suspicion of murder? Which means, and you'll have to correct me if I'm wrong, that you think he and I colluded somehow?" George said nothing. "Well? Is that it?"

"I'd like to talk about Gemma Radford," George said finally.

"Gemma Radford? You are joking? You had Wesley down as a witness. Now he's supposed to be part of it, is he? You're a joke, Inspector, and believe me, this doesn't end here. I don't care what the outcome is, this does not end here."

George made a show of not understanding fully.

"Is that some kind of threat?" he said.

"You interpret it how you see fit—"

"Is that standard procedure, Ewan?" George asked. "Like a natural reflex of some kind? To threaten somebody. To abuse what little power you have."

"Like I said," he replied. "You interpret it how you see fit, but you mark my words, I'll be out of here, and I'll hear what you say to Wesley. I'll get the recordings, so you make sure you keep to the script, because if you don't, your world is going to come tumbling down."

"My world already came tumbling down," George said, smiling softly. "It can't tumble any further. But rest assured, everything I do and say will be fully above board."

"Can I see him?" he said. "My boy. I just want to know he's okay."

"Wesley is being processed, Mr Harris," Ivy said. "Once that's complete, he'll be taken to a holding cell. When we're finished with you, one of two things will happen. Either you'll be released, or you'll also be taken to a cell: a different cell to your son."

"What do you mean, processed?"

"It means that his fingerprints, DNA, and photographs are being taken—"

"You can't do that. He's a minor—"

"He's a minor under arrest," George said. "So, before you attempt to remind me of the law, let's just get the facts straight, shall we. Unlike you, Wesley has agreed to have a duty solicitor present. She is independent of the police force, and therefore a party with no vested interest in this investigation. Does that satisfy you?"

"I'll be satisfied when he's home," Harris said.

"For the benefit of the recording, I am now showing Mr Harris evidence number HC-038," George said, sliding the piece of paper towards Harris. "Can you tell me what this is?"

"It's a map."

"Okay, have you seen this map before?"

"Have I seen a map of the country park before? Of course, I have."

"Have you seen this particular map before?"

"Not that I recall."

"Can you please read the title of the map?" George asked. "It's there at the top of the sheet."

"Proposed Archaeological Survey. Snipe Dales Country Park. Lincolnshire," he said.

"And the word in the centre of the page?" George said. "Stamped in red ink."

"Rejected," he said. "Look, I'm sorry, but—"

"Are you sure you haven't seen this before?" George asked, which seems to rattle Harris.

"What? Yes. I just told you I haven't seen it before."

"You haven't seen any document like this?"

"Well, yes. I've seen these before. We get requests all the time."

"All the time?"

"Every few years, yes. Of course we do. The country park is an untouched area that is neither private property nor a farm. It means nobody has disturbed it. It's a prime source of information for archaeologists."

"The previous requests," George started. "Have these come by you before?"

"Well, yes. I've seen one or two."

"And have you approved them in the past?"

"Yes, *we* have approved them."

"We?"

"The committee," he said. "It's not down to me. I might have a say, but we live in a democracy, you know?"

"And you haven't seen this."

"No," he said. "Look, if you are explaining why this is relevant to me and my son being arrested, I wish you'd just come out and bloody well say it."

"Tell me about your relationship with Gemma Radford," George said, changing tack.

"Ah, here we go. What do you want to hear?"

"I want to hear how you felt about her," George told him, and Harris leaned forward.

"You want to know how I felt about her? I felt nothing for

her," he said. "Not a scrap of emotion. She might as well not exist for all I care."

"She doesn't exist," Ivy said.

"Well, that worked out well then, didn't it?"

"Sounds like hatred to me," Ivy said. "That's a strong emotion, right, guv?"

"Right," George agreed.

"No," Harris continued. "No, it's not hatred. It's nothing. She was one of life's losers. She was a thorn in society's side."

"Not your side?"

"Your words, not mine," Harris said. "She was the type of person who...I don't know, had something missing from her own life, so she spent her time forcing her opinions on others. You know the type. The type that twists everything you say to make you sound racist, or sexist, or whatever happens to be her latest cause. I'm political. It serves me best to remain neutral on most topics. There are a few that require my backing, but for the most part, I take no sides except that of my constituents." He stabbed a finger at the table. "So, when I fail to give a statement on a topic, like solar, or wind farms, or..." he grinned, "fly-tipping, then she turns that into a negative. She convinces the world that I'm pro-whatever it is. You want to know about Gemma Radford, that's who she was." He tapped his temple this time. "She was mental. She destroys people and takes great pleasure in it. I couldn't care less about her," he said. "But did I kill her?" he laughed and sat back in his seat. "Come on, Inspector. You can do better than that, surely?"

"What about this?" George said, slipping another image from the file, watching Harris's eyes as he did.

"What's that?"

"For the recording, Mr Harris is now viewing HC-002," George said. "Surely you recognise it, Ewan."

"It's a carpet."

"Correct," George said. "Recognise it?"

"Should I?" he replied. "I presume this is what the girl was found in?"

"The carpet *your son* found her in, you mean?" Ivy said. "After she'd had a hessian sack pulled over her head, after she had suffered through God knows what, and after somebody put their hand over her mouth and snuffed her life out."

"A hessian sack?" He peered at her and then shook his head as if she had spoken another language.

"Yes, it is that carpet," George added, bringing his attention back to the image. "Doesn't ring any bells then, no?"

"It rings no bells," Harris said, tearing his inquisitive gaze from Ivy to meet George's stare.

A knock at the door prevented George from saying what was on his mind, and perhaps that was for the best, he thought, as his temper simmered.

"Enter," he called out.

Maguire pushed into the room, handed George a folded slip of paper, and then waited. George read the note, passed it to Ivy, and then nodded thanks to Maguire, dismissing him.

Only when the door closed and Ivy had refolded the note did George continue.

"What?" Harris said when he saw the new look in George's eyes. "What is that?"

"It's a question," George replied.

"What?"

"A question. A simple one, so don't worry." George retrieved the documents and slid them back into his folder before closing it and resting his hands on the top. "Did you kill Gemma Radford, Ewan?"

"What? No, I told you, I—"

"You held a grudge against her, though."

"A grudge?"

"She was a thorn in your side, no?"

"She was a thorn in everyone's side. If that makes me a

suspect, then you're going to need more cells, Inspector, because she was a thorn in every other person's side."

"I'm not interested in every other person," George told him. "But to summarise, you do agree that you and her didn't see eye-to-eye."

"What? Yes, we didn't see eye-to-eye. She was trying to destroy my career, for God's sake."

"And you didn't seek some kind of revenge?"

"No," he said. "I'm a politician, not a bloody psycho."

"She went to the country park, Ewan. The country park that backs onto your property."

"So?"

"She was investigating why that archaeological dig," George said, stabbing at the file before him, "was rejected. Now, Sergeant Hart and I have been to see your friends at the Environment Agency. Mr Holloway. Does that name ring any bells?"

"Course it does. I get daily emails from him, and if it's not him, it's one of his hippy team."

"The fly-tipping?"

"Yes, the fly-tipping. Though God knows what he expects me to do about it. We spend half the bloody budget picking that crap up, and people wonder why we can only afford to cut the grass verges twice a year."

"You see, Mr Holloway explained that the archaeological dig would have come through you before it was sent to him."

"So?"

"He never received it."

"Neither did I," Harris said. "Try further up the food chain."

"No," George said. "No, I'm comfortable nibbling this particular morsel for the time being. You see, when you've been doing this job as long as I have, you get to notice certain things. Certain similarities, shall we say?"

"Christ almighty, you really are delusional—"

"Everywhere we look, Ewan, everyone we speak to, every

shred of evidence, and every twinge in my stomach, and believe me, they're as reliable as DNA, it all leads me to you."

"Such as?" Harris said. "You said you had evidence. What evidence?"

"Well, for a start, there are your ongoing interactions with Gemma Radford."

"Ongoing interactions," he scoffed. "There were no ongoing interactions. The ongoing interaction was her bloody slander—"

"And then there's the proximity of your property to the crime scene."

"Oh, come on. That doesn't mean anything—"

"Your land backs onto the country park Ewan. All you had to do was step over the fence."

"Right," he replied. "Except I was three miles away at an event." He stared at them both, daring them to argue.

And then his confidence waned, and George smiled.

"You told us you were at an event, didn't you?"

"I did," he replied. "I was in a bloody tuxedo, for God's sake. You don't think I—"

George opened the note, and Harris's words faded as he read Maguire's handwriting.

"What is that?"

"It's a note," George told him.

"I can see that. What does it say?"

"It says, you're a liar," George told him, folding the note once more. "Now then. Let's start from the beginning, shall we?"

CHAPTER FORTY-EIGHT

Five faces looked up from their laptops the moment George shoved into the fishbowl, each one wearing a look of hope, promise, and anticipation.

George said nothing. He dropped into his seat at the central table, and Ivy took her place at the side of the room, leaning against the glass with her arms folded.

"Christ, I'll bet you're always the last one to open your Christmas presents, guv, eh?" Maguire said, breaking the silence. "You hang in there, controlling your urges, resisting temptation while everyone else tears the paper off theirs."

George ignored the comment. He leaned across the table, took hold of Campbell's notepad, and then dragged it towards him.

"Guv?" she said.

Again, George said nothing. He copied an address from his file onto the notepad and then slid it back to her.

"What's this?"

"Maguire?" George asked. "Care to explain your little note?"

"Me? Aye, well, I called the place, you know? The place in

Ormsby. That's where the event took place-the event on Sunday. You know? The one—"

"The point, Maguire, please," George said, realising that he was doing very little for the officer's nerves, but hadn't the time to manage feelings.

"Well, long story short. I called the place, and they put me in touch with some Coppin fella. Works on the council, you know? Project Manager or something." He waited for a response, but George raised an eyebrow, which moved him along. "Well, he said that Harris was there at the event. It was a networking thing, you know?"

"Maguire?"

"Aye, right," he said. "Well, I got back in touch with the place. You know, to check Coppin's story out, and they checked their CCTV."

"And?" O'Hara asked.

"Harris left early. Slipped out around two p.m.."

"In time to meet Gemma Radford," Ivy said.

"Right," Maguire agreed, then eyed George cautiously. "That's about it, guv. I came downstairs as soon as I found out."

"It's fine," he said. "It's good. It should have been done a lot sooner, but it's fine. There's no harm done."

"I don't get it," Byrne said. "Am I missing something? What's the address you just gave Campbell?"

"That's where he says he was," George replied, turning to Campbell. "Are you still here?"

"Sorry?"

"Go," he said. "Don't call the house, don't call any mobile telephones. Just get down there. Byrne, you can go with her, please. That address is a ten-minute drive from Ormsby. Was he really there? What time did he get there? What was he wearing? What was he driving? Had he had a drink? How was his behaviour? Ask questions. Take notes. Press hard. Go," he said, ushering them out of the door and checking his watch. "I want a phone call in under thirty minutes, and it better be good news."

They left in a flurry of jackets and hushed whispers, and George closed his eyes to gather his thoughts.

"What if it's not good news?" Maguire asked when the door closed behind them.

George laughed to himself. He hadn't meant to, it just escaped.

"Nothing," he replied. "It's a figure of speech." He sighed. "Good work on the Harris thing, by the way. I mean it."

"Aye, cheers, guv."

"Ruby? Anything?"

She shook her head.

"I've been all over his social media," she said. "To be fair to him, he has as many fans as he has haters."

"Well, that much must be true, or else he wouldn't be going for MP, would he?"

"I suppose," she said.

"Alright," he said, realising they were hitting more walls. "Let's say this Coppin character turns out to be a dud. Where does that leave us?"

"With Harris in the frame?" Maguire said.

"Add to that the proximity of his land to the crime scene, and the social media stuff," O'Hara added. "And all we need is a hessian sack." She waited for a response and checked Maguire's expression. But they were all waiting for George, who smiled to acknowledge their patience, but was still processing the information.

"Gemma Radford drops Matthew Cooper off at the pub around midday," he began. "She then drives to the country park, yes?"

"According to the photo she posted of the fly-tipping, yes, guv," Ivy said.

"And she couldn't have stopped to pick anybody up?"

"It's possible, but there's nothing to say she did. The car's clean, guv."

"So, she went alone," he said. "On a mission, maybe? On a mission to look into this." He slid the map from the folder and shoved it into the middle of the table so they could all see. "Now, Harris says he hasn't seen this before. He said it wasn't him who rejected it, yet Holloway, the man who manages the park's environmental interests, says it would have been him. How do we prove Harris is lying?"

"His laptop, guv," Ivy said. "There would be some kind of email trail."

"Ruby, how are we doing with that search warrant?"

She pointed to the new printer that sat quietly against the far wall.

"Ready when you are," she said.

"Thank you," he replied, then continued. "She's suspicious about the rejection. How does she know about the rejection?"

"Guv?" Ivy said.

"How did she know about the rejection? Surely that kind of thing is confidential?" he said. "Come on. How do we find out how Gemma Radford knew about the rejected archaeological dig?"

"Her laptop," Ruby said.

"And how's that going? The tech team have had it for days now."

"Slow," she replied. "I'll chase them."

"Tell them to pull their finger out," he told her, then resumed his narration. "She turns up at the country park. She must know something. She must have known something that we don't."

"All we have is the rejected proposal, guv," Ivy said.

"And a laptop," he replied. "She printed the map, but what else is on her laptop? What information could be on there that could tell us what she knew? A hint? Come on, let's think."

"Something about Harris, guv?" Maguire suggested.

"Right, what about him?"

"I don't know," he said, without thinking. "Something that might destroy his career."

"She liked destroying careers," George said, clicking his fingers. "That's what she did. She did it to Ingram. She destroyed him online."

"Yeah, but she had video evidence, guv," O'Hara said. "It couldn't have been hard."

"People listened to her," George said. "But she wasn't stupid. Whatever it was, she hadn't gone public yet. Sunday was the day she intended to find out. Sunday, when she parked up at the country park, she knew where to look."

"The bones?" Maguire said.

"The bones," he replied. "I don't know how she knew, but she knew, and somebody else knew that she knew and met her there." He watched them all process that complex statement. "Following?"

"Yes, guv," O'Hara replied.

"Ivy?"

"Guv," she said calmly.

"Good. It's Ewan Harris. The old man is too, well...old to chase after her, and the boys are too young to bring her down. It's Ewan Harris. Picturing it?"

"Yes, guv," Maguire replied.

"He chased her and catches her in the car park, where he finds the carpet and the rest of the rubbish. What does he do?"

"Eh?" Maguire said.

"What does he do?"

"Well, according to the pathologist, he pulls a hessian sack over her head to disorientate her, then smothered her with his hands."

"Right," George agreed, and then waited for them to catch up.

"Where did he get the sack from?"

"Well..." Maguire started, taking a deep breath. "He knew

Gemma Radford was close. Holloway sent him the images and asked for the rubbish to be removed—"

"According to Harris, he didn't see any images from Holloway."

"Well, then he's probably lying."

"And Holloway didn't say anything about the images being sent from Gemma Radford. He just said he received them from somebody. Could be anybody. So how did Ewan Harris know that Gemma Radford was in the country park? How did he know she was researching the archaeological dig and therefore seeking to destroy him? Why was somebody's DNA found on her chest, and why the bloody hell would Ewan Harris be carrying a sack? If he intended to kill her, surely there are more effective ways of doing so than a bag with holes in?"

The silence that followed was awful. Maguire let out a long exhale, and Ruby resumed typing.

"It's not him, is it?" O'Hara said.

"I'm not ready to cross him off yet," George replied. "But, it's not looking good."

"Where is he? You haven't let him go, have you?"

"He's in a cell," Ivy answered on George's behalf, "until Byrne and Campbell call in. Unless we can put answers to the guv's questions, then I can't see how we're going to keep him."

Maguire looked despondently at George, shaking his head, as if he'd really thought they could wrap the investigation up.

"It's the way it goes," George told him. "You get knocked down. You get back up."

"Guv?" Ruby said, and he slowly looked up at her. There was a strength to her voice, where the rest of the team had shied from his raised voice. Perhaps it was due to having grown up in a predominantly white county with dark skin. But that strength was good. It was a rope to cling to when the world around him was falling apart.

"Ruby?"

"I've had an email from Katy Southwell," she said. "She's processed the latest DNA samples."

"And?"

"It answers *one* of your questions," she said, and George sat up in hope, but she shook her head sadly, deflating him before his chest had fully expanded. "But it doesn't solve the crime."

CHAPTER FORTY-NINE

"Detective Sergeant Ivy Hart," Ivy announced for the recording. "Joining me is Detective Inspector George Larson, Miss Harriet Bronson—"

"Mrs," the duty solicitor corrected.

"Miss Lucy Sherman," Ivy continued, to which the social worker smiled briefly. "And Wesley Harris."

"Thank you, Ivy," George said. "And before we begin, thank you both for joining us. I appreciate it's last minute." He nodded at the solicitor and the social worker in turn. "Miss Sherman, I understand you are acting as Wesley's appropriate adult. Is that right?"

"That's correct," she replied, her voice light but confident.

Wesley Harris glanced nervously at the women on either side of him, then at George, perhaps hoping for all of this to just go away.

"Can I ask that if at any point at all, you feel the conversation is too graphic or inappropriate, then you let me know. I'm guided by the law, but in instances like this, I have to find the blurred line between that and...well, Wesley's feelings. I'll need your help with that."

"That's fine," she said, and George was comfortable that he had established a rapport with her, which is more than he could say for the solicitor, who sat with her pen in her hand and A4 notepad on her lap, just waiting for him to make a mistake.

"Now then," he said, straightening his folder so that it aligned with the edge of the desk. "Wesley Harris, you have been arrested on suspicion of conspiracy to murder. You do not have to say anything but, it may harm your defence if you do not mention when, questioned, something which you later rely on in court. Anything you do say may be given in evidence. Now, before I begin, does that statement make sense to you? Would you like me to explain it further?"

He looked to his solicitor, who nodded once.

"I get it," he said.

"You get it?" George said, for confirmation.

"Yeah, it makes sense, like."

"Good, good," George replied, and he settled in his seat, glancing briefly at Ivy and then at the two women. Finally, he drew Wesley Harris's gaze from the floor. "Do you know why you've been arrested, Wesley?"

The boy sought support from his solicitor once more, who whispered in his ear.

"You suspect me of having something to do with... you know? That woman. But I never, I—"

George held a hand up to stop him and offered a smile to appease him.

"It's okay, it's okay. We can get to all of that," he said. "But that's not *why* you've been arrested, Wesley. That's the charge. The reason you're here, along with Miss Sherman and Mrs Bronson, is because there's a discrepancy in the statement you provided us when we came to your home."

"A what?"

"Something you told us contradicts what your friends told us,"

George said. "In fact, there's more than one contradiction." He felt Ivy's questioning stare, but moved on.

"No," he said. "It's the same as what they said."

"And how would you know what they told us?"

"Because..." he started. "Well, because we were all there, weren't we?"

"Are you good friends?" George asked, to which the boy shrugged.

"Suppose, yeah."

"I had good friends when I was your age," George mused. "And do you know what? I could rely on them for anything. Anything at all. Whatever tricks and pranks we got up to, I knew they would have my back, just like I'd have theirs." The story was permeating, and slowly, Wesley was being drawn in. "Do you have their backs, Wesley? Or should I ask if they have yours?"

He shook his head.

"I don't know. I mean, they live next door to each other, don't they. I suppose I'm the odd one out. They see each other more than I do, but we're still mates."

"But you have to walk some distance to see them. Is that right?"

"It's only ten minutes."

"But you can't call over the fence to them, can you?"

"Well, no. We don't really have a fence. Unless you count the barbed wire over the fields."

"Well, it might surprise you to learn Wesley, that they do have your back. In fact, it took my officers two attempts to get the truth out of them."

"The truth?"

"And before I tell you what they told my officers, you should know that, as far as I can tell, they had no intention of getting anybody into any trouble."

"Trouble? What do you mean, trouble?"

"Whose idea was it to take the sofa and make a den, Wesley?" George asked.

"Eh?" He was stalling for time while he thought of the answer, so George waited patiently. "Louis's, I think."

"And who carried it?"

"Erm, we all did. I think. It weren't that heavy, really."

"Okay, and the carpet?"

"Oh, that was me and Oscar. Louis was up ahead while we carried it."

"But whose idea was that?"

"Eh?"

George waited once more, and the solicitor made notes, just itching for him to make the wrong move.

"Was it your idea, Wesley?" George asked eventually.

"I don't know. I suppose, it could have—"

"It was your idea," George told him.

"But I didn't know—"

"That's okay, that's okay," George said, holding his hands up. "We're just talking, alright? It's just a conversation to iron out a few details." He pointed to Mrs Bronson. "She'll tell you about details. If we don't have our facts one hundred per cent straight, then whoever did that to that woman will very likely walk free. We don't want that, do we?"

"Suppose not," he said.

George leaned forward and linked his fingers on the desk. It was a passive posture that George hoped would ease the boy's nerves.

"And when you unrolled the carpet, and the woman rolled out—"

"Erm, I think we should exclude graphic details where we can," Sherman started.

"It's fine," he replied. "It's a brief reference, that's all." He refocused on Wesley. "When you found what you found, what happened next? You all ran, is that right?"

"Well, yeah," Wesley said.

"To the road?"

"Erm, yeah. I think so."

"You think so?"

"It was the road, yeah," he said.

"Oh, good," George replied. "And at some point, Louis phoned his dad, is that right?"

"Yeah. He did."

"So, I'm guessing you stopped somewhere to make the call?"

"No," he said. "We were terrified. We ran to the road and called him."

"But you didn't call your dad?"

"No—"

"Why?" George asked. "Why not call your dad. Your house is closer, is it not?"

"Well, yeah, but..." He faltered. "He's nicer."

"Your dad is nicer?"

"No, Louis's dad. My dad's always so...so angry. I hate calling him."

"What about Janet? Could you have called her?"

"God no," he said. "She'd have told him."

"I see," George said, feigning an understanding. "You hoped that nobody would find out. That all of this would blow over?"

"Yeah," he said. "Dad's always going on about how anything I do has an impact on his job. If I make a mistake, if I mess up at school, then people will know, and it'll make his life harder. So I have to be good. I have to just stay out of trouble."

"Well, your dad is under immense pressure," George explained. "And he's right to a certain extent, but surely you could go to him?"

"No," he said. "No, he's not like the other dads. He doesn't really get involved."

George turned to Ivy, who was making her own notes, and

waited for her to nod her agreement that it was time to reveal their hand.

He addressed Sherman before he continued.

"A word of warning," he started. "I will need to touch on some... sensitive matters. I'll do my best to keep my language appropriate, but please be mindful we have a job to do, and if Wesley ends up in court over this, then I can assure you, sensitivities will not be a factor. So it's best if we air this here and now."

"I understand," she replied.

"Wesley, there's no easy way to say this, but I'm afraid there's a flaw in your statement."

"Eh?"

George shook his head.

"The call wasn't made from the road, was it?"

"Yeah, it was," he said.

"You didn't all run, did you?"

"What? Yeah, we all ran."

"You arrived at least ten minutes after Louis and Oscar. In fact, Mr Foxon was already there when you arrived, wasn't he?"

Wesley Harris stared at George, wide-eyed and with his mouth ajar.

"I presume you can evidence this, Inspector—" the solicitor began.

"We can," Ivy said, closing her down, then nodding for George to continue.

"Wesley, how old are you?"

"Thirteen," he replied.

"Thirteen. Have you been taught about DNA at school?"

"Eh?"

George smiled.

"You see, we found DNA on the body you discovered. Now, in case you're not aware, DNA is specific to individuals. We all have it, but no two people have the *same* DNA. It's unique to us, and it means that when we match an individual's DNA with a sample we take from a body, for example, we can be 99.99 per cent sure of its accuracy. It's groundbreaking, frankly. We didn't have it when I started in the force, but these days, the technology is, well, it's virtually infallible."

"What do you mean?"

"I think you know what I mean," George said, turning to Ivy. "Stop the recording."

"Guv?"

"Stop the recording," he said, and she did as requested, before George turned to Wesley. "Nobody is going to judge you, Wesley. Nobody is going to say a word." He laid his hands flat on the table. "But I need you to tell me the truth. Do that, and I'll do what I can."

"That sounds like coercion," Bronson said.

"You call it what you like, missy. I call it being human," George told her. "This is your client's only chance of walking out of here." The solicitor sucked in a breath, then replaced the cap on her pen, and folded her arms. It was the decent thing to do, and George smiled warmly at her. "Now, Wesley. You don't need to go into detail, but I need you to confirm that the DNA we found on Gemma Radford's clothing, namely her blouse, was yours."

Wesley Harris closed his eyes. He flushed red, and his chest rose and fell in panic.

Sherman shook her head and closed her notepad, and Ivy followed suit.

Eventually, Wesley opened his eyes and stared at the only other male in the room.

"I just..." he started, quietly. "I don't know why I did it. I just..."

"It's okay," George said. "Take your time."

"It's mine," he said. "She was just...she was so pretty."

CHAPTER FIFTY

There were only three faces to look up from their work when George and Ivy returned to the incident room this time, but each was as unique as the personalities behind them.

"How did it go?" O'Hara asked. "Did he give you anything more?"

"We didn't interview Ewan Harris," George replied, checking his watch. "He's still in his cell."

"Right, so..." Maguire started.

"Wesley Harris," George announced, before the questions that were sure to follow interrupted his train of thought. "We interviewed the boy."

"Wesley Harris? What's he got to do with it?"

What he really needed, more than anything, was a strong coffee, a dark room, and some peace and quiet. Instead, the fishbowl was filled with light, reverberated their voices, and a distinct lack of refreshment.

"There were flaws in his statement," George replied, as he settled into the chair at the central table, where he mused briefly that he'd only sat at his new desk three times, and one of those occasions had been to see if the placement felt right. "It was his idea to use the carpet."

He watched O'Hara and Maguire exchange bemused expressions.

"Right?" Maguire said, his Southern Irish somehow sliding an O into the word before the I. "Surely a defence lawyer would put that down to trauma?"

"They would, yes, and I'd agree," George said. "It's not the fact he suggested they use the carpet, it's the fact that his statement had a flaw, which, if you wish to continue using a courtroom analogy, a prosecution lawyer would use to pull the rest of his statement to bits. If there's one flaw, then who's to say there isn't one more, or two more, or ten more? What part of the statement is actually credible?"

"Right, gotcha," Maguire replied.

"Which then led me onto the timing. In the initial statements that we took, the boys found the body, then ran out to the road," he continued. "Only during the second interviews did we learn they stopped to make a call."

"So they're all flawed?" O'Hara asked.

"And that's when we discovered that Wesley wasn't with them when they made the call, and when they ran to the road to meet Mr Foxon. Again, you could put this down to trauma, but seeing as this critical piece of evidence came from Mr Foxon, who, as far as we know, is not involved—"

"Yet," Maguire added.

"Is not yet involved," George corrected himself, "it does carry a certain amount of credibility. Add to that, Oscar Wyman's revised statement supports that notion, which means that there was a ten to fifteen minute gap between Louis Foxon and Oscar Wyman running from the body, and Wesley Harris catching them up at the road."

"Right..." Maguire started, again clearly not falling in with where George was leading them.

"It's a five-minute walk from the crime scene to the road," George said. "So, either he took a wrong turn, which is highly unlikely, or he stayed behind."

"Jesus, why would he stay behind—?"

"Which leads us to another critical piece of evidence that, for all our efforts, we have not been able to slot into any of our theories. Think about it. Think about the theories we've discussed. About Gemma Radford arriving at the car park, buying a parking ticket, photographing the fly-tipping, and then going about her business, investigating the archaeological proposal. Not once have we been able to find a solution as to when and why she was found with semen on her chest."

"I just figured the killer did it," O'Hara said. "You know, like he gets off on what he'd done."

"Then why hide the body? Why not just leave her there? Why go to all those lengths, dragging her over to the rubbish heap, heaving a carpet down, and rolling her up in it? Why do that? He might as well have signed his name on her forehead, or left us his business card."

"Oh God," Maguire said, his face becoming almost elastic in an animated expression of disgust. "Wesley Harris?"

"I'm afraid so," George said.

"What on earth possesses anybody to do that?" he replied, as Ruby's desk phone rang and she tore herself from the discussion to answer it. "I mean, she was dead, for God's sake. That's depraved."

"Guv?" Ruby called out, holding the phone's handset in the air. "Campbell."

"Loudspeaker?"

She pressed a button, and the room was immediately filled with ambient noise. A gentle breeze tickled the microphone, and bird song decorated the background, the creatures oblivious to mankind's incessant desire to self-destruct.

"Campbell?" he called out. "You're on loudspeaker. What have you got?"

"Checks out, guv," she replied, getting straight to the point. He had a lot of time for Campbell. She rarely minced her words, seldom sought attention or praise, and always provided results. Only once, that George could recall, had she bent the rulebook so far it had very nearly snapped in half. "Simon Coppin. Thirty-seven years old. He's a project manager for the council. No criminal record, no history, and doesn't even have any points on his driving licence."

"What are you saying, that he's a credible alibi?"

"Well, he's not in politics, for a start," she said. "Clean house, nothing that really alarmed me."

"And he backed Harris, did he?"

"He was reluctant at first, but yes, guv. He even showed us his doorbell camera on his phone. Harris arrives at two-fifteen. He's there for a few hours, and then leaves."

"And what was the purpose of his visit? What are they, old friends?"

"In a way, yes, guv," she said, and her smile was evident in her tone.

"Campbell? Are they old friends or not?"

"They're lovers, guv," she replied.

"They're what?" Maguire called out, then quietened at George's glare.

"Lovers?" George said. "Did I hear that correctly?"

"You did, guv. Been seeing each other for years."

"Years?" Maguire called out again.

"Maguire, if you keep on, I'll ask you to go and work in the car park."

"Sorry, guv," he said. "But Jesus, he's supposed to be an upstanding member of the public. He's going for MP, for God's sake."

"So?" Ivy said. "He's gay. Does that mean he can't be an MP?

I'll bet there's more gay MPs in parliament than anybody knows about, and does it matter?"

"Well, no. It doesn't matter to me. I'm not homophobic. I mean, I know loads of gay people—"

"We're police officers. An individual's sexuality is not our concern," George stated, before Maguire dug himself a hole he couldn't climb out of. "However, as liberal as we might like to think *we* are, that sentiment is not mirrored by society. A man in Ewan Harris's position might prefer to keep that kind of thing to himself. There's plenty of people out there who, believe it or not, still cling to traditional values, shall we say? Voters. It's a divisive topic, especially among certain generations, and this place..." He tapped the board, specifically isolating the name of the crime scene, "is where many of that particular generation live."

"Are you suggesting that the local population is homophobic, guv?" Ruby asked.

"No, I'm saying that there are those who were raised in a different time, and a large percentage of the local population is of that generation. Why would a man who, let's face it, needs all the votes he can get, limit his chances by announcing something that many, not all, but many, might see as controversial?"

"I don't think it matters," Ivy said.

"None of us thinks his sexuality matters," George said. "Who people choose to spend their lives with is their own business—"

"No, I mean, it doesn't matter what he is, or what he does," she said. "The fact remains that he wasn't at the crime scene when Gemma Radford was killed." She let that fact hang in the air for a moment. "His alibi stacks up."

"Explains why the kid is messed up," Maguire muttered.

"Sorry, what was that?" George asked.

"Nothing, guv."

"No, you said something about Wesley Harris. What was it?"

"I said, it explains why he... you know. Why he did what he did." He tapped his temple. "He's messed up."

"What, because his dad—"

"Alright, alright," George said. "Let's not get into a debate about the effects of a parent's sexuality on a child. None of us is an expert on the subject." He sighed and physically deflated. "Ivy's right, though. Ewan Harris couldn't have been there."

The silence that followed was broken by Campbell and Byrne, whispering to themselves on the other end of the phone.

"What do you want us to do, guv?" Campbell asked.

George shoved his chair back and pushed himself to his feet.

"Come back," he said, then turned to O'Hara and Maguire. "Go and give them the good news, will you?"

"You're letting him go?" Maguire asked.

"He didn't kill Gemma Radford," George replied. "And if he did, then until we can prove he had a hand in it, I see no reason why he should stay. I doubt we've heard the last from him anyway. With any luck, as long as we all keep his little secret to ourselves, he won't find a way to make our lives any harder."

"How could he do that?"

"Because he's a politician," George replied. "And politicians know people. They rub shoulders with people, namely, chief constables and assistant chief constables. See where I'm going with that?"

"What about the lad?" Maguire asked, to which George gave a few seconds thought.

"Him too," he said.

"What? But he—"

"I know what he did, and there's no way I can condone his actions, but did he cause Gemma Radford's death?"

"Not that we know of, but—"

"Then we let him go," George replied. "You may wish to make an example of him, but I for one am not in favour of destroying a young man's life before it's even begun. Not for one mistake, no matter how messed up you think he might be." He strode over to the printer and snatched up the piece of paper in the tray, which he then held in the air. He caught Ruby's eye. "Is this for me?"

"It is, guv, yes," she replied, as he started out of the door.

"Where are you off to?" Maguire called.

"I'm going for a walk," he replied. "I need to find somewhere cool, dark, and quiet to clear my head."

"Looking for another one of those roads in, are you?" Maguire asked, referring to the analogy he had used earlier in the week. George smiled to himself, but provided no direct answer.

"We need a reset," he said. "We need to take a step back."

"Jesus, if I step back any further, I'll be downstairs in the car park," Maguire said.

"Matthew Cooper," he said.

"Oh, come on, we've cleared him—"

"Why was Gemma with him?"

"She was using him. We know that," Maguire said. "She accessed the council's CCTV through him, which she then used to destroy Corbyn."

"Corbyn?" he replied. "Corbyn is a nobody. Corbyn was a lucky by-product of something bigger."

"Guv?" Ivy said, sounding concerned.

"Gemma Radford wasn't with Cooper to bring down people like Corbyn. She wouldn't invite a man like that into her home just to bring down a fly-tipper or some other little business. She was onto something. Something bigger. Much bigger."

"Harris?" Maguire said, to which George simply looked at him unable to put into words what was playing out in his mind.

"Guv, you heard what he said," Ivy told him. "Until we have something on him, I say we steer clear. You said it yourself. He rubs shoulders with the ACC, for God's sake. We could lose our jobs."

"Or," he said. "Or we could just do our jobs."

"I'm going with you," she said, and he stopped to appraise her.

"No," he said from the doorway. "No, where I'm going is far

too foggy, and if I'm wrong... if I get lost in the fog... well, it's better if it's just me." He gave her a smile. "You keep an eye on things here. It's better if I walk this road alone."

"Guv, if you walk out that door, you might never be back," she said, which seemed to stun the team into silence. "If you go after Harris again, he'll destroy you. Is that what you want?"

"If I go after Ewan Harris?" he replied. "Who said anything about going after Ewan Harris?"

CHAPTER FIFTY-ONE

There was no doubt about it, the house was incredibly impressive. Had it been modernised, George imagined it would sell for multiple seven figures. But the windows were old, the plumbing and electrics were very likely afterthoughts and therefore surface-mounted, and he dared not think what the heating bill must have been like.

From the moment he passed through the wrought iron gates, a sense of what he could only describe as dread washed over him, as if a dark cloud hung over the property in perpetuity.

It was a place with history, a place where hopes were built but were ultimately dashed. Where dreams were born and ultimately destroyed, and where countless lives had begun, from Wesley Harris all the way back to God knows when. Born beneath that dark and formidable cloud.

His imagination ran wild, perhaps as a result of those Gothic windows, dormers, decorative cornices, and huge doors.

Climbing ivy had been allowed to roam across areas of stone work, clinging to the mortar with its tiny tendrils, exploring every weakness, exposing every crack. But like the world in which

Wesley Harris lived, the invasive perennial had been clipped to keep it in check, to prevent growth. To wonder what might lie just out of reach.

Of the two huge front doors, the right side was ajar, and when George climbed the few steps, he called out. There was no sign of Harris's car. No doubt he and his son would be on their way home.

"Hello," he called. "Janet?" He nudged the door, expecting it to creak, but it swung freely. "Janet, it's Detective Inspector Larson." Nobody called back, and there was no sound of approaching footsteps. "Anybody home?" He called again, now fully inside.

Before him, the ornate staircase led up to the first floor, where the house divided into two wings. On either side of the staircase were two doors, while to his right, another door, which appeared to be Ewan Harris's study. He peered through the open door and took the scene in. The room was thirty feet by fifteen, with oak panelled walls, a wall of ceiling-high book cases, and a partner's desk so opulent that it almost seemed a shame to sit at it.

He noted the closed laptop and spread of paperwork on the desk, and moved on to the door to the right of the staircase. He knocked but barely waited for a response before opening.

"Hello?" he called again. Should anyone accuse him of trespassing, he would at least know he had tried to make his presence known.

The doorway led through to an old parlour, with a staircase leading down. He took the stairs, feeling the temperature drop with every step, as he ventured into what must have been below ground to a large country kitchen. With high-level windows offering a decent amount of light, he could almost imagine a cook of old and her assistant preparing food for whatever guests the owners had invited that evening. He pictured a plump and red-faced lady, shuffling about the flagstone floor with a towel over her shoulder, barking orders, and despite having an endless list of complaints, she would have no doubt produced fine foods fit for the finest that Lincolnshire had to offer.

The modern additions, a range with a digital clock, two electric ovens set into the cupboard wall, and an electric kettle, somewhat tainted his daydream. He wondered briefly what the woman in his dream might have made of them.

At the far end of the kitchen was a door he presumed to be the larder or pantry, but when he opened it, he noticed the back wall had been broken through and another door had been fitted, through which led him into a large living space decorated with an old pine dresser, a floral three piece suite, and an old TV, the type that needs two people to lift and an entire cabinet to house it. The floor was a continuation of the flagstone with two more doors off the living space, one at the far end of the room, which was open and revealed a comfy double bed, neatly made, and a second which took him out into what could have been a scullery which, given its proximity to the kitchen, would have made the main living space the servants dining room. The entire ground floor, which had once been where the staff had gone about their business, had been converted into accommodation.

With decades of experience behind him, there was one thing he had come to terms with. The sense of intrusion never went away. He could have had a folder filled with warrants under his arm, and still, he would have felt it; that pang of guilt. That sense of betrayal. The entire cellar was partially below ground, meaning the only natural light came from the high-level windows. He stood on tiptoes to peer out. He dragged a small stool closer to the wall, took one step up, and from there he could see across the property. The forest that merged with that of the country park was several hundred metres away to the left and centre. To the right of his view, he could just make out the ancient roofs of what could have been old stables or a store. The foreground was tamed for the first hundred metres or so, with topiary box trees establishing the ends of three ornamental beds. The lawns would be striped, loved and vibrant green, he guessed, unlike George's own lawn, which was bathed in the shade of the surrounding trees all year round.

A sudden noise nearly knocked him off his stool, and he had to hold onto the wall for fear of falling.

He snatched his phone from his pocket, saw the name on the screen and hit the green button to answer the call.

"Bloody hell, Ruby, you..." He caught himself before he said something he might regret. "You nearly killed me."

"Sorry, guv. You okay?" she asked, as he stepped down and perched on the arm of the sofa to compose himself.

"Yes. Yes, I'm fine. You just startled me, that's all."

"We were wondering...you were," she replied.

"Sorry?"

"Guv?"

"Can you hear me?"

"We wondered where...are, guv?"

"The line's breaking up," he said his voice loud in the near silence. "Hang on. I'll go upstairs."

He held the phone to his ear while retracing his footsteps back through the kitchen, up the stairs, along the little corridor and into the main hallway.

"Hear me now?" he asked.

"Yep, I can hear you," she replied. "Sounded like you were underground. Where are you?"

"It doesn't matter," he replied. "Just getting some air. Nowhere that matters."

"Right," she said, clearly not believing a word of what he said.

"What do you need anyway?" he said.

"I thought you'd want an update," she replied.

"Don't tell me, our mystery man has handed himself in with a note around his neck?"

"Not quite," she replied. "It's about the bones."

"The bones?"

"Well, the bones and the carpet."

"Carpet first?" he said.

"According to Southwell's team, the whole thing has been washed down with glyphosate."

"Glyphosate?"

"Yes, guv. It's the main chemical used in—"

"Weed sprayer," he finished.

"That's right. Does that mean anything to you?"

"Bones. Talk to me about bones," he said, pressing on.

"We've got a partial DNA match," she told him.

"Don't tease me, Ruby," he said. "I don't have the luxury of time, here."

"They match the DNA from Gemma Radford's chest, guv," she said. "Southwell's been working her way through every sample she's got, from every suspect, every bit of rubbish, and...well, everything."

"Sorry, did you say the bones are a match to Wesley Harris's? Am I on loudspeaker? Is Ivy there?"

"Yes, yes, and a *partial* match," she said. "A direct match would mean the bones belong to him, and unless he's walking around without a metacarpal or a phalange, I very much doubt they're his."

"Well, yes, I know that, but..." He stared at the beautiful staircase, which in all likelihood had been carved from oaks from the estate. He pictured a young Wesley Harris descending those stairs, and alongside him, a faceless sibling held his hand. "Did Wesley Harris have a sister or a brother?"

"No," Ivy called out. "Not that we can find. The only people alive who would have a partial DNA match with Wesley Harris are his parents."

"Alive?"

She paused.

"That's my point," she said.

"Jesus, Ivy," George muttered, and that faceless sibling faded away only to be replaced by a woman. "Ruby?"

"Guv?"

"Do we have access to Harris's phone records yet?"

"We do. It came through with the search warrant."

"Look through it," he told her. "All of you look through it. Take a page each if you have to."

"Guv?"

"Just..." He took a breath to calm himself. "Just do as I ask, please."

"What are we looking for?" Ivy asked.

"We're looking for a phone number," he said. "What's Wesley Harris's birthday?"

"What? Guv, what on earth—"

"Just do as I ask. I'll explain later," he said, hearing Ruby typing in the background.

"It was last week," she said after a few moments.

"Right, check Harris's phone records," George told her as he started back down the stairs. "Wesley's mum sends him a birthday message every year, and every year, he tries to call her back, but she never answers. That means that on Harris's phone statement, there'll be an SMS from a number, which he'll try to call sometime afterwards. There won't be any charges, as the call doesn't connect."

"I've got one," Maguire called out. "I've got a number. Six days ago. SMS comes through. He attempts a call an hour later."

"How far back do those phone statements go?"

"Three years," Ruby replied.

"Go back another year."

"What?"

"Just, do it," he said, as he burst into what was once a servant's dining room and now a living space. "The same number should have sent an SMS, and he would have tried to call it again."

"Here we go," O'Hara said, and there was a pause while he imagined they were comparing numbers.

"It's..." Maguire started, but the line cut out. "Guv?"

"Say it again," he said. "The line's bad down here."

"We said that we've...." Again, the line cut out.

He lowered the phone to his side, counted to five to calm his racing heart, and then checked the signal. The little symbol in the top right corner suggested he had just one bar, which then dropped to no bars and the call disconnected.

He let his head fall back, and he squeezed his eyes closed, doing everything he could to put the pieces into some semblance of order.

And then he heard it.

A vibration, faint and alien to that underground world. He moved around the room, venturing into the bedroom, but the vibration grew distant. Quietly, he crept, closing his eyes once more, guided by his hearing until slowly, inch by inch, he honed in on the noise.

He was standing before the pine dresser staring at a photo of the Highlands.

The noise drew his gaze upwards. Up and up, until there was nothing but a heavy oak beam and the wattle and daub ceiling.

Still, the noise came, taunting him, coaxing him on. Daring him to venture further, pushing him past the limits of his imagination, to where empathy mattered not one iota, until he reached up and ran his hand blindly across the top of the dresser among the dust and detritus.

And there it was.

An old Nokia phone. The type that stayed charged for days, unlike modern phones.

He pressed the green button, and slowly, held the phone to his ear.

"Guv?" Ivy's voice said. "Is that you?"

He opened his mouth to answer, the fragments of the puzzle coming together, but not quite fitting into place, when the crunch of car tyres on gravel came through that row of high-level windows behind him.

"I need you here," George rasped. "We've got him."

CHAPTER FIFTY-TWO

It was like reading the words of a ghost.

He scrolled through the spectral text messages. *Wishing my beloved boy a happy birthday, Ewan. Tell him I miss him. Merry Christmas to my darling son. One day we'll be together.* Make sure he reads this, Ewan. Make sure he knows.

It was that last message that turned George's stomach.

The loving texts from an apparent lost mother — her stolen voice trapped in an old Nokia and messages back, written for eyes that could no longer read.

He pored through the hundreds of missed calls from Ewan Harris's number, some in the middle of the night. Others spaced days apart, maybe when the weight of guilt crept in, or loneliness had hit him like a wave. Each unanswered call, a small, private panic, a man desperately trying to cling to something that was so far out of his mortal reach.

He ascended the stairs and had expected to find Ewan Harris in the hallway, but it was empty, devoid of life.

A car door slammed — more like a gunshot cutting through the peace than the slam of a door.

He moved to the front door, edging closer to peer out, hearing the sound of footsteps on gravel, quick, heavy and laboured.

George ventured outside, and the fresh air washed over him, cleansing him, refreshing him. There was nobody in sight. He bent a little to peer into the car, thinking that Harris might still be inside, or had got back in. But he couldn't see a soul.

Then a gate banged somewhere to his right. He turned and saw the old wooden panel blowing in the breeze, its hinges issuing a faint protest as it swung open again.

Slowly, George made his way towards it, towards the rear of the old house, where he stepped into the open, finding a similar view to that he'd seen through the basement windows, only from a higher perspective.

The first was his left and centre, a few hundred metres away, and over to the right, at the edge of the trees, a line of what had once been stables stood proudly before an open paddock.

The lawn he had only just been able to see through the basement window was indeed mowed and rolled, leaving precise stripes at least forty inches across. The blades of grass in the first stripe had been rolled to the right, and the next stripe to the left, creating the illusion of stripes that would fade in a day or two, until the lawn was next mown.

But that picture of perfection was tainted. Like a polished car with mud across its bonnet, a series of footsteps had cut across the lawn, each one as clear as the nose on George's face, and each one leading him towards those tantalising roofs in the distance.

His footprints joined those that had been left previously and cut a trail towards the distant stables some two hundred metres away. He rounded the ornamental beds, which served as a decorative mask to shield the obscenities that lay beyond. Piles of discarded wood, old plasterboard, wiring, and broken glass had been strewn into a pile, and beyond that, the trees offered the first real taste of security.

The pitched roofs jutted from the tree line like foul teeth

from pert lips, and as George moved closer, his senses became attuned to the surroundings.

The forest was young, and the buildings were old, perhaps little more than acorns, when the first stones were laid. But now they dwarfed the old stables, casting them into shadow, and that same ivy that had been tamed against the house walls ran riot, claiming every inch of mortar it could cling to, smothering, penetrating, and hiding whatever lay inside.

He pressed his back against the stable's side wall and focused his mind beyond the thumping heartbeat and rush of blood in his ears until the low hum of a man's voice came to him, as if it called his name.

Before him, set into trees and covered in an old canvas tarp, the contents of a woodpile had tumbled, spilling across the ground in the shadow of a tall oak. The logs had recently been cut, perhaps with a chain saw, as their bright ends, devoid of burrs almost shone in the gloom, like light bulbs lighting the darkened soil, and with every passing minute, those lights faded. One day, a month from now, maybe two, their glow would be muted.

But the glow that emanated from those virgin logs was not muted. They lit the way. They beckoned George, despite the raised voices in the distance, despite the weight of what might be. He strode towards the light - toward those virgin logs. Not all of them. Most were insignificant, but one of them, one log, whose bright and pale end, looked up to the sky almost vertically, where the rest of them looked out across the paddock.

He dropped to a crouch and reached down for it. Only a few inches had been visible from where he had stood with his back against the stable wall, but now he was closer, now he was standing over it, he saw it was longer. Two feet, he guessed, and two-thirds of it was in a hole - a freshly dug hole, perhaps four feet across and nearly two feet deep.

He collected a handful of soil, letting it crumble between his fingers and scatter to the ground.

"No," somebody yelled, and he shoved himself to his feet, making his way back to the safety of the stable wall.

He checked his watch. It had been close to ten minutes since he had spoken to Ivy, and her journey played in his mind. One minute to get down to her car. Six minutes to get to the country park and another two or three to reach the house. Perhaps she'd go inside. He'd left the door open and now cursed himself for it.

Three minutes? he thought. Three minutes to realise the house was empty and to venture into the grounds.

"Let me go," that voice yelled.

"Harris," he whispered to himself, praying that Ivy and the team would come bounding across those manicured lawns any moment now.

He rounded the corner, prepared for the worst, but finding a run of concrete that connected each of the three stables. The top half of the first stable door was open, pinned back to the wall with a hasp and staple. He peered inside. For little more than a place for horses to rest and feed, it was a large space. Ten feet by twenty, he guessed.

The first was used as storage. Makeshift racks had been built, on which were all manner of things, from plant pots to old rope, and boxes of God knows what.

But on the ground, tucked into one corner, he made the connection, and another piece of the puzzle slotted into place.

A light had been left on in the next stable, and the walls were whitewashed, almost blinding compared to the storeroom next door. An old cabinet stood against one wall, atop which were a series of boxes. The rest of the room appeared to be habitable, with an old brown leather sofa, a lamp, and a footstool similar to the one Grace used to have.

Briefly, he wondered what had happened to it. Then as the tenor rumble of male voices drew his conscious mind back to the here and now and the situation at hand, he found himself staring at the floor. It was as if a light had been turned on, and all those stupid theories he'd developed, those ridiculous analogies he'd convinced the team to use, and those moments where he'd felt as if the entire investigation had been lost, fell into shadow.

Out of the stable he strode, no longer fearful of being heard, no longer hoping that Ivy and the team would come bounding into view, and with a kick as hard as he could summon, he sent the last stable door crashing open and stepped into the room.

The daylight that spilt in from behind George found the shiny steel blade, and a single droplet of blood dripped onto a writhing hessian sack.

CHAPTER FIFTY-THREE

"Put the knife down, Ewan," George said. "It's over."

"Not yet, it's not," Harris replied. "Get out of here, Inspector. This isn't your fight."

"I'm afraid I can't do that. You know I can't," George told him. "Where's Wesley?"

"At the house," he replied.

"Well, I suggest you think about him. Think about his future."

"He has no future," Harris said, shifting his position so that he faced George, should he try to rush him. He kicked at his quarry. "*He* saw to that."

"John?" George said. "John, are you okay?"

"He... He stabbed me. I'm bleeding, here."

"Shut it," Ewan yelled, and he kicked out once more, so that John rolled onto his front. Everything that Ewan had needed had been in that first stable. The rope that bound his hands and the sack that had been pulled over his head.

"I know you're upset, Ewan—"

"You know nothing," he called back. "Nothing."

"We spoke to... your friend. Mr Coppin," George said. "You're a free man, Ewan. I know it wasn't you who killed Gemma Radford."

"Oh, I killed her alright," he replied, his upper lip curling in distaste to reveal a row of almost perfect white teeth. "I may not have pulled that sack over her, and I may not have smothered her, and I certainly didn't wrap her in that carpet, but I killed her, Inspector."

George slid his hands into his trouser pockets. A calm demeanour was what the situation called for, which he worked hard to portray.

"Let me get him to the hospital," he said, taking a step further into the room.

"Stay there," Harris yelled at him, holding the knife out as a warning. "You don't move. You hear me. You don't move a bloody muscle."

"Fine," George said calmly. "I'll just stand here and watch, shall I? I'll just stand here and witness you murder John. Look at him, Ewan. Look at him."

"I don't want to look at him," he scoffed. "I don't want to see his face."

"Ah, now I see. Hence the sack, yes?" George said. "Well, I suppose I could stand here and watch, but to be honest, I've a few places to be—"

"You just stay right there. I told you, don't move, so you don't bloody move. Okay?"

"There you go again," George said. "Making demands. Tell me, is that an inherited entitlement, or did you learn that when you got into politics?"

"Don't be smart with me."

"Well, I'd beg you to be smart with me," George replied. "Do you honestly think I'm going to stand here and watch you slot poor John."

"Poor John? Poor John," he hissed. "You know what he did."

"No. No, I don't. Well...I have a version of events. But, why don't you tell me?"

"You're buying time," he said. "You're waiting for that little bitch of yours to arrive."

"Well, yes and no," George told him. "I mean, yes, she's on her way, and she won't be alone, but I doubt they'll find us for a while. I imagine they'll see my car parked out on the road. Then they'll assume we're in the house somewhere. It's a big house, so what do you think? Five of them. Ten minutes? Less, maybe?"

"I need help," John said, as he rolled once more and revealed his blood soaked shirt and the blood that had begun to pool beneath him. "I'm getting cold. I want my wife."

Ewan eyed him, and it seemed as if the skin on his face was being pulled back, creating a vicious sneer.

"You want your wife?" he said, leaning down and raising the knife behind him. "You want your bloody wife?" His arm shot down in a fit of rage and plunged into his back, and the old man bellowed like a wounded bear, arching his back. George instinctively stepped forward, but Ewan was ready. He wrenched the blade from John's back and held it out before him. "Back," he warned. "Get back, Inspector. There's no going back from this."

On the ground, John groaned and writhed, and although George couldn't see his face, he knew how it would look - scared and agonised.

"I want *my* wife," Ewan yelled. "*My* wife. I want her. But I can't have her, can I? I want her back, and you took her. From me. You took her from me and Wesley."

"No," John said, curling into a ball as best he could to ready himself for another blow.

"Ewan, listen to me," George pleaded. "Just listen. It doesn't have to end this way."

"I knew it," he said. "I think I've always known. The signs were all there, but...but at the police station, when you showed me those photos." A moment of realisation hit George. He'd given Ewan everything he had needed to make the connection before him. "The carpet," he continued. "You showed the bloody carpet, and I knew. I knew, Inspector." He straightened and let the knife hang by his side. "I've had him renovating this place for three weeks now," he said. "Somewhere for Wesley to come and play. Somewhere he could have all his games and whatever. And do you know why? Do you know why I chose here?"

"No," George replied, sensing the man was on the verge of tears. "No, I don't."

"Because this is where I came to play," he said. "Me. When I was his age. That carpet. That carpet was down since before I was born. I'd know it anywhere. It was what my mum and dad had installed when the place was converted from stables. I crawled on it, Inspector. I crawled and played, and spent nearly every day of my bloody childhood rolling around on it, so yes. I recognised it like it was the back of my hand." He held up his free hand as if to support his claim. "And the sacks," he said with a laugh that faded to despair. "We've got a pile of them in the store room. She bought them. She bought them for all the bloody vegetables she wanted to grow."

"Who?"

"Who? My wife, that's who," he yelled. "You told me. You told me that Gemma Radford had a hessian sack pulled over her head. You told me that she suffered. She was bound, and then, when the suffering was done, somebody put a hand over her mouth and... " he shook his head as if the very idea of her death was abhorrent to him. "Snuffed her life out."

"I did tell you that," George said. "And it's the truth."

"Well, I worked it out, Inspector, before you. I worked it all out, and now he's got a bag over his head. Now he's the one who's suffering."

"Stop," John pleaded, a pool of clear liquid running from beneath him and merging with the blood. "I need help. I can explain."

"You've had your chance," Ewan shouted. "You've had your chance, and now it's my time. It's my time. You hear me? It's my time." He dropped to one knee beside John and grabbed his shoulder to hold him still. John stiffened at his touch.

"Please," he whimpered. "Please. Stop him."

"Ewan, listen to me—"

"No," Harris replied. "No, I've got to do this. I've got to do this for Wesley. How can I go on now? How can I go on knowing that I knew who took his mum away, and I did nothing about it? That's not a man, Inspector. That's not courage."

"Courage?" George said, slightly alarmed at the word. "Courage? Is that what this is?" He stepped closer, and although Ewan held the knife up, he offered no warning. "Do you think that by doing this, your boy will think you a hero? Is that it? That he'll think you're brave? He needs a father figure, Ewan. A father. A father isn't a man who uses violence to prove himself."

"You don't know him—"

"A father is a man who is there when his child needs him. A father is a man who, above all else, puts his child first. Before his own problems, before his own ego, and do you know what, Ewan? Before his own career."

"Do you have children, Inspector Larson?" Harris asked, lowering the blade to the sack, just above John's shoulder.

"No," he replied quietly. "No, we were never blessed in that way."

"Well, I have, and you'll excuse me for not paying heed to your fatherly advise."

There were a thousand things that George could have said to buy more time. A hundred different ways he could have moved or reacted to delay the death of the old man. To seek justice by some other means.

But he said nothing.

He didn't move.

He just watched.

And that calm was enough to unsettle Harris. Tentatively, he pressed down on the blade, searching blindly for that soft spot between the shoulder and the skull.

"I'll do it," he said.

"I'm sure you will," George replied, and as Harris took a deep breath, preparing himself to deliver the fatal blow, George revealed his final card. "Just as you should be sure that John murdered your wife, Ewan."

Harris stopped.

"What?"

"I just meant that, what you're about to do. You need to be sure of it."

"I am sure," he said. "I saw the carpet and the sacks, and Gemma bloody Radford has been trying to get to me for years. I know why he did it. Radford made the link. The archaeology dig. She worked it out long before anybody else did, and she was *this* bloody close when he found her." He held his thumb and forefinger an inch apart. "She thought that I killed my own wife, and my guess is that Radford found her. She would have had this whole place torn apart by police. Of course, he killed her. He was saving his own skin."

"Well, in that case, Ewan," George said, as the blade cut through the hessian fabric and found skin. "Ask yourself why he killed your wife." Harris stopped. His gaze wandered to the pool of blood at his knee. "You can't answer me, can you? You can't give a reason for why he might have killed Georgina, and do you know why?" Harris stared at him, then tore his eyes away and focused on the blade in his hand. "Because he didn't do it, Ewan."

Slowly, Harris raised his head to stare at George, but his gaze found a far more sinister subject somewhere behind him, as a shadow formed at George's feet and stretched to the pool of blood.

George sighed, but remained facing Ewan Harris.

"I'm right, aren't I?" he said to the newcomer. "I'm right, aren't I, Janet?"

"You are," she said, that lullaby Scottish accent adding a sweetness to those cold, harsh words. George turned to find her standing in the doorway with Wesley at her side. That gentle, motherly gaze of hers resting helplessly on her husband's dying form. "But I'm afraid it's too late for any of us to do anything about it, now."

CHAPTER FIFTY-FOUR

"John?" she called out, swallowing hard to overcome her emotions. "John, can you hear me?" The sack had long since stopped moving, and several minutes had passed since George had heard him groan. He lowered his eyes in sorrow. "Ewie?" she said. "My God, Ewie, what have you done, boy?"

"I..." he started, staring down at the knife in his hand, questioning everything he knew. His gaze wandered around the room, as if he was lost in a dream or a memory, or perhaps he was rebuilding his own version of events with this new information, with the doubt that George so delicately planted. Then he settled on her, and the confused expression he had worn tightened into a foul sneer. "You?"

"Is he..." she hissed, unable to properly form the words. "Have you..." She swallowed again, her breath deep and panicked. "John?"

"You killed Georgina?" Harris said.

She stared at him in disbelief, but at the accusation or the fact that her husband was dead, George couldn't tell.

"What have you done, boy?"

He rose to his feet, the knife hanging limply by his side.

"You killed Georgina? It was you? All this time."

"Ewan, stay where you are," George said, placing himself between them. "Nobody move. Ewan, put the knife down."

Harris shook his head slowly and started towards her until George's hand found his chest, and he felt resistance. It would have been all too easy for a man with Harris's youth on his side to overcome George, whose strength seemed to wane with every passing day.

But the effort to push past George was halted the moment Janet wrapped an arm around Wesley's neck and dragged him close.

"Janet?" the boy cried. "Janet, let go—"

"You stay," she told Harris, fumbling in her apron for whatever she could find. Eventually, she drew out a pen and pressed the nib against Wesley's neck. The young boy closed his eyes, grimacing with terror, bracing for the onslaught of pain. "I'll do it," she said. "I'll bloody do it. I should have done it years ago, when you were a wee bairn."

"Janet, that's enough," George yelled, but his words had little effect. "Let him go."

"You're sick, Ewie. You're sick, just like your pa was, and just like this one." She tapped her temple with her pen hand. "All of you. You're all twisted. Haven't a good bone in your bodies. Any of you." She turned to George. "I'll be doing yous a favour," she spat, then softened when she looked down at her husband again. "I'll be doing yous all a favour. The whole world."

"All this time," Harris said. "All this bloody time. You sat with me, you evil cow. You sat with me and held my hand when she left. I cried on your bloody shoulder, for God's sake."

"And may God strike me down for it," she spat back at him. "You think I'm proud of it? You think I'm proud of what I did, eh? It wasn't planned. I didn't..." Her chest rose and fell, and the corners of her mouth formed a miserable arc. "I didn't mean to do it, Ewie. I was... I was protecting you, laddie. I was looking after my wee boy."

"I'm not your boy, you evil witch."

"I didn't have a choice," she yelled desperately, then shook her head at the memory. "I didn't see any other way."

"Any other way of what, Janet?" George asked, to which she simply gazed at him like he'd spoken in another language.

"Of protecting him, of course," she said. "She was going to destroy him. After all his hard work. She was going to ruin him." She shook her head sadly. "I couldn't let it happen. Don't you see? I couldn't."

"Why don't we let Wesley go, Janet?" George suggested. "We can all calm down. Nobody else needs to be hurt."

She looked down at the boy in her arm, and that motherly instinct oozed from every muscle in her face. She laughed, as if the whole thing had been a joke, and then dropped the pen to the ground before running a hand over his head to smooth his hair.

"That's my wee boy," she said. "I didn't mean it. Aye? I didn't mean it."

"Let him go," George said, with more force in his tone than before.

He slipped from her grasp, and she stood there, in the open, alone.

"Come," Harris called to his son, holding a hand out. "Come here, Wes."

The boy wanted to, but the knife in his father's hand deterred him and he froze, unsure what to do. Harris tossed the blade away to one side.

"Come on, son. Come to me."

George nodded to him, hoping to provide some level of comfort to the young man, who in the past few days had seen more than most men in their twenties. Eventually, Wesley Harris ran to his father, and the two embraced, as father and son should.

George turned his attention to Janet, waiting for her to begin her story.

"What I have to say," she started, then nodded at Wesley. "It's not... well, a wee bairn shouldn't hear it. Not about his father."

All eyes turned on Wesley, who clung to his dad's arm, and probably for the first time in his memory felt some warmth in return.

"I know," he said, and Harris looked up at George, concerned.

"What do you mean, you know?" George asked. "You know what, exactly."

"About Simon," he said, and then braved his father's expression. "I've always known." He smiled warmly, affectionately, and under such volatile circumstances, the scene was oddly and grotesquely warming. "You don't have to hide it, Dad."

"Simon Coppin?" George asked, to which the boy nodded sincerely.

"I'm sorry," Harris said, as if the two were the only people there. "I... I should have tried harder—"

"No," he said. "No, Dad. You shouldn't have hidden it at all. You didn't need to hide it. You don't. Not anymore."

It was a bittersweet scene. The boy had longed for a father, likely for as long as he could remember, and now he had found him. He had found a connection, and when the day was over, George would be compelled to take it away.

"Janet?" he said, as he stepped out of the stables and looked to his right, where a group of people were adding fresh prints to that flawless lawn. "This might be your only chance. The boy needs to hear it."

She looked to her left briefly at George's cue and took a deep breath.

"I heard her," she said. "I don't know what I was doing, exactly. It was so long ago now, but I was upstairs, and I heard her. Crying, she was. Sobbing into the phone to... I don't know, one of her friends, I imagine. I listened. I know I shouldn't have, but I listened by the door. She was moving about in the bedroom, opening drawers and cupboards and whatnot, sobbing at her friend, saying that she was going to leave him this time. That she couldn't bear to share a bed with him anymore. Not with...you know, that type of man. She said she'd go to the papers, and that she'd make sure everyone knew. She said the people deserved to know who he really was."

"She found out about Ewan's sexual preference?" George asked. "Is that what you mean?"

"Aye," she replied sounding more like a cough than a word. "Then I heard it. The zipper. Her suitcase. I heard her tug it from the bed and drop it to the floor, and I heard her end her call, saying that she'd call whoever it was when she got there."

"Got where?"

"I don't know. I suppose I must have missed that part of the conversation. Then she found me. I wasn't ready. She just came bursting out of the room in a flurry of tears and sobs, and she found me." She shook her head again, perhaps in denial. "I don't know what possessed me to do it."

"Do what?" George asked. "Listen to her conversation?"

"No," she said, and her lower lip began to tremble. "I... I pushed her. I just don't know why. Everything was so... so right. She was going to ruin it all. I had my wee bairn," she said, nodding at Wesley. "We were like a family, and she was going to take that away, all because of something that Ewie had no control over? I couldn't let it happen." She stared up at Harris. "I couldn't let it happen. Don't you see?"

"And then what?" George pressed, before the emotions set in and the tale came to a grinding halt.

"Ah," she replied, looking fondly at Wesley. "I'm so sorry, laddie. Your mother, she..." She inhaled again, forcing herself to tell the story he needed to hear.

"He has to hear it, Janet. You can't leave him with questions that haven't been answered. You owe him that much."

"Aye," she said. "Aye, I do. I don't know if it helps. Nobody can know, but she wasn't breathing when I ran to the bottom of the stairs. John thought she'd broken her neck during the fall, and he said that she wouldn't have suffered. I suppose I took some comfort in that. I'm not a bad person, Mr Larson. I'm really not."

"What happened, Janet?" he asked. "You mentioned your husband. Did he help you?"

"I had to tell somebody," she said. "I couldn't just leave her there, all..."

"All what?"

She looked away at the woodpile to the side of the stables.

"All twisted up," she said quietly. "We brought her down here. Ewan never used the place any more, and it wasn't fit for a wee bairn. You were only a lad then. Too young to be down here on your own, that's for sure."

"And you just made out that she'd left?" George pressed. "You fabricated a truth, and nobody ever questioned it?"

"I thought somebody would find out. You know, come looking for her. For the life of me, I don't know how I got through it. Nearly ended it myself, truth be told. And I would have, had it not been for..." She looked to her husband once more. "For John. Aye, he was a rock, alright. She'd told whoever it was that she was leaving, and there was a note for Ewie on the dressing table. All we had to do was get rid of the suitcase and the clothes, and..."

"Bury her beside the stables?" George said, and Ewan Harris emitted a groan as if he'd been punched in the gut. "And then you kept it up. You kept the whole charade going?" To his right, Ivy and the team were closing in, so he held up a hand to keep them at bay. "You kept her phone and you sent birthday messages and the like?"

"I had to," she said. "I mean, she was going away. The note said she wouldn't be back, but that she wanted the wee bairn to know she loved him very much. It seemed worse not to, you know? Not to send a message. At least he had a mother."

"But the mother was you, Janet—"

"Aye, and I'd have been a damn better mother than she ever was," she spat in a moment of bitter spite.

"We'll never know, will we?" Harris said. For the first time during the horrific episode, he had lost his scorn and scowls and had been reduced to a victim holding onto his son, as if it was just the two of them against the world. "You took that chance away."

"Aye, and if I could turn back time," she replied. "I'd do it all again."

CHAPTER FIFTY-FIVE

"Janet—" George started, but she hushed him with a swipe of her hand through the air.

"You're better than she ever was, Ewie. You just need to be yourself. It's all you've ever needed to be. Look at what you've done. Look how far you've come. You don't have her to thank for that. You've got yourself, the boy, and me. You know, I see those emails people send you. I see them all. And do you know what? It makes me proud."

"The hate emails?" George asked, slightly confused.

"Aye, I see them," she said. "But I'm talking about the fans. The people you please, Ewie. Aye, there's the Gemma bloody Radford's of this world, but there's far more people out there who like you than don't. You did that. You earned that, and it makes me proud, Ewie. Proud."

"And you have the nerve to call me twisted—" Harris said quietly.

"Wait," George said, wanting to hear more. "You read Ewan's emails?"

"She moderates them for me," Harris said. "It saves me time. Anything from the constituents, she responds to or brings to my attention. Anything else she leaves for me. You have to under-stand, I get hundreds of emails every day—"

"The archaeology dig," George said, cutting him off. "You read the email requesting the dig."

Despite everything she had just confessed to, Janet looked more ashamed at this particular act.

"Aye, I read it, and aye, I printed it off and stamped it with his wee stamp thing," she said. "They wanted to dig the place up."

"And if they'd done that, then they might have found Georgina," George finished for her, shaking his head. "But Gemma Radford got hold of the rejected proposal."

"Aye, of course she did. Little minx could sleep her way to a peerage had she put her mind to it. Had her nose in all manner of things, she did, little cow. He saw her," she said. "John. He saw her nosing about here, on private property, I might add. So he got hold of her and she started asking all these questions about Ewie's wife, where she was, and if she could talk to her. She said that it was strange how somebody could just disappear like that, and that she thought Ewie might have done something. That he couldn't be trusted, and how evil he was because of the whole wind farm thing. She said he's a selfish man, and he's not. He's really not, he's just... he's Ewie." She shook her head again, as if George might somehow empathise. "She had to be stopped, Mr Larson. She had to. If John hadn't—"

"And if she had been allowed to go about her business—"

"She'd have had this whole place dug up," Janet continued. "There wouldn't have been a patch of ground without a spade in it if she'd had her way."

"And John couldn't let that happen, could he?" George said. "He couldn't let her walk away, knowing what she knew." He nodded, the pieces coming together to form an image he would never forget. "So he killed her." Those four words put so bluntly snatched her from the past to the present. "He put a bag over her head. The first thing he found to hand, is that right?"

"He told me," she said quietly. "He told me that he didn't want to do it. He had to find out what she knew."

"So he put the sack over her head and forced her in here?"

"Aye," she said.

"And he pressed her. Disorientated her. Forced her to tell him how much she knew," George said, knowingly. "And judging by the outcome, she knew enough that she posed a risk to you and what you'd done to Georgina?"

"He was just protecting me," she said, pleadingly. "He wouldn't have hurt a fly."

"So, he smothered her, and then what? Did he come to you?"

"Aye, he did," she replied. "Ewie had had an email from the environment place, about the fly-tipping business. And well, we had the carpet that John had ripped out of this place. It's only through the trees there, and with the two of us. Well, we managed just fine."

"And Georgina?"

"She had to go," Janet replied. "We couldn't leave her there. What if Gemma Radford had left something on her computer or told somebody? We had to move her. John did it. I couldn't deal with it. It was all too much. So John did it. He waited until all the fuss had died down and took her over the meadow over the way, there. Said it was for the best. Said that with all the police and whatnot around, that somebody might find her and that she could be laid to rest. And that the wee boy might know the truth."

"The truth?"

"That she's dead, Mr Larson," she replied. "That's all he needed to know." She puffed her cheeks and dabbed at her eyes with the corner of her apron. "And there you are. That's my story, and..." She stared down at her husband one last time. "And let that be an end to it all."

George nodded. The loose ends had fallen into place. A family had been both united and torn apart, but the truth was out there. The only thing that remained was for justice to be served.

He waved to Ivy for her to bring the team, and gestured that she needed to make a call, hoping that she would interpret that as an ambulance would be needed.

"Ewan Harris," he said to Ivy as she approached. "Murder of John Ferguson."

Maguire and the team took the scene in open mouthed.

"Lock the place down. We'll need uniformed support, CSI, and the FME," George told them. "Nobody touches a thing."

"Guv," Campbell replied, and assumed the lead, directing each of them to a particular job.

George followed Janet's vacant stare into the stable, where Ivy was pulling Ewan Harris's arms behind his back. Wesley held onto him, clinging to whatever last touches he might have with the father he had longed for.

"And then there were two," Janet said sadly.

"And then there were two," he agreed, standing before her. "Janet Ferguson, I am arresting you on suspicion of murder. You—"

"I need help," somebody called out, their voice wet and thick. George turned on his heels to find the team all staring at each other, wondering who on earth had called out. It was Janet who saw him first. The hessian sack twitched, and with a groan, John Ferguson rolled onto his side. "Somebody?"

"John?" Janet called out as she rushed to his side. "John, dear? It's me." Ivy shoved Ewan Harris to one side, dropped to her knee, and tugged the bag from John Ferguson's head, and he breathed as if he had never tasted air so sweet. Janet dropped down beside him and leaned over him, holding and kissing his face. "Oh, dear. You're going to be fine, dear. They've got an ambulance coming. It's coming for you. You're going to be fine."

George placed a hand on her shoulder, and she stiffened at his touch.

"And you?" John asked, a trickle of sticky blood running free from the corner of his mouth. He eyed George, perhaps begging silently for one more moment with his wife.

"It had to end one day, dear," she said softly, raising his hand to her mouth and planting several affectionate kisses on it. "It had to end one day. And we did right. When all's said and done, everything we did, we did it for good."

He nodded, and George allowed a few more seconds before tightening his grip on her shoulder and nodding for Ivy to step in. The handcuffs she had intended to use on Ewan Harris were placed on Janet's wrists, and from there, George took over. He led her from the stable, but as they reached the doorway, stepping into that bright summer sun, John called out.

"I love you, Janet Ferguson," he said, and she turned and smiled at him.

"And I love you, John," she said. "With every fibre of my heart."

If the old couple were anything like Grace and George had been, before Grace had succumbed to dementia, they could have stayed that way for hours, staring lovingly at each other, never wanting the moment to end.

But like she had said, it had to end one day.

"Janet Ferguson," he started, for the second time. "You are under arrest on suspicion of murder. You do not have to say anything, but it may harm your defence if you do not mention, when questioned, something which you later—"

"No," somebody yelled, and mid-sentence, George sensed a commotion behind him. He turned just in time to find Wesley Harris holding the knife his father had used on John Ferguson. His arm was drawn back, his face was a picture of hatred, and the only thing stopping him from ending all of their lives, was his father, who clung to his boy's arm with everything he had.

Wesley struggled a moment longer, then dropped the knife to the ground for George to kick towards Ivy. The boy's bitter expression seemed to loosen, then sag into a look of utter despair, before his strength waned, and his knees buckled.

Ewan Harris held onto his son, lowering him to the ground and then joining him there, where they clung to one another, where something quite wonderful took root. Something that would stand the test of time. Something that had endured terrible episodes and emerged stronger than ever before. Like the trees in the surrounding forest, like the old house that George led Janet towards, and like the fields behind them, with a history that should never be unearthed.

CHAPTER FIFTY-SIX

From the fishbowl window, the sunset over the station's car park was the most beautiful George could remember.

The feathery edges of cotton-ball clouds glowed pink, as if they blushed at his admiration, and shied at his affection.

In the car park below, long shadows stretched across the tarmac, like yawning arms reaching languidly, as though sighing with relief that the day was coming to an end.

The investigation that had felt like a winding road with an invisible finish line was over, but Janet's words of wisdom hung in the warm evening air.

All things came to an end, George knew — Grace, childhood, investigations. Even the longest of days which he was putting off until tomorrow, collating statements, gathering evidence, and preparing the file to hand over to the CPS.

It all had to end, eventually.

"What do you think will happen to them?" somebody behind him asked, his accent as rich and vibrant as the lawn at the Harris's house.

"She'll be held on remand," he replied without turning. "Her husband will either recover in hospital, or he won't. If he does, he'll also be held until the trial." He cleared his throat and savoured the last remnants of the dying sun. "And I imagine that will be the last they see of each other," he added.

"I meant the Harris's," Maguire said.

"Oh?" he replied, giving it some thought. "Well, I suppose that all depends on two things. If John Ferguson wants to press charges, then he's well within his rights?"

"Even though he buried the man's wife?"

"Even though he buried the man's wife," George agreed.

"And the other thing?" O'Hara asked. "You said it depends on two things."

"Oh, that'll be us," he said. "If the CPS want to press charges, wounding with intent, for example. Then, they will."

"Will he serve time?" Byrne asked, and George realised that he wasn't just talking to one or two of his team. They were all sitting around the table watching him and waiting to close the investigation off.

"Not if I had anything to do with it," he replied, then winked. "Thankfully, I don't get to make those decisions."

"But you get some say, surely?" Maguire asked.

"Not really," he said. "I suppose how I word my report might knock a potential charge off balance."

"And how will you word your report?"

"Weighted," he replied with a smile. "To one side."

"And what about the boy? If it hadn't been for his dad, the old lady would have been toast."

"Oh, really?" George said, again smiling himself. "I don't remember that. Unless any of you do?"

The team were stunned into silence, but had any of them disagreed, they would have spoken up.

"Can I ask something?" Campbell said, to which George responded with raised eyebrows, expectantly. "What made you go back?"

"To Harris's house?"

"Yeah. I mean, you came up here after talking to Wesley Harris. You told us about his... you know? His little mistake."

"Right?"

"And we told you that Simon Coppin had confirmed Harris's alibi," she said.

"I didn't know," he replied flatly.

"Sorry?" she said, looking around the team for some support. "You said that he couldn't have been there if Simon Coppin was telling the truth."

"Yes, I know what I said, but I didn't *know*. Not for certain. What I *did* know, however, is that Gemma Radford was a tenacious young woman who stood up for the underdog. Somebody who fought for justice, and that she would never, and I mean *never*, allow a man like Matthew Cooper into her life without good cause."

"The big fish?" Byrne said.

"The big fish," he replied. "Gemma Radford thought Ewan Harris was responsible for Georgina's disappearance. She thought she could prove it, and when the tech team finally get around to getting inside her laptop, shall I tell you what they're going to find? In fact, I don't even need to see their report. I know what they'll find. They're going to look at her files and her internet search history. There will no doubt be photos of the country park, as well as Harris's property, and all manner of research into him and his private life. In her web history, there will be research into every aspect of his political career. The local wind farms, the local solar farms, fly-tipping, you name it, the research will all be on there. It'll be a timeline of her quest to destroy Harris, much like the wall of her office, Ivy. Remember the wall? Do you remember all those little projects that she was so against?"

"I do, guv, yes," she replied.

"And on that timeline, there will be a point when she made a key discovery. Something that clinched it for her. Something that she just couldn't let go of."

"Georgina Harris?" Ivy said, and he pointed at her.

"Georgina Harris. The missing wife."

"Why?" Maguire asked.

"Well, where would you look if you were looking for dirt on a man who claimed to be separated from the mother of his child?"

"The mother of his child," Maguire replied, falling in with where George was leading them.

"Right. Who else would know the ins and outs of his life better than anybody? His wife, correct? And what would you do if, no matter how hard you looked, you just couldn't find her? If she had just vanished into thin air?"

"Seek professional help?" Maguire suggested. "A PI or something, maybe?"

"And if they couldn't find her?"

"Presume the worst," Campbell said. "Or at least look into the possibility?"

"Right," he said. "Let's face it, her opinion of him was hardly glowing, was it? It wouldn't have taken much for her to at least have an inclination that he might have done something to her."

"But that's all it would have been," Maguire said. "An inclination."

"It was enough for her to start digging," he replied. "Not literally, but what she needed was a source of information. Somewhere she could go to get her hands on dirt. And where do you get dirt?"

"The ground?" Maguire said, unsure of his response. He looked around at the team for some kind of support, but received only shrugs.

"Alright," George said. "Ruby, can you bring up those photos that Ivy took in Gemma Radford's office, please?"

The apparent change in direction confused her a little, but she did as she was asked, and in a few moments, the images were up on her screen, which she turned for the team to see.

"What do you all see?" George asked.

"A wall of printed papers," Maguire said, leaning across the table.

"They're her projects," Campbell said. "Look, that one's about the wind farm, and then there's the solar farm."

"Yeah, there's loads about fly-tipping," Byrne added.

"And the archaeology proposal is in the middle," George said. "But look closer. What else is there?"

Maguire shook his head and sat back in his seat, exhaling through pursed lips.

"It's like one of those magic eye pictures or something."

"It's staring you in the face," George said. "It's been staring us all in the face since Ivy and I went there." He looked at them all, hoping that at least one of them would see the connection. "No?"

"A coffee stain?" Campbell said. "Look, on the wind farm document."

"Bingo," George said excitedly. "A coffee stain."

"Jesus, I really am not following," Maguire announced.

"What about the solar farm document?" Byrne added. "That looks like somebody's wiped their backside with it."

"Not their backside, but close," George said, looking at Ivy, who appeared to have just clicked what he was referring to.

"They're all grubby?" Maguire said.

"Why are they grubby?" George asked. "Come on, you're so close. Why do they all look like they've been crumpled up and flattened?"

"They were thrown away," Campbell said, and she sighed heavily. "They're from his bin?"

"They're from his bin," George said, clapping once. "Where better to get dirt on people than their waste bin?"

"All of them?"

"Every single one," George told them. "The wind farms, the solar farm, the fly-tipping, and most importantly..."

"The archaeology proposal," Maguire said.

"And we're there," George said with a smile. "That's how she knew everything. That's how she was getting to him. Janet Ferguson even told us they had a problem with foxes getting into their bins. It was all there. We, like Gemma, were just looking in the wrong place. We were trying to match the suspect to the crime, but it wasn't the suspect, it was the place."

"But he said he hadn't seen the proposal," Byrne added.

"No, *he* hadn't. But Janet Ferguson had. When we first spoke to her, she told us how she dealt with his emails, how she pretty much ran his life and his home for him. She had access to it all. She printed the proposal, stamped it with his rejection stamp, and then scanned it. What did she do with the original? I'll bet a month's salary she didn't file it where he might find it. She couldn't risk Georgina's bones being found by an archaeology team."

"But wasn't she buried on his land?"

"She was," he said. "But not by much. Metres in fact. You could spit from the stables into the country park. What if they found something and wanted to expand? It was a risk."

"Jesus," Maguire said. "She was binning stuff, and Gemma Radford was pulling it out and using it against him."

"Okay, so why did she need Cooper? How did he help her get to the big fish, as you called it?"

"Well, that's where we *will* need her laptop to prove my theory," George admitted. "Although I suspect it has something to do with Simon Coppin."

"Eh?" Maguire said, and George looked to Ivy, hoping she might add some insight based on what he'd just revealed.

"Coppin is a project manager for the council," she said. "So he works at the council offices."

"Where Harris would have been," Campbell joined in.

"And where there are, no doubt, many cameras," Ivy continued. "All managed by Admiral Security."

"All managed by Admiral Security," George said with a smile.

"I don't know how she got wind of their relationship. Maybe it was a rumour she heard, who knows? But my guess is that once she could prove that Ewan Harris's wife was dead, she was going to use that information and probably video evidence of his secret relationship to destroy him."

"And she was close, right?"

"She was close to finding out that Georgina was dead, yes. But, like us, she was going after the wrong person. We made the same mistakes as she did. We hit dead end after dead end, just as she did. Do you know why? Because she was trying to make Ewan Harris fit the crime. She was trying to prove something that wasn't true. She thought it was true. In fact, she was convinced it was true. Just like we were. The mistake we all made was following the clues to identify a person. Ewan Harris. If we'd have just followed the clues to identify a *place*, then things might have turned out differently. We might not have been so blinkered."

"The Harris house?" Ivy said.

"The Harris house," he repeated. "It backs onto the country park. Who even considered that she might have parked in the country park merely to access his land?"

"Not me," Maguire said.

"What about Georgina? Who among us even questioned her whereabouts? She disappeared years ago. She was out of the picture, and we had suspects coming out of our ears."

Ivy shook her head.

"It was the place," he said quietly. "And if it couldn't have been Ewan Harris because he was with his lover, then who else could it have been? Who else knew Georgina? Who else had access to Harris's laptop? The fact is that the key to all of this lies in Gemma Radford's pursuit for justice. She wanted to bring Ewan Harris down, and she would go to great lengths to achieve that."

"Even though she was wrong about him," Maguire added.

"Wrong?" George said. "Or just on the wrong road? I wonder if she would have tried another path if she hit another dead end."

"Yeah, but I mean Harris wasn't lying, was he? He didn't know about his wife. When all's said and done, what has he really done?"

"Apart from putting a man in critical condition with a knife, you mean?" O'Hara said.

"Before that," Maguire said, dismissing her reply. "I mean, he didn't kill his wife, and all the stuff about solar and wind and whatnot. That's just politics, right?"

"Right," George agreed. "It makes you wonder, doesn't it? It makes me wonder, anyway? If she hadn't been killed, and if she had tried to expose him, all this might have come out some other way. It always does, you know?"

"What does?"

"Lies," George said. He smiled at the young PC fondly and leaned on the back of the nearest chair to address them all. "We've worked on a few investigations together now," he began, then looked across at Ivy. "Some of us have worked on what seems like hundreds together. But if there's one thing you should all take away from every investigation we've worked on as well as those we'll work on in the future, it's that every single crime is based on a lie. All the heartache we see. It's all rooted in lies. All the deceit, the fights, the arguments, and the families that are torn apart through death, it's all rooted in lies." He took a moment to make sure that they weren't just listening, but that they were truly hearing him. "We're in a position here where what we do, the decisions we make, and the way in which we portray ourselves have a real impact on people's lives. The only way through it is to tell the truth. No, more than that. To seek the truth. Don't settle for ticked boxes. Find the truth." He looked up at Ivy, and she averted her eyes briefly, before finding him again. "The truth, no matter what way you spin it, always works out for the best. Remember that. You'll all be doing this long after I'm dead and buried, and I hope that when that time comes, when you're faced with a dilemma, no matter how hard it might seem, and no matter what the consequences, you'll seek the truth, because that, my friends, is how you sleep at night."

"Even if that particular path is foggy?" Maguire asked, grinning.

"Especially if that path is foggy," he replied, straightening and stretching his aching back. "And on that little pearl of wisdom, I think I'll bid you all goodnight."

He collected his bag while a thoughtful silence hung in the air.

"Night, guv," Ruby said, as he made his way to the door.

"Yeah, good night, guv," Maguire added.

The door to the fishbowl closed silently behind him, and he worked his way through the remaining CID officers to the main door. He was halfway through it when a voice called out behind him, and Ivy joined him in the corridor.

"Everything okay?" he asked, sensing some urgency on her face.

"Why do I get the feeling that last little speech was aimed at me?" she asked, to which he cocked his head to one side, studied the sincerity in her eyes, then considered his response.

"I don't know," he said, feigning ignorance. He checked nobody was listening in, then stepped close to her, touching her arm the way a father might hold his daughter. "We're all on our own journey," he told her. "We all have to make our own way through this crazy place we call life. Sometimes the road is flat and smooth, and you can see for miles—"

"And sometimes there's a fog?" she said. "I'm getting tired of that analogy."

"To be honest, so am I. But it's still relevant," he replied with a gentle squeeze. "See you at home, yes?" She nodded almost imperceptibly, and he left her standing there. "Don't work too late," he called back over his shoulder, and as he reached the stairwell, he looked back at her. "And don't let the team work late, either. Get them home. Paperwork tomorrow, remember? The fun part."

She laughed once and watched him leave.

"Guv?" she called out as the doors were closing behind him. He stepped back, waiting to hear what she had to say.

"I just wanted to say," she began, faltering, as if she'd changed her mind and beamed warmly at him instead. "I'll see you at home."

CHAPTER FIFTY-SEVEN

George hauled the bulging bin bag out to the wheelie bin by the fence. As the kitchen door shut behind him, the world around him shifted — birdsong returned, the soft hush of wind rustled through the trees, and a neighbour's sprinkler whispered its rhythmic *tff-tff-tff* across the lawn - the gentle soundtrack of a peaceful summer's day.

If only it knew.

Just beyond the brick walls, Hattie and Theo's shrieks ricocheted throughout the house, dulled only slightly by distance and a layer of brick and mortar. He couldn't fathom how their tiny vocal cords hadn't given out, nor how Ivy and Jamie had endured the constant chaos. It was like living inside a kettle that never stopped boiling.

He was also astonished at how quickly Ivy's two children accumulated rubbish, from snack wrappers, juice boxes, and scrap paper to broken crayons, not to mention the fairy princess castle Hattie had built from old cardboard boxes and Theo had destroyed whilst pretending to be a tornado.

George turned to face the house — his home, his safe place, his haven.

How could two children in two hours have turned it into a madhouse?

But he'd been the one to ask Ivy to stay, knowing she'd have the kids every other weekend. And now he was facing the consequences. A Sunday afternoon of playing jousting knights, making forts with his good pillows, and letting Hattie give him a princess-style makeover.

He dumped the bin bag, closed the bin, and savoured the silence.

It took a few moments for what he'd seen to register, and he stopped, doubting his own eyes.

Slowly, he opened the bin lid once more, peering inside as if what he'd seen might leap out at him.

But it didn't leap out, and any doubt he'd had faded.

He removed the bin bag, dropped it to the floor and reached inside the bin to remove the item.

It was Ivy's lamp. The monstrosity that did indeed belong in a bin, but still, it saddened George to see it there.

He brushed a rogue leaf from one of its clam-shell shade decorations, and once he'd dumped the bag again, carried it inside, awkwardly navigating the low kitchen doorframe.

The noise from the living room hit him the moment he stepped inside, a full-frontal assault on his senses.

George carried the lamp to the corner of the kitchen where, he hated to admit it, it sat perfectly in line with the counters.

He stepped back and tilted his head, appraising the monstrosity. Admittedly, the purple fringe did go quite nicely with the oak countertops, and he quite liked the idea of having soft lighting to eat by, as opposed to the harsh overheads.

The living room door burst open.

"Grandpa George, Grandpa George!"

Before he could do anything about it, two kids had run up to him and clung to his legs like monkeys. The girl had blonde ringlets and striking blue eyes, while the boy was round-faced with a quieter, more contemplative disposition, yet no less likely to leap from a coffee table onto the sofa at his sister's suggestion.

Ivy followed them into the kitchen, leaned against the doorframe, and smiled.

"Come play pirates with us!" Hattie yelled.

"You can play that on your own," Ivy said firmly. "Go on. Both of you."

They looked between her and George, as though deciding who had the final say. But a single head tilt and raised eyebrows from Ivy made it clear, and they tore from the room like a whirlwind.

"I'm sorry for the chaos," she said.

"It's okay," he chuckled. "Really."

"I understand, you know, why you and Grace never had kids." She rubbed her forehead. It was strange to see the usually calm, silent, dependable force, if sometimes a little hostile, visibly stressed. "I mean, I love them, of course I do. But they are hard work, especially at this age."

"You know, I never particularly wanted kids. I wasn't too upset when we learned that we never would," George said calmly. "But I always wanted grandkids." He laughed. "I know that doesn't make sense."

Ivy smiled. "You get to give them back at the end of the day."

"Ah," he said, nodding. "Something I'm struggling to come to terms with." She checked on the children, then closed the door to lower the noise, before making a point of standing before him. And although she appeared to have something to say, her eyes were closed with doubt. "Ivy?"

"Sorry, I just..."

"Is there something you want to tell me?"

"There is," she said, awkwardly stuffing her hands into her jeans pockets. "Actually, it's about your little speech in the incident room. You know? The one about seeking the truth."

"Ah," he said, leaving her room to explore the possibilities before her.

"I... I haven't been entirely honest with you," she told him.

"Oh?"

"You invited me to stay here because I told you that Jamie had thrown me out. I said that it was him who was driving the break-up, and that I was no longer welcome." She forced herself to look him in the eye. "I lied," she said.

"Okay," he replied, nodding, but not yet ready to intervene.

"It was me. Jamie wanted me to stay. It was me who made the decision to leave my family. I just told you that it was him so you wouldn't lecture me on family values, or whatever."

"Right," he said.

"Is that it? Is that all you're going to say?"

"What should I say?"

"I don't know. Maybe you could have a go at me for lying to you? Tell me how selfish I've been?"

"And what good would that serve?" he said. "Besides, I already knew."

She peered up at him quizzically.

"You what? You knew?"

"Oh, Ivy, I've always known."

"And you let me carry on about how Jamie was being unfair—"

"I did what you wanted me to do," he said. "The decisions you make are no business of mine, Ivy. All I could do was give you somewhere to stay. Try to stop you from committing to buying a tiny little house from which there would be no going back."

"I don't understand."

"Well, the four of you can't live in that tiny little house you've been looking at, can you?"

"The four of us?"

"You are planning on getting your family back together, I presume."

"Well, yes, but—"

"And it won't be long, Ivy, until you're running the team. Your life's dream. Jamie wouldn't deny you that."

"You've spoken to him."

"Once," he said. "He showed up when I was clearing out my Mablethorpe house." He grinned, safe in the knowledge that the only flaw in his actions had been to keep her secret from herself. "I'll bet, if you called him right now, he'd be here like a shot."

"You..." She turned away and then stiffened at the sight of the lamp. She stared at him, bemused. "Where did that come from?"

"Oh, that old thing?" he said with a laugh. "It's amazing what you find in the bins, isn't it?" She shook her head in disbelief, but for the first time in as long as he could remember, she was speechless. He touched her shoulder and gave it a squeeze before moving over to the door. "Now, if you'll excuse me, I think I'll go play at being grandpa," he said, averting his gaze while she dabbed at her eye. She beamed at him, like a daughter might beam at her father, and a rush of warmth surged through him. "Why don't you give him a call, eh? Take all the time you need."

He left her there and was just closing the door behind him when she spoke.

"Guv?" she said, and he waited expectantly, but everything she had to say was written in her eyes, and he closed the door softly.

"Right then," he shouted to the kids, who stopped running and stared at him as if terrified he might be angry at something. "Who wants to slay the monster?"

The End.

BOOK SIX - PROLOGUE

All that was familiar and comforting by day, the fresh, green flicker of field maples, the looping, playful roads that wound as fallen ribbons might between the hills, the charming cottages nestled like sugary surprises in the folds of the land, became strange and unwelcoming after midnight in the Wolds.

By day, the dappled sunlight through the trees cast rippling shadows on the tarmac, like the flat sands of a shallow tropical seabed.

But at night, when those slivers of light had succumbed to the ever-swelling shadows, the landscape rolled over to expose nature's seedy darker side.

Gnarled branches clawed at the low moon like mangled, groping fingers, and the hedgerows, which by day were alive with birdsong, had become dense, black barricades with toothlike thorns. The narrow lanes no longer wound playfully through the hills but seemed to lie in wait like a snake ready to strike. Every corner held its breath. Eyes, bright, wild, and accusatory watched from the undergrowth, waiting for a lonely driver like Lori to make a mistake.

And she felt it, deep in her spine, the conviction that nobody should be out here.

Not alone, not at this time of night.

Even the steering wheel felt unfamiliar in her grip. As did the tone of the wind, which had shifted from a gentle breeze to a thin, unsettling whisper, the same whisper that warned the rabbits return to their burrows and the birds to their nests.

She heard it too.

But Lori couldn't go home. Not now. Not anymore, and maybe never again.

"Mummy, where are we going?"

She heard the fear in her daughter's voice — the innocent teetering, the threat of breaking, like when she came into their room after a nightmare.

Lori glanced in the mirror at the five-year-old girl who clutched Pierre, her cuddly toy horse, to her chest, the one they'd bought on holiday in Saint Malo.

"Get some sleep, darling," she replied, hoping her daughter could make out her weak smile in the mirror.

The truth was that she didn't know where they were going. The road ahead was so dark, it was almost impossible to see at all. The only thing she could do was head towards the one place she knew was safe. Towards the one person she knew would always take them in, no matter what.

"Mummy!" Angel screamed. "Where are we going?"

"We're going to Auntie Claire's," Lori said quickly.

"Why? It's not New Year's Eve, is it?"

"No," she whispered. "It's not New Year's Eve."

"Then why are we up so late?"

"Just go to sleep if you're tired, okay?" she said, and took advantage of a stretch of straight road to reach behind and give her knee a squeeze.

"Will there be fireworks there?"

Lori frowned. "Where?"

"At Aunt Claire's?"

"No," she snapped. "I just told you, it's not New Year's Eve."

"I don't understand," she said. The wobble of her lip shook her words. "Where's Daddy?"

"I don't know," Lori said quietly, the same fear threatening to break her own voice. "Don't w-w-worry, darling," she said, her old, outgrown speech impediment shining through as she pronounced her Rs as Ws.

That was the problem with loving Jules. Every time he let her down, her confidence plummeted to such lows that she fell back into her old patterns of self-loathing, and this was more than just a let-down. It was a betrayal.

A disaster.

"Will he be at Auntie Claire's?"

Lori swallowed. "No."

"Who will read me a bedtime story?"

"I don't know," she said. "I will, probably."

"But Daddy does the voices."

"Well then, I'll do the bloody voices," she said, her patience as thin as the glare of the headlights. "Alright?"

Lori knew she was driving too fast. She knew her hard press on the pedal was due to adrenaline rather than reason. But the dark tarmac came at her all at once, piercing her racing thoughts with a single path to follow. Beyond the headlights was a black abyss, feeding her road inch by inch, allowing her only the immediate moment.

When she blinked, when the road disappeared for even a millisecond, all she could see was *her*. The strange woman in Lori's living room. The woman on *her* sofa. The woman waiting for *her* husband. She had been so beautiful, so tall and slim and long-legged, all the things Lori was not, wearing all the things Lori could not — lace and mesh and leather, and the confidence of a woman unbridled by shame and self-loathing.

She tried to shake away the old, cruel rhyme they'd sung

around her as a child in the playground, growing louder and louder in her ear like a bout of tinnitus: *Red lorry, yellow lorry, fat Lori, spotty Lori, she can't even say lorry!*

"I want to go home," Angel muttered.

"We *can't* go home," Lori said, taking a hand off the wheel to wipe away tears. She blinked to clear her eyes. "Not right now."

"*When* can we go home?" she whined.

"I don't know, Angel."

"But I want to go home!" she screamed, letting out that ear-splitting scream she reserved usually for public places like supermarkets and airports. "I want Daddy!"

She started kicking the back of the passenger seat.

"Angel, calm down. Mummy needs to concentrate," she said, reaching blindly for her daughter's feet with one hand, and navigating that black snake, feverish with promise of prey, with the other.

"I need you to be a big girl now, okay?" she said.

"I just want to see Daddy," Angel sniffed.

"You will soon, okay? Just not tonight. But you will, I promise," she said, finding her daughter's shining eyes in the gloomy mirror. "We'll be okay. I promise you, everything will be—"

Lori was unable to finish her promise to her daughter.

A terrible scream overpowered her words as Angel's moist eyes widened in fear. High-beam headlights before them, tore through the night, blinding Lori, and the gentlest caress of wing mirror on wing mirror, almost a kiss, brief and soft in the darkness, like a lover's was it took.

It changed everything. It threw their entire life's journey off course. The right kiss could do that, Lori couldn't help but think, as the soft touch sent her spiralling out of control. The long grass to the side of the road seemed to reach up and grip the car's front end, snatching the steering wheel from Lori's hands, and in that moment of terrible chaos, of spinning like a star, she felt Jules's lips on hers like the very first time.

It was the final image she held, his face, his freckles, his eyelashes as he bent down to kiss her, sending shivers down her spine as they spun from the road onto the hillside.

The abyss came at them, closer and closer, through the windscreen, and in a terrible crunch of metal, everything turned upside down, throwing them against the windows as the car flipped over and over. She could do nothing but pray for it to end.

And like all first moments with lovers, it ended too soon, with a neck-straining abruptness and the tinkle of shattered glass.

She had hoped it would be quick, those final moments. She had hoped it would all turn black. Like falling asleep.

But sleep was lingered somewhere in the darkness.

The first thing she saw was smoke or steam. Then, through its wisps, the dark field beyond lit by a single headlight, and even, in the dreamlike absurdity of the moment, a few cows mooing somewhere in the distance, perhaps angered at the disruption.

Blood rushed to her head. Her seatbelt suspended her like a cradle over her fate, as she hung in suspended animation, and the water bottle she always carried rolled to a stop on the roof.

"Angel," she whispered.

A pain in her neck like a stab wound as she turned to her daughter. She, too, hung like an unused puppet, limp and lifeless, her hair and limbs succumbing to the overwhelming power of gravity.

"Baby, wake up," Lori said, just as she did every morning, waking her daughter for school. "Please, Angel. It's time to wake up now."

Her little chest rose and fell as softly as small waves upon a lake's shore — the only sign of life. She slapped her daughter's face lightly, but her efforts yielded little results. A sickening cut on the side of her forehead, deep and terrifying, like a chasm left by an earthquake shone in the dashboard's weak lights.

"Angel," she whispered. "My angel."

The windscreen was now a wall of white, the smoke from the

engine thickening like dense fog. Nature's whisper that had seemed threatening earlier now warned her in no uncertain terms: *You have to get out*.

Lori gripped the side of the car and lowered her foot onto the broken car window, bracing herself before unbuckling her belt, but still dropping like a stone into a messy collapse on the upturned roof.

"Come here, darling," she said, scrambling to reach into the back.

She tried to unbuckle her daughter's seatbelt with the same care she took when she fell asleep in the back. But it was stuck.

"No, no, no," she whispered, eyeing the thickening smoke, that seemed to sniff tentatively at the broken windows, as if tasting blood in the air. "*Please*."

Then she heard it.

The crunch of footsteps on dry grass, grass that hadn't seen rain for weeks.

"Hello?" she said. The footsteps stopped. "Help us!"

The footsteps continued, growing closer like oncoming thunder, like the promise of rain.

"Who is it? Help us, please!" she cried. "It's my daughter. I need help."

She yanked at Angel's belt, but it only tightened across her chest. The steps grew closer still, and a pair of smart, leather boots appeared through the window on the grass outside. Her heart filled with relief. They were going to be okay. Someone was here. Everything was going to be okay.

Just like she'd promised.

"Help her," she said, her voice thick with the irony taste of blood. She coughed and tried again. "Help my daughter. Please."

The shoes waited a moment, then backed off into the darkness.

"No, don't go!"

Outside, the grass crunched in a slow circle around the car, fading in and out with the breath of the breeze until it had gone full circle, and returned to her window.

"Please," she said, groping her way through the broken glass, until she could pull herself into the night, where she looked up at the figure, who calmly pulled on his gloves and peered curiously down at her.

"Hello, Lori," he said, and he grinned a grin that had haunted her for most of her adult life. "Where do you think you're going?"

ALSO BY JACK CARTWRIGHT

The Deadly Wolds Murder Mysteries

When The Storm Dies

The Harder They Fall

Until Death Do Us Part

The Devil Inside Her

Secrets From The Grave

When Blood Runs Dry

The Wild Fens Murder Mysteries

Secrets In Blood

One For Sorrow

In Cold Blood

Suffer In Silence

Dying To Tell

Never To Return

Lie Beside Me

Dance With Death

In Dead Water

One Deadly Night

Her Dying Mind

Into Death's Arms

No More Blood

Burden of Truth

Run From Evil

Deadly Little Secret

Waiting For Death

The DCI Cook Murder Mysteries

A Winter of Blood

A Secret to Die For

VIP READER CLUB

Your FREE ebook is waiting for you now.

Get your FREE copy of the prequel story to the Wild Fens Murder Mystery series, and learn how Freya came to give up everything she had to start a new life in Lincolnshire.

Visit www.jackcartwrightbooks.com to join the VIP Reader Club.

I'll see you there.

Jack Cartwright

AUTHOR

A NOTE FROM THE AUTHOR

Locations are as important to the story as the characters are, sometimes even more so.

I have heard it said on many occasions that Lincolnshire is as much of a character in my work as George, Ivy, and the rest of the team. That is mainly due to the fact that I visit the places used within my stories to see with my own eyes, breathe the air, and to listen to the sounds.

However, there are times when I am compelled to create a fictional place within a real environment.

For example, in the story you have just read, the towns and villages mentioned are all real places. However, most of the houses and buildings in the story are entirely fictitious, and any references to farms and businesses highlight little more than figments of my imagination.

The reason I create fictional places is so that I can be sure not to cast any real location, setting, business, street, or feature in a negative light. Nobody wants to see their beloved home described as a scene for a murder, or any business portrayed as anything but excellent.

If any names of bonafide locations and businesses appear in my books, I ensure they bask in a positive light, because I truly believe that Lincolnshire has so much to offer and that these locations should be celebrated with vehemence.

I hope you agree.

Jack Cartwright

AUTHOR

AFTERWORD

Because reviews are critical to an author's career, if you have enjoyed this novel, you could do me a huge favour by leaving a review on Amazon.

Reviews allow other readers to find my books. Your help in leaving one would make a big difference to this author.

Thank you for taking the time to read *Secrets From The Grave*.

Best wishes,

Jack Cartwright

AUTHOR

COPYRIGHT